A MICHEL

A NOVEL OF EARLY AMERICA AND THE ILL FATED NARVAEZ EXPEDITION OF 1528.

PART I

BY

ROBERT CHAMPION WILSON JR.

To my daughter, Bobbi Ellen, and my grandchildren, Zachery, Gavin, Landon, and especially the Princess, Riley Ray.

TABLE OF CONTENTS

CHAPTER 01

Panfilo

Panfilo de Narvaez

A fearsome warrior, over six feet tall, legs like ship masts and a barrel chest that resonated his voice, it was rumored that Narvaez couldn't even whisper without someone on the next island hearing every word. His voice sounded like it came from deep in the earth.

01 August, 1527

Approaching the Windward Islands

From above, the five ships looked minuscule against the enormity of earth, sea, and sky that surrounded them. *El Rabiforcado*...The Magnificent Frigatebird looked down at the tiny vessels in momentary wonder as they slowly moved across the endless expanse of sea, that extended to the horizons. The spray of the whitecaps dotted the seascape, each imparting a momentary flare that softly subsided back into the blue tapestry. A spirited southeast wind billowed the sails...a profusion of whiteness against the azure blue of the endless *Oceano Atlantico*. Hoping for discarded morsels, swirls of gulls followed in the wakes that imparted only a momentary disturbance in the water. Off the bows, pods of dolphin...*el delfines*, frolicked in the spray. From the masts and yards flew brightly colored flags and pennants, some dipping low enough to catch a momentary wave. On the mainsail was emblazoned the red emblem of *Spanish Castile*.

Still out of sight of the vessels below, a broad sweep of islands began to form on the distant horizon. Like jewels glistening in the sun, they lay on the fringes of the *Caribbean Sea*. These are the beginnings of the West Indies...*Las Antillas*. The first to be encountered are the *Windward* Islands. Haphazardly forming a giant arc, they are the first recipients of the southern trade winds that have their origins in the great *Sahara*. Heated in the unrelenting desert, these dry air masses tumble off the coast of *Africa* carrying suspended sand and boundless energy. Their journey across the *Atlantic* uplifts enormous amounts of moisture, the vapor condensing on the dust particles form towering cumulonimbus megaliths that rocket into the stratosphere. These "cells" then impart their own brand of fury with violent winds and prodigious rainfall. When conditions are right and the ocean's upper layers have been heated by the summer sun, the cells can develop into enormous dynamos of energy covering thousands of square miles...monsters that become the hurricanes...*el huracans* of the *Caribbean*.

At the point where the island chain begins to bend northwest are the *Leeward* Islands. The "*Leewards*" are downwind of the great trades. The long arc of islands, the *Windwards* and *Leewards*, are collectively called the *Lesser Antilles*. Further west still, are the largest islands of *Las Antillas*. These are the *Greater Antilles*. Beginning with *Puerto Rico*, they include *Hispaniola, Jamaica,* and *Cuba*.

On this day, the air is clear and bright with only a distant uprising of clouds far to the northeast. High above, the Frigatebird broadens its circular flight, searching for an uplifting thermal of heated air. Closer now, the island's presence becomes suspect to the seamen...*marineros,* riding atop the ship's great masts. What is first visible is the sky above these emerging archipelagos...it is different. Moisture rising from the biomass condenses in the air above, forming a characteristic smudge of cloud. The lookouts recognize this anomaly and soon the call of "*La Tierra, La Tierra*" rises above the wind noise and the flapping of the sails. On deck, the soldiers and settlers crowd the rails in anticipation of their first sight of this New Land...*Nuevo Tierra*.

The sun, directly overhead, hangs in the sky like a torch, pouring its heat and light onto everything below. The frigatebird, gliding above, casts a shadow that skims the water's surface, dropping into troughs and climbing over the crests of waves. No one notices, for all eyes are looking ahead for the emerging islands.

Slightly forward in the small flotilla is a vessel marked by the banner of the *capitan-general.* This is the flagship. At 120 *toneles...tons,* it is not a new vessel, but it is the largest. It is a type called *caravela,* developed by the *Portuguese* and modeled after early *Arab* fishing boats. Fast, shallow drafted, and able to sail close to the wind, the *caravela* was adopted and further improved by Henry the Navigator during *Portugal's* circumvention of *Africa.* When converted from lateen sails to square rigging, the *caravela* could take advantage of the constant *Atlantic* trade winds. In this configuration, it is called a *caravela redonda.* Christopher Columbus used two such caravels, the *Nina* and *Pinta,* on his first voyage.

This journey, however, began over a month before, leaving the *Spanish* port of *San Lucar de Barrameda* on June 17, 1527. It is the Narvaez expedition, named after its leader Panfilo de Narvaez, and backed by the King of *Spain* and Holy Roman Emperor, Charles V. The voyage will explore and populate the vast tract of land to the north and northwest of the *Greater Antilles.* As the King's official representative, the *capitan-general* is also awarded the title of governor...*Adelantado.* Today, *Narvaez* is standing in the bow of the flagship, re-christened in honor of his wife Maria. It is now; "Maria of the Southern Seas...*Maria de la Meridionales Mares.*"

01 August, 1527

On Board the Caravel Maria de la Meridionales Mares

Scanning the horizon for a view of the island sighted only moments before, Panfilo Narvaez knows that here on the deck, it will be some time before anything appears. He looks with satisfaction at the other four ships loosely clustered around him. They have made good time and the weather, for the most part, has been good. He knows that this part of the journey is coming to an end. The expedition will follow the ring of islands to *Hispaniola* and the harbor at *Santo Domingo.*

He studies the people on deck, some clustered in boisterous groups, others quietly standing alone and gazing out to sea. As is customary, he has allowed all to come topside at once, for this will be a momentous occasion in their life.

Born in *Castile* of high means, the young *Narvaez* migrated to *Hispaniola* as a soldier, to claim his riches in the New World. He first made his presence known in the province of *Higuey* where he and his compatriots, under the governor's lieutenant Juan de Esquivel, subjugated the native *Tianos*. Those had been exciting times…the newness of pristine land, the thrill of battle, riches, and above all…the women. The *conquistadors* took their liberties, often segregating whole villages by sex and age. There were unspeakable acts of brutality. All males, children, older and less attractive women…*la indeseables*, were removed…sold into slavery to provide a labor force.

What remained were the young attractive females. Many had seen their husbands and sons killed or led off into slavery…some watched in horror as their newborns were dashed against a tree. They sat in clusters, wailing and tearing at their hair. The soldiers seemed not to hear.

First to choose were the leaders and *capitans*, the other soldiers making their choices in turn. A loose guard was posted around the town, not so much for security, but to ensure that the inhabitants didn't escape. The raping would continue for hours, women being passed from one to the other of the marauding soldiers. Many were violently savaged, tortured, and sodomized.

When finally the conquistadors were spent, the very fairest of the women were taken as personal slaves; the others were added to the slave labor force. This outrageous behavior was justified…the *Indianos* were not *Christian*. Even the holy men, the friars that often accompanied the conquistadors, looked the other way…some even participated.

After *Hispaniola*, Narvaez accompanied Esquivel in the conquest of *Jamaica*. Again, the relatively small groups of *Spaniards* pursued the natives across this island paradise. The atrocities learned in *Hispaniola* were now committed by new arrivals from *Spain*, eager to show their mettle. For the most part, the *Indianos* fought well, even ferociously, but they were Stone Age warriors and no match for the *Spaniard's* steel weapons, armor, and horses.

Recognized for his fearlessness, Panfilo was promoted. At the request of the new governor, Diego de Velazquez, he led a company of crossbowmen into the largest Island, *Caobana,* by the native population. The native *Ciboney* and *Tiano* cultures, collectively called *Caobanas*, were rapidly overwhelmed.

Narvaez commanded the *Spanish entrada* that attacked and massacred the Indian village of *Caonao in 1513*. Before the attack, the *Indians* had greeted the one hundred well-armed *Spaniards* with gifts of food; cassava bread and fish. 2000 *Indians* were squatted down in the village square, all very frightened at the sight of the *Spanish* horses. Another group of 500 remained in a nearby large house called a *bohio*. Distribution of the food had begun under the watchful eye of a *Dominican* friar named Bartolomeo de Las Casas. During the distribution, a crazed *Spaniard* suddenly drew his sword and began hacking at the defenseless men, women, and children. The rest of the *Spaniards* drew their weapons and joined in the killing.

Narvaez dispassionately sat astride his horse while the slaughter continued around him. Seeing the *Dominican* friar, Narvaez called out.

"How does Your Honor like what our *Spaniards* have done?"

Appalled and deeply troubled Las Casas answered.

"To you and your men, I command you to the devil!"

Panfillo had done well in this land of the *Caobanas*…now pronounced by the conquistadors as "*Cuba*". Devotion to the governor advanced his career and his fortunes. He became Velazquez's second in command and traveled tirelessly throughout the island. After the subjugation of the *Caobana*, the *Spaniards* helped themselves to their land. Panfilo acquired large tracts in *San Salvador de Bayamo* and immediately set to using the conquered indigenous population as slave labor. Busy with the various military affairs throughout the country, Panfilo's wife, Maria de Valenzuela, became the operational head of the newly acquired properties.

Panfilo's reflections were interrupted by a commotion. In an effort to get a better view, one of the colonists had become entangled in the ratlines. Now hanging upside down, he became the subject of amusement and ridicule by those on deck. Arms swinging wildly, the coins in his pockets rattled onto the deck below. There was much laughter as the *marineros* struggled to free him.

Panfilo chuckled to himself, watching the man's discomfort, "It is good, the morale is high and hopes abound with the first sighting of land."

A fearsome warrior, over six feet tall, legs like ship masts, and a barrel chest that resonated his voice, it was rumored that Narvaez couldn't even whisper without someone on the next island hearing every word. His voice sounded like it came from deep in the earth. Fearless in battle, his one great shortcoming was himself…rash, impetuous, and quick to anger.

Still, he moved easily within the *Spanish* ruling class and was well-liked by all who served with him.

On board, Panfilo was uncomfortable, and he had to stoop to pass through doorways. Many had witnessed his volcanic wrath when he struck his head. These were ships for the small men of the time, not giants like Narvaez. His powerful arms and huge hands could lift a normal man off his feet. His head, with the shock of red hair and unruly beard, looked out of proportion to the rest of his body. His right eye socket, dark and foreboding…was empty, mostly filled now with loose skin. As if to accentuate the eye, scar tissue ran from his forehead, across the socket, and down to his cheekbone. Still, his good eye seemed to capture everything.

Panfilo Narvaez had lost the eye in *New Spain*.

In 1518, Governor Velazquez sent his brother-in-law, Hernan Cortes, to explore and report on the mainland to the west, a land inhabited by the *Mexica-Aztec* culture. Velazquez became disenchanted, however, and feared that Cortes would exceed his authority. True to form, it was reported that Cortes had found vast wealth and was hoarding it for himself. Narvaez, with a superior force, was sent to remove Cortes from command and bring him back to *Cuba* in chains. Panfilo even boasted that he would personally capture and hang Cortes on the spot.

Things did not go well for Narvaez.

Cortes used treachery and bribes to turn Panfilo's men against him. In the end, it was only with a small contingent of loyal followers that Narvaez confronted Cortes at the *Totonac* town of *Cempoalla*. The battle was no more than a skirmish. Cortes's men isolated Narvaez at his command post atop a Great Temple built by the *Aztecs*. Under orders to be captured alive, the soldiers surrounded him, but none could put Panfilo to the ground. Swinging his *montante*, a two-handed broadsword, like a hammer, the fighting was fierce. Turning to meet his next assailant, Narvaez received a lance point in the eye thrust by a pikeman standing on the steps just below.

He bellowed in rage as blood streamed down his face, "Holy Mary, protect me, for they have killed me and destroyed my eye."

Looking up at the now crazed red-haired giant, Cortes's' men were momentarily intimidated and backed off. Attached only by nerve and muscle tissue, the severed eye swung back and forth from the gaping eye socket. Panfillo's head was bathed in blood. Through this gore, the remaining wild eye shone with an eerie brilliance.

But...he wasn't dead. Narvaez and his small following continued to fight until finally withdrawing into a thatched shrine on top of the pyramid. The fight ebbed and flowed until Cortes's men set fire to the structure. In a gasping rush, Panfilo and his men ran from the burning enclosure only to tumble down the steep temple stairway, swords and armor clattering on the steps.

It was over.

Ridiculed by Cortes, he spent the next 6 years in confinement while Cortes continued on with the subjugation of the *Aztec* empire. Now 50 years old, a bitter Narvaez was finally released and returned to his home in *Bayomo* to recuperate. Here, under the care and influence of Maria, he made a decision to travel to *Spain* and petition the king for compensation. To be sure, there were monetary and personal losses...chained like an animal in *Vera Cruz*, his resentment had festered. More than that, however, he had watched as Cortes grew rich beyond his wildest dreams.

At the royal court in *Spain*, Charles V was unmoved by the claim for compensation. Fearing he would be dismissed out of hand, Panfilo quickly modified his request. He asked instead that the King grant a claim to settle the territory yet untouched by Cortes.

Cortes had secured all the lands in *New Spain* northward to a region known as *Panuco*. To the north, *Panuco* was bordered by the "*River of Palms*". What remained was an enormous area, extending north and east to the peninsula of *La Florida*. This was a vague area known only as "*Amichel*".

To be sure, no one really knew much of anything about *Amichel*, save for a few slavers on the lookout for Indians to capture. What existed inland from the shoreline was only a guess. Rumors abounded. Some believed that a navigable route existed to the *Orient*; others spoke of tribes of warrior women who procreated with their captive men before killing them. *Amazons!*

In his *audiencia* with Charles V, Panfilo played upon this unknown. An *Aztec* medicine man that Panfilo had met while imprisoned spoke of the lands to the north as "endless". Surely, the gold and riches of the *Aztec* empire were only a precursor to the riches that waited in the expanse of *Amichel*.

Like most Europeans, Charles V had little comprehension of the enormity of the new world. He regaled in the stories and exploits of the conquistadors and was fascinated by the parade of artwork, jewelry, and *Indianos* that were presented to him. More than that, however, was the gold and silver that was enriching his royal coffers. Even now, relays of galleons were bringing fabulous riches to *Spain's* shores. This is what Charles V most cared about, and Narvaez's request piqued his interest.

On December 16, 1526, Charles V granted the license and bestowed upon Panfilo de Narvaez the title of *adelantado*. He was given claim to all land to the north and east of *Panuco* which, in turn, was defined by the *River of Palms*. He had one year to begin an expedition that required the establishment of two settlements and the garrisoning of two forts at sites chosen at his discretion. He would populate the expedition with people from *Spain*. More importantly, the expedition would include friars who would spread *Christianity* to the native populations.

Narvaez had no sooner left the royal court than he began petitioning friends and former colleagues for funds to finance the expedition. Tales coming back from the New World and the riches of the *Aztec* Empire had transfixed the population. Interest still hadn't abated, and investors were plentiful. Handbills had been posted throughout *Spain* and Panfilo traveled tirelessly, seeking and recruiting colonists, seamen, and soldiers. Audiences sat transfixed as he spoke of the glory, riches, slaves and fertile land to be had. At the ale houses and in the company of other men, he talked of the native women that abounded in the New World. With his deep booming voice, the eye patch, and jovial mannerisms, Panfilo often related his own experiences in *La Espanola, Jamaica, Cuba,* and *New Spain.*

Narvaez chose most of the military officers for the expedition. Some were men that Panfilo had served with or had knowledge of. Others had political connections that could not be overlooked. All had seen military action. For Narvaez, this was a requirement. He felt most comfortable around the military men of the time, men who had proven themselves in battle.

As in any royal decree, Narvaez was obligated to include officials of the royal court as legal officers, tax assessors, and guardians of the crown's property. Alonso de Solis was the crown's tax agent and inspector, a rather short middle-aged man whose nose seemed to dominate his face.

Alonso Enriquez would be the comptroller. The direct opposite of de Solis, Enriquez was tall and gaunt, his eyes set deep into his skull. Of these two, Panfilo knew very little, but both were favorites of the royal court, and protocol dictated that he treat them with respect.

His second in command would be the royal treasurer, Alvar Nunez Cabeza de Vaca, a 28-year-old from *Andalusia.* Of de Vaca, Narvaez had a slight acquaintance…he was well placed, with a military background and a famous family history. Although likable, Narvaez found de Vaca somewhat difficult; still, the young treasurer seemed to be well-educated, perceptive, and had battle experience.

As soon as investors were found, the ships were secured and brought to the *San Lucar de Barrameda* port at the mouth of the *Guadalquivir River.* It was here that most of the expeditions to the New World embarked. Even the great admiral, *Cristobol Colombo,* had embarked from here years before.

The caravel "The South Wind...*El Viento del Sur"* was the first to be purchased. Three other ships followed in progression, "Princess Margaret...*Princesa Margarita*," "The Dolphin...*El Delfin*," and "Queen of Naples...*Reina de Napoli."* Each had its own history and all had been well used. Ships carpenters, caulkers, and sailmakers had to be brought in to bring them back to seaworthiness. The governor's own flagship was purchased from a *Portuguese* merchant involved in the spice trade. Countless trips across the *Mediterranean* to ports in *Greece, Turkey,* and *Egypt* had taken their toll, but the price was right and the craftsmen at *San Lucar* soon restored the *Maria.*

01 August, 1527

On Board the Caravel Maria De La Meridionales Mares

The wind shifted slightly and Panfilo felt a subtle change. He grabbed a line and instinctively looked up to the masts. *Marineros* scrambled into the rigging to adjust the sails. The wind was freshening to the south, and the red pennant attached to the mainmast slowly arced more to starboard. In the aft castle, Boatswain Miguel Alvarez chided the seaman to rapidly complete their tasks.

From his vantage point in the bow, Panfilo took in the panorama before him. The sighted land was still not in view to the people on deck, but the water abounded with signs of its presence. Branches, leaves, and an occasional coconut were pointed out with glee. It had become a game as to who would first see them. Far to the northeast, the thunderhead had all but disappeared. He drifted back into thought.

On the day of departure, the harbor at *San Lucar* had throbbed with activity. The horses that had been stabled on shore were brought to the ships and lowered into the hold. Loading the animals was always the last operation performed. The horses were critical to any journey to the new world and it was imperative to keep them healthy. In normal conditions, the animals would fare well for about two months of sea travel. In their small stanchion, each was held in semi-suspension with wide leather belts attached to brackets on the ceiling and stable walls. Each belt had to be carefully adjusted so that the animal could still support itself, but not enough to thrash about. Both, the fore and hindquarters, were shackled, and a retainer was attached on each side of the bridle to keep the neck and head stable. Directly in front of the horse's head, a makeshift trough was hung to feed and water them during the journey. On the floor below, a liberal amount of straw was spread to soak up the inevitable urine and manure. This was periodically thrown overboard, but not before remnants filtered through the straw and wood decking and into the ship's bilge, adding to an almost unbearable stench.

Narvaez had brought a few private mounts...all breeding stock. He would sell these in *Santo Domingo* and *Cuba.* These *Spanish* horses of good pedigree were in demand and he was assured a good price. Horses of lesser pedigree, purchased from local ranchers, would be used for the expedition. This would minimize travel loses during the *Atlantic* crossing, and the sale of these animals would help defray some of the costs.

Already below deck was a multitude of provisions for the journey, carefully placed to properly balance the ship. Casks of various sizes...*tonels, botas, quintelenos, and botijas,* held most of the provisions...water, salt pork, salted fish, biscuits, beans, wine, vinegar, oil, black powder, and nails. If not stored in casks, other items were stored in bales or crates. This included cloth, firewood, animal feed, trade items, weaponry, and a host of personal belongings, carefully regulated and stored.

Along with the horses, the soldiers brought the war dogs on board. These were the great mastiffs and greyhounds that were trained to kill. Panfilo had realized the value of these animals while fighting in *Hispanola, Jamaica,* and *Cuba.* Terrified by its presence, one war dog could keep an entire village of *Indianos* at bay. Each dog was housed in a separate kennel and watched over by its handler. The last of the animals stored on board were the expedition's collection of hogs. Unlike horses, the hogs were not individually restrained, but rather combined in large slatted pens. Resilient to sea travel and quick to reproduce, hogs provided a low-maintenance food source, both aboard ship and on land. As they were loaded and moved about, the squeals added to the already boisterous activity. The stench from their excrement quickly mixed with the foulness emanating from below deck.

In the weeks before departure, Panfilo had supervised it all. As the merchandise was delivered, he had been there to inspect and verify the quantities. Aboard the ships, he was a constant presence, confirming with the military captains and pilots of each ship that all the material had been properly stored and inventoried. On the docks, family members and well-wishers had mingled about while colonists, soldiers, and *marineros* made final preparations to come aboard. Vendors plied the dock with bread, cheese, wine, shoes, clothing, and cure alls. All about was a kaleidoscope of movement, sounds, and smells.

Of the many souls on the five *Spanish* ships, each had their own purpose. For some it was to escape the law, for others without noble ties, it was the promise of a new life where one could own land. For most, however, fantastic riches, adventure, and power were the overwhelming attractions. Aboard were *marineros*, colonists, friars, and soldiers collected from the former kingdoms and communities of Old *Spain*. There were miners from *Extremedura*, coopers, an *Aztec* Prince, wheelwrights, and carpenters from *Andalusia*, farmers and metal workers from *Aragon*, fishermen from *Galicia*, and boat builders from *Catalonia*. Also represented were *Portuguese* and *Greeks*. In greatest attendance, however, were the soldiers and gentry class… *hidalgos*…from Old *Castile*, that central expanse of the *Iberian Peninsula* that had been so instrumental in the final expulsion of the *Muslims* from that part of *Europe*. Now, out of work, they searched for gold and glory in the New World. Finally, interspersed among these nobles were *Moors* and black *Africans*…slaves and servants that did their bidding.

There were also women on board. Fifteen in all. Several of the colonists and a few soldiers brought their wives…there were ten married women and two female mulatto servants. Among the colonists, three women were unaccompanied. These were harlots or fishmongers of Seville who, by whatever means, had accumulated the money to ensure a place on the expedition. Women were in demand in the Indies and those able to make it to *Santo Domingo*, *Havana*, or *Santiago* were guaranteed to capture a husband. On board, they performed valuable services by washing clothes and seamstress duties…and, of course, sexual favors to the crew, other colonists, or for that matter, anyone willing to pay the price. One of the married women, Rita, stood out from the rest.

Rita was a rawboned, barmaid from a local tavern in *San Lucas*. Her husband, Bonito Pina, was the ship's carpenter. Rita had heard of the voyage and rapidly needed a man to give her some legitimacy. Finding the carpenter to her liking, she plied him with strong drink and sexual promises. A three-day drinking spree ensued. By the time sobriety returned to the poor wretch, he learned he was married and signed on for the expedition. Rita was a large woman with hands and forearms that spoke of years of hard work. She was as adept at rousting drunken seaman as she was in hoisting drams of *cerveza*. Rita would occasionally take a seaman to her bed but was more selective than the other barmaids plying the tavern. Those who did experience an evening with Rita would tell amazing stories of rabid lovemaking and physical exhaustion. She became known as *Rita la Salvaje*…Rita, the wild one.

A natural leader, Rita had taken the other women of the expedition under her wing. She had even approached the *adelantado* about securing a private area for the women to perform their toiletries…an area not subject to the leering eyes of the *marineros*. Narvaez, for once taken aback, had agreed, and a makeshift screen was soon constructed on the aft deck.

El Delfin had been the first of the five vessels to be pushed from the dock. Two harbor tugs attached to opposite sides of the bow had pulled the caravel through the congested harbor and out into the bay. The tugs were nothing more than huge rowboats, ten oarsmen, five to a side, straining at their oars to get the caravel moving. A single port assistant...*ayudante del Puerto* sat in the stern of the tug, directing the oarsmen and communicating with the ship through shouts and hand signals. Once clear, the tugs disconnected and the bow sail was unfurled. Depending on the wind, the bow sail allowed just enough forward movement for the caravel to proceed further out into the bay where it weighed anchor.

Panfilo was the last to leave *San Lucar.* As the flagship *Maria* was towed into the Bay, it made ready for sail. The bow sail was deployed, but instead of seeking anchorage, the flagship continued seaward. Soon, the main and topsails were lowered. The other four vessels followed in turn, and the procession began its westward journey.

01 August, 1527

On Board the Caravel Maria de la Meridionales Mares

C*apitan, capitan!"*

Someone was pulling at his sleeve. Panfilo stirred from his reverie. He was now sitting on the aft rail with one leg up on the starboard rail looking landward.

"*Capitan,* here is some water, you have been standing in the sun for over an hour."

It was Campo…his young page.

"Ah…Campo…*gracias*, I have been day dreaming…*sueno de dia*! The wind and the rocking of this boat have almost put me to sleep. Yes, I could use a drink."

Even dressed in his light sleeveless tunic, the heat was becoming oppressive. Taking the tin cup, Panfilo drained it in one gulp. Campo, carrying a pail, immediately refilled it. The water tasted stale like the inside of a boot, but that was to be expected on board a ship. He grimaced to the taste and then wiped a big forearm across his mouth. Panfilo reached out and tussled the youngster's mop of curly blond hair and handed back the cup. Campo proceeded on to other crew members and some soldiers who were talking together. Panfilo thought of how he had discovered Campo in *San Lucar*.

He had just left the Boars Head…*Cabeza de Varraco,* one of the many taverns that permeated this rough harbor town. Just off the street, two *hidalgos* were roughing up what appeared to be a street urchin. Panfilo recognized the two men…both had signed on to the expedition just the day before. One had a knife and was holding the young boy by his hair.

"Maybe I should cut off a piece of his ear."

The other also brandished a knife…"I think I'll cut off his nose!"

Surprisingly, the boy didn't appear to be intimidated and kicked one of the *hildagos* in the shin.

"You little shit…*Justed poca mierda*" cried the hildago, as he momentarily released his grip on the boy. Seizing the opportunity, the boy lurched away from his assailants and turned to run down the street…right into Panfilo Narvaez, who grabbed a handful of shirt and lifted the thrashing youth off the ground.

"What's going on here?"

The two *hildagos* were somewhat taken aback. *"Adelantado* Narvaez, we caught this little *ladron* stealing and, by the grace of God, we thought to teach him a lesson.

Panfilo turned to the urchin. "Hah, so you're no better than a little *rata* stealing cheese from the larder…what's your name boy?"

"What's it to you, you big oaf…let me down!"

With that, Panfilo let out a belly laugh while still holding the boy high in the air. "He's a feisty one. You two go about your business, I'll take care of little *rata.*"

Unable to free himself from Panfilo's iron grip, he looked at the bearded giant and audibly gulped.

"Now tell me young one, why shouldn't I take you down to the constable? Besides, what would your parents think?"

"I have no parents".

Panfilo blinked. "No parents…everyone has parents, surely yours are around here somewhere."

"I never had *un padre* and *mi madre* died from the fever", the boy repeated.

Setting the boy down, Panfilo maintained his grip and sat down on a step in the alleyway. "How old are you boy"?

"Twelve…what happened to your eye?"

Another laugh by Panfilo, "it's a long story, perhaps I'll tell you sometime. When did you last eat?"

"Two days ago…is it true you are a governor...*Adelantado*"?

"Yes, I am. Now, you tell me your name and we will get something to eat".

The little urchin's eyes brightened and Panfilo released his grip.

"Governor, my name is Campo...*Adelantado mi Nombre es Campo.*"

That was how it had started. Narvaez had fed the boy and then asked him if he would serve him as page on a great voyage. Campo had eagerly agreed.

Now, watching the youngster making his way among the crew, Panfilo could only wonder what his life would have been if that chance encounter had not occurred. Looking up into the almost cloudless sky, Panfilo noticed the frigatebird circling high above. The thought flashed through his mind what this spectacle of ships must look like from that height. He drifted back into thought.

At San Lucar, Campo followed Narvaez everywhere. His sole purpose was to assist the governor and at this, he excelled, but the trip across the ocean sea had not been easy. Almost as soon as the flotilla cleared the harbor at San Lucar, Campo began to feel a bad taste rising in his throat. It was something he never had experienced…the rolling climb and crash of the bow as it mounted a swell, hesitated and then crashed into the trough below made his head swim. First, there was nothing but sky, and then the churning green maelstrom of water, foam, and spray. It all terrified him. Much to the delight of the *marineros,* he couldn't walk without falling and sliding across the wet deck, flailing for a handhold.

Then the vomiting began.

This was no ordinary *vomito*. He had been sick before, but this was much different. At first, there was the dizziness…then, he gagged as the bile crept up his esophagus. What happened next was a violent contraction of the stomach muscles. Involuntarily, he made a bellowing noise. The contents of the last three meals came out in a brown projectile stream, fouling and spreading across the deck.

It didn't stop there, three more followed in quick succession. He was shaking from the exertion. Worse, the violent contractions caused him to lose control of his bowels. Campo felt he was about to die and began to sob.

It was at this moment that Panfilo appeared out of nowhere. Seeing the youngster was covered in vomit and excrement, Narvaez grabbed a bucket and threw the contents on the young page.

The water was cold and the salt stung his eyes. As he fought for his breath, Campo momentarily forgot about the dizziness in his head.

"Pull off those *pantalones*", Narvaez barked.

Turning them inside out, Panfilo tied the *pantalones* to a line and threw them over the side. "That should clean them"! Panfilo threw two more buckets on the shivering Campo and then wrapped him in a blanket.

Taking the boy up on the aft castle, Narvaez pointed out at the horizon. "Look out at the sea, focus on that line of sky in the distance. Do not think about the ship and its movements…soon it will no longer bother you".

Campo followed the governor's advice, and although he would succumb to seasickness many times after this, the effects became increasingly less pronounced. He was further enjoined by watching the number of soldiers and colonists that also fell victim. He had not been the only one. Eventually, Campo would conquer the seasickness and weather the foulest of rough seas.

Narvaez continued to watch over the boy, guiding him in this new life. A homeless urchin in *San Lucar*, Campo now had someone who cared about him. His devotion to the red-headed giant was cemented into an unbreakable bond.

Once again, Panfilo was shaken from his reverie. There was commotion on the deck below him. It was Campo, involved in some mischievousness with one of the *marineros*. He watched in amusement as the seaman chased the page around the deck after having suffered the indignity of one of Campo's practical jokes. It was all in good fun and Panfilo joined in the laughter. It was good to laugh. For almost a year now, he had been absorbed with the expedition...his council with the King, raising funds, procuring ships, crews, soldiers, colonists, provisions, animals, and the myriad of other details necessary for an expedition of this size. The stress had been enormous.

Now, with the expedition successfully underway, Panfilo could feel himself relaxing. Soon, he would be back in *Cuba* where the final stages of preparation would be put into place. *Habana* would be their final port of call before embarking for *New Spain,* and the region of *Panuco* and the *River of Palms*. First, however, would be visits to *Santo Domingo* and *Santiago*. Here, he expected to secure additional funding and supplies.

He thought of Maria waiting for him at his *Ranchero* in *Bayomo*. He planned an overland visit from *Santiago*. It had been a lengthy separation and he longed for her touch. Panfilo loved his wife...she was his rock, the motivational power in his life. He had been with many women during his time in the Indies, but they were just dalliances. She alone was his true desire. Her beauty was beyond description. While in *Bayomo,* they would plan for her journey to *Habana,* meeting up one more time before the expedition sailed for *Panuco.*

Beginning in the south at the *Rio Tuxpan, Panuco* is a poorly defined area in central Mexico. It is named for, and centered around, the *Rio Panuco,* a 500-kilometer river system that drains the valley of Mexico. The *Sierra Madre Oriental,* the easternmost mountain range of the immense North American cordillera, roughly marks *Panuco's* western extent.

There was a problem, however.

In the official royal grant, the northern boundary of *Panuco* was defined by the *Rio De Las Palmas*, the River of Palms, but, which River of Palms? A vast unknown, there had only been limited forays into the land beyond, and at least three northern rivers exhibited vast stands of palms at their deltas. This was a fact unknown by Narvaez in his negotiations with the royal representatives of Charles V. Thirty leagues north of *Rio Panuco,* the *Rio de Soto la Marina* empties into the Gulf of Mexico. At its delta, mangrove thickets give way to stands of palm trees extending to the water's edge. Navigable for three leagues inland, the palm forests finally give way to the sparser vegetation of the drier uplands.

Much further north up the coast, another large river system enters into the Gulf. Also prolific with palm forests, this is the *Rio Grande,* a system extending almost 3000 km inland and draining a vast watershed. To the early explorers who had seen one but not the others, they each represented the "River of Palms" and, as such, there was much confusion.

Looking astern, Panfilo spied the expeditions chief pilot, Janero Flores, watching with amusement at the commotion below. The passengers were anticipating their first sight of land and the mood was becoming festive. Even the *padres* on deck, normally subdued in their relationships, were laughing and joking.

With numerous trips across *Oceano Atlantico* and an unprecedented knowledge of the *Lesser Antilles*, Janero Flores had been just the man that Narvaez needed to guide the expedition. He had admitted early on, however, that his knowledge of *Amichel* was limited. Appreciating his frankness, Panfilo would seek a local pilot to assist in the last stages of the journey. He knew that around *Hispaniola* and *Cuba,* numerous forays to the mainland were conducted by illegal slave-collecting expeditions. Finding a knowledgeable pilot to assist Flores should be no problem.

Panfilo recalled his earlier conversation with Flores about the final destination. It had been mid-voyage and on one becalmed afternoon, while both tarried on deck, they had idly talked of their experiences. The talk had somehow turned to *Panuco,* and Flores related the confusion of the *Rio de las Palmas'.* Panfilo was thunderstruck at first but then realized this could be an advantage. He, of course, would choose the most southern of the rivers and if rebuked, had the perfect excuse. After the scheduled refit and supply in *Cuba,* they would proceed to *Panoco* and the southernmost *"River of Palms"*.

As the bow of the *Maria* sliced through the water, Panfilo stared down at the frothy bow wave, the wake emanating out into a large V that spread and then disappeared in the ocean swells. Ahead of the wave, flying fish broke the water's surface and skittered just above the waves. While their large pectoral fins were held rigid, the strong tails continued to beat back and forth. Even minimal contact with the water's surface would extend the flight and leave tell-tale swirls on the surface. In flight, their green bodies would contrast with the deep blue of the ocean. Inertia spent, they would fold their over sized fins and knife back into the water with hardly a splash.

There was another strong presence in *Panuco* that gave Panfilo pause. His name was Nuno Beltran de Guzman. On November 4, 1525, the crown had appointed him governor of the area of *Panuco.* Panfilo knew of this appointment and became increasingly concerned. Guzman was already in *Panuco* and rumors abounded that he had designs on the country to the north...the same area promised to Narvaez.

Guzman...Guzman, the name echoed in his head. Panfilo thought of the man he had never met, who gave every indication of interfering with the area promised to him. "What was he doing at this very minute"?

When they landed in *Santo Domingo,* he would immediately make discrete inquiries. Most certainly there was someone newly returned from *Panuco* with a story to tell.

His fists clenched, Panfilo could not help but vocalize his feelings, "I will hang the son of a bitch...*hijo de a perra*!"

At his side with the water cask, Campo's questioning eyes looked up at the conquistador. "What is it you're saying *mi capitan*".

"Ah, Campo you are good at sneaking up on me".

Pouring another glass of water, Campo handed it up to Panfilo, "*Capitan*, who were you speaking to?"

Finishing the water in one gulp, Panfilo looked at Campo, "I was thinking aloud my little friend...thinking of an enemy I would like to squash!"

There was more commotion on deck. People were pointing over the port side of the bow and straining to see. Panfilo turned to look in that direction. At first, there was nothing, but as the *Maria* crested, a small, dark, outline interrupted the otherwise flat contour of the horizon. At last, after their long and uncomfortable journey, there was something out there besides the endless sea. From here until they docked in *Hispaniola,* the strange and wonderful islands of the *Indies* would be close at hand. The most dangerous part of the journey, crossing the unpredictable *Océano Atlántico,* was over. A milestone had been passed and Panfilo secretly rejoiced and gave thanks. He thought again of the series of events during the last few years and the challenges yet to come. He thought again of Cortes.

While languishing in captivity, Panfilo had followed the politics of *New Spain* with interest. At first, his subjugation had been harsh, chained like an animal in the corner of a filthy hovel in *Vera Cruz.* But conditions improved, and after a time, he was moved to a better location and even allowed to move about. As Cortes' heart softened, the chains were eventually removed and he was held, on his honor, in a condition resembling house arrest. Many of his captors were former compatriots who had served with him in *Hispaniola, Jamaica,* and *Cuba.* Each day's news on the progress of *New Spain* was discussed at length. When Cortes suffered his defeat and retreated from *Tenochtitlan,* Panfilo secretly applauded the news. Later, he watched in amazement as Cortes reorganized his forces and prepared to return. In a span of only five months, he was on the attack again. The ensuing battle was long and protracted. As news filtered into *Vera Cruz,* Panfilo had to admit a grudging respect for his old adversary. In August of 1520, the *Aztec* empire was defeated, and even Panfilo was caught up in the celebration and feelings of euphoria.

Before being released from imprisonment, Narvaez had been invited by Cortes to visit him at *Mexico City*, the former *Tenochtitlan.* So, with a guard of five horsemen, he had proceeded from *Vera Cruz* along the same paths followed by Cortes and his army only a few months before. Riding along the circuitous route, Panfilo was astounded by the roughness of the country. His respect for Cortes grew with each league passed over. For days, they rode until finally, Panfilo was on the summit overlooking the *Valley of Mexico.* On this day, the view was intoxicating...even the guards paused and took in the grandeur spread out below them. The deep blue of *Lake Texcoco* shimmered in the high mountain air and the ring of volcanic mountains seemed to frame the city below.

Cortes himself had greeted Narvaez and together, they entered the city that once was the center of the grand *Aztec* empire. Dismissing the guards, Cortes took Narvaez on a detailed tour. All around was new construction, but here and there, signs of the pre-conquest city remained. They visited the towering great pyramid built to appease the twin Gods *Huitzilopochtli* and *Tlaloc.* High above, Narvaez could see that a giant wooden crucifix now adorned the top of the heathen temple where so many had been sacrificed. They visited Montezuma's grand palace and Narvaez noted that Cortes spoke fondly of the *Aztec* emperor. At various locations along the way, Cortes would stop to recount the battles fought and the men lost in a particular area. Many times, he would recite from memory the names of common soldiers killed by the *Mexica.*

It was at one particular location that Cortes suddenly stopped and dismounted. They were on the remains of one of the great causeways that connected *Tenochtitlan* to the mainland. Hands folded in front of him, Cortes stared out into the lake. Quietly in a voice choked with emotion, he explained that this was the site of the sad night...*Noche Triste*. Here, his forces had been ambushed as they attempted to leave *Tenochtitlan,* with much loss of life.

Riding back to the city, Cortes explained the battle and recounted the horrors of that night. Even now, years later, he would wake in the quiet hours of the morning bathed in sweat, remembering the awful things that had happened there. It was then that Narvaez suddenly reined in his horse and came to a stop. A surprised Cortes also reined in his mount.

In his characteristic booming voice, Narvaez had lamented, "*El Capitan*, when I was defeated by you at *Cempoallan,* you related to me that my capture was one of the least of things accomplished in New Spain. To that statement, I now concur. What I have seen this day marks the accomplishments of a great *caudillo"*.

Taken somewhat aback, Cortes only answered, "My only wish is to glorify God and serve our great King."

Janero Flores had joined Narvaez on the foredeck. Looking westward, the upcoming island was now clearly visible in the distance. Somewhat further north another spit of land began to make its presence above the horizon.

"Janero, your navigation is unerring. As a humble soldier, I am always in awe of seamen such as yourself."

Flores just shrugged. "*Capitan*, I have been walking these decks since the age of 13. You mastered the sword and crossbow, I learned the quadrant and cross-staff. I know every knot and line and listen while the ship talks to me. It is all a matter of perspective."

Narvaez eyed Flores with new respect, "I suppose we are good at what we do best."

They laughed and then Flores seemed to notice something on the boltsprit, Panfilo had no idea what. The pilot hurried back to the stern to chide a *marinero* who had failed to set one of the spirit sails to his liking. The wind changed slightly and Panfilo felt the soft force of it on his face. He felt the *Maria* respond, a subtle shift in the caravel's attitude. A curtain of spray burst upward from the bow and fell heavily on the deck. Thoroughly doused himself, Panfilo let out a belly laugh as he watched the cluster of onlookers below him react to the drenching.

Looking forward again to the upcoming island, Panfilo again thought of that last meeting with Cortes. It marked the last time he saw him. Later that evening, Cortes had been called to address a problem in one of the outlying areas. Narvaez spent two more days in *Tenochtitlan* before being escorted back to *Vera Cruz* and freedom, his hatred towards the conqueror greatly diminished. He never forgot *Tenochtitlan* and the riches that he observed there. The land beyond *New Spain,* this land called *Amichel,* now beckoned him.

CHAPTER 02

Red Dawn

Rojo Amanecer

The sunrise this morning had been one of the grandest Alvar had ever witnessed. Even before the sun's orb broke the surface of the horizon, it cast a brilliant crimson hue on the frothy clouds that hung motionless in the sky. In the half-light, the bow waves cascaded with luminescence, as they spilled across the surface. Only a light breeze propelled the El Viento across a calm sea that reflected the glow. For a time, the masts, sails, and rigging were tinged with red. A short distance to starboard, the Princesa Margarita was also ringed with a strange luminescence. For a moment, even the veteran marineros stopped what they were doing to gaze in wonderment at the display. But, the moment passed. The sun rose higher and the effect was lost. The morning was perfect...too perfect.

01 August, 1527

Aboard the Caravel El Viento Del Sur

Alvar stared out at his first sight of the New Land. The mountainous island of *Dominica*, its crumpled green profile abruptly rising from the horizon. He had hurried to the bow for an unobstructed look. There, watching the island materialize in the distance, he recalled the stories of Columbus. So enraptured with its beauty, the great Admiral had simply given it the *Latin* name for the day on which it was discovered—*Dominica*...Sunday! Once asked what the island looked like, Columbus had jokingly taken a piece of parchment, crumpled it, and thrown it on a table, "This is how *Dominica* appears!"

Alvar Nunez Cabeza De Vaca was somewhat taller than the average Spaniard and of a lithe build. He moved with a touch of regality that somewhat annoyed those who didn't know him. He listened more than talked and spoke with a preciseness that made it clear to all who were listening what his intentions were. His brown hair and neatly trimmed beard framed clear, blue eyes and a somewhat sharp, Roman nose.

Born i*n Jerez de la Frontera, Andalusia* to a family of wealth, his paternal grandfather, Pedro de Vera, led the movement that eliminated the native population from *Grand Canary*. His unbelievable barbarism resulted in the massacre or indenture of the aboriginal *Guanches* and the capitulation of the islands to *Spanish* rule.

From his maternal line, Alvar had chosen the strange surname *Cabeza De Vaca* meaning "head of the cow" from an ancestor who helped the Christian army at *Las Navas de Tolosa* defeat the invading *Moors* by marking a secret trail with a cow's skull. King Sancho of *Navarre* awarded the surname.

As a youth, Alvar lived well. He was educated and accustomed to a life assisted by slaves. Slavery was an institution in *Spain. Moors, Berbers, Guanches,* and black *Africans* were bought, sold, and used extensively by the family.

Alvar's first sexual experience had been with a 14-year-old *Berber* girl assigned to his mother as a cook's servant. His mother had been furious when the girl showed signs of pregnancy. She was immediately sold to one of the many slave markets that dotted the *Iberian* coast.

Growing up, De Vaca displayed the arrogance that was typical of all young *hidalgos* of the time. They believed in themselves, *Spain,* and absolute devotion to the Catholic Church. *Spain* had been a nation at war, a war against the *Islamic* intruders that had invaded the country in the 13th century. Not until 1492 was the last of these intruders vanquished. It was still a nation of warriors where young men of status were expected to show their mettle in battle. He learned his trade at the battle of *Ravenna* and then in the *Comuneros* revolt. Alvar, however, had a boundless thirst for knowledge and took every opportunity to expand his understanding of the world around him.

He followed closely the stories that filtered back from the New Land, particularly the conquest of *Mexico* by Hernan Cortes. It became quite the rage in *Spanish* society. At a public viewing in *Valladolid*, he had even been a witness to the unbelievable *Aztec* riches sent back by Cortes. Silver, pearls, exquisite featherwork, engravings, exotic birds, and above all...gold...tons of it! It was here that Alvar had made up his mind to experience the New Land for himself.

The opportunity for the Narvaez expedition came along at the right time. Active in high places, Alvar was awarded for his loyalty, and appointed treasurer and second in command. In his position, Alvar was given overall command of the *El Viento del Sur*...The South Wind. Command, however, was restricted only to military matters. The real operation of *El Viento* in all things nautical, would be by the ship's pilot. This was very much agreeable to Alvar, whose knowledge of sailing and the sea was minimal. True, he had grown up in *Jerez* not far from the great seaport at *Cadez*, but Alvar's life had been consumed with education.

From the moment the expedition left *San Lucar*, Alvar made his presence known on deck. At every opportunity, he asked questions, watched the mariners perform their tasks, and even became familiar with the ship's components. He memorized the 32 points of the compass, learned to sight the cross-staff, calculate latitude, and even joined in on such mundane tasks as sail repair. One particularly clear evening, he spent all night with the ship's pages as they performed their 4-hour sea watches, throwing the knot line, reading the compass, and entering the results on the traverse board.

Aboard, pilot Bartalome Valdez was subject to Alvar's constant presence and questions. Valdez was a meticulous and thorough man who made notes of everything encountered on the voyage. He quietly went about his work and enlisted the boatswain to carry out his deck commands. At first, Alvar was a nuisance, but as time passed and Valdez realized De Vaca was sincere, he began to volunteer information and take him into his confidence. And so it was...the rest of the crew soon lost the rigid formality of the time and greeted Alvar with a smile or a nod of the head.

As *El Viento del Sur* closed on the island, more of its particulars became visible. From his vantage point, Alvar could easily see that Columbus' analogy was quite correct. Nowhere was there even an acre of flat ground. The mountains extended down to the water's edge and all were covered with lush green vegetation. Above the thick canopy, flocks of birds made their way through the dark valleys, their bright plumage contrasting with the deep forest hues. But it was the smell that most surprised him. Carried by the shore breezes, the sweet perfumed scent of the island played upon his senses.

High above the deck, a *marinero* hollered, *"Tierra al estibor...Land to starboard*!"

Alvar shifted his gaze to the starboard side of the ship. Although not yet visible to those on deck, a tell-tale cloud bank marked the presence of another island.

Moving back to the aft deck, Alvar joined Bartalome Valdez. Valdez was pointing out landmarks to his apprentice pilot, Angel Jimenez. Behind them, the boatswain kept an eye on the workings of the ship and waited for any commands from pilot Valdez.

"Senor De Veca, we pilots call these *Islas de Barlovento,* for they are windward of the trades. What you will see on the starboard side is *Marigalante*...gallant Mary...named for the Admiral's flagship on his second voyage. I had hoped we would be a little further to the north, but this will do quite nicely. As we draw nearer, you will see the much larger mass of *Santa Maria de Guadeloupe* in the background.

Marigalante was now coming into full view. To Alvar, it looked like a *galleta*...cookie, floating on the water, so different from the mountainous *Dominica* only a few leagues to the south.

Now, a small cluster of Islands on the starboard side began to materialize as *Santa Maria de Guadeloupe* loomed further to the north. Valdez continued his narrative, "These are the *Islas de Los Santos* discovered by Columbus on November 4, 1493...All Saints Day! As soon as they are well astern, we will turn somewhat northerly and parallel the beaches of *Maria de Guadeloupe* until nightfall. At that time, we will tack further to sea to avoid any unforeseen landfalls in the darkness.

Alvar felt the slight shift in direction as the *Islas de Santos* passed well astern. The feeling of the wind on his face changed ever so slightly. The beauty of the land before him was mesmerizing.

He felt a hand on his shoulder, it was Valdez. "*Alguacil*, do not become too enthralled with this beautiful place for we are now in the waters of the *Caribs*, they are cannibals capable of unbelievable violence. I call these waters the 'sea of the Caribs'...*mars de Caribs*. If we became shipwrecked here, the chances of you ending up in a stew pot are very good!"

With that, Valdez briefly touched the medallion he wore around his neck.

Bartalome Valdez had accompanied Christopher Columbus on his fourth voyage to the new world in 1502 as an 18-year-old apprentice pilot. He had grown up in the *Spanish* seaport town of *Cadiz* in a middle-class family. Big for his age, Bartalome was the oldest of the nine Valdez children. His father had been a minor magistrate in *Cadiz* but died in the cholera epidemic of 1496. With eight younger children at home, his mother and relatives could not afford to support all the children. In 1497, his uncle had arranged for him to serve as a page aboard a *Mediterranean* merchantman. Bartalome had so impressed the ship's captain that he was brought forward as an apprentice seaman in 1499 in preparation for pilot training. After plying the many ports of the Mediterranean for three years, he passed his examination in 1501 at the *Seville* Board of Trade—the youngest ever.

Valdez was a natural navigator with unmistakable talent, some would say a sense, for reading the seas and the weather. He made few mistakes and began to build a reputation as an exceptional pilot. In between voyages in 1501, he was approached by Bartholomew Columbus, brother to the great Admiral, and was asked to accompany them on their upcoming voyage...their fourth to the New Land. This, Bartalome accepted, for the idea of serving with the Admiral was an honor like no other. The fleet's four vessels sailed out of *Cadiz* on April 2, 1502.

The voyage was a surreal adventure for Bartalome Valdez. At *Hispaniola,* he experienced his first Caribbean hurricane, a terrifying ordeal even for a hardened seaman. In *Panama,* his ship had been stranded in the *Rio Belen* and surrounded by vicious *Indians.* Men had died, and Bartalome had taken his first life in the melee. It was there that he removed a copper talisman from the slain *Indio* and put it around his own neck. From that moment on, it was always with him. After being shipwrecked in *Jamaica* for a year, the remnants of the expedition made it back to *San Lucar* in November of 1504.

So began Bartalome Valdez's life as a pilot in the *Indies.* In the years after 1504, he sailed on excursions throughout the area. Usually, his returns to *Spain* were brief. Trade and travel to the New Land was increasing at phenomenal rates and demand for experienced pilots was always high. While at *Cadiz* in April 1527, Bartalome had responded to the town criers' request for experienced seamen for the upcoming Narvaez expedition. It promised to be a journey to the mysterious *Amichel*. For this alone, he would agree to go.

As evening approached, *Maria de Guadeloupe* began to fall astern and Alvar, once again, felt the shift in direction as *El Viento del Sur* turned further out to sea.

The sun was like a hot ember as it dropped toward the western horizon. One of the finest evenings Alvar had yet experienced on this trip across the *Oceano Atlantico*.

From above another call, *"Tierra al estibor...Land to starboard*!"

Absently sitting on a keg and whittling a stick, Bartalome Valdez looked up as Alvar approached, "*Alguacil,* I would imagine you are ready to walk on dry land again, I know I am."

 "I would have thought, pilot Valdez, that you prefer this life to one ashore."

Valdez laughed aloud, *Alguacil*, it is my profession and I am good at it but I would still prefer a warm bed that doesn't rock back and forth and the accompaniment of a beautiful woman."

Alvar smiled at this. He liked Valdez. "What is this island that we now approach?"

"Ah, this is one that I know very little about. The Admiral passed it by on his second voyage. Other *Indios* had told him it was uninhabited because of raids by the *Caribs*. To this day there is no *Spanish* presence on it."

"What is it called?"

Valdez thought for a moment. "The only name I have heard is from the *Carib* language. They call it *Alliouagana.*

Alvar shook his head. "Pilot Valdez, How do you know these things?"

"When you have been at sea as many years as me, you meet people and hear many things!"

With the sun fading, the mountainous island the Indians called *Alliouagan* passed slowly by as *El Viento del Sur,* and the other ships proceeded into the night.

02 August, 1527

Off the Coast of st Kitts and Nevis

At first light, Alvar rushed on deck to check the horizon. On the port side, there was nothing but ocean and the still darkness of the western sky. To the east, however, and directly starboard, was the rugged outline of a mountainous Island. Framed in the foreground by the rising sun, the western side of the island was still in shadow, making the whiteness of the breakers against the beach stand out. It was a beautiful sight.

"*Alguacil*, you are up early!" It was Valdez.

"*Si* Pilot Valdez, I have never seen sights such as this. Tell me what you know of this island." Alvar made a broad gesture toward the island.

"Ahhh, there are four islands in a row here, I call them 'The Four Sisters'. All were seen by the Admiral on his 2nd voyage of discovery, but he came ashore on only one...the one you see before you. The first of the four we passed before the morning light. If you look toward the bow, the third island is now just emerging. You will see the telltale view of a volcano's cone."

Alvar squinted hard and even took a step or two up the rat line to get a better view. Sure enough, there it was, low on the horizon.

"The fourth 'Sister' will come into view before noon. This one is very small and also formed by a volcano. There are almost no beaches. It is the point at which we will turn west toward *Borinquen*."

Alvar did not recognize the name *"Borinquen"*.

Valdez, picking up on De Vaca's blank look, elaborated. *"Borinquen* is the *Indio* name for the island, the Admiral called it *San Juan Bautista*. Now many just call it, The Rich Port...*Puerto Rico."*

It was a grand day with high clear skies and a strong following wind. Sure enough, just before noon, the fourth Island came into view. Narvaezs' flagship *Maria de la Meridionales Mares."* was the first to come about in a westerly tack, followed by the other four. They passed no more than a league from this unusual island, the remains of a large volcano staring down at them. The *marinos* called this *Isla Peligrosa*...dangerous Island. Indeed, when first sighted by Columbus, he had refused to land here because of the perilous rock shores.

After altering course at *Isla Peligrosa,* the five ships of the Narvaez expedition took a heading north-north, west. At dusk, the setting sun seemed to hang on the bowsprit until finally dropping below the horizon. On this evening, the afterglow was spectacular, coloring the sky with an orange incandescence. A light to medium south wind heeled the ships to starboard as dolphins glided in the wakes. It was a magical evening.

03 August, 1527

Passing St Croix

With the morning light, Panfilo Narvaez was up early to observe the progress of the expedition. He was accompanied, as usual, by Campo, who hoovered just behind the *Adelentado,* ready to respond to his every need.

"Look there, Campo!" Narvaez pointed to the port side, amidships to an island whose shape was just emerging in the early light. The island appeared very hilly.

"I see it *Adelentado*, what is this island called?"

"The Great Admiral landed here on his second voyage and called it *Isla de la Santa Cruz*...Island of the Holy Cross. It is one of the last waypoints before we come to *Borinquen* and then, after that, *Hispaniola*.

To Campo whose life as a street urchin had been limited, this was an adventure on a grand scale. He could not contain his excitement.

"Tell me about this island, *Adelentado*. Are there *Spaniards* living there?"

Narvaez let out one of his belly laughs. He tussled Campo's hair.

"No one lives there, my little *rata*. A few hearty souls have tried to establish farms and villages, but the *Caribs* have killed them all. It is a very dangerous place."

Campos's eyes were wide with wonder. "Are these the *Indios* that eat people?"

Narvaez only chuckled, "Yes they are my little friend, yes they are."

The ships of the Narvaez expedition continued on, still enjoying clear skies and mild seas. At noon, an island on the starboard side became visible in the distance. Columbus had seen this on his second voyage but had bypassed it. The *Tiano* inhabitants had given it a name that the *Spaniards* interpreted as *Isla de Vieques*...small island. Very soon after sighting *Isla de Vieques,* a much larger land mass seemed to spread across the horizon. This was the eastern end of *Borinquen,* the last large island before reaching *Hispaniola.* From here, they would follow the shoreline while staying well out to sea. As the darkness began to fall, only a red smudge illuminated the western sky. In the east, the stars shone brightly. It would be a clear night. To starboard, an occasional light could be seen on shore. A bonfire, a residence? One could only guess.

04 August, 1527

Approaching the Coast of Peurto Rico

The southerly wind had remained steady during the night, and they sailed in a broad reach across the expanse of *Borinquen's* southern shore. Just at midnight, the ships turned to port to increase the distance from the island. This was to avoid several smaller islands that jutted out from the central coast.

Alvar had come up on deck just as the direction change was taking place. Moving to the stern, he urinated into the water below. The altered course of the ship was marked by the bio-luminescence that trailed off and eventually disappeared into the distance.

From somewhere amidships, the voice of Bartolome Valdez called out to one of the *marineros* who was adjusting the rigging. Alvar moved toward him.

"Pilot Valdez, do you ever sleep?"

Valdez left the question unanswered. "Alguacil, what brings you on deck at this late hour?"

"My mind is very active this evening and I can't sleep. We are getting close to our destination and so much has to be done. Besides, I had to piss."

Valdez laughed, "That's as good a reason as any. After this course change, we will sail in almost a straight line to the port at *Santo Domingo*. That is, of course, if the wind direction holds."

Alvar retired back to his berth but lay awake for a long time listening to the sounds of the night.

At morning's first light, the south shore of *Puerto Rico* loomed large on the starboard side of *El Viento del Sur.*

04 August, 1527

Off the Southwest Coast of Puerto Rico on Board

Maria De La Meridionales Mares

Panfilo Narvaez watched as the southern coast of *Borinquen* slowly slipped by. Further west, but still out of sight, was the westernmost terminus of the island. Beyond that, there was only ocean until they arrived at the harbor at *Santo Domingo* in *Hispaniola*. He had only been in *Borinquen* on one occasion and that was a brief stop at the harbor in *Puerto Rico de San Juan Bautista* on the island's north shore. He sighed thinking of that visit, for it had been almost 17 years ago. He had been a much younger man back then, full of fight and enthusiasm. Now at 47, he was embarking on one of his biggest challenges. As he looked across the expanse of water, he could see the glistening white beaches and the mysterious forests behind. He was sure that the lands of *Amichel*, to which the King had granted him governorship, would be equally mysterious and a source of unequaled wealth. Surely, if Hernan Cortes could stumble upon the untold riches of the *Aztecs* there had to be more such rich kingdoms in this massive land.

05 August, 1527

Leaving the West coast of Puerto Rico on board

Reina de Napoles

Alonzo del Castillo finally found time to sit down on a barrel head that was lashed to the aft mast. He had spent the morning looking after the *soldatos* in his charge. Mostly, they were a sorry lot prone to arguments and insubordination. For this, he had no tolerance and several had tasted the lash as a result of their actions. There were some who showed promise, however, and he would use these as his nucleus to form a competent fighting force in the new world.

He looked past the stern and could see the island of *Borinquen* disappearing in the distance. God willing, tomorrow would bring them into the port at *Santo Domingo* where, finally, he could walk on dry land again. Castillo hated being on a ship and suffered mightily from sea sickness. Turning toward the bow, he could see the other four ships spread out before him with the governor's flagship, *Maria de la Meridionales Mares* in the lead. Scanning the horizon ahead, there was no sight of land but the pilot Dario Quiroz had assured him that their destination was not far off.

"Praise God!"

06 August, 1527

Just South of Isla De Mona

It was very early morning. The horizon ahead was still very dark. At the stern, the very first faint blush of light began to tinge the eastern sky. Overhead, the stars so visible just minutes before began to wink out with the coming daylight. The winds during the night had been weak and contrary and the progress of the Narvaez fleet had been reduced to only 15 leagues. Bartolome Valdez checked the compass and confirmed that they were on course. He looked toward the bow and could just make out the outline of the flagship, *Maria de la Meridionales Mares.*

Bartolome thought to himself, "So far my friend, Janero Florez, as pilot of the flagship has done an unerring job." They had been friends for years. Now, as the first tinges of light touched the top of the masts, the wispy surface haze began to disperse.

"Ah, there it is, right where it is supposed to be!" To starboard, Bartolome saw the characteristic flatness of *Isla de Mona* just making itself visible. This little island, no more than two leagues across, marked the halfway point between *Borinquen* and *Hispaniola.* The island had received its name from the *Tiano Indians,* and this crossing was increasingly called *El Pasaje de Mona*...the *Mona* Passage.

06 August, 1527

Approaching Saona Island Aboard El Viento Del Sur

It was noon and now the day was brilliantly clear, *Isla Mona* had slipped astern several hours past. Now, another projection made itself known just off the bow. The *Isla Saona* rose in the distance. The pilot immediately corrected his course somewhat to the south, for the *Isla Saona* marked the southeast terminus of the island of *Hispaniola*. Alvar could hardly contain his enthusiasm. Here, the great Admiral of the ocean sea had named the island on his second voyage of discovery. Growing up in *Andalucia*, De Vaca had been spellbound by the stories of the great seafarers of the time. Now, by God's providence, here he was looking with his own eyes at the same miracles viewed by the great Admiral.

Rounding the *Isla Saona,* Alvar thought it to be a paradise. The whiteness of the perfect beaches was blinding in the sun. Onshore, the towering palms gently swayed to the ever-present sea breezes. The white sand extended far out into the water and even at a distance one could see schools of fish gliding just beneath the waves. It seemed to Alvar that each island was more beautiful than the one previous.

From the moment that land was first sighted at *Dominca,* the decks remained crowded. The people pointed at new wonders and talked excitedly of their hopes in the New Land. Normally, the pilot and boatswain would have cleared the decks, for congestion impeded the operation of the ship, but the weather was perfect and these people deserved to share the experience.

Then, just after reaching *Isla Saona's* eastern shore, the winds ceased to blow for a period of 18 hours. Becalmed, the vessels of the expedition floated like statues on an emerald sea, sails flaccid, pennants hanging limply from the masts.

Not until the early morning of the next day did the wind reestablish itself, first as a light breeze that just cooled the cheek and forehead.

Finally, at the hour of Vespers, the wind picked up to a steady southerly blow. Masts and yardarms creaked and groaned while the canvas sails popped to and began propelling the vessels forward. With darkness, however, the winds calmed and once again the vessels sat idly in the water.

In the morning, a steady breeze came up and the expedition was once again underway. Behind *Isla Saona, Hispaniola* had come into view, the coast receding to the north and then making a gradual arc to the west. Soon, another Island rose from the horizon, this one *Santa Catalina,* also identified by The Admiral during his second voyage. *Catalina* marked the point at which the shoreline of *Hispaniola* continued on in a westerly direction. From here, the pilots would be on the alert for the mouth of the *Rio Ozama* and the protected harbor at *Santo Domingo.*

10 September, 1527

The Port at Santo Domingo, Hispaniola

Santo Domingo was a bustling town of opportunity. Most voyages to and from the New World stopped here and it was so with the Narvaez fleet. Although somewhat in decline, the port at *Santa Domingo* was a cacophony of everything needed to sustain the massive *Spanish* effort in the *Caribbean, New Spain,* and *South America.* There were hustlers, whorehouses, food markets, blacksmiths, shipwrights, livestock, metal smiths, sail wrights, carpenters, slave blocks and lumber mills. The hills around the port were dotted with small farms, elaborate *haciendas,* and fields of sugar cane tended by *Tiano* and black slaves.

There was always a need for artisans, farmers, and men of all types. The local authorities actively solicited visitors to the port. The Narvaez expedition was no different. Many of the colonists and even some of the soldiers deserted the ship and disappeared into the countryside...about one hundred and forty in all.

The population around *Santo Domingo* was sympathetic and actively protected the deserters. Narvaez was enraged that these local *"paridos"* would interfere with his expedition, but he needed the support of the authorities and was forced to overlook the desertions. In any case, the deserters would have to be replaced with other recruits from the surrounding areas and *Cuba*. It would take time to gather the necessary people and restock the expedition.

While in *Santo Domingo*, the colonists and soldiers had been free to stay on the ships, but many chose to set up quarters elsewhere. In port, life on the ship was hectic. Livestock was offloaded, bilges were pumped, hulls scraped, and ballast readjusted, while a variety of on-board repairs were underway. The harbor was alive with the sound of hammers, saws, blacksmith anvils, and the rough talk of the tradesmen going about their duties. Those who could afford it paid for lodging at a local home or farm. Others constructed crude hovels in the fields around town.

Alvar's duties while in the port at *Santa Domingo* were largely administrative and mundane. Repairs, supply acquisitions, and dispute arbitrations filled his days and nights. Still, whenever he could free himself, Alvar regaled in touring the city and the countryside, visiting the plantations and farms. He marveled at the *Alcazar de Colon*, the governor's home and seat of government built by Diego Colon in 1510. Several of the trips into the countryside had been with Narvaez. In *Hispaniola*, Narvaez had numerous friends and acquaintances. Alvar was astounded at the old warriors' abilities at horse-trading. He wandered tirelessly throughout the area, displaying the royal charter, and seeking new recruits, horses, and supplies.

Three high-placed acquaintances provided additional funding in the form of cash advances. With this funding, Narvaez purchased another caravel, *La Doncella De Plata*, to assist in transporting the horses he intended on taking to *Panuco*. Narvaez was aware that any military campaign conducted in this new land hinged on the number of cavalry that the commander was able to put into the field.

Ten of the pedigreed horses brought from Spain rapidly sold and the returns easily purchased twenty more of lesser provenance...all that were available in *Hispaniola*. After 42 days on the island, Narvaez had exhausted most of the sources of supply. The ships had all been repaired and any more time spent in *Santo Domingo* stood the chance of further desertions. Narvaez was impatient to continue on to *Cuba* where his real influence lay. It was with some relief then, that Narvaez announced his intent to leave *Santa Domingo* and continue on to *Santiago, Cuba.* It was also no coincidence that the sprawling Narvaez *ranchero* was 20 leagues from *Santiago* near the agricultural town of *San Salvador de Bayomo*. His wife Maria, ever the astute businesswoman, had originally suggested he purchase quality breeding stock in *Spain* to gain a substantial profit in the *Indies*. The prize studs, quartered on the Narvaez flagship would be supplementing his own herds at *Bayamo,* to be replaced with horses of lesser pedigree.

On October 21, 1527, the fleet, now six vessels, left the protected port of S*anto Domingo* and began the journey to *Santiago* on the island of *Cuba.*

21 October, 1527

Aboard the Caravel El Viento Del Sur

The day of departure from the port at *Santo Domingo* had been gray and rainy. A lackluster south wind propelled the flotilla along at a slow pace. Depending on conditions, head pilot Jenero Flores in the flagship, followed the shoreline from a distance of 1 to 2 leagues. The low haze obscured the mountains on shore and filtered down into the valleys below. Flores continued thus for 10 leagues and then adjusted the course westward at noon. Here, the shoreline ran east-west for another 10 leagues. This course took the fleet into *Bahia de Ocoa.* It was in this bay that Columbus, on his fourth voyage, had avoided the terrible hurricane that sank the *Torres* gold fleet in the *Mona* Passage.

As the evening progressed, the fog thickened, the wind fell to nil and darkness closed in around them. The vessels displayed their storm lanterns and the formation grouped together. Here in *Bahia de Ocoa* an eerie glow and sinister shadows played upon the deck. Sitting on an empty *pipa,* Alvar thought of the fierce Carib *Indians* that frequented these waters. The practice of eating their victims gave Alvar reason to cross himself several times during the night. Seaward, only drifting, pinpoints of light marked the other ships. Occasionally, one would momentarily blink as a *marinero* or sentinel passed in front of it.

Sometime after midnight...*medianoche...*the wind came back up. On the deck, Alvar had fallen asleep. He was roused by the commands and the commotion on deck. The fog was abating and the wind was freshening. Overhead, the canvas sails flapped and then filled. *El Viento* began to move. In the darkness, Pilot Flores steered a course well offshore. By daybreak, the fleet was progressing rapidly under a southeast wind. Ahead, *Cabo Beata* came into view. South of the cape was *Isla Beata,* just visible in the morning sky. From here, the coastline of *Hispaniola* dropped back to the north. The fleet continued on past *Isla Beata* not wanting to chance the shallow waters between the mainland and the island. Instead, Pilot Flores made his turn to the west in the passage between *Isla Beata* and the smaller *Isla Alto Velo* just to the south.

From his vantage point, Pilot Flores watched as both islands, one to starboard and the other to larboard, passed. Like most other landmarks on this voyage, these two islands had been first seen by Columbus on his second voyage. Alvar was impressed at the quantity and breadth of discoveries made by the great admiral, now more than 35 years prior. As evening came upon them, the fleet continued to the northwest, staying far out from the mainland. In the morning, there was no land in sight. Here, the *Hispaniola* coastline had receded to the north. By late afternoon, the low smudge on the northern horizon indicated that the coastline was, once again, coming into view. In the evening, the fleet passed very close to a peninsula that jutted out from the mainland. The sails were reefed and the ships now idled along as night closed in around them.

Alvar questioned Bartalome Valdez as to why the ships were slowing.

"*Algaucil*, tomorrow we will approach a small island off the coast of *Hispaniola*. This island is our waypoint. From here, we will turn north for the final run to *Santiago* harbor. Sailing at full speed in the darkness would increase our chance of missing the island altogether."

The journey along *Hispaniola's* shore had been uneventful but wonderfully scenic. The rugged coast slid by in a profusion of mountains, islands, forests, cliffs, sand, and sea. The days were clear and the winds favorable. Finally, in the morning, the western terminus of *Hispaniola, Cape San Miguel*, passed astern and the small island of *Navaza* lay just ahead.

Alvar knew of *Navaza*, for it was here that two Spaniards had performed a legendary feat of seamanship. In 1503, Diego Mendez, Bartolomeo Fieschi, and six Indians paddled a canoe from *Jamaica* to *Hispaniola* to bring help for their shipwrecked comrades. Their efforts saved what was left of Columbus' fourth and final voyage of discovery. Across 40 leagues of open water, the feat would not have been possible had they not chanced on *Navaza* Island. Almost consumed by thirst, the island provided refuge and a fresh water source before continuing onto the mainland, another 10 leagues distant. Being a member of the fourth voyage, Bartalome Valdez knew both Mendez and Fieschi well and spent many an evening talking of their heroism.

Passing by *Navaza,* Alvar's ship, *El Viento,* was the closest, being not more than several hundred yards...*varas* to starboard. True to the stories Alvar had heard, the island was virtually flat; a large gray bubble on the water's surface. Limestone cliffs rose 40 feet or more to the plateau above. Sea waves colliding with these buttresses sent plumes of spray bounding into the air. On the plateau, a field of grasses and stunted shrubs struggled to survive in the barren environment – but it was the birds that were most impressive. Thousands of them! Everywhere they wheeled and circled, filling the air with a riot of color and noise.

On this day, the wind was quartering astern from the northeast. As *El Viento* sailed by the island, a pungent smell permeated the air, its intensity getting stronger as the vessel passed to the leeward side.

It watered Alvar's eyes. Looking around, he noticed the pilot Bartalome Valdez watching him with a grin on his face.

"Bird shit...*Mierda del pajavo!*"

At *Navaza,* the *Narvaez* Expedition turned north and pointed their bows toward *Santiago, Cuba.*

25 October, 1527

Aboard the Caravel El Viento Del Sur

Located near the eastern tip of *Cuba, Santiago* was a magnificent natural harbor. A steep bluff, projecting high into the air, hid the inlet until the vessels were almost upon it. Once past the narrow entrance, the harbor opened into a wide bay that meandered inland for a league or more. The town looked down on the waterfront vista below. Even in the foulest of weather, *Santiago* was a harbor like no other.

The expedition had arrived off *Santiago* late in the evening but had elected to remain offshore until daybreak. As the sails were unfurled and the anchors dropped, Narvaez was rowed ashore to begin the negotiations for men and supplies.

In the morning, the air was alive with activity. Sounds of the port carried across the water...one could hear the blacksmith forges, the sharp ringing of the hammers in the carpentry shops, and the rough talk and laughter emanating from the docks. As *El Viento* drew nearer, Alvar began to recognize the unique smells. The aroma of hot pitch and burning charcoal mixed with rotted fish, waste from the butcher shops, animal manure, and human excrement, all using the bay as a receptacle. To be sure, there were sweet enticements as well...the fresh smell of baking bread, chicken cooking, and fragrances from the abundant greenery that surrounded the bay. All of this wafted across the water to greet the new arrivals.

The docking process was always time-consuming, but on this day, *El Viento* was the first to be secured to the wharf...*embarcadero*, a large wooden structure still under construction. Alvar immediately set upon unloading the eight horses on board, for keeping the horses healthy was a priority. As to the colonists and soldiers on board, Narvaez had placed severe restrictions, not wanting to repeat the personnel losses experienced in *Santo Domingo*. They would be released under close supervision and only for a limited amount of time.

In the harbor, other ships were being serviced as well. Alvar counted eight. The expedition vessels would have to wait their turn. Next to the *Viento* a large carrack, the *Senora de Sevilla*, was loading supplies for *Vera Cruz* in *New Spain*. Alvar had stopped briefly to talk with the pilot, a fellow countryman from *Cadez*.

Next to them, a line of laborers were struggling under the weight of *botijas* of wine being loaded aboard the *Senora*.

"It looks like the soldiers of Cortes won't have a problem finding wine for holy communion," Alvar noted.

With a laugh, the pilot waved his hand as if to encompass all of the supplies. "It used to be gunpowder and horses...but now with the *Mexica* defeated, they are living the good life."

Here, as in *Santo Domingo,* the workers were *Indio* slaves under the supervision of a tough labor boss...*jefe de trabajo.* Alvar couldn't help but notice the blank stares as they performed their drudgery. It was as though a light had been removed from their soul. Shirtless, all were marked with welts...some recent. The *jefe* eyed each one and tapped a short ratline, a *rebenque,* against his leg. *Indians* didn't hold up well, in a few months most of these would be dead and replaced by others.

Alvar noticed that the *Adelantado* standing on the hill above talking to a well-dressed *Spaniard.* Excusing himself, Alvar took the path up the hill, noticing on the way, the panoramic view of the bay spread out below him.

As he approached, Narvaez looked over, "Ah De Vaca, how are the horses holding up?"

"They appear to be in fine shape, your excellency. We are unloading the last one now but I will need some kind of enclosure to hold them."

"May I suggest the corral just to the north...about half a league." It was the well-dressed *Spaniard.*

Narvaez spoke up, "My apologies De Vaca, this is my good friend Vasco Porcallo de Figuerora. Here in the *Indies,* we have much history together." Wrapping his huge hand around the back of Porcallo's neck, Narvaez gently shook him. "He was kind enough to meet me here today with offers of additional supplies and horses.

"It is a pleasure *Senior* Porcallo."

Alvar mentally appraised the gentleman now standing before him. He knew the name. Porcallo's fame as a warrior both in *Spain* and in the *Indies* was well known. Early in the conquest of *Cuba,* he and Narvaez had fought side by side. Both had been well rewarded for their efforts.

In 1519 Porcallo had joined Narvaez in the ill-fated expedition to *New Spain* to arrest Hernan Cortes. After Narvaez's defeat at *Cempoallan*, however, Porcallo returned to *Cuba* in chains while Narvaez remained in *Vera Cruz*. In *Cuba*, once free of Cortes' influence, he was immediately released. Since then, he had concentrated his efforts in *Cuba*, expanding his holdings in both land and slaves.

Porcallo was now one of the richest men in *Cuba*. Somewhat younger than Narvaez, he was showing signs of the good life. Impeccably dressed, the added pounds were apparent even under the richly embroidered tunic. Around his neck hung a gaudy gold pendant. Only the scar that ran across his right cheek and the lobe of an ear missing betrayed he was once a warrior.

Porcallo watched Alvar intently as Narvaez continued, "Senior Porcallo has promised the expedition horses, swine, and supplies of cassava bread, smoked bacon, and maize from his *ranchero* in *Trinidad*."

"Senior Porcallo, that is most gracious", Alvar bowed slightly at the waist.

"Ha!" Narvaez's laugh carried across the waterfront. "De Vaca, don't let this sly *caballero* completely fool you. There is always a motive for such gifts."

"Panfilo, you misjudge me. My intentions are honorable." Porcallo spread his hands in front of him and feigned a look of disbelief.

He continued. "But of course, if the land is rich in *Indios* I could use a few to supplement my workforce here in *Cuba*."

"Vasco, my friend, for such a gift we will bring you back all the brown *hibridos* you can use...especially the females." Narvaez winked at Alvar, but the effect was lost because of the eyepatch.

"But enough of business Vasco, let us sit down at the *cantina* and talk of old times."

Porcallo turned to Alvar, "Will you join us?"

"You are most gracious Senior Porcallo, but my duties require that I return to the ship."

Leaving, Narvaez gestured to Alvar, "After the horses are sufficiently rested we should proceed directly to *Trinidad* to take advantage of Senor Porcallo's kind offer."

Narvaez looked back at Porcallo, "Before he changes his mind!"

Porcallo laughed and slapped Narvaez on the back, "Let us go drink."

Alvar watched the two companions walk towards the town and then made his way down the hill, back to *El Viento.*

26 October, 1527

The Cantina El Galleon De Oro in Santiago, Cuba

As the two men approached the single-story brick building, Narvaez noticed the new sign hanging from the porch rafters. In large letters *"El Galleon de Oro"*, was neatly lettered on the weathered boards. Below it, in somewhat smaller font, was *cerveza y vino*...beer and wine.

Narvaez smiled, "Ah, friend Vasco we have passed many a good time in this establishment."

Porcallo stopped abruptly in front of the *Cantina,*

Narvaez, with a questioning look also stopped.

"Panfilo, I have a surprise for you."

Narvaez spread his hands and shrugged his shoulders, "A surprise! What else besides your generous offer could you surprise me with?"

"Let us go inside *La Cantina* and I will show you."

Narvaez had to bend slightly as passed through the door. Inside, it was cool. He stood a moment, acclimating his eyesight to the darker interior. It was very bright outside, and inside, the window shades had been pulled shut.

He scanned the room.

The bartender and several *cabelleros* were looking at him with large smiles on their faces. Friends and fellow soldiers from the past.

"*Madre de Dios*!"

Then, he felt another presence in the room, far in a corner. From behind a table, a woman of impeccable beauty stood up. She was tall and gracefully built, with long black hair falling far below her shoulders. Her blouse, low cut, revealed large breasts pushed together to form an inviting cleavage. Even from a distance, her dark eyes shone with a brilliance.

"Panfillo, *mi querido*, welcome home!"

Dumbfounded for a moment, Narvaez could only utter, "Maria? And then again, "Maria?"

Her laugh filled the bar, "Of course it is me, you big oaf!"

Surging forward, Narvaez upset a chair as he crossed the room. Coming together, both embraced to the cheers of all in the room.

27 October, 1527

Aboard the Caravel El Viento Del Sur, Santiago, Cuba

On *El Viento*, Fray Juan Velazquesz de Salazar had just completed Sunday mass and after some small talk with the passengers had approached Alvar with his usual good-natured mannerisms.

"*Algacil*, it is my understanding that we will not be long at this location before sailing to *Trinidad*."

"Fray Velazquesz, that is my understanding as well. The expedition needs to replenish men who deserted at *Santo Domingo*, and we are loading supplies. After that, we will proceed to *Trinidad* for horses and salt pork...all provided by a friend of the *Adelentado*."

Velazquesz thought on this a moment, "I ask these questions not of myself, but to be more knowledgeable when asked by those aboard this ship."

"I understand."

"So, *Senor* De Vaca when do you think we will leave *Santiago*."

"Ha, good fray, of that I am uncertain. Until last night I thought our stay would be brief." Alvar nodded towards the town.

Velazquesz chuckled, "That was quite a party last night. I hear the *Adelentado* is still not up."

Without thinking, Alvar answered, "Who would be, with a woman like that to share your bed!"

Velazquesz summed up his most pious look and stared at De Vaca.

"Oh, excuse me, Father Juan, I...ah...meant no disrespect."

Fray Velazquesz let out a huge belly laugh as he put his hand on Alvar's shoulder. "*Alguacil*, my vows of celibacy only go so far...I am still allowed to look. The *Adelentado's* wife is indeed a beautiful woman."

With that, Velazquesz collected his assortment of vestments and walked back to his quarters, still chuckling to himself.

Alvar stepped off the ship onto the rough planking of the dock and proceeded up the hill towards the town. There was still much to do.

30 October, 1527

The Harbor at Cabo Cruz, Cuba

The fleet had exited the harbor at *Santiago*. They had sailed throughout the night. Now, the next day, the weather was clear and the winds were favorable.

The stop at *Santiago* had provided six more horses and a quantity of other supplies. After three days in *Santiago*, Maria had returned to the large ranch in *Bayomo*. With much fanfare, the *Adelentado* himself had escorted her out of town. Now focused on the expedition once again, Narvaez was anxious to pick up Porcalo's offerings in *Trinidad* and then move on to *Habana* where he would acquire additional stores and set up a resupply ship. Of course, Maria had promised to visit him in *Habana* as well. From *Habana,* the expedition would begin the journey to the territory of *Panuco* and the *River of Palms*.

It was well past noon. As they coasted along the *Cuban* shoreline, Narvaez suddenly instructed the fleet to detour to a small harbor at *Cabo Santa Cruz,* the southernmost tip of *Cuba*. Here, while at anchor, the officers and Vasco Porcalo were rowed ashore for a meeting.

The harbor itself was nothing more than a small fishing village, but it offered a refuge and a place to discuss the situation at hand. A rather unkempt and portly individual greeted them as the ship's boats were pulled onto the beach. Narvaez, the first to land, jumped out and rushed to the man.

"Julio! How long has it been?" Narvaez picked him up like a rag doll.

"*Capitan,* I looked from the hill and couldn't believe it was you". Julio Rios looked perplexed.

"Ha! It's not *capitan* anymore dear friend, now I am *Adelantado* and all the ships you see are mine." Narvaez gestured out to the harbor.

Just then Julio spied another familiar face, "Vasco, is it truly you?"

"Ah, Julio, the greatest swordsman in all of *Cuba*", Vasco Porcalo stepped up and clapped the man on the back.

While the rest of the officers and their crews pulled up onto the beach, the threesome continued their discourse, obviously happy to see each other. Suddenly, Narvaez stepped back, drew his sword, and held it high in the air.

"This is Julio Rios...the best *soldado* I have ever served with. We fought together on *Hispaniola, Jamaica,* and here in *Cuba*...right on this beach. Many times has he pulled my *gonadas* out of the fire."

"Mine as well," echoed Porcalo, grabbing his crotch.

Alvar looked at the disheveled individual and could not conjure up the vision of a warrior. Rios, like Naravez, looked to be approaching 50, his curly brown hair and beard streaked with gray.

"Now we will meet in his *hacienda* and talk of our strategy".

With that, Narvaez sheathed his sword and trudged up the beach to a rundown enclosure located on a small hill overlooking the harbor, a bewildered Rios following close behind.

The "*hacienda*" was nothing more than a one-room living space. Outside was one cane chair, a crude table, and several logs. Interspersed between these were all manner of items...shoes, fishing nets, a set of oars, and, strangely, a grinding wheel. Alvar and the others loitered outside while Narvaez and Rios frantically looked around for another meeting location.

Quickly poking his head through the narrow door, Alvar noticed that the interior was similar in arrangement. The single bed was of a bare wooden frame and a thatched mattress. Various articles of clothing hung from pegs pounded into the brick walls while a plate, chicken bones, and *botellas* of wine littered the floor.

Around the officers, several young *mestizos* frolicked in the yard, their mothers involved with a variety of tasks. The mothers, obviously *Indians*, probably *Tianos,* may have been attractive earlier in life but were now haggard and overweight. The children were lighter in complexion with hair that departed from the straightness seen in their mothers. Their resemblance to the old conquistador was obvious.

Further down, a rough carpentry shop had a collection of logs and rough-sawn lumber. It was here that Narvaez finally assembled his captains. Back on the beach, the boat crews remained at their stations, while behind them the six vessels of the expedition sat idly at anchor.

Finding seats among the stumps, rocks, and other clutter scattered throughout the lumberyard, the party settled itself in a rough semicircle around its leader, each boat group more or less sitting together.

Alvar spied Bartalome and stepped up next to him.

Sitting with Narvaez was the military *capitan* of the flagship *Maria de la Meridionales Mares,* Alejandro Tellez, and the head pilot Janero Flores.

The *Princessa Margarita* was represented by military *capitan* Alonso Pantoja and Pilot Baudelio Reyes. From *El Delfin Capitan* Enrique Penalosa and Pilot Jose Eraso. For *Reina de Napoli*, military capitan Alonso de Castillo and Pilot Dario Quiroz.

And for the newest Caravel *La Doncella de Plata,* Capitan Diego Valenzuela, and Pilot Amado Lucero.

Fray Juan Xuarez stepped into the center of the circle. Head bowed, hands clasped in front, he silently held this position. The leaders and royal officials dropped to one knee, crossed themselves and, as one, became silent. The good father then thrust his hands into the air and looked heavenwards as if searching for guidance in the clouds above. Finally breaking the prolonged meditation, Xuarez commenced into a litany that seemed to have no end.

Fray Xuarez was a Franciscan...a Greyfriar...so called for the dark grey *cappa* worn over a white habit. In the tropics, however, the cappa was only worn on special occasions, its dark color concentrating the sun's heat. Normally, Fray Xuarez was seen attired in the white habit as he commingled among the members of the expedition. Always hanging around his neck was a silver cross of *Tau*, unique in its resemblance to the Greek letter and a symbol of the *Franciscan* order. A friendly and fastidious man, he managed to uplift all he came in contact with, albeit with a strong tendency to prolong conversations. In addition to his responsibilities as the head religious leader, Fray Xuarez was the expedition commissary, no small responsibility on an expedition where food and water could at times be in great demand. Quartered on the *Maria,* he was a favorite of Narvaez, the two often conversing about a wide range of subjects. The remaining four friars on the expedition, also of the *Franciscan* Order, were divided up between the other vessels of the expedition. Only the newly purchased caravel, *La Doncella de Plata,* was without a religious representative.

As his kneeling position became increasingly uncomfortable, Alvar's attention diverted to a fiddler crab scurrying beneath him. With surprising dexterity, the oversized claw bobbed up and down, fending off all comers to the tiny hole the creature defended in the sand.

Fray Xuarez's lamentations faded into the background.

Alvar started when the holy man placed a hand on his shoulder and then proceeded around the circle to bless each man in turn. After a final tribute to the trinity and "amens" all around, the party resumed their former positions.

Narvaez entered the center of the circle. "Fray Xuarez has blessed us with his presence and given us a new piece of mind in our journey to the New World, Glory to God and our King".

Everyone murmured "Amen" again.

Narvaez went on, "Because our blessed savior has been with us in our travels and kept us safe, we unite here on this *Cabo Santa Cruz* so close to our entry into the lands awarded by our most noble and benevolent emperor."

Narvaez stopped and looked carefully at each of his compatriots.

"As you know my good friend Vasco Porcalo has graciously promised our expedition horses and supplies from his *hacienda* in *Trinidad*." Narvaez looked over at Porcalo seated on a log. Porcalo half bowed his head while performing a half-sweeping motion of recognition with his hand.

"I have decided to divide our effort and have Capitan Pantoja in the *Princesa Margarita* proceed with Senor Porcalo to Trinidad. My second in command, Alvar Nunez Cabeza de Vaca, will accompany Capitan Pantoja in *El Viento del Sur*." Narvaez briefly nodded at Alvar and then continued, "Because we are still much in need of additional horses and men, the rest of the expedition will continue to the east, stopping again at *Santiago* and then onto *Puerto Naranjo*, *Varadero*, and finally *Habana*.

There was a murmur of voices.

Narvaez continued, "I will disembark at *Santiago* and continue inland towards *Habana* with a small party. Using whatever influence I have, I will procure additional horses and supplies along the way. These I hope to forward to the ports previously mentioned."

Alvar thought on Narvaez's decision and silently agreed. Splitting their effort to procure additional supplies and men had merit. The *Cuban* countryside was full of acquaintances who could be counted on to lend support to the upcoming expedition, especially if there was some kind of profit to be made.

"Governor"! It was Elonso Enriquez.

"*Senor* Enriquez", Narvaez turned to face the expedition comptroller.

"What of the *Princesa Margarita* and *El Viento del Sur* after the *Alguacil* and *Capitan* Pantoja complete their collection of material in *Trinidad*?"

"They will continue west to the port of *Jagua* with papers of introduction to several acquaintances I have there. After *Jagua*, they will proceed around the west coast of *Cuba* and continue on to the port at *Habana*. At *Habana,* we will all again unite for our journey to *Panuco.*"

Narvaez slowly surveyed all of those around him.

"If there are no more questions I suggest that *El Viento* and *Margarita* disembark as soon as possible and continue on to *Trinidad.* I will visit with my friend for a time before returning to the ships."

At that point, the meeting broke up. Narvaez and Rios trudged over to a collection of small huts and, hopefully, a drink of rum. The pilots huddled together and discussed the best routes to accomplish their respective journeys, some drawing coastlines and routes in the sand. The men assigned to *El Viento* and *Margarita* hurried to the boats so as to get underway.

31 October, 1527

Aboard the Caravel El Viento Del Sur

The journey from *Cabo Cruz* had been delightful. Quartering south winds and smooth seas accompanied the two ships. The sunrise this morning had been one of the grandest Alvar had ever witnessed. Even before the sun's orb broke the surface of the horizon it cast a brilliant crimson hue on the frothy clouds that hung motionless in the sky. In the half-light, the bow waves cascaded with luminescence as they spilled across the surface. A moderate breeze propelled the *El Viento* across a calm sea that reflected the glow. For a time the masts, sails, and rigging were tinged with red. A short distance to starboard the *Princesa Margarita* was also ringed with a strange luminescence. For a moment even the veteran *marineros* stopped what they were doing to gaze in wonderment at the display. But, the moment passed. The sun rose higher and the effect was lost. The morning was perfect...too perfect.

The attitudes of the *marineros* began to change. They huddled in small groups and talked amongst themselves. The display this morning had not been a good omen. Although *El Viento* was sailing in almost perfect conditions, there was an ominous feeling that began to permeate the caravel. Even Alvar felt uneasy. One of the crew complained of aching bones, a condition, he claimed, that only occurred before great storms.

And yet, the morning was glorious. Just beyond the *Princesa Margarita* the shimmering islands of the *Jardines de la Reina* slowly passed astern. So tranquil and beautiful from this distance that Alvar wished he had a moment to explore each one and revel in its uniqueness. Here, on his second voyage, Columbus had felt equally inspired to name them in honor of his queen...*The Gardens of Reina.* Still, the great beauty that passed them by did nothing to change the feeling of foreboding. As evening approached the islands of the *Jardines* fell away to the north and the two ships turned north north-west to begin their final haul into *Trinidad.*

CHAPTER 03

Hurricane

Hurican

The noise outside the small hut was overpowering, a constant throbbing din punctuated by the crash of rain, thunder, and airborne projectiles against the sides of the building. The roof was leaking now and water poured in from a multitude of locations...Outside, the blackness was total with only the lightening providing a momentary glimpse at the world around them.

01 November, 1527

Aboard the Caravel El Viento Del Sur

Although the last *cayo* of the *Jardines de la Reina* had long ago passed from sight, Alvar noticed that the archipelago seemed to continue on...underwater. Today a long line of shoals and reefs remained visible just below the surface, the water a shimmering pale green in contrast to the deep blue further out. Occasionally, a spit of sand and rock would rise above water level, providing a tenuous hold to new mangrove growth. They sailed close to the submerged archipelago in deep water, for the seabed dropped precipitously not more than half a league south of it.

At noon a small island appeared just off the bow. It was here the pilots ordered a turn toward the mainland. From previous experience, the pilots knew that a deep channel would allow them to enter a broad bay whose northern terminus would be the port at Trinidad.

The two caravels reduced sail and proceeded slowly northwest into the bay. Lookouts were posted and soundings were taken continuously. These were shallow waters.

What had been a perfect sea was now strangely different. At first, it was the large swell that passed under the *El Viento* like a serpent, the caravel skidding up one side and then plunging down the other. Curiously, after this, the sea continued calm.

A half-hour passed before another swell rolled under the ship. Alvar watched it move to starboard and then further on to the *Princesa Margarita,* her masts exaggerating its passing.

Bartalome Valdez stood on the aft deck, apprentice Jimenez close by his side. Both were clearly concerned. Alvar noticed a tenseness he had not seen before. Bartalome Valdez nervously fingered the medallion about his neck.

The journey through the bay lasted about four hours. Ahead, the mainland of Cuba became more defined. To larboard, a peninsula extended into the bay. Here the pilots called for a course correction to the west-northwest. Signs of habitation were visible. Cleared land, hulks of small boats, and an occasional fishing shack dotted the shore. Further up, what appeared to be a league or so from shore, was the town of *Trinidad,* the bell tower of the church just discernible above the trees. In the far distance, the glaucous blue ridges of the *Sierra del Escambray* stretched across the expanse. From his vantage point, Alvar could see the occasional swells impacting the beach, their crests rolling over into large breakers. The faint sounds of the surf carried across the water.

With all but the mizzen sails struck, both caravels inched their way closer to shore. The bay was broad and shallow. Only slightly protected here, the vessels were still subject to the wind and seaborne swells that would be exaggerated by the shallow depth. It was clearly not a good anchorage.

Valdez called for the anchor and watched as the boatswain supervised the multitude of tasks involved with securing an ocean-going vessel. Jimenez remained at his side watching the crew deploy both bow and stern anchors. The bow anchor bottomed quickly in the shallow harbor and then was allowed to play out as the ship followed the wind in a short arc. The ship's boat was launched and five *marineros* manually rowed the stern anchor a distance before releasing it. At this point, the lines were winched tight.

Close enough to shout between the two vessels, Bartalome cupped his hands and hailed his counterpart on the *Princessa Margarita*, Baudelio Reyes.

On the aft deck of the *Pincessa* the short, barrel-chested pilot held onto a thick rope and leaned out over the water so as to be better heard.

"Friend Bartalome, tell *Senor* De Vaca that Capitan Pantoja and *Senor* Porcallo will be leaving immediately. They are requesting *Senor* De Vaca's presence and as many *marineros* as you can spare".

Valdez turned to Alvar, "*Senor* De Vaca, should this weather turn as I suspect it will, this harbor is untenable. It is most important that we conclude our business here and move to a more suitable anchorage. What are your orders?"

Alvar answered, "Bartalome, I will stay on the ship to supervise the loading. Have the boatswain dispatch the ship's boat with as many men as we can spare so that this task can be completed. My compliments to Capt Pantoja and *Senor* Porcallo but emphasize that time is of the essence."

On board, the crews prepared to leave. Hauling supplies from shore was not an easy task. Ropes, tie-downs, and winches had to be transported ashore. Once on shore, it was hoped that a barge would be made available for transporting the heavier supplies and horses to the ships. On the ships, holds were opened and cleared while the winches and lines were set up to hoist up the supplies.

Pantoja and Portallo had been quickly rowed ashore. Shortly after, men from both ships were rowed to shore to assist with the loading. Several return trips were required before all the personnel and equipment were in place.

Observing the activity, Alvar noted that the rough harbor contained only a single quay. Because of this, they would be limited as to how many boats could be loaded at once. Scattered about was the detritus present at any harbor... broken casks, boxes, planking...but no material staged and ready for loading. Leading to the shore was a single rough-cut road leading immediately into a heavy thicket brake. Earlier, Alvar watched as Pantoja and Portallo mounted horses, that were hastily provided to them, and disappeared up the road with a small contingent of men. Several *Indians* from the town accompanied them. Supplies and horses coming from *Senor* Portallo's storage areas would have to be transported from town, almost half a league away. A returning seaman confirmed this. It was going to take time to complete this transfer.

The weather was still clear with light seas but the frequency of swells had increased; riding in the shallow anchorage, the ships raised and rolled with each passing, and the breakers rode high onto the shore.

Bartalome Valdez was visibly agitated. Both he and Jimenez had just returned from a short trip over to *Pincessa Margaritta* to confer with pilot Baudillo Reyes. All agreed that the swells were a harbinger of activity further out in the Caribbean Sea. In these waters, it was better to be safe, especially in an unprotected location such as this. It had become obvious that they would be spending the night, and depending on the proximity of Portallo's supply sources it could be much longer.

Valdez and Jimenez approached De Vaca, *"Alguacil,* this transfer is going to take time."

Alvar nodded, "What are pilot Reyes' thoughts?"

Valdez chuckled, "Friend Baudillo has never been known for understatement."

Alvar looked at Valdez to continue.

"His and my feelings are much the same. I think we best conclude our business here as soon as possible. This miserable excuse for a port will provide us no protection."

Alvar considered his answer for a moment, "If our stay here is prolonged, what are your suggestions?"

"*Senor* De Vaca, not more than 10 leagues from here is the harbor at *Xugua*, a natural enclosure well protected from the sea. I suggest we consider relocating *El Viento* and *Princessa Margarita* to that location until the necessary supplies are in place and ready to load."

Alvar considered his answer. The logic was sound and 10 leagues were only a short half-day's sail away. Before such a decision was made, however, he would have to coordinate with Pantoja and Portalo, both of whom were currently unreachable.

Alvar looked up at the clear sky and scanned the seaward horizon, "Bartalome, I agree with your suggestion for the port at *Xugua*, but until I can confer with *Capitan* Pantoja and our guest we must remain. Thankfully, the sky is clear and the seas are calm. We will remain here tonight and by tomorrow morning be better able to make decisions."

Alvar stopped and considered. If indeed they did leave now, a runner could be sent to Capitan Pantoja describing their intentions. Soon, however, it would be the hour of Vespers and if under sail, *El Viento* and *Princessa Margarita* would be making their way in the dark.

"Yes, better that we stay the night". Alvar repeated himself.

Even now, some of the mariners were returning to the ship, well aware that no activity would commence today. Some stayed ashore, however, as advance teams to assist in the disposition of the supplies.

Margarita's bell rang 4 times. The *ampolleta* was turned and the young page boy, head bowed, began his evening litany.

02 November, 1527

Aboard the Caravel El Viento Del Sur

Sometime after midnight, the mild southerly breeze had shifted to the southeast. At first, the shift was imperceptible, but as the wind increased, its passage was marked by whistles and moans in the overhead masts, yards, and rigging. Skyward, the broad expanse of stars so clear in the early evening was eclipsed by a membrane of clouds. By morning the sky had become queerly amorphous.

Rousing himself from a fitful night of sleep, Alvar watched the subdued light announce the beginning of a new day. The frequency of seaborne swells had increased during the night. Now the swells rocked *El Viento* every two or three minutes. There was still no word from Pantoja or Portello on the status of the promised supplies or as to when the loading would begin.

The wind freshened and a fickle rain fell but stopped almost as abruptly as it started. For a time the skies seemed to lighten and Alvar noticed sunlight shafts hitting the inland tree canopy and even the distant mountain tops...but they disappeared as if someone had pulled a shade. Then the outline of the mountains themselves faded from view.

Again, a splattering of rain started to fall. Winds gusted briefly and then fell dead calm, the water's surface like a mirror. Looking seaward, a diagonal stripe of rain dragged across the expanse toward the anchorage. Alvar could see the rain's frothy impact on the water as it neared them.

With the rain, a wind skittered across the harbor in staccato bursts. A torrent of profanity sliced the air as a *marinero*, working on the main spar, lost his hat in a gust. Alvar, Valdez, and Jimenez stopped to watch the head cover spiral toward the water below.

There was commotion on the deck. A canoe was making its way towards *El Viento*. Abruptly the band of rain moved further down the shoreline and the wind ceased. Pulling alongside, the occupants were two *Spaniards* and three *Indians,* two paddling and one providing steerage.

"Ho the ship", one of the *Spaniards* called out.

Alvar moved to the rail and looked down.

Seeing Alvar, the *Spaniard* stood up. "Are you *Senor* De Vaca?"

Cupping his hand, Alvar answered the hail, "I am...what is your business?"

"*Senor* De Vaca, I have a letter for you, we will remain until we have your answer."

With that, the *Spaniard* reached into an oiled pouch and pulled out a piece of paper.

The same seaman who had lost his hat clamored over the side, holding to a shroud line. With the next swell, the canoe raised up and he grabbed the letter from the outstretched hand of the *Spaniard.* Holding the letter in his teeth, the seaman regained the deck and handed the letter to Alvar. Valdez and Jimenez gathered around him.

"It is a request from a *Senor* Viela. It says that Pantoja and Porcallo have both ridden north to bring back five additional horses and they had left directions to cache all the available stores in the town before proceeding to the ships. Porcallo's people have been working all night and the supplies are now ready to begin transport. Viela requests that I come ashore as soon as possible for a final inventory."

Alvar put down the letter and considered a moment, then made his way to the side rail closest to the canoe. The canoe had pulled back somewhat but was still within easy-hailing distance.

"Are either of you gentleman *Senor* Viela?"

The *Spaniard* that had handed the letter tried to stand but thought better of it when the canoe wobbled precariously.

"I am Dario Vargas..." Turning to his side he gestured towards the other *Spaniard* in the boat, "...and this is my brother Tomas. We are both employees of Vasco Porcallo de Figuerola. Rafael Viela is the *Alcalde* of *Trinidad*."

Alvar was amused by the formalization of Porcallo's name. "Why is it that you need my presence ashore?"

"*Senor* De Vaca, we have accumulated a multitude of supplies in three warehouses. *Alcalde* Viela insists that someone of authority be present before it is released."

Alvar was somewhat annoyed. Obviously, this Viela was exercising his control as a small-town bureaucrat and wasn't concerned with their situation in this damnable harbor.

"My compliments to *Alcalde* Viela but my responsibilities are here and time is of the essence. If it pleases, I will sign a note giving him authority to release all of the material." The two *Spaniards* shared a look but nodded in agreement.

With that, Alvar hurried back to the aft castle for a pen and ink. On the back of the rough parchment note he wrote.

"I Alvar Nunez Cabeza de Vaca appointed by His Majesty and Holy Roman Emperor Charles V as treasurer and alguacil mayor for the expedition under the auspices of Governor Panfilo de Narvaez, do hereby grant Rafael Viega, as the alcalde of Trinidad, Cuba, authority to release all stores provided by Vasco Porcallo de Figerola for immediate transport to the vessels El Viento del sur and Princesa Margarita under the command of myself."

Signed,

Alvar Nunez Cabeza de Vaca

Port of Trinidad, 04 November, 1527

Alvar made the letter as official-looking as possible, hoping that it would satisfy the *alcaldes* bureaucratic wishes.

Blotting the wet ink and then carefully folding the document, Alvar handed it to the seaman who again clamored over the side to deliver it.

Dario Vargas rapidly read the note and inserted it back into the oiled pouch. He hoped that De Vaca's answer would suffice, but he knew the *alcade* and how peculiar he was.

"*Senor* Vargas, please deliver this to *alcade* Viela as soon as possible. I believe we have deteriorating weather and it is to our advantage to be quickly underway. We have a crew ashore and can begin loading as soon as the supplies reach the dock."

"Gracios *Senor* De Vaca, I will forward this to the *alcade* as soon as we return".

With that, the *Indio* oarsmen turned the canoe and paddled back. Except for the occasional swell, the sea was still calm and the canoe glided gently onto the beach. A light misting rain had begun to fall again as the two *Spaniards* mounted their horses and disappeared up the road leading into town. If the note satisfied the *alcade*, Alvar was still hopeful that they could conclude their business here and leave for the port at *Xuaga*. If Capitans Pantoja and Porcallo were delayed, they could easily transit the short distance overland and meet them.

The ship's boat had returned from the beach. One of the *marineros*, a burly fellow named Elcano, climbed to the deck and approached Alvar.

Elcano was unique among the crewmen. He was a *Vasco*...a *Basque*, and for a time had been a whaler in the far north Atlantic. It seemed as if his whole upper body was covered with tattoos. At times Alvar had caught himself staring at the artwork; there were symbols of all types...stars, flowers, a giant crucifix on his right forearm, and like-nesses of ships, harpoons, and, of course, whales. Some crewman even said they had spied tattoos on his *pene* but the very thought caused Alvar to cringe.

Elcano was a prized seaman with great strength who could do the work and drink more rum than three ordinary men.

In a thick accent Elcano spoke, "*Senor* De Vaca, the men on shore have done what they could to prepare for the transport. The beach is without shelter and with this infernal rain the men are sodden and cold. With your permission, we will return to the ships until the sup-plies arrive."

Alvar readily agreed but first directed Angel Jimenez to take the ship's boat and update Baudillo Reyes and the crew on the *Princesa Margarita*.

The light rain continued, intermittently at first but then constant and somewhat heavier as noon approached. For most of the morning, the winds had been becalmed, with only an occasional offshore breeze. Just after the fourth watch, there was a noticeable reversal in the elements. Now, the situation changed rapidly. Gusts, unimpeded in their journey across the *Caribbean* sea, began to buffet and swirl around *El Viento.*

The sea toughened. Lines of breakers developed, the gusts decapitating their crests into frothy whitecaps. Watching the lines of surf slide across the bow was dizzying. Alvar steadied himself against a bulkhead.

Bartalome approached him. "*Senor* De Vaca, the skies and sea are strange and foreboding. I have been through many a storm in three different oceans, but have only seen conditions such as these one other time."

Alvar waited for him to continue.

"At times the sea has a predictable way about it. This is what a pilot looks for. Other times you use your experience and make decisions. On my voyage with the Admiral, we encountered a terrible cyclone shortly after arriving at *La Hispaniola.* If not for his experience and seamanship, we all would have perished. The conditions then were much as they are now. The *Indios* call these cyclones '*huracans'* and I fear the worst."

As if to accentuate the situation, another swell rocked *El Viento,* only this time more pronounced than any before.

Looking up, Alvar noticed several *marineros* pointing toward shore. Following their gaze he could see activity on the beach. Two men had arrived by horseback leading a third riderless horse. Even from this distance, Alvar could see that it was the *Spaniards* Dario and Tomas. In addition, a small carriage pulled into the clearing behind them.

Again the two men hurried to a waiting canoe and pushed off into the surf. The short journey this time was obviously more difficult. Both men held tenuously to the gunnels as the *Indians* struggled to paddle into the wind. Sheets of spray exploded from the bow as the canoe cut though the breakers. Finally, after what seemed like an eternity, the canoe entered the somewhat protected area on the leeward side of the ship. Still, the paddlers had difficulty maintaining their position. A line was thrown to them.

Alvar called out, "*Senor* Vargas, please tell me the situation on shore for I am under advise to leave this port and return when the weather is more accommodating."

Dario tried standing in the narrow canoe with some difficulty. Another passing swell caused him to immediately sit down. The canoe rocked dangerously.

"*Senor* De Vaca, my apologies. I have *alcade* Viela's return letter here, but I will summarize it to save us both time. He insists that since Pantoja and Porcalo have not returned, only you have the authority to inventory and release the collected material."

Alvar looked down and shook his head.

Dario saw the movement and tried to explain, "I can tell you that there have been issues in the past with corruption. Being a very careful man, Viela will not take responsibility on his own.

Alvar was becoming frustrated and not of good humor. He paused to collect himself.

"*Senor* Vargas, I understand that you are but the messenger and I hold no animosity towards you but the *alcade* is costing us valuable time...time that we could have used to load these ships and be underway."

Alvar made a broad gesture that encompassed everything around him, "Now, we face worsening weather and I'm not sure we can even begin the transfer under these conditions."

From the canoe, Dario responded, "*Senor*, I beseech you, to accompany us back to *El Trinidad*. We have brought an extra horse and a carriage to transport you."

At that moment the wind laid down and the rain stopped. Above the anchorage, a strip of blue appeared in the overcast sky, a shaft of light hitting the beach in the distance. Alvar looked up and then continued his conversation, "I must excuse myself, but my responsibilities are still with these ships. Tell Vargas that I insist that he begin transport." Dario's countenance seemed to sink and he turned to confer with his brother.

On deck, Bartalome moved up close to Alvar, Elcano was by his side.

"*Senor* De Vaca, as a pilot I can only advise but it may make sense to accompany these men back to *Trinidad* and clear this issue up. While there, you can evaluate the amount of stores that must be transported and determine the time we will need in port to complete this mission. For this determination you should take Jimenez and Elcano who have experience."

Alvar stepped back form the rail deep in thought.

Bartalome continued, "If the stores and operation are in a state of disarray, as I suspect, you can make a determination to leave this place and return at a more appropriate time."

Alvar, clearly frustrated, whispered under his breath, "This Rafeal Viela is an *idiota*!"

At this moment Elcano made his presence known, "*Senor* De Vaca, tomorrow is Sunday. If this weather subsides and your decision is to stay we will all attend mass in the town and then begin our work in earnest."

Alvar stepped to the rail, "*Senor* Vargas, I have reconsidered and will accompany you. Please ready my horse and the carriage for I will be bringing two additional men with me."

In the canoe, Dario Vargas was visibly relieved. After a halfhearted wave of understanding, he instructed the *Indio* oarsmen to return to the beach. Alvar gave instructions to lower the boat.

Before leaving, Alvar turned to Bartalome, "Friend Bartalome, I will strive to get this problem resolved and return to the ship as soon as possible. Should the weather worsen to a point where you feel in great danger, run the vessels ashore so that the men and horses might be saved. We can always rebuild ships, we can't replace men".

From the aft castle, Bartalome Valdez watched the ship's boat disgorge its three travelers on shore. Immediately the rowing crew pushed the boat back into the oncoming waves and began the journey back. He noticed they were pulling hard against the wind and waves.

On shore, De Vaca mounted the extra horse while Jimenez and Elcano settled into the carriage. The little group rapidly disappeared up the trail.

02 November, 1527

Aboard the Caravel El Viento Del Sur

Bartalome Valdez was greatly distressed. No more than an hour after the ship's boat had deposited De Vaca, Jimenez, and Elcano on shore the winds became exceedingly strong. The wind direction changed as well, first blowing fiercely from the south and then east.

The vessels were in jeopardy. They had been anchored fore and aft with the bow seaward. As the winds moved to the east, the constricted ships labored and rolled dangerously, plumes of spray and seawater falling on the decks. The seas were too rough to recover the aft anchor and Valdez ordered the line cut. Before releasing the line, however, the *marineros* tied another buoy to it. Anchors were expensive and the floating buoys would allow later recovery.

On board, the *Margarita* Baudelio Reyes was performing a similar maneuver. Almost as one the two aft anchor lines were severed and the ships swung in a large arc to leeward. No longer rolling, the bows now took the brunt of the waves head-on.

Moving towards the aft castle ladder Valdez was knocked off his feet by a blast of wind coming from starboard. Falling heavily on the first step he heard a crack on his left side. Momentarily dazed, he tumbled down the stairs to land on the deck below. Everything seemed to happen so slowly. As if detached from his body he watched each step go by in the fall.

"*Madre de dios*!", he was lying on his back looking up at the main mast. A seaman had hurried over to help, pulling on his left arm.

"Aaaaaaaahhhh", the pain was like a knife and he gasped for air as the seaman released his grip. With his right arm, Bartalome managed to roll to a sitting position. He looked up at the seaman, his head swimming.

"A thousand pardons *Senor* Veldez, it appears that you might have broken some ribs. Sit a moment until your head clears."

After a moment, the seaman, whom he thought his name, Munoz, gently helped him to his feet.

"*Gracios* Munoz, I think I can make it from here. Check on the hatches and make sure everything is dogged down tightly."

"Yes, *Senor* Veldez", the seaman replied as he started to move away. Stopping in the mid-stride he turned back towards Bartalome. "*Senor* Veldez, what are your thoughts on our predicament in this place?"

Bartalome looked out at the stretched anchor line...the wind was shifting more to the north. "I think, Munoz, that we should make our peace with God, for by this time tomorrow we may all be in paradise with our savior."

Munoz's face paled but he said nothing. Crossing himself he hurried off.

Bartalome was angered at himself. The northerly shift in the wind would eliminate the possibility of running the ships aground, for it was blowing from the shore. If only he had made that decision an hour earlier. His only hope now was for another wind reversal...that's if they could hold against this tempest.

The shifting wind did bring some relief...although slight. Wind blowing from the shore lessened the severity of the waves. However, there was another danger. The fierce winds blowing against the ships were putting severe strain on the anchors. Early in the evening, Bartalome had felt it loose its tenuous hold on the sea floor...a lurching feeling of helplessness. For a brief moment, *El Viento* had started its slide toward the open sea only to abruptly jerk to a stop as the anchor found new footing. Bartalome hoped it would hold.

02 November, 1527

On the Road to the Village at Trinidad, Cuba

On shore, Alvar and his escort had stopped briefly on a little escarpment that provided a somewhat shielded view of the harbor below. Dismounting, he walked to the edge to get a better view of the vessels. The wind was pushing up the hillside in staccato bursts and Alvar found himself having to concentrate on each step. Looking seaward, the Caribbean was a cauldron of churning water, echelons of white-capped waves moving slowly shoreward.

To his horror, he saw that both vessels had shed their stern anchors and had swung seaward. Both were pulling hard on the remaining bow anchor.

"The wind has shifted to the north *Senor* De Vaca." Angel Jimenez had joined him. "There is no chance of running the ships aground now."

"What of releasing the anchor and confronting the elements in open water?"

Jimenez pondered his answer for a moment, gazing intently at the drama below. "In the harbor, even as bad as it is, there is a chance they can make the shore. There are no rocks or reefs nearby, we can only pray that the remaining anchor will hold and a contrary wind will develop."

Alvar steadied himself as another gust descended on them. "I should have left this infernal anchorage yesterday, now I fear it is too late!"

"*Senor* De Vaca, Bartalome Veldez is a fine pilot and seaman. In such a predicament as this, I would want no other in charge. By God's grace, he will find a way to save the ships and crews."

Far out to sea, the horizon was illuminated in a prolonged but undefined flash. For a brief second the dark wall clouds could be seen descending to the surface. As Alvar and Angel made their way back to the path the ominous low rumbles of thunder could just be heard over the sound of the wind.

02 November, 1527

Aboard the Caravel El Viento Del Sur

Darkness came early. Below deck, the air was already stale. Light from two lanterns suspended on deck supports was all that penetrated the gloom, the whale oil fumes adding to the thickness of the air. Hobbled horses fidgeted nervously in restraining slings. Men not assigned to the pumps huddled in groups staring blankly at the ceiling, the sounds of the sea played tricks. Each clatter, bump, and roar was followed like an imaginary sprite in the mind's eye. Some, looking up beyond the earthly vestments offered lamentations to their God and savior.

Above decks, Bartalome squinted as the rain and salt spray stung his eyes. His side was hurting. Only one storm lantern illuminated his surroundings under the quarter deck, the others having long blown out in the wind and sprayed. The darkness beyond his confine was absolute, broken only by the flashes of lightening. These brief views provided a surreal look at the sea, sky, and clouds. During one particularly long discharge, he thought he caught the silhouette of the *Princesa Margarita*.

Bartalome's thoughts drifted back to that time many years ago when he shared the deck with the great Admiral. Denied access to the protected harbor at *Santa Domingo* they had finally found sanctuary in an isolated estuary. It was there that the terrible *huracan* of 1502 fell upon them. He remembered the terror and knew what was coming.

02 November, 1527

Arriving at the Village of Trinidad, Cuba

Alvar had arrived in the dark. It was raining. Not hard, but a constant drizzle punctuated periodically by a driving squall. Drenched to the skin, the party had immediately sought shelter. First to greet them was the mayor, Rafeal Viela, who, from the doorway, ushered them into one of the few brick-and-mortar buildings. *Indio* slaves quickly unsaddled and corralled the horses.

Inside a fire had been prepared. The travelers stood in front of the crude fireplace, steam rising from their wet clothing. Viela, a portly man obviously used to a pampered life, offered drams of rum. A beautiful *mestizo* girl of about 16 distributed the libation. Alvar couldn't keep his eyes off her, the passion rising in him. It had been months since that last night in *San Lucar* with his Maria. He loved his wife dearly but distractions such as this were hard to control. Alvar noticed that her beauty was not lost to Angel Jimenez and Elcano. They openly leered as her supple body passed tantalizingly close to him. She, in turn, was well aware of the effect her presence was having on the newcomers and the hint of a smile curled her lips.

Viela spoke first, "*Senor* De Vaca, my apologies for the weather, I had hoped we could conclude this transfer and have you on your way, but the situation has grown critical. My *Indios* tell me that this is just a portend to the coming tempest."

Alvar, still watching the servant girl as she disappeared behind a curtain, was slow to answer.

Viela noticed. "She is a real beauty, is she not?"

Brought abruptly out of his reverie Alvar answered curtly. "*Alcade,* at the moment I care only for the safety of my men and ships. When I last looked a contrary wind was blowing from the shore and I fear the worst."

"As well you should," Viela answered. "We can only hope by the grace of God that this coming tempest will subside long enough for them to escape its wrath."

Viela paused as wind-blown debris clattered on the roof. "I have dispatched two teams of my finest oarsman to the beach. Should the opportunity manifest itself they will assist in removing your people from the ships. At last report, however, the seas and wind are much too fierce."

Alvar was impressed with this effort. "My thanks for your prompt action *alcade.* "

Changing the subject, Alvar continued, "What of the supplies?"

Vaega gestured, "At the end of this street is a fine new church we have completed work on, *Nuestra Senora de la Trinidad.* It is brick and mortar and of substantial construction. We have chosen to store the more perishable commodities within its walls. Other materials we have stored in buildings close by. Just to the north, we have a corral with a few horses but I anticipate these numbers to increase when *Senors* Pantoja and Porcallo return. I have an accounting of all the materials."

With that Viela pushed several documents across the table for Alvar to review.

Just then another crash resounded from the roof. All eyes looked toward the ceiling.

Vaega continued, "I doubt very much, however, that Pantoja and Porcallo are traveling today."

Alvar was thoughtful, "*Senor* Vaega, do you know the extent of their journey?"

"*Senor* Porcallo has several holdings in this area and a *ranchero* ten leagues to the north." Vaega hesitated, "Malita, more drinks for our guests!"

The young *mestizo* girl immediately appeared from behind a curtain with a tray of drinks and deserts. Alvar concentrated on the subject at hand but could not control his quick glimpses. She was dressed in the style of the Indies, white cotton blouse and a skirt that hung down to mid-calf. Her tanned legs, ankles, and bare feet were intoxicating. Bending to refill his glass, her blouse shifted and Alvar had a momentary view of her breasts unrestrained under the clothing.

She brushed against him as she moved to fill another glass. He could smell her essence.

Looking across the table at Angel Jimenez, his eyes were as big as saucers as they followed Malita around the room. Beside him, Elcano looked like he might explode.

Again Viela noticed...chuckling, "You should see her mother!"

It was time to defuse this situation. Handing the inventory list to Jimenez, Alvar gathered himself, "Take Elcano to the church with you and see to the status of our supplies. I will join you shortly".

Both men rose and moved toward the doorway, Elcano wolfing down a piece of bread on the way. At the door, which opened outwards, the force of the wind pulled it from Angel's hand and it banged loudly against the side of the building. With a blast, rain and wind cascaded though the opening, the sounds of the storm invading the structure. Papers that Viela had sitting on the table swirled into the air and empty drinking cups clattered to the floor. Quickly jumping outside, both Jimenez and Elcano grabbed the door and closed it behind them.

For a moment Alvar and Viela looked at each other as Malita began to gather the loose articles.

Viela was the first to speak, "*Senor* De Vaca, I will tell you truthfully, I think your ships and *marineros* are in grave danger. This *viento de diablo* is much like one we suffered two years ago. The *Cubaneos* call them *huracans* and they are much feared by the natives...their ferocity is beyond belief. If your pilots are not able to run the ships onto the shore I feel that they all will be lost."

Alvar nodded, "I am in despair sir, for I was the last to leave and now my friends and comrades may perish. There is nothing I can now do. The supplies that we have been sent to collect are now the least of my concerns. My only solace is the seamanship of our excellent pilot and the hope that, somehow, he can prevail in this maelstrom."

Outside, the wind increased in intensity and another limb clattered onto the roof above, its noise momentarily halting the conversation.

"*Senor* Viela, I think I will join my men outside and see to the disposition of the supplies. At this point, I think the effort is futile, but I need to be alone with my thoughts."

Viela gestured towards an adjacent room, "When you have completed your task a bed has been prepared for you here. Your *compatriotas* will be staying at the church. I have directed that sleeping mats and blankets be provided to them.

Thanking his host, Alvar donned his cloak and stepped out into the elements, this time only partially opening the door while squeezing though the opening. Closing the door he caught a momentary view of Malita peering at him from behind a curtain.

03 November, 1527

Aboard the Caravel El Viento Del Sur

Bartalome peered out from beneath the quarter-deck. The darkness was coming to an end. Almost imperceptibly the world around him began to focus. At first, he could just make out the Main mast and the immediate area in front of him, but then other parts of the ship came into view. Looking outward, the sea was still dark and foreboding, remaining invisible except for explosions of whitecaps streaming in an ocean of black.

More light began to filter through the thick overcast and with it the angry sea made its presence known. Turning astern he was surprised to see the vague outline of *Princesa Margarita* still at anchor but several hundreds of yards from where she had been the night previous. In reality, both ships had moved in the night. Just after midnight, the offshore winds had increased dramatically and Bartolome had felt the anchor giving way, the ship backsliding toward the open ocean. But, every time the anchor found another hold, *El Viento* would grind to a stop.

For the moment, the winds had abated somewhat, at least for the moment, although a thin drizzle continued to fall.

In front of him, a group of five soldiers nervously paced back and forth. At about midnight, they had forced themselves on deck, refusing to stay below. The wind, the noise, the uncertainty, and the stench of the hold had finally gotten to them. In battle they were fearless, but here, with no control over the environment, they were terrified. Others below lay scattered in writhing agony, succumbing to the gut-wrenching effects of motion sickness. Others hid their fear and stared into the darkness. The two friars on board continued their supplications throughout the night, their droning background noise lending an air of hopelessness.

And....there was nothing he could do!

Nothing that is, unless a change in the wind direction allowed them a run at the beach. Even that would be risky, but certainly better than the predicament they were no in.

"*Senor* Veldez!" It was Pasqual Aguayo, captain of the soldier contingent on board.

He looked terrible and smelled of vomit.

"*Capitan* Aguayo I did not see you come up. How are things below?" Bartalome was sorry he asked the question almost before it cleared his lips.

Aguayo shook his head at the question. Looking up, he could just see the shoreline becoming visible in the morning light. "The wind has dropped, shouldn't we release a boat and row to shore...it doesn't appear that far...with several trips, we could save ourselves."

Although the wind speed had dropped, Bartalome guessed it was still blowing steady at 15 knots and the swells were approaching six feet... He tried to convince Aguayo, "In good weather, it's a considerable row to shore. With these headwinds and the high seas it would be a challenge just to keep the boat pointed in the right direction."

"Is there nothing we can do?"

Looking at the fear in the retched young captain's eyes he felt pity. "I would say, *Senor Capitan* now is the time to make your peace with our savior and ask for his forgiveness. If our Lord provides a contrary wind we may have a chance to gain the shore, but, if not, today we surely will enter the Kingdom of Heaven."

Aguayo stared at him for a moment and then, dejected, retired to the company of the soldiers on deck.

Bartalome noticed that several others had made their way topside but didn't think anything of it. He was desperately tired and the pain in his side was getting worse. Any deep breath would rack him. Clutching his chest Bartalome sat down and closed his eyes. If he could just rest for a moment. Slumped to the side, head resting on his chest, the sleep washed over him.

As he languished in a state of vague consciousness Bartalome began to become aware of a commotion. The cobwebs of sleep were overpowering, however, and he drifted back into the semi-lucid world of exhaustion.

"Bartalome, Bartalome!" It was the boatswain Fermin Morales.

"What is it Fermin?" his mouth was dry and it took a moment to collect himself. Fermin and he had a long history of sailing together and they easily addressed each other by first names.

"Bartalome, some of the soldiers are taking the ship's boat."

Standing, Bartalome was instantly awake. Amidships several of the soldiers were standing on deck with swords drawn, and others were lowering the boat. A small crowd of seaman and soldiers were circled about them. Pushing himself through the onlookers Bartalome came face to face with one of the swordsmen who stepped in his way. Apparently directing the activities was Capitan Aguayo.

"What is the meaning of this sir, I gave no order to lower the boat?'

Aguayo dropped the rope he was working with and stepped toward Bartalome. "Pilot Veldez, we are doomed on this ship unless we can make shore. The wind has dropped and I have chosen six of my strongest men. If we hurry I believe we can make the shore with eight passengers including myself. Once ashore, four men will return in the empty boat for another load."

Bartalome was incredulous, "Captain Aguayo you will never make the shore, the distance is too far and the wind and tide are too strong.

Many of the seasoned mariners standing around nodded their heads in agreement.

"And besides, if you do make it, who among your 6 rowers is going to jeopardize their life and return to the ship?"

All eyes focused on the *capitan*, but it was too late for talk. There was a wildness in his eyes and Bartalome saw that nothing was going to stop them.

"Stand aside Pilot Veldez, if we die in this attempt at least we died trying.

With that, the soldiers pushed Bartalome back into the crowd and roughly began to winch the boat to the sea surface.

03 Novmber, 1527

The Home of Alcade Rafeal Viela, Trinidad, Cuba

Alvar awoke to the sound of a loose shutter banging in the wind. The sound of the rain was heavy on the roof and the gusty winds made strange noises as they coursed through and around the buildings outside. Slowly he untangled himself from the embrace of Malita who was snoring softly beside him. Sitting up, he looked down at her naked body splayed across the bed. He could feel the desire rising in him once again.

Last night he had left the cabin and the company of the town's mayor, Rafael Viela, to inspect the horde of supplies in the church and surrounding structures. With that completed, Angel Jimenez and Elcano returned to the church to spend the night, and Alvar returned to the cabin.

On entering, only Malita was there to greet him. Helping him out of his sodden coat she hung it on a wooden chair next to the fire. With that, she disappeared behind the curtain. Removing his boots he carefully placed them next to the fire and then took a moment of reflection to stare into the embers.

Alvar had felt her presence. He turned.

Stepping from behind the curtain Malita stood in the candlelight, totally naked. She paused unashamed while his eyes languished on her perfect body. Slowly she began to walk towards him, every step more sensuous than the one before. Pausing just in front of him she reached for the buttons on his tunic and slowly began to unbutton each one.

Their eyes locked together. Alvar was transfixed. He placed his hands on her waist and then slowly slid them down over her hips and legs. He had almost forgotten how soft a woman could be. Grabbing his hand, Malita brought it to her lips and then turning, led him to her bedroom.

What a night it had been, the storm raged outside while he labored inside to satisfy Malita's unlimited sexual appetite. Alvar was sure he loved his wife but no man on earth could have rejected this. Never in his wildest dreams had he ever experienced such pleasure. She was uninhibited and unrelenting and by the time she had had enough Alvar was utterly exhausted.

But...this morning he felt ashamed. Not even a league away his friends and compatriots were involved in a life-and-death struggle while he was enjoying the menstruations of a beautiful *mestizo*.

Covering the sleeping Malita with a blanket Alvar pickup up his pantaloons from the floor, still wet from the night before. In the main room, the fire had long since gone out but at least his boots and coat were dry.

There was a knock on the door and Alvar hurried to it. Angel Jimenez quickly stepped inside to avoid the runoff water cascading off the roof. It was raining hard outside, another squall line was passing over the town.

"*Senor* De Vaca, there is a promontory not far from here with an excellent view of the harbor. One of the mayor's men has agreed to show us the way. He says that it is a rough path but we...."

Jimenez's words froze in his throat.

Behind them, Malita stepped out of the bedroom as naked as the night before, "Who is it, my love?"

Alvar rapidly threw on his coat, "There's no time to lose, we must be on our way!" He ushered Angel out, almost having to force him through the doorway.

Meeting the guide, Alvar, Jimenez, and Elcano made their way in the heavy rain. The path though the village was awash in water. The mud clung to his boots and he found himself walking in the grass to the side of the road to avoid its burden. Just after they had passed the last building, the guide turned off the road and entered a path through the heavy palmetto and pine forest. Here the overburden protected them somewhat from the wind. Overhead the sound of the wind continued in a dreadful groan. Single file they continued down the path and then started a slow incline up a modest hill.

Ahead Alvar could see a break in the trees. A short climb up a rocky outcrop and the entire coast was before them. Here the wind was unencumbered and its full force surged against the hillside. Electricity filled the air. Ugly diagonal gray lines marked the areas of heaviest rain. Fast-moving clouds skudded across the sky, some almost touching the surface. The seas were in turmoil, echelons of white waves marched in columns toward the shore. This spectacle continued on for as far as the eye could see. Waves colliding with the rocky shore sent spray high into the air. A continuous pall of windblown sand coursed along the shore. From this vantage point, the storm was at once awe-inspiring and terrifying.

The three *Spaniards* strained to catch site of their ships. Far in the distance and to their northwest, the harbor was obstructed by yet another squall line moving across the area. Finally, looking like a ghost ship emerging through the rain and mist, *El Viento* was the first to materialize. Alvar was immediately struck by its smallness in this world of turmoil. Its bow pointed at the shore, the small caravel strained at its anchor, waves streaming past it. Behind it, the *Princesa Margarita* was much further out in the bay. Both vessels had obviously slipped further seaward, but the *Princesa* was in the greatest jeopardy. Not far off shore the seafloor drooped precipitously...once that point was reached, the anchor would become ineffective.

"Look there!". Pointing, it was Elcano who first noticed something unusual occurring on *El Viento*. Off the starboard side what appeared to be the ship's boat separated from the larger vessel. Just a speck at this distance it slowly pulled away from *El Viento,* struggling to make headway into the wind.

As if transfixed, they watched the boat slowly inch towards the shore. Alvar could only imagine the strain on the oarsman as they fought to keep the small vessel moving forward into the wind.

The rain increased to a torrent and from their vantage point the view of the harbor faded and then disappeared. All three men were wet to the skin. The force of the rain was beginning to sting their faces and each had to turn away. Alvar, holding onto his hat with one hand constantly wiped the the rain from his eyes with the other. Losing his footing in a gust, Angel struggled to keep his balance, his felt hat lifted off his head and spiraled down the hillside. The *Tiano* guide stepped back into the wooded area.

The torrent passed and slowly the harbor came back into view. Each of the men was not prepared for the sight that greeted them. The boat had capsized and was rapidly being blown out to sea. Several men could be seen holding on to the overturned vessel mere dark specks bobbing in the water around the craft. One man could be seen making a futile attempt to swim towards shore.

Alvar, Angel, and Elcano watched in despair as the swimmer disappeared under a wave. Slowly, each of the specks in the water also disappeared. The boat, drifting quickly, was now well beyond the two ships when another torrent passed over the hill obscuring the harbor once again.

It was Elcano who first spoke, "They are gone, God be with them."

Disheartened, the *Spaniards* made their way back to the village. The force of the wind was increasing, the roar overhead constant. Limbs falling from above filled the air. Even above the sound of the wind and thunder, the occasional crack of a tree echoed through the forest.

The full force of the *huracan* was almost upon them.

03 November, 1527

Aboard the Caravel El Viento Del Sur

El Viento was again slipping seaward in the wind, Bartalome could feel the shudder as the anchor released its hold and then abruptly found a new hold on the seafloor. The wind had increased to such a force that even being on deck presented the chance of being blown overboard. Still, several of the soldiers were afraid to remain below, clinging to the main mast on the open deck.

The ship's boat was gone. Bartalome had watched in vain as the oarsman strained to make headway into the wind. For a moment he felt they had a chance. The wind had relented somewhat and the oarsmen were pulling hard, the spray cascading over the bow. But then, the energy seemed to leave them. Ever so slowly the wind took control, pushing the small craft broadside to the waves. In a moment it had rolled over, trapping men beneath it. Captain Aguayo who had been standing in the stern was thrown clear and amid the confusion of men and floating oars began to swim towards the shore. At first, he was able to ride over the oncoming waves, pulling himself along with strong strokes. Soon, however, he seemed to tire and each wave momentarily engulfed him. Surfacing, he continued shoreward only to be engulfed by each succeeding wave. Finally, totally spent, a final wave cascaded over the lone swimmer and Bartalome watched in vain as he failed to surface on the other side.

In the heavy wind, the overturned boat drifted rapidly past *El Viento,* close enough for Bartalome to see the terrified look in the eyes of those still clinging to the hull.

But, there was nothing he could do. The boat receded into the distance, men still clinging desperately to the hull. It disappeared from view in the mist and spray.

The winds continued unabated. For the moment *El Viento* seemed to hold position but under the quarterdeck, Bartalome gazed across the expanse at the *Princesa,* now well aft of their position. With each successive band of rain, she would momentarily disappear from view only to reappear still further aft. Bartalome knew that the shallow bottom of the harbor rapidly fell off at some distance from shore. Once blown into this deeper water the anchor would lose its tenuous hold and the *Princesa* would be rapidly blown out to sea.

Another squall line passed over them and the rain fell in torrents. The air, thick with moisture, permeated everything. Bartalome's clothes were sodden and clung to him like a cold blanket. He had begun to shiver uncontrollably and even breathing was difficult in the driving rain. Through clenched teeth, he guarded against inhaling water. Still, he would be racked by spasms of coughing as water passed into his lungs. On deck one of the soldiers who had been clinging to the mast abruptly rose to his feet and jumped overboard followed by the other two. All three surfaced a short distance from the ship and began to swim towards shore. Over the waves and down into the troughs the swimmers valiantly floundered against the oncoming wind and surf. Soon all three were spent and began to tread water, their heads mere specks in the violent sea. They too were swept out to sea one by one disappearing in the haze. Bartalome crossed himself and said a silent Ava Maria.

Another phenomenon began to play out in *El Viento*. The mass of humanity huddled below decks had had enough of the movement, the stench, and the terror. One by one they began to concentrate on the main deck, their moans and lamentations at times louder than the wind. Soldiers and sailors alike hung onto whatever rope or projection could keep them from being washed overboard. Bartalome made no attempt to stop them...better to face death head-on than die with the animals in the dark squalor below decks.

"The *Princesa!*" A voice in the crowd caused Bartalome to jerk around in the direction of the companion ship.

A particularly strong blast of wind had dislodged the *Princesa* from its anchorage for good. The anchor, not finding a hold on the increasingly deeper sea floor, bounced along the sandy bottom. Still functioning as a sea anchor the bow maintained its position in the wind, but the ship was rapidly moving out to sea. There was movement on the decks but the distance was too great and Bartalome could not distinguish any one in particular. He could only imagine the grief that his friend Baudelio Reyes was feeling. Watching the *Princesa* slide out to sea he thought he saw a rigid figure in the aft castle standing alone, but this vision rapidly faded as a slight shift in wind rotated the craft and obscured a clear view of the stern. The ship remained visible for some time, its outline diminishing with each passing minute.

And so it continued for the next four hours, the wind steadily growing in strength. Amazingly, the anchor continued to hold in the shallow harbor but the buffeting of wind and sea was taking a toll on *El Viento*. Battered and under stress the hull planking was losing its integrity. *Marineros* plugged off gaps as best they could while relays of men labored at the pumps. Still, the accumulation of seawater began to build. After his last inspection tour, Bartalome knew it was just a matter of time. The ship was becoming heavy in the water.

03 November, 1527

Aboard the Caravel *El Viento Del Sur*

The light was fading. Although the sun was still high at these latitudes, the thick layer of clouds and mist made it seem much later. After taking a turn at the pumps Bartalome returned to the deck. The wind was of such velocity that he was forced to crawl or crab walk from place to place while maintaining a grip on lines or stanchions. It was blowing steady now, rain and sea mist stinging his face. To stand on the deck in an unprotected area was impossible. The noise was deafening. Bartalome noticed that most of the wretched souls that had wondered on deck earlier in the day had returned below. A few still huddled in protected corners of the aft deck, shivering and miserable. Others had been blown overboard. He made eye contact with one man he recognized as a crossbowman, his eyes questioning and full of terror. Bartalome looked away.

Huddled in a corner of the aft castle Bartalome watched the shoreline slowly disappear from view in the fading light. Although still only late afternoon, the density of the clouds so obstructed the sky that darkness would soon envelope them. Spray cascaded over the length of the ship. Physically exhausted and lightheaded from lack of sleep and food he, at first, didn't notice their position relative to the shore. It finally came to him in a start. Where before the shore had been directly off the bow it had now moved slightly to starboard. Slowly *El Viento* was pivoting on its anchor line...the wind direction was changing.

Bartalome struggled to his feet. Instincts told him that as the storm passed over them the wind direction would continue to change. At some point, it would blow toward the shore providing them with a last chance to save themselves. He had to have help.

Struggling to open the hatch he negotiated the steps with difficulty. He was looking for the boatswain. All about wretched bodies were sprawled about the lower deck. Some looked up at him as he entered their area but others just stared ahead as if in a trance. It was the look in their eyes that most caught him off guard. It was vacant as if the life had gone out of their soul...these were already dead men. It angered Bartalome and he began to kick the prostrate figures. Kicking and cursing, the frustrations of the storm, the exhaustion, and their situation overwhelmed him. The onslaught continued until strong arms grabbed him from behind.

It was Fermin Morales, the boatswain, "*Senor* Valdez, for the love of God, you must desist, these people are frozen with fear. It will do no good to further injure them."

Bartalome spun around, still in a rage. He grabbed Morales's shoulders with both hands and shook him, "The wind is shifting to shore...there is a chance to escape this tempest but I need help."

Suddenly there was a ray of hope in Morales's eyes, "What is it you need us to do, I will find the men."

03 November, 1527

The Home of Alcade Rafeal Viela, Trinidad, Cuba

The noise outside the small hut was overpowering, a constant throbbing din punctuated by the crash of rain, thunder, and air-borne projectiles against the sides of the building. The roof was leaking now and water poured in from a multitude of locations. In a corner Malita, softly whimpering, was crouched down holding a blanket about herself. Where only hours before she had been the ultimate sex partner, Malita now appeared only as a terrified child. With each lightening flash and clap of thunder, she shuddered and seemed to sink deeper into the blanket. Alvar sat at the table trying to protect the single candle from blowing out in the drafty enclosure...it was their only source of light. Outside, the blackness was total with only the lightening providing a momentary glimpse at the world around them.

Above the noise of the storm, a loud crack reverberated through the night. Alvar looked at Malita who stared back with saucer-sized eyes, full of fear.

Suddenly the room itself seemed to explode. Alvar was thrown from his chair and fell heavily on the floor. Momentarily dazed and in complete darkness, something heavy lay across his chest pinning him to the floor.

He struggled to collect his thoughts. "What had happened?"

The rain and wind were now all around him. Debris was swirling around the room and the amount of rain running down his face forced him to breath through clenched teeth. In a lightning flash, he could see a tree limb lying across his chest, leaves, and branches everywhere. Slowly his dazed brain came back into focus. A large tree on the windward side of the building had crashed through the roof, pulverizing the small building.

A wave of panic momentarily flooded over him and he struggled to free himself of the entanglement. Slowly sliding to one side, the downward force of the limb began to somewhat abate. Pushing with both arms and raising his knees he was able to slide under the branch. Pushing leaves and limbs out of the way, Alvar struggled to sit upright. Overhead, water cascaded on top of him from what remained of the roof. The sound of the wind made it hard to concentrate and now pieces of wind-driven debris were stinging his exposed skin. For a moment he checked his appendages to see if anything was broken. Other than a very sore shoulder and what felt like a deep cut on his face, everything seemed to be all right. Crawling forward he moved toward a remnant of the remaining wall where the force of the wind was somewhat reduced.

The lightning was almost continuous now and it revealed the table at which he had been sitting. It had been crushed and undoubtedly had protected him from the full force of the limb as it crashed through the room. Toward the other side of the room was the main trunk. It had easily passed through the roof and side wall, scattering bricks, timbers, and roofing beneath it.

"Malita?" Alvar called out, but the sound of his voice was swallowed by the wind. At that moment he thought how strange it was that he couldn't hear himself. In the phosphorus glow of the lightning, he made his way toward the corner where she had last been.

Climbing over limbs and building remnants he made his way to the bulk of the tree. What remained of the building was now all but unrecognizable in the profusion of limbs, branches, and leaves. Looking back at the crushed table and then finding the remnants of the door jamb Alvar began to come to the terrible realization that the tree had fallen almost directly on where Malita had been sitting. Still, there was a possibility she had avoided it somehow. Crawling on hands and knees, the shattered masonry cut into him. With each flash of lightning, Alvar moved further along the tree feeling around him for any sign of Malita. The storm raged...pieces of the roof, sticks, sand, leaves, rain...swirled about in the air above him.

A continuous flash of lightning revealed what looked like a blanket just ahead. He moved slowly forward, ducking under one limb, and crawling over another. Feeling he must be close, Alvar paused and felt the area in front of him, slowly moving his hands back and forth. His fingers located the blanket. Grabbing a fistful of the fabric he slowly pulled it. It came freely for a moment and then abruptly stopped...the blanket was wedged under the bulk of the tree. It was then that his nostrils detected the sickening odor of feces. Even through the wind and rain, it was unmistakable. Alvar waited for another lightning flash to illuminate the area.

What he saw made him recoil in horror. Entangled in the blanket were the remains of Malita's left leg from the knee down, the remainder disappearing under the huge tree. Next to it, her entire left arm lay at a grotesque angle, palm up. Thick black hair covered a visible part of the shoulder. All around him blood, feces, and bodily fluids were collected in the wetness of the pouring rain.

Panicked, Alvar lurched from his position and crashed through the branches...he had to get out. First stumbling and then falling he flailed his arms in desperation to be free of the entanglements. Finally able to stand, he crouched low and moved with hands extended in front like a blind man. Lightening revealed an opening in the wall and he lurched forward out into the yard.

The effort to get away left him bruised and bleeding. Free of the tree, he sat huddled behind a section of the front wall. Here he was somewhat protected from the wind and debris. The ferocity of the storm continued unabated, the sounds of breaking trees discernible above the wind. Still shaken, he thought of the scene he had just witnessed...of Malina. In his mind, he thought of the times he had stepped on an insect and watched the innards squirt out across the floor. He vomited and then retched until his stomach hurt.

03 November, 1527

Aboard the Caravel El Viento Del Sur

With each lightning flash a line of whiteness stood out against the dark background. Now, directly off the stern, Bartalome knew that this was surf impacting the beach no more than half a league from where they were now anchored. The wind had turned. There had been a brief period of relative calm only to be replaced by a raging tumult. The storm surge was strong, much stronger than before. Now huge waves broke over the bow of *El Viento*, the spray blasting high over the main mast. The added pounding was taking its tole. Bartalome could feel the ship riding lower in the water. The pumps were no match for the amount of sea water now coming through the damaged hull. It would not last much longer. Their time for action was now, they had to make the effort to run the ship into the shore.

Morales had done well in accumulating several of the *marineros*. At the right moment, two of the men would cut the anchor line. Bartalome would like to have partially hauled in the anchor and trailed it as a sea anchor. This would have allowed a stern-first approach to the shore, but there was no possibility of hauling in the anchor in these conditions. With such a weight it was even difficult to winch in calm seas. His alternative was to cut the anchor line during a period of reduced violence while setting a remnant of storm sail. Hopefully, this would rapidly rotate *El Viento* and minimize the amount of time it would lay broadside to the waves. Once rotated, the sail would accelerate the ship towards shore, giving it as much forward momentum as possible. Bartalome knew that, once grounded, the ship would be blown broadside and rapidly break up in the mountainous surf. It was their only chance. Out here all would die. Ashore, some may have a chance to survive.

Morales signaled that all was ready.

Bartalome noted the sequence of the waves and listened carefully to the sounds of the storm. Although the winds now were blowing constantly, there were surges that intensified its effect. He would try and avoid these.

Concentrating intensely, he was about to signal on several occasions but hesitated...it didn't feel right. Next to him the two *marineros,* each wielding a sharp ax, waited in anticipation. The anchor was attached to a chain, *el cadena del ancla,* which extended up for twenty feet. This *"cadena"* was then attached to a thick rope that made up the majority of the anchor line. The rope passed through an opening in the bow, *el escoben,* to the ships, windless. The rope itself was thick and very resilient. The two *marineros* would have to work fast to get it cut.

For a moment the sound of the wind abated ever so slightly as another wave broke against the bow. Water poured down on them. Now was the time. Bartalome gave the signal and then moved rapidly to the bow to help with the storm sail.

The forecastle was being pummeled by wind, waves, and rain. It would be difficult for a man to venture out into the exposed area. Two *marineros* were huddled beneath the steps clutching ropes, tackle, and a canvas sail. Bartalome crawled over to them. Behind him the the two axemen chopped feverishly. The anchor line separated with a loud snap and the ship lurched with the release of tension.

Immediately there was movement. *El Viento* began its rotation to starboard...but slowly. The wind which had been directly off the bow was now coursing to the port side. Bartalome and the two *marineros* scrambled up the ladder. Once in the open, the force was breathtaking, his feet were blown out from under him and he landed heavily on the slippery deck. He gasped but only got a mouthful of rain and seawater. Choking, the force of the wind blew him against the starboard gunwale and he struggled to grab a line or handhold to steady himself.

Turning, Bartalome saw that the two *marineros* had reached the heel of the bow sprint. One was trying to pass an attached line around the forestay. With this, they could anchor a corner of the sail, but the wind blew the rope out of his hand and he lurched across the other man, falling in a heap. Losing his grip on the canvas sail, it billowed in the wind and tore from his grasp. The sail lifted skyward. Draped around the seaman, the attached line became taunt around his neck. Releasing his grip, he briefly struggled to free himself but the force of the wind was too much. The lifeless body was dragged across the deck and then into the air. Now only a few feet above him, Bartalome watched in horrified fascination as the dead *marinero's* arms and legs gesticulated wildly in the turbulent air. Strangely, he thought of the puppet shows he watched as a child growing up in *Cadez.*

El Viento was being pushed backward, its rate of rotation increasing. Things began to happen fast.

The port side of the ship now felt the full force of the wind and began to roll heavily. Still hanging to the starboard gunwale, Bartalome was only inches above the water. Looking shoreward he could just see the pounding breakers getting closer.

On deck, the miserable inhabitants sequestered below began to stream out the hatch, their screams, and lamentations lost in the sounds of the storm. Hanging on to whatever handhold was available, many began to push and shove for choice locations. Blown from their precarious perches some were already in the water...heads bobbing like melons in the waves.

A loud crash next to Bartalome - the headless body of the *marinero* released from the sail line - the abrasive rope completely severing the head. Above, the loose sail continued to flap noisily in the wind.

Time seemed to slow and Bartalome's thoughts became more lucid. There was nothing he could do now...soon *El Viento* would roll, trapping him beneath its bulk.

He had to get away from the ship.

Grasping the amulet around his neck Bartalome said a silent *Ave Maria* before he pushed off into the turbulent waters. Swimming strongly, he put several yards between himself and the floundering *El Viento* only to be grasped from behind by another man in the water. Forced under, he fought to free himself but the crazed swimmer seemed to have abnormal strength. The man grabbed at anything he could hold onto...Bartalome's tunic, his hair, his belt. Even underwater the man's incoherent screams sounded above the water noise. The waves and current rolled both of them deeper until, suddenly, the man released his grip, stepping on Bartalome's shoulders to get to the surface.

His lungs aching, Bartalome desperately needed air. He struggled to the surface, gasping for as much air as his lungs could hold. The other man was nowhere in sight. A wave broke over him and again he tumbled through the water. Rising again, Bartalome was lifted on a swell and, in the distance, saw the breakers hitting the shoreline.

He thought, "I may yet live" and began treading water. The waves and wind would push him to shore soon enough.

Behind him, *El Viento,* broadside to the shore, rocked violently back and forth with the wave and wind action. It would roll to its starboard gunwales and then partially right itself as the next wave passed, the masts making majestic arcs in the sky. The tremendous weight of the water in its hold was stabilizing the caravel. Both the doomed ship and Bartalome were moving toward shore at the same speed.

Bartalome had turned towards the shore and didn't see the drama playing out behind him. Probably a good thing, for *El Viento,* moving rapidly in the surf, struck bottom. The effect was catastrophic. Stopping abruptly, the energy stored in its movement through the water was transferred to the hull and masts. The ship rolled rapidly to starboard. Like a medieval *trebushet*, the masts at the end of the arc moved at tremendous speed.

In one instant Pilot Bartalome Valdez floated on the surface of the storm surge, his eyes and efforts affixed to the oncoming shoreline and survival. The next instant a two-ton mast exploded into the water...a spray of red...everything obliterated beneath it.

There was no warning, no pain...only blackness.

CHAPTER 04

The Medallion

Los Medallon

The beach appeared to be clear, nothing but seabirds as far as he could see. Sheathing the sword Alvar bent over to pick up the saddle cloth that was lying in the sand. Beneath the cloth, something shone brightly in the morning sun. He reached to pick it up... He stared at the article in his hand, dropped to his knees, and crossed himself. Still attached to the gold chain, it was the medallion that had been worn by his friend Bartalome.

03 November, 1527

Trinidad, Cuba

Unable to sleep during the night, mayor Viela had made his way to the church to check on the supplies that were stored there. Not long after arriving, the church had also suffered grievously, first losing its roof and then a wall, blown down by the force of the wind. The violence of the storm had increased such that Viela, Elcano, Jimenez, and others had locked arms to keep from being carried off. Somehow, Alvar, stumbling through the streets, had found them, with only the illumination of lightning strikes to guide his way. Others had joined them. Throughout the night they sat in a circle, praying for deliverance from this terrible onslaught. They were shivering, pelted with debris and all were cut and bruised. Talking above the tumult had been impossible, for the wind screamed and made unearthly noises such as no one had ever heard. At its worst Alvar had thought he heard demons' voices, bells, and musical instruments. He could only think of the Hell described to him as a boy in the *Catechisms*.

In the morning, daylight had come upon them slowly and although the rain was continuous, the wind began to abate. When able, Alvar, Elcano, and Jimenez had carefully made their way to the cliff overlooking the harbor, but for as far as they could see nothing interrupted the ocean surface but angry rolling whitecaps. Of the caravels *El Viento del Sur* and *Princesa Margarita*, the sea had swallowed them up.

04 November, 1527

On the Beach at Trinidad, Cuba

Alvar stepped over a ship's mast half buried in the wet sand, the lines and fixtures spread about it like a spider web. With him were Angel Jimenez and Elcano. They walked together, each harboring their own thoughts on the magnitude of damage around them. Along the beach, not a single tree remained upright for miles, trunks, and limbs scattered about. Further inland the trunks remained upright, but only as bare sticks pointing skyward like lone sentinels. Huge mounds of sand randomly dotted the landscape, piled there by the intervening waves and wind. Inter spaced between, deep furrows of erosion extended hundreds of yards inland, water still draining seaward, dark with mud and debris.

Before the storm, the harbor area had been a sparse collection of storage huts and a single wharf. Scattered about had been the remnants of the town's commerce. Small fishing boats, barrels, boxes, nets, wagons, ropes and tools. Nothing remained. Now, except for an occasional piling stuck in the sand, all had washed away.

It was still raining. A mist-like drizzle that, even at this latitude, was chilling. Gray clouds scudded rapidly across the sky bringing an occasional squall and heavier rain. The wind, so strong mere hours ago, had calmed considerably. A heavy breeze now blew inland, occasionally interspersed with gusts that lifted the loose sand in swirling clouds.

Immense waves continued to assail the beach, the thunderous breakers deafening amongst all the destruction. Far out to sea, shafts of sunlight briefly thrust themselves earthward through the grayness. The *huracan* had spent itself out.

Other than the single mast laying in the sand, the only sign of *El Viento del Sur* and *Princesa Margareta* were the lone anchor buoys riding in the surf.

Alvar had never seen destruction like this. Nothing in *Spanish Andalusia* had prepared him for this level of destruction. He sat down on the mast and put his head in his hands.

To no one, he lamented, "I was in charge, I am responsible for this." His shoulders shook with emotion.

Further down, a smattering of people filtered onto the beach; other crew members who had remained ashore to prepare the supplies for loading, townspeople, the brothers Dario and Tomas Vargas, and even the mayor, who had not been in the building when the tree had destroyed his house.

Elcano and Angel Jimenez continued their trek along the beach, poking among the tangle of debris for any sign of their crew mates. Rising, at last, Alvar joined them in their search. Together they walked until traveling a fair piece down the beach.

"*Senor* De Vaca", it was Elcano..."I suggest that we turn into the forest, the beach has been cleaned by the waves."

Moving inland they crawled over trees and moved tangles of debris out of the way. Here they searched for several hours until fatigued by the exertion, lack of food, and sleep. The evening was approaching as they made their way out of the tangled forest.

It was Alvar who noticed it first.

High above, straddled between two massive limbs was one of the ship's small boats, its sides caved in, but still recognizable. The three *Spaniards* stared at it without comment and slowly turned to begin their walk back to what was left of *Trinidad.*

Aboard the caravels, *El Viento del Sur* and *Princesa Margareta* 60 men, 20 horses, and five war dogs had perished.

05 November, 1527

The Shoreline East of Trinidad, Cuba

For two days after the great *huracan,* Alvar had traveled the beach looking for a sign of the ships and people that were lost. Borrowing a horse, he traveled alone, riding a distance and then walking into the tortured forest to look for anything unusual. Attached to the saddle was his sword, a water gourd, and a short shovel, for if there were bodies he was determined to give them a *Christian* burial.

This day he had ridden most of the morning, lost in thought while he surveyed the shore and scanned the forest beyond. To be sure, the expanse of shoreline that stretched endlessly into the haze was blanketed with storm remnants...mostly trees and branches, but occasionally dead animals, fish, and sea birds. In one area he had found a massive fishing net with cork floats still attached. Along the way, there were remnants of small fishing boats, native canoes, paddles, and even a whalers harpoon. Strangely, nothing from the *Princessa Margarita* or *El Viento.*

Here the shoreline turned rocky and he guided the borrowed gelding closer to the trees, carefully avoiding snags and outcroppings. Alvar paused in a clear area as a colony of land crabs skittered in front of him intent on reaching some undefined goal. Unwrapping the gourd from his saddle he took a long drink and then reinserted the wooden plug. At the tree line, something caught his eye. A shape that, somehow, didn't conform to the tangled mess of storm damage.

Tying the horse he moved into the treeline, stopping frequently to get his bearings and scan the area ahead. Closer, he determined there were two shapes...each suspended from the limbs of a huge uprooted oak tree. Below them, what looked like ship storage containers littered the ground. Closer still, Alvar instinctively knew they were bodies and hesitated ever so slightly in his forward movement. As he neared the downed oak, the smell of putrefying flesh wafted through the air and he tried desperately to breath only through his mouth.

Now, directly beneath one, he could make out two arms hanging down. The corpse was upside down and the coat the man was wearing obscured his head. Above him twisted legs rose into the air at odd angles, the bare feet pointing in opposite directions.

Further on, the other corpse was lower. By standing on a log, Alvar could look directly at it. He immediately recognized the coat. He had seen it on one of *El Viento's marineros,* conspicuous by its red bunting on the collar. The head, covered with flies was battered and unrecognizable. The smell was overpowering and Alvar had to step down to get away from it. Falling to his knees, he retched several times, the bile taste burned his throat and filled his mouth. Slowly he rose and walked back to the gelding to retrieve the shovel. He would bury both men beneath the downed oak.

The sand dug easily but the heat was intense and Alvar soon determined to put both bodies in one grave. Climbing partially up the tree he used a long stick to prod the first corpse in hopes of dislodging it. The body was blotted almost twice its normal size and it took considerable effort to move. Pushing with the stick he could feel the soft fleshy parts yielding until finally, the corpse released, hitting the ground below like a tomato. The other corpse was easily dislodged from its position.

He dragged both bodies to the grave site and as ceremoniously as possible rolled them into the freshly dug hole. Filling the hole was almost as strenuous as digging it. The day's shadows were getting long as Alvar patted down the mound of sand. Using straps stripped from saddle leather he fashioned a crude cross and pushed it into the soft sand. Exhausted, he stood there, shovel in hand, and mouthed a short prayer.

Shuffling back to the horse Alvar stowed the shovel and mounted the animal. After riding only a short distance he stopped at a stretch of open beach. Dismounting, he waded into the surf and let the swirling seawater remove the stench of death.

05 November, 1527

The Shoreline East of Trinidad, Cuba

The ride had taken Alvar further then he realized. He had tarried too long in the surf, relaxing in its freshness and thinking of the horrors both of the men he just buried had experienced. Looking seaward, the sun was just sinking below the horizon in a beautiful clear sky. *Trinidad* was still a good two hours away and riding at night would not be smart on the debris-strewn shoreline. He would search for a place to bed down. Coming to a narrow estuary he had passed earlier in the day Alvar determined to spend the night. Here he could get fresh water from the small stream that still flowed strong from the storm run-off waters. The day had been exceedingly hot and he was sure he would be quite comfortable with the evening temperatures. He would use the saddle blanket for a ground cover and sleep under the stars.

The evening had begun well enough. The darkness came on quickly and a moonless night revealed thousands of stars that, at times, seemed to be close enough to touch. In the clearness he watched meteorites flash across the sky. A moderate breeze blew in from the ocean. The ever-present sound of the waves and the occasional movement of the gelding were the only distractions. Tired from the day's labor, he quickly fell asleep.

It was late, probably after midnight when Alvar was started awake. Momentarily disoriented, he lay there gathering his thoughts. The sky was still exceedingly clear and he recognized several of the constellations that Bartalome had showed him. His favorite was one called "The Hunter"...three prominent bright stars represented the belt, and others outlined the head, shoulders, and sword. Alvar would always remember these and think of his friend Bartalome.

Far out to sea, a prolonged flash danced across the sky. The momentary brilliance revealed a line of distant clouds low in the sky. Alvar began to slide back into sleep when a different noise permeated his senses.

He lay there listening...maybe he had just dreamed it.

Then, over the noise of the waves, it drifted to him again, "*Aronka ti sombu*". Human voices in a language he didn't understand. Fully awake now, Alvar quickly rose and located his sword. It was very dark and only the occasional lightning flashes far out to sea provided any visual aide. He squatted in the sand, holding his sword and straining to hear. More talking...it sounded as if it was coming from the water...the unmistakable sound of an oar striking the side of a boat. More talking again...the sounds drifting further down the beach. Someone expelling gas in a raucous explosion...laughing...more talk.

Alvar, frozen in his stance, continued to listen as the disruption moved down the beach and eventually died away. He remembered a conversation with Bartalome about the *Caribs*, a group of *Indians* that continued to frequent all of the *Indies*. Unlike other tribes of the islands, they had never been defeated and roamed freely, capturing women for mates, and men and boys for food. The *Caribs* were cannibals and many a shipwrecked *Spaniard* had been taken by these savages.

Only the roar of the breakers remained.

Terrified, Alvar could not sleep. To scared to move, he remained sitting for, what seemed an eternity, listening into the night for anything out of the ordinary. Once, the gelding had stomped his foot. Alvar jumped up...spun around....pointed his sword at the source of the noise, his heart pounding in his throat. Again the horse made a movement and Alvar recognized it for what it was. Feeling ridiculous he sat back down and continued his vigil. Sometime just before dawn, sleep again came over him and he lay there on the sand, gently snoring, still clutching the sword.

The sun was well up before Alvar opened his eyes. He had been sleeping deeply and for a moment the reality of his situation didn't come to him. Finally, remembering last night and the *Caribs* he jumped to his feet in a start. The sudden movement made him light-headed and he steadied himself on a piece of driftwood close at hand.

The beach appeared to be clear, nothing but seabirds as far as he could see. Sheathing the sword Alvar bent over to pick up the saddle cloth that was lying in the sand. Beneath the cloth, something shone brightly in the morning sun. He reached to pick it up.

A feeling of overpowering bewilderment flooded his senses. How...how did it get here? What were the chances of finding it in all this sand? Unconsciously, Alvar looked around him for other wreck remnants...but there was nothing. He stared at the article in his hand, dropped to his knees, and crossed himself. Still attached to the gold chain, it was the medallion that had been worn by his friend Bartalome.

05 November, 1527

Trinidad, Cuba

Alvar stood on the hill overlooking the harbor. From his vantage point, he could make out four sets of sails only now rising up from the horizon to reveal the ship's structure below. He had been alerted to the sighting by several of the town inhabitants only minutes before. He was sure they must be Narvaez and the rest of the expedition, but the day was hazy and the vessels were too far away to be identified. To be sure, these were not the first visitors to *Trinidad* after the *huracan*. Other vessels had stopped here. Some limped in with shattered masts and only tatters for sails...two had sunk in the harbor after arriving. Several traveling from *Vera Cruz* had stopped to lend assistance and...of course...profit in the sale of much-needed items.

It had been almost two days since the terrible *huracan* had taken his ships, soldiers, crews, horses, and supplies. He could be thankful for one thing...only three settlers had died in the storm. A farmer and his two sons. The rest had elected to return to *Santiago* with Narvaez. He tried to picture the farmer in his mind, but couldn't. The name...Gomara...maybe. Others, like Alvar, had been spared. Those that had left the ship to make ready the supplies had all survived the terrible wind...about 30 in all.

A few days after the storm Captain Pantoja and Vasco Porcallo had returned to the ruined city accompanied by four of Porcallo's slaves. They were all on foot and severely stressed. They had been leading a group of six horses back to *Trinidad* when the storm caught them. Dismounting, the travelers had attempted to lead the animals but the winds were too severe and they were forced to hole up under a protected cliff, the animals tied to a picket line only a short distance away. As the storm increased in fury the animals became more distressed and for fear of injury Porcallo had the hobbles removed from their forelegs. During a particularly bad squall, lightning had struck close to the picket line, splitting a large Banyon tree and setting it afire. The noise had been tremendous and for a moment the *Spaniards* sat stunned, momentarily blinded by the flash as the rain beat around them. Finally rising, Porcallo and his men hurried to check on the horses. Two lay dead, still attached to the severed line, a wisp of smoke emanating from their steel-shod hoofs. The other horses had bolted and were nowhere in sight.

Behind Alvar, the sounds of construction permeated the air. Men were working to rebuild what the storm had destroyed. It had been extensive. Every structure in *Trinidad* had been severely damaged. Many dwellings had collapsed upon themselves from the force of the wind, others had been the victims of downed trees and airborne projectiles. Even the church, built entirely of stone, had lost its belfry and a partial wall. In the town, 13 people died and many were injured.

The *ranchos* and *haciendas* surrounding *Trinidad* had suffered even worse, many being completely obliterated by the storm's fury. People had streamed into town needing aid, but there was little available. There was almost no shelter and very little food. In the fields, animals had been killed by the dozens and had to be disposed of. For weeks farmers had scoured the countryside rounding up stray livestock.

The recovery had been slow, and to his credit, the town mayor, Rafael Viela, who had survived the onslaught, took immediate control. Work parties were organized and everything that could be useful was brought to the center of town. The church had been the first priority and everyone assisted the masons and carpenters in its recovery. Even the pious friars had helped move debris, mix mortar, and mend fences.

At the water's edge, several small boats had been salvaged and were now being used to collect fish for the town's larder. For the most part, many of the *Indio's* canoes had remained intact. Nets were being repaired, and lobster and crab traps had to be built. Most importantly, the town's salt supply had been decimated by the storm. Without it, nothing could be stored. Parties had been sent out to collect salt from as far away as *La Evangelista* and *Havana*.

Now, still standing on the overlook, Alvar wondered what decisions Narvaez would make now that he had lost two of his ships.

Angel Jimenez and Elcano joined him on the hill.

After long years at sea, Elcano had the best vision of the three. Shading his eyes he squinted into the distance, the lead vessel now was almost completely above the horizon. "*Senor* De Vaca, the large ship in front is truly the *Maria*. She rides low in the bow. Behind her...I think is *Reina,* by the set of her sails. Amazed at the seaman's eyesight, Jimenez sighed in relief, "Praise God, they survived the storm".

Since the *huracan,* the three *Spaniards* had become good friends. Still, Alvar was the expedition's royal representative and had to be treated with some deference, but the events of the last few months had bonded them. The three friends were further joined by other members of the doomed ships who had survived the storm. Most were the advance *marineros* who had gone ashore to begin the acquisition and loading of supplies. Several soldiers had also accompanied them, happy to remove themselves from the undulating decks of *El Viento del Sur* and *Princessa Margarita*. Two *Franciscan* friars, Juan Velazquesz de Salazar and Juan de Palos, each from their respective ship had also gone ashore to administer to the souls of *Trinidad*. Little did they know at the time that it would save their lives. Now, on this hill, they conducted a short mass to celebrate the return of the expedition.

05 November, 1527

Harbor at Trinidad, Cuba

No sooner had the flagship *Maria de la Meridionales Mares* settled into the bay then the ship's boat could be seen lowering into the water. Standing in the bow was the unmistakable form of Narvaez, his booming voice carrying across the water as the *marineros* strained at the oars.

Back on the flagship, there was a flurry of activity. The anchor was lowered, sails furled and the multitude of ropes and rigging were tied off and stowed. Behind the *Maria* the *Reina de Naploles* slowly glided past, its crew just beginning the same procedure. Further out

El Delfín and *La Doncella de Plata* were beginning to drop their sails.

They watched as Narvaez drew closer. Behind them a single carriage attended by three *Tiano's* moved down the road to transport the *Adelantado*.

With one last look, Alvar left the overlook and returned to the village. There was much to do. First, he would organize some kind of reception and a lunch for Narvaez...someplace they could meet and discuss the dreadful happenings and the future of the expedition.

CHAPTER 05

Like Fat Whales

Ballenas Gordas

He picked up the closest thing at hand...a belaying pin...and threw it at Miruello who was still sitting on the deck rubbing his head. The pin missed the pilot and clattered along the deck. All movement stopped and everyone turned to watch. Miruello scurried up the aft stairway.

"Now we are beached like fat whales, ballenas gordas!"

20 February, 1528

The Anchorage at Jagua, Cuba

The expedition lay at anchor in the protected bay at *Jagua*. It was a perfect day; clear blue sky and warm with a slight breeze from the southeast. Besides the normal boat traffic in the bay, the ships of the Narvaez expedition where a hub of activity. Tenders bringing supplies, animals, and people darted to and fro between each vessel. *Marineros* working high in the masts were making last-minute repairs and adjustments to the rigging and sails. These ships would soon be underway.

Before the storm, Narvaez had tarried at *Cabo Santa Cruz* before setting sail and continuing north along the coast. His destination was a place called *Puerto Manzanillo,* where he had planned on collecting additional horses and supplies from his *ranchero* in *Bayomo.*

Actually, *Manzanillo* was only two structures and a dilapidated quay that extended out into the water...it was hardly a port at all. Surrounded by reefs and sandbars there was only one channel leading to the primitive dock. It was said that the name, *Manzanillo* came from the occupants of a shipwrecked caravel carrying a cargo of sherry from the port of *Sanlucar de Barrameda in Cadiz, Andalusia, Spain*. The sherry, called *Manzanillo*, was consumed by the survivors who stayed drunk for weeks.

There was no hurry, for Narvaez had told De Vaca to continue on to the port at *Jagua* after obtaining Porcallo's supplies in *Trinidad*. At *Jagua* De Vaca would await the rest of the ships of the expedition before continuing around the west coast of *Cuba* to *Havana*. Narvaez would continue overland to *Havana* using his considerable influence to procure additional supplies and funding along the way.

Things, however, did not turn out as planned.

As they coasted northward in the *Gulfo de Guacanayabo*, the weather had worsened dramatically. Nearing their destination, pilot Janero Flores had advised Narvaez to bypass *Manzanillo* and continue on to the *Rio Cauto*. *Manzanillo* was a relatively unprotected harbor and here the ships would surely be lost. The large delta system of the *Rio Cauto* could provide them with any number of protected sanctuaries from which to escape the worsening storm.

Nearing the river, a terrible gust of wind blew down on the *Maria* and sheared the mizzen mast. It made a terrible noise as it separated from the rigging and clattered down onto the deck below. The *marineros* struggled to extricate the debris from an increasingly unstable deck.

Suddenly from above. "*Rio al estribor*"! On the starboard side, the lookout had sighted the river's entrance into the bay.

Ahead the shoreline opened and all aboard praised God, for the mouth of the river was at hand. It was a risky passage, to be sure, bordered on one side by mangrove tangles and the other by sand bars that extended into the river channel. All of the vessels entered successfully, a strong quartering wind allowing them to continue against the current. As the river narrowed, the water deepened and they continued until almost a league upriver to a small backwater. At that point, all immediately proceeded to set anchors. On board the *Maria* the shattered mizzen was cut free and lashed to the deck. Below decks the friars huddled with the colonists and soldiers, taking confessions and asking forgiveness.

In the darkness, the eastern fringe of the *huracan* had descended upon them. Even in the protected river, the wind blew with unrelenting fury. On board the stress was great. From the holds, lamentations from the terrified inhabitants had continued throughout the night. It wasn't until early morning that the winds began to diminish. At first light, Panfilo had ventured out to survey the damage. The deck and rigging were strewn with limbs and leaves blown from the shore. From the protected cove he could see that the river was running high. The huge carcasses of trees rolled in the current. Overhead, the clouds scudded rapidly across the sky. The wind rippled the surface of the water, gusting across its length. Rain still fell in isolated bursts. Surprisingly, however, the damage was light. This sanctuary in the *Rio Cauto* had served them well. There was no thought now about landing at *Manzanillo*. Narvaez was deeply concerned about the fate of the two ships and he ordered the expedition to proceed as quickly as possible to *Trinidad*.

The short journey to the bay had been difficult. The *Maria,* with its deeper draft, had briefly run aground on a sandbar that extended into the river's channel. In the still-strong current the stern swung completely around, dragging the encumbered bow behind it. Just as rapidly, the bow slid free. *Marineros* had struggled mightily to turn the big caravel and somehow got it done just as the vessels emerged into the litter-strewn bay.

The journey had been sorrowful. All around, evidence of the recent calamity was evident. Sailing westward, the coastline was a mass of refuse. From the aftcastle, Panfilo watched the detritus pass below him. Forward, an occasional floating log impacted the hull, sending its vibration throughout the ship. More often carcasses of all manner of animals could be seen floating in the still turbid waters. Deer, horses, cattle...even dolphin and at least one dead whale was observed, its lifeless fluke waving at them in the rolling surf.

Arriving on 05 November, 1527 what greeted them at Trinidad was beyond comprehension. It was obvious that the worst of the storm had been centered here. All of those aboard the returning ships had friends or acquaintances who had been lost. Many walked the beach, others searched inland for any sign of the lost ships. Quickly constructed crosses were hammered into the sand. Strangely, only bits and pieces of the *Princesa Margareta* and *El Viento del Sur* were ever found.

So afraid were the people of the expedition that Narvaez had reluctantly agreed to winter in *Cuba* until Spring. The fleet would relocate to the protected harbor at *Jagua,* only 10 leagues further west. This small settlement was located next to a deep inland bay accessible only through a narrow dog-legged inlet that provided unprecedented protection from the sea.

On the 7th of November, they entered the port of *Xuaga* and set up winter quarters, forming a sub-community that operated both out of the ships and hastily constructed shelters on shore. Here the carpenters re-caulked leaking hulls and repaired storm damage. Several of the vessels were intentionally run onto sandbars and careened, their hulls scrapped clean of speed-robbing barnacles.

Not one to remain idle, Panfilo and a small contingent of followers off-loaded horses and traveled some 10 leagues across *Cuba* to the port city of *Havana.* Maria had met him there, making the overland journey from the *ranchero* at *Bayomo.* While in *Havana* Narvaez would do what he could to procure additional funding, replenish supplies, and draft more volunteers. Things had gone well. Several friends had taken an interest in the expedition and contributed enough for the purchase of a caravel, *Santo del Aqua Azul...*Saint of the Blue Water. On the *Aqua* he designated one of those accompanying him, Alvaro de Cerda as its military captain. The *Aqua* would remain in *Havana* as a re-supply ship with 40 men and 12 horses to be called upon later as the expedition needed them.

His business in *Havana* concluded, and Narvaez returned overland to *Trinidad.* While there, a small lateen-rigged, brigantine, *La Estrella*, had entered the bay. The ship's master, a fisherman, was getting on in years and was looking to sell the craft. Narvaez immediately jumped at the opportunity and purchased it at a good price. Its small size and shallow draft would be ideal for exploring the multitude of bays and rivers they were certain to encounter.

Shortly after purchasing *La Estrella,* Narvaez and the contingent of men and horses with him set out to reunite with the expedition at *Jagua,* arriving on the 18th of February.

20 February, 1528

The Anchorage at Jagua, Cuba

He sat on the rough-planked dock watching the last of the horses being winched onto the caravel *La Doncella de Plata*. The ship sat at anchor only thirty *yara* from the dock, a tender barge close alongside. Further out, three additional caravels and a brigantine also rode at anchor, their decks and rigging busy with *marineros* preparing to get underway. A diagonal beam rigged to the ship's main mast supported a crude block and tackle that provided the mechanical advantage to lift the nervous animal. As the weight shifted to the beam, the fulcrum effect heeled the entire ship toward the barge. The horse was hoisted until somewhat higher than *Doncella's* deck. With its bulk supported entirely by a leather sling, the animal quieted, its legs dangling downward. Now, with pull ropes attached to the end of the diagonal beam, laborers began to pull the beam with its suspended load towards the deck. At the crotch end of the beam, other laborers liberally coated the mast with lard to lessen the resistance as it rotated. After passing over the deck, *back-pullers* slowed the rotation and positioned the animal over the open hold. Carefully, the block and tackle lowered it into position. It was a well-rehearsed routine but always subject to the unexpected. This rangy black stallion had been a problem. Before being completely restrained, it had laid low one of the *Indio* laborers with a well-placed kick. The man had been brought back from the barge and dumped unceremoniously on the dock. Crumpled to one side, he was moaning and holding his upper arm. It was obviously broken. It hung at an odd angle and there was a trickle of blood slowly dripping onto the planks below. Judging from the blood, the severed bone had pierced the skin.

With a sigh Fray Juan Xuarez rose to his feet and walked towards the writhing man. He knew that no one else would help the poor wretch. The overseer of the *Indian* work crew was a hard, ungodly man who had no reservations about working these men until they dropped. To stop and help an injured comrade was to invite a stinging reproach from the overseer's whip. Xuarez was even surprised that they had taken the time to bring him back to the dock.

"Was this not one of God's creatures in need of attention?"

Xuarez stooped down and gently rolled the native over. It was a bad break and the man was clearly lapsing into shock, the pain tremendous. Carefully he cleaned the wound around the protuberance and then looking up searched for someone to assist him. Further down the dock, another Friar was having a discussion with the expeditions blacksmith, Jorge Nazario.

"Father Palos, bring the blacksmith and assist me!" It was a command and not a request and both men rushed to his side.

Quickly he assigned the blacksmith to hold tightly to the *Indio* while Father Palos was to sit on his legs and begin pulling the injured arm. Xuarez would guide and manipulate the broken bones into place. Stuffing part of his vestment into the young laborer's mouth he directed him to bite down as the pain increased. Through glazed eyes, the young *Indian* nodded his understanding.

Xuarez signaled to his assistants.

With that Father Palos began to pull the injured arm. Xuarez held the skin back as the bone slid beneath the surface. Holding tightly to the arm, he could feel the movement within. Strong as he was, the blacksmith could hardly contain the man's agony as his back arched up and the legs jerked spasmodically. Guttural screams echoed across the waterfront until suddenly, the body went limp. The *Indian* had lost consciousness.

As best as he could tell, the underlying bone had seemed to slide into place and Xuarez hurried to construct a crude splint, wrapping it tightly with cloth strips. Carefully they picked the man up and moved him to a comfortable location. Xuarez looked down at the results of his efforts and hoped that it would heal. They had done all they could do and all three men returned to the wharf.

Father Juan Xuarez was the expeditions commissary and leader of a contingent of five *Franciscan* priests who would accompany the Narvaez expedition. They were responsible for bringing true faith to whatever cultures they would encounter and maintaining religious discipline with the soldiers, sailors, and colonists. Chosen personally by Narvaez because of his experience in *New Spain*, particularly the area called *Panuco*, Xuarez had chosen Friar Juan de Palos as his assistant. Three other *Franciscan* friars, each assigned a ship, would also accompany them.

As expedition commissary, Xuarez had to check each vessel before departure to insure the necessary supplies were aboard and stored correctly. With this last horse now safely loaded aboard *Doncella,* the laborers and *marineros* were dismantling the lifting device. It would shortly be time for his inspection. Father Palos would accompany him...the *Doncella* was his ship. The blacksmith would wait for Xuarez to return, for both were quartered on the expedition's flagship, *Maria de la Meridionales Mares.*

20 February, 1528

Aboard the Caravel Maria De La Meridionales Mares

Panfilo Narvaez paced nervously. There was a favoring wind and he was anxious to get under way. With him on the aft deck was pilot Janero Flores calmly watching the *marineros* preparing the ship for sail.

"Friend Janero, it is time to leave this place. Our time here was unfortunate...we must now move with the greatest haste to begin again what has been, so far, denied us."

"I agree *Adelentado*".

The ship's boat pushed off from the dock and began making its way. A nervous Narvaez could just make out his commissary and blacksmith sitting in the bow.

 "Ah, good, Fray Xuarez and Senor Nazario are returning from *La Doncella,* we will be getting underway as soon as they arrive."

Ten minutes later the ship's boat was being winched aboard. As soon as it had cleared the gunnels the *marineros* were well into their routine of hoisting the anchor. Four men strained at the capstan while water and harbor mud streamed off the chain and ran out the scuppers. The anchor was coming up and the distinctive sound of canvas dropping from the yardarms echoed across the harbor. On the deck below, after Father Xuarez and the blacksmith collected their things and moved below. The ship's boat was overturned on the deck and lashed down tight.

As they entered the narrow channel leading to the open ocean a most unusual anomaly presented itself. Somewhat east of the entrance, a large whirlpool had formed. Slowly rotating around its outer perimeter harbor flotsam moved ever inward. Closer to the center the concentration of material increased until at its vortex a giant jumble of debris boiled in the spinning water. It was no threat to the vessels, but all aboard watched the phenomenon with rapt attention.

With a questioning look, Panfilo turned to his pilot for an explanation.

"In all my years in *Cuba*, I have never seen such a thing!"

Flores didn't turn to answer but remained focused on the strange sight.

"Nor I, *adelantado*, but I was warned by the locals of its existence. Only when the wind and tide are right does it make its presence known. They call it *bano de diablo...*the devil's bath."

On the deck below, a cluster of the women were also watching the strange sight. Among them, Rita la Salvaje stood, pointing at the whirlpool.

"There, see? Such strange sights most have never seen. It is a sign. The old woman in the *San Lucar* war right, this journey is cursed!"

Rita turned and slowly looked up at the aft castle where for a moment Panfilo met her gaze.

"I wonder what that crazy bitch is saying now!"

Flores turned to see, but Rita had already looked away. He didn't comment. Everyone knew of Rita la Salvaje and her experience with the old *Moor* witch. The *bruja* had related that all but a select few on this expedition would ever return. Flores tried not to think about it, but being a man of the sea, superstitions were a way of life.

Each ship cleared the channel and keyed up behind the *Maria*. Offshore, the wind was brisk from the northwest. They set their yards to sail in a broad reach to SSW. The expedition was again underway.

21 February, 1528

Aboard the Caravel Maria De La Meridionales

Mares

It is called "The Gulf of Dogfishes". In this *Golfo de Cazones,* the seafloor rapidly drops. Here along the deep trenches, where nutrients are plentiful, these small sharks congregate. Because of their habit of hunting in large packs, the name dogfish originated. Looking down from the rigging it wasn't uncommon to see hundreds...even thousands of them on a clear day.

After leaving *Xuaga* the expedition had sailed into the night, but at much reduced sail. Slowly they had crept forward until dawn. With the sun, all ships were again at full sail and moving rapidly. There was a feeling of optimism on board.

On the *Maria,* another pilot had stepped forward to assist Flores. His name was Diego Miruelo and Narvaez had purchased his services in *Havana.* Miruelo had extensive experience along the expansive length of *Amichel* as well as northwest *Cuba.* He had been a slaver for much of his seafaring life, making lightning strikes along the populated coastline that extended from *Panuco* to *La Florida*...or so he said. Flores would maintain his head pilot status in the operation of the vessel, but Miruelo would guide the expedition from this point on.

Diego Miruelo was thin, almost emaciated, and looked somewhat disheveled. When not directly involved in a conversation he would hang back, his look sullen and disinterested. Flores was immediately suspicious of the new addition but held his opinions to himself. Miruelo seemed to have a fair knowledge of all things nautical and he spoke with some authority on the land to the north. Perhaps this distrust reflected his opinion on sailors that participated in the slave trade. Janero Flores had no issues with slavery, but he had seen the stinking slave ships and all manner of horror that went with them. Even the animals of the *Spanish* were treated better than the chattel that was crammed below decks on these ships. And, yes, somewhere deep in his subconscious he knew that the *Indians* were human beings like himself.

Miruello called for a course change, "A little south of due west". The rudder was brought over and teams of *marineros* adjusted the yardarms in unison. In this westerly course, they would be "close hauled" to the wind and both pilot and helmsman would have to remain alert. The other four vessels trailing the *Maria* followed suit. To starboard the coastline of *Cuba* remained very much in view and Miruelo, busy watching the passing landmarks, repeatedly called for small course adjustments.

Requesting a sharp-eyed lookout to send aloft, Miruelo explained that soon the shoreline would begin dropping off to the north. This would mark the beginning of a large inlet, *Bahia de Cochinos*...Bay of Trigger fishes. Once they passed this bay and the western shore hove into view the lookout should be alert for a sandy shoal that extended 3 leagues from the shore. It would be marked by several rocky spits of land just visible above the water. It was called *Cayo Piedra*...Rocky Key. Thismarked the point at which the deep bottom of the *Golfo de Cazones* began to rise up to meet the *Archipielago de los Canarreos*.

Comprising a string of nearly 60 leagues of shoals, reefs, and keys, the *Archipielago de los Cannarreos* had at its center a large, heavily forested island. Columbus had called it *La Evangelista*. It had other names, *Isla de Cotorrus* and, most recently, *Isla de Pinus*.

The enormous expanse of water between the archipelago and the mainland was a gauntlet of hidden reefs, shoals, and sandbars, ever-changing with weather and tidal currents. This is the *Gulfo de Bata-bano.* During the *Pleistocene,* this was manifest as a vast coastal plain where mastodon and giant sloth made their home. As the earth warmed the towering ice sheets of the northern hemisphere released enormous quantities of water that flowed down the *Mississippi* and *St. Lawerence river* channels. The earth's oceans rose. What was once a coastal plain became a swamp, a tidal basin, and finally, a shallow enclave.

It was into this gulf that Miruelo would lead the expedition. Through a narrow bottleneck surrounded by enormous sand shoals. This was the passageway called *Pasillo de las Canerreos.*

22 February, 1528

Aboard the Caravel Maria De La Meridionales Mares

It was unclear to Janero why Miruello had chosen this route instead of bypassing *La Evangelista* to the south and deep water. When questioned he became defensive and difficult. He gave a vague explanation that the shallow gulf would provide protection from the spring storms that blew through the area. Janero had no knowledge of this and had to acquiesce to Miruello's experience. Late that afternoon the expedition neared the *Canarreos* corridor.

From the aft castle, Flores looked out at the ocean around him. The coloration of the water was startling. Far to port the water was greenish-white, an indication of shallowness. The sun's rays reflected off the sand only a few feet under the surface. As the depth increased so did the hue of green until in deep water the green was replaced by a deep blue. Forward near the bow, the linesman, balancing himself on the gunnel, walked the sounding line and called the depth back to the pilot. From above, a *marinero* was also watching the water and calling down directions. So far they were still in deep water...the sounding line continued to drop without finding a bottom. A league forward of their present position, however, the water color was dramatically lighter.

The other vessels had closed and were now sailing in a loose "V" formation with the *Maria* at the apex. All had dropped significant sail. Being the largest caravel, the *Maria* carried the most draft...fully loaded, about 2 *vara* below the water. They were closing on the area of lighter water color. Miruello called for a change in course slightly to starboard. They would keep the shallow water off their port side.

Progress now slowed considerably. Lookouts intently scanned the water and depth readings were continuous. The bottom rose to 8 yara, dropped to 10, and then back to 8, a pattern that continued for the next hour. So far they were steering a clear course through the corridor. As the day progressed, however, the sun became lower in the west and the angled rays reflected off the water into the lookout's eyes. The color differentiation disappeared. The vessels groped along, relying only on the sounding line. *Mariners* stayed aloft, prepared at a moment's notice to drop sail. Two hours before sunset the bottom once again began to fall away. The pilot called for more sail and the speed increased. Miruello hoped to travel on for another hour before anchoring for the night.

It was then it happened.

Far to starboard the *Reina de Napoles* suddenly lurched to a stop.

From above, "*La Reina es encallada!*" A pause. "*Bajios al estribor!*" The *Reina* was aground, a vast shoal extending outward, directly in their path.

Aboard *Maria* the bottom soundings came up rapidly. *Marineros* struggled above. Tension on yardarms was released. Sails lufted noisily. The wind was SSW and blowing briskly.

Even as the sounding line was being withdrawn and readied for another throw the lookout on the *Maria* came to life, "*Bajios, bajios a continuacion!*" They were fast approaching a shoal, dead ahead. Only the slightest ripple in the water had alerted the lookout. This deep water valley they had been following abruptly ended in an immense sand bar that was only a few feet below the surface, unseen in the fading light.

They were surrounded. The small fleet had sailed into a redoubt of tidal and wind-washed shoals.

The rudder was laid hard to starboard...but to no use. At first, it was a light scrapping noise and then a roar as the forward momentum of the *Maria* carried her high onto the bar. Behind and beside them the other vessels, turning port and starboard in their confusion, could not avoid the snare. Even the shallow drafted brigantine, much lighter than the others, continued higher still onto the shoal...so much so that it listed heavily to starboard as it came to rest.

Panfilo, like the others had been thrown to the deck with the impact. Miruello was catapulted down the stairs, landing in a heap on the main deck. Flores had slid into the mizzen mast. Throughout the ship, crew members were pulling themselves off the deck. Campo, sporting a scuff on his knee, was already beside Narvaez helping him to his feet. Below deck, there had been some panic but it subsided as people streamed onto the deck. Overhead a crew member had fallen from the rigging only to land in the shallow water. Even now his fellow crew members were helping the sputtering *marinero* back on board. The *Maria* was listing, only slightly, to starboard. Panfilo made his way to the bow and leaned out as far as possible to survey the situation. Amazingly, there was only two to three feet of water lapping at the hull. The sandy bottom was clearly visible. Panfilo focused on a star fish laying on the bottom. Behind them, the *Maria* had gouged out a furrow in the sand and was securely bound. He felt the blood rushing to his face.

"*Madre de dios,*" Panfilo looked up at the sky, his hands outstretched. "*Madre de Dios*, I have never seen such a thing...how can this happen?"

He picked up the closest thing at hand...a belaying pin...and threw it at Miruello who was still sitting on the deck rubbing his head. The pin missed the pilot and clattered along the deck. All movement stopped and everyone turned to watch. Miruello scurried up the aft stairway.

"Now we are beached like fat whales, *ballenas gordas!*"

Narvaez reached for another pin. Everyone discretely moved behind protection. Even little Campo backed up, wide-eyed.

Pointing the belaying pin at Janero Flores, Narvaez's enraged voice resonated through the salt air.

"Pilot Flores, get us off these shoals"!

Flores stepped forward, didn't answer, but turned to the *marineros* and ordered the ship's boat to be released. To no one he uttered, "First we must determine the extent of the damage."

Turning, Narvaez dropped the pin and then angrily kicked it across the deck.

All along the arc of stranded vessels the small boats milled about in the water surveying the situation and evaluating damage. Even as the last rays of daylight disappeared into the western sky the boats remained, some setting small oil lamps to see by. On board the larger vessels storm lanterns were lit and the smells of cooking drifted into the wind.

Later in the evening, each *capitan* reported to a sullen Narvaez. In all of the ships, injuries had only been slight and there was virtually no structural damage. All of the ships were "hard into" the sand. It would take a major effort to release any of them. Luckily, the weather was mild and there was no immediate danger. At first light, the crews would begin working on *La Estrella*, the brigantine, which was the lightest and most shallow drafted.

01 March, 1528

Aboard the Caravel Maria De La Meridionales

Mares

On clear days sunrise on the open ocean can be explosive. This morning had been no different. At first light an orange hue filled the eastern sky, its glow touched the tips of the masts. Campo had watched the band of illumination move downward, enveloping the yardarms, the shrouds, ratlines, stays...until, with a blinding presence, the very tip of the sun rose above the water, bathing everything with its light.

Today was Sunday and even now the holy Friars were assembling on the deck making ready for morning services. Campo was a *Christian*...at least he thought he was. In the rough sea town of *San Lucar,* he was never introduced to the specifics of the written word. In truth, he had never thought about it much. He had lived singly or with small groups of other street children. His time was spent surviving and although he was aware of *Christian* generalities, the few holy men who frequented the docks were seen as just another resource. Things were now so much different.

Narvaez had seen to his religious education, assigning Father Xuarez to spend part of every day with him. The good father had started with the scriptures, but then, realizing that his charge could neither read nor write, Xuarez had broadened the education. Now, still with difficulty, Campo could slowly read aloud the Bible passages that were assigned to him.

Part of his duties as a page to Narvaez, his *Capitan*, was to take his turn at the night watches and assist Father Xuarez as his acolyte whenever needed. Now, standing on deck, adorned in the white vestment, he tried to remember the *Latin* phases that had been put to memory. In services past he had fumbled with the words causing snickers from the gathered throng.

"Father Xuarez, the Lord be with you!" It was Narvaez, his booming voice alerting everyone on deck.

"And to you, *Adelantado*."

"Father, although it is the Lord's day we have much work to do. I would ask that you abbreviate this morning's service as much as possible."

"*Adelantado*, today is a sabbath of solemn rest, holy to the Lord."

"Father, of that I am aware, but if we don't extricate ourselves from these shoals we will all die here. For now, I would choose to break the sabbath rather than end up as a pious skeleton!"

With that Narvaez dropped to one knee, crossed himself, rose, and strode off in the direction of the ship's boat, even now being lowered into the water.

Campo had never seen Narvaez so aggravated. They had been 7 days trapped in the sand and his temper was unrelenting.

They had tried everything and all that had been accomplished was to turn *La Estrella* back in the direction from whence she came.

Today another effort would be made to free the brigantine from the sands grip. It had been offloaded of everything but the horses. The people and supplies had been redistributed to the other vessels. Both anchors had been carefully placed in the ship's boats and rowed out to deeper water, the mooring lines, borrowed from the other vessels, trailing behind.

When the boats reached the desired point, four stout crewmen labored to push the anchor overboard, the other four crewmen leaned far out over the gunnels to counterbalance the weight. Once released, the loss of the anchor's weight would pop that side of the boat up like a cork. The crewmen had to scramble to keep from capsizing.

On the *Maria* the soldiers, colonists, and *marineros* filled the deck, all watching the spectacle unfold. Looking outward, Campo could see spectators on the other vessels as well. Mired in the sandy shoals the vessels were all enclosed in a small arc. It was like an amphitheater at sea.

The first boat released its anchor with no problem. Aboard the ships, a cheer went up. The other boat was having some problems. This anchor was heavier and the men were having trouble pushing it into the water. The starboard side of the boat was raised high in the air with the four seamen stretched out as far as possible to compensate for the weight. Finally, with great effort, the men on the port side managed to slide the anchor into the sea.

The boat rolled and bounded upward.

The men providing counterbalance had over extended themselves and rapidly disappeared beneath the waves while the men on the port side were catapulted into the air. The boat had turned turtle....it was upside down in the water. There was a moment of hushed wonderment aboard all the vessels, but when 8 heads bobbed up around the overturned hull there was cheering and laughter.

The anchor lines now extended out in a large "V" from *La Estrella.* On board the brigantine Narvaez directed the operation, his booming voice resonating out over the shoals. Even as the overturned boat and crew were collected, the *marineros* aboard *La Estrella* began to turn the capstan, tightening the lines and, hopefully, pulling the brigantine off the shoal.

Grasping the capstan bars the *marineros* walked in a circle, ever tightening the line. As it became taunt sprays of seawater flicked off the fibers. They strained with each step. Finally, the capstan would move no further. Even the addition of Narvaezs' great strength couldn't budge another bit of turn. They jammed the capstan secure and went in search of longer bars.

On board *Maria,* Campo was seated behind two *marineros* watching the proceedings with rapt attention.

"She'd be stuck to the bottom like a load of whale shit!" They both chuckled.

"You know, if his excellency, the *Adelentado* would remove his fat *punta* from *La Estrella* she'd probably float away like a cork!"

Now there was more laughter and they rocked back and forth in their mirth.

It was almost mid-afternoon by the time longer capstan handles could be shaped and brought aboard *La Estrella.* With the longer handles, the *marineros* again strained at the capstan.

At first, there was no movement...but...slowly, they began to notice a slackening of the line. The tension was taken up and again the line slackened...was the brigantine moving or were the anchors releasing their grip on the bottom?

Again they took up the slack. Narvaez peered over the side and through the clear water. He spied a starfish just off the port bow. This time, almost imperceptibly, he could see the hull move forward in the sand in relation to the immobile sea creature.

"*Madre de maria de Jesus*, we are moving!" He cried out.

04 March, 1528

Aboard the Brigantine La Estrella

They had worked three days slowly pulling *La Estrella* off the shoal. Near midnight the movement stopped. The lines were brought up tight once again and the capstan locked down. The exhausted sailors sat or lay down on the deck. Narvaez, still on board, paced nervously. An hour passed, and then two. They were beginning to lose hope. At 2:30 a shudder reverberated through the ship and...suddenly the anchor lines were limp. The *marineros* jumped to the capstan and began cranking anew. The brigantine was moving again.

At mid-morning the shoal gave way to deeper water and *La Estrella* floated on her own. The rest of the day was spent moving people and equipment back to *La Estrella* and reducing the load on the next lightest vessel, *El Delphin.* Like *Estrella,* she would first have to be turned. Because of possible damage to the rudder, pulling a vessel off the sand, stern first, was not an option.

06 March, 1528

Aboard the Caravel El Delphin

Four more days had passed. Progress had been slow. Even unloaded, *El Delfin's* keel rested on the bottom. During periods of high tide, the situation improved slightly but still, it remained mired. Turning the vessel under these conditions was much like the process of careening the hull. An anchor was set out about 50 *vara* from amidships and a block and tackle was attached to the main mast. As the vessel was hove over, other anchor points on the bow and stern would pull in opposite directions to rotate the ship on its axis.

But there was a problem. On board there were 20 horses and nowhere to off load them. Teams had come aboard to truss the animals up like Egyptian mummies. This would protect them from flailing about in their slings, but the animals were already stressed in the unventilated holds. This action would undoubtedly take its toll, but it had to be done.

07 March, 1528

Aboard the Caravel Maria De La Meridionales

Mares

From his vantage point on the *Maria*, Janero Flores scanned the morning horizon, a routine he had followed for years. The early morning sky told him much. It was also a quiet time where he could contemplate his decisions and consider the day's actions. Since their entrapment, the weather had remained mild and dry with a constant northwest breeze. Remarkably, not even an afternoon thunderstorm had appeared. But, this morning, things were changing. The wind had dropped noticeably...in fact, it seemed to be directionless. Looking up, the flag of *Castile* hung listlessly, occasionally being disturbed by halfhearted puffs. Drawing on his many years at sea, Flores knew that changes in weather were usually predicated by storms but, so far, the sky didn't exhibit any change. All indications were that it would be another clear day, and with the wind diminished...hot!

Drinking water was becoming critical. The animals on board consumed prodigious amounts of fluid and the human cargo had already begun rationing water. Food, on the other hand, was not a problem. Fish were plentiful. Colonists and soldiers alike would drop baited lines into the water and almost immediately bring back a catch of some consequence.

Yesterday, *El Delphin* had finally been turned, but the caravel, now upright, was still held fast by the shoal. Even at this early hour, teams of *marineros* were busy removing ballast rocks from deep in the hold. These had to be hoisted top side in buckets and then carefully deposited into the boats alongside. From here the heavy rocks were rowed to an exposed sand bar where they were deposited. When (and if) *El Delphin* was floated free they would have to be reloaded.

Just to the east, now drifting out to the deeper water where *La Estrella* was anchored, Flores watched the corps of a dead horse floating in the water. The mare had died yesterday in the hold of *La Doncella de Plata* and had been thrown overboard. Now, as he watched, the water around the dead animal boiled as the sharks feasted.

"Senor Flores, what are your thoughts this morning?" It was Narvaez joining him.

"Ah, *Adelantado*, I was lost in thought, I didn't see you approach."

Narvaez motioned toward the dead horse, "If we don't get off these shoals soon, there will be many more carcasses floating in the water...ours included."

"I agree, our progress is slow and the water stores are running low."

Narvaez contemplated for a moment.

"Senor Flores I am going to send *La Estrella* back to *Jagua* with as many as it will hold. I will instruct *Senor* de Vaca to resupply it with water and fodder and return as quickly as possible. I estimate it will take at least 5 such trips."

Flores knew that this had been a difficult decision for the governor, but one that had to be made.

"When will *Senor* De Vaca leave for *Xuaga*."

"We will begin loading today, and he will sail in the morning."

08 March, 1528

Aboard the Caravel Maria De La Meridionales Mares

The noise woke him. In the haze of sleep, Janero wasn't sure what it was. The day before had been hot, the evening sultry, and he had bedded down on the aft deck. Others had also, and all around him the snores and heavy breathing continued unabated.

There it was again. He recognized it now, the low rumble...almost sub-audible sound of thunder, barely distinguishable over the sound of waves lapping the hull.

He sat up, the sleep still heavy in his body. A soft momentary glow illuminated the sky.

Lightning.

Standing, Flores looked out into the darkness. Stars were still overhead and the moon was just rising in the east...it was almost full. The water sparkled in the new moonlight.

Another flash in the southwest...not definitive, but a general illumination low on the horizon. A breeze puffed against his face, it felt different somehow, the faint smell of rain.

He stood there for 15 minutes watching the sky, trying to get a feel for the storm's direction. It was large, the lightning encompassing all of the western and most of the southern horizons. The flashes became more numerous and began to highlight an angry cloud structure. Overhead the stars were still visible, but wispy *Colas de yeguas*...mares tails, began to dim their view.

Time to alert Narvaez.

It was Campo's watch and Flores caught site of the young page walking on the main deck below him. He hissed out a call.

"Campo!"

Surprised, Campo looked around to see who would be calling his name at this hour. Squinting into the darkness he finally fixed on the pilot standing above him. He hurried up the stairs being careful not to disturb the people sprawled on the deck.

"*Senor* Flores, it is very early!"

"Campo, I need you to wake the governor, there is a storm coming and we need to prepare."

Once awoken, Narvaez had wasted no time in alerting the other ships of the expedition. He had commanded the signal cannon to be fired and a boat launched immediately to insure all were forewarned. No sooner had the boat returned than a south wind began to blow with some authority.

But then the wind stopped. The water was like a mill pond, the air was still.

Others on the *Maria* looked around expectantly. Flores rushed to the rail to have a look. At that moment the sun rose as if in a tunnel, a thick cloud layer just above the eastern horizon and the sea below. A red pallor reflected off the clouds. The ship was illuminated in an eerie glow. Everyone was looking east.

Narvaez joined him at the rail. Overhead the clouds scudded by and a few wayward drops of rain fell on the dry deck leaving momentary discolorations. Still, the wind was laid.

Campo saw it first. "My *Capitan*!" He was tugging at Narvaez's tunic and pointing.

Everyone turned.

Materializing out of the inky blackness was what looked like a long, low cloud moving across the water directly at them. At first, there was silence and they watched, transfixed, as it closed. Then...a great wailing sound filled the air...and it was upon them. The *Maria* shuddered as if impacted by a great hammer.

The wind raced across the top of the waves, shearing the crests into frothy whitecaps that pummeled the windward side of the vessels. The normally placid water overlaying the sandy shoals was now in turmoil. Great rollers began to march across the endless sand flats. The sun, which only moments ago shown through the clouds, was now gone as if someone had pulled a shade.

With the majority of their weight still resting on their keels in the sand, the vessels rocked unnaturally. The worst to suffer was *El Delphin*. The combination of waves and wind slid the small caravel sideways while heeling her hard to starboard. The storm was completely reversing the efforts of the *marineros* not two days before. The wind continued to blow with unmitigated fury and the temperature was dropping rapidly. A tremendous bolt of lightning split the sky and a great clasp of thunder momentarily deafened all aboard the *Maria*.

Flores was holding tightly to the railing and blinked hard to remove the light spots in his eyes. Narvaez was still by his side. Campo too...but everyone else, save a few *marineros* had scurried below.

"Look!", Narvaez' voice boomed through the noise of the wind.

El Delphin appeared to be moving. It was. Free of cargo and ballast the wind carried the lightened ship off the shoal.

"*Adelentado*, how many men on *El Delphin?*

"Only ten!"

Flores could only imagine the terror on board *El Delphin* as it lurched off the shoal, broadside. Driven now across the deeper water by the force of the wind the caravel suddenly came about. The anchors that had been set for the previous day's operation were still in place and the caravel swung in a wide arc until it abruptly stopped, the ship's bow into the wind.

"She's free!" Narvaez couldn't believe what he'd seen.

Just as suddenly as the wind had started, it abated. It was raining now...huge, cold drops that seemed to explode on the deck. Interspaced between the rain drops, pea size balls of ice...*el granizo*...bounced high into the air. It had begun to hail. Narvaez held out his hand and watched in amazement. He had never seen this in the *Indies*.

The hail fell in spurts and then died out altogether. Another tremendous clap of thunder and the rain began to fall in torrents. The wall cloud had passed. Now individual squalls within the storm began to cycle through the area.

The heaviest of the lightning and thunder seemed to be passing to the east, but on board the *Maria* another sound coursed through the ship. It was felt more than heard. The hull was dragging on the shoal below.

They were moving!

The storm surge had raised the water level and the *Maria* was being pushed along the sandy bottom. Narvaez rushed to the rail to look out at the other ships. It was hard to see in the rain and spray but he was sure of it.

"*Dios de la alabanza*...praise God, they are all moving! We are free of these shoals!"

The rasping sound on the hull below had ceased and the *Maria* moved into deeper water. The wind was still fierce but the *marineros* clambered over the ship making it ready for sail. The first order was to turn the vessel. A forward staysail was set. The bow imme-diately responded, the drag of the sail pulling it around. The *Maria* rolled heavily as it momentarily drifted abeam to the wind. But, the rotation continued and soon the big caravel was answering her rud-der. Now, with directional stability, they would "run before the wind" until well clear of this area that had so tormented them.

08 March, 1528

Aboard the Caravel Maria De La Meridionales Mares

The storm had passed as quickly as it came, its only evidence a low darkness in the eastern sky. The five vessels were "hove to" all floating in close proximity to each other.

To the side of *Maria de la Meridionales Mare* were tied the launches from the other four vessels.

A meeting between Narvaez, the pilots, and the captains was just breaking up. The topic of discussion had been whether to return to *Jagua* or continue on. There was much debate, but in the end, Nar-vaez had persuaded all that they must continue on. The wind had shifted to the east and they were now well into the *Bayo Batabano.* Returning to *Jagua* in this contrary wind would be difficult and by his best estimates, it would take only 10 days to reach *Habana.* Once there they would restock the ships, exercise the animals, and make preparations for the final push to *Panuco.*

Some languished aboard the *Maria,* talking in small groups, while others began drifting back to the launches. Finally, all had departed to their respective ships. Soon, the expedition was underway, but this time the shallow drafted brigantine, *La Estrella,* and its captain, Alvar Nunez Cabeza de Vaca, would take the lead.

CHAPTER 06

White Horses

Caballos Blancos

In this starboard tack the monumental waves the marineros called "caballos blancos" broke across the deck from right to left. These ridges of water moved across the seascape in long columns, the crests and troughs alternately rolling and plunging the ship. The wind, blowing along the surface, would shear the wave crests off into frothy wisps of foam, appearing like the white mane and tail of a horse at full gallop.

The storm had blown the expedition off the Shoals of Canerreos by a strange trick of geography and weather. Tidal action in the Golfo de Batabano is slight, but winds have a major effect on water levels. Depending on speed and duration, a wind blowing from the northern quadrant will lower the level...northwest winds being the most severe. Conversely, winds from the south will raise the level of water...southwest winds being the most severe. Sea levels near the shoals can vary significantly during these periods. The five ships had chanced onto the shoals during a period of a prolonged northwester when sea levels were unusually low. Pilot Miruelo had followed the same course he had sailed several times before, but this time nature had changed the rules. It was only the advent of an early spring storm that swept the expedition off the shoals.

10 March, 1528

Aboard the Brigantine La Estrella

The sun was low in the evening sky. There was still no indication from the flagship, but Alvar knew that the order to "hove to and anchor" would come soon. Narvaez, of course, would make that decision.

Yesterday they had favorable winds and even under reduced sail the progress had been good. As the lead ship it was *La Estrella's* responsibility to set course through this vast expanse of hazards. Its shallow draft made it the obvious choice. The new pilot Diego Miruelo, who was familiar with the area, had been transferred on board. Angle Jimenez, the acting pilot, was happy to have him and the two seemed to work amiably together. However, to Alvar, pilot Miruelo was stiff and difficult to talk with. Alvar was uncomfortable with the situation and tried repeatedly to gain the man's confidence. All to no avail...their relationship remained strained.

"Boom!", the concussion broke across the water. Turning his head Alvar could see the gray smoke from *Maria's* deck gun, its drift only slightly faster than the speed of the ship. It was time to strike sail and set anchor. *La Estrella's* decks become a hub of activity.

Letting the forward momentum slow, the *marineros,* released the lashings, and the anchor swung free just below the Hawes hole. They waited for a sign. The pilot nodded to the boatswain. He, in turn, pointed to the men on deck. The slip shackle was released and the anchor rode rattled loudly as it passed through the opening. There was a loud splash next to the bow. The anchor line, coiled in huge circles on the deck, began to uncoil. In the shallow water, the anchor bottomed quickly. The line played out until the last coil disappeared and then tightened. *La Estrella* came about, its bow now windward.

Jimenez jumped down to the main deck and grasped the anchor rope, its vibrations a tell tale sign of how the anchor was setting. There is some slip...he can feel this in the line, but quickly the flukes dig into the sandy bottom and hold fast.

Already the activity on board had started. As the hour of Vespers approached, Friar Juan Velazquesz was preparing his vestments and table for the nightly communion. Below, the *fogones*...cook stoves, were being lit in preparation for the evening meal...the same as the night before, and the one before that...*garbanzo* and *cazon* mixed together with a stale biscuit.

The fires of the cook stoves are tended by the slaves on the expedition. The ship's pages and the personal pages of those on board served the meal.

"Peas and fish, fish and peas.." Alvar looked behind him to see Elcano scrunched in a corner looking down at his plate with disgust. The *Basque* seaman was now the boatswain of *La Estrella*, a position awarded to him after the loss of *El Viento del Sur* and *Princessa Margarita*.

Alvar set his own plate down. The thought of peas and fish...again...didn't particularly excite him either. He looked out across the broad expanse of now placid water that surrounded them. The wind had dropped and only the slightest breeze touched the side of his face. To the south, he could see the mass of *La Evangalista,* the deep green of its forests still visible in the fading light. In front of it, and no more than a league distant, was a line of small islands and keys that generally curved back to the southeast. To the north, another line of *cayos.* Between them, there was a clear water opening. Tomorrow they would pass between these two points and turn southwest. Pilot Miruello had indicated that, after this, there was one more passage before they would be rid of this shallow sea of hazards. He had a name for it. One that Alvar felt some foreboding for. *Canal del diablo*...Channel of the Devil.

"Senor De Vaca." It was Elcano. Alvar turned.

"Senor De Vaca, if you won't be eating I would be most gratified to have your plate".

Alvar laughed, "Boatswain Elcano, I cannot face the prospect of fish and peas again tonight...they are yours."

11 March, 1528

Aboard the Brigantine La Estrella

The day had begun with a striking sunrise and a cloudless sky.

Already under sail at first light, the early morning shadows extended far out in front of the five ships. Ahead of them, the profile of *Cuba* covered the horizon, the ridges of the *Cordillera de Guaniguanico* just stood out in the clear morning sky. Off the port bow was the severe line of shoals and small islands (*Los Cayos San Felipe*) that extended almost to the coast of *Cuba*.

Almost.

No more than a league distance from *Cuba*, the shoals came to an abrupt end. A channel, scoured deep by severe tides and winf-induced currents, provided passage out of the *Bay of Batabano*. Prone to storms and rough seas, this was what Murello called *Canal del Diablo*.

Somewhat close hauled and on a port tack, a south wind had propelled them along at a good rate. Miruelo estimated they would be through this last passage and in the deep waters of the *Caribbean Sea* by the hour of Vespers. As mid-day arrived, however, the western sky behind the *Cordillera de Guaniguanico* began to change. No longer clear, it took on a dull gray appearance that seemed to grow in intensity.

Nearing the coast of *Cuba*, they turned further to the south. Just ahead lay the *Canal del Diablo*. It had begun to rain and the wind vacillated in speed and direction. At times the gusts became so severe that all were forced to reduce sail. When the wind suddenly moved to the southwest all of the vessels were "in irons" and forced to drop all but the lateen sails on the missen. Miruelo considered turning and "running" before the wind while they still had light. Surely there was a protected bay on the *Cuban* coast. But, the wind shifted again, this time off-shore.

"Perfect!" They would sprint for the passage. From the yardarms the canvas dropped with loud "pops" and *marineros* hauled on the shroud lines. Picking up speed and heeling hard to port the vessels lurched forward. It was raining harder and with the thick overcast the light was fading fast. Lightning began to split the air. Thunder added to the wind and sea noise. To the east, the last of the shoals passed behind them. To the west paralleled a broad white beach...the mainland of *Cuba*, now so close it felt as if only a short swim away.

Clear of *Canal del Diablo,* Miruelo turned the expedition south-southeast, away from the shore and out to deeper water. The storm was growing worse... much worse...and close-in to land was not a good place to be.

12 March, 1528

Aboard the Caravel Reina De Napoles

The caravel *Reina de Napoles* heeled over and dropped from the crest into a cavernous trough. The plunge lifted everything that wasn't tied down. All around the roar of the storm stifled the screams of anguish.

Below decks Andre Dorantes watched in amazement as the man across from him was bludgeoned into the low ceiling, an audible "crack" resounded as his head and neck contacted the ceiling timbers. He fell back to the floor and slid against the wall, his body limp.

He recognized the man as one of the conscripts picked up in *Santiago* and assigned to his company.

Loose material flew around the enclosure and skittered across the floor. Andres deflected a loose helmet that crashed against his forearm.

Andres Dorantes de Carranza was from *Bejar, Spain*, a town on the border of *Extremadura* and *Castilla La Mancha*; communities or divisions of *Spain* that had united in their expulsion of the Moors. Born into an influential family, Andre had offered his services to

Spain at an early age. Shorter than most, he had a natural authority that was enhanced by his strength. Thick through the chest, his thick neck looked as if placed on the massive shoulders as an afterthought. However, with his dark complexion and curly black hair, he was a handsome man. Andre cared for those who served under him and was well-liked and respected by his men. In *Spain,* he had supported Charles I in the *Comuneros* revolt and made a name for himself. With his family's support, Andre had been able to sustain a gentle-man's lifestyle in *Spain,* but stories from the New World made him anxious and he longed to make the journey. The call to join Narvaez provided that opportunity. As *Capitan,* Andre Dorantes commanded 40 men. They were a support unit composed of infantry.

Many had joined the expedition in *Spain* with promises of glory and riches. Upon reaching *Santo Domingo,* however, almost half of his *infanteria* command had deserted. Influenced by the local *ciuda-danos*…citizens, with promises of free land, 18 men had chosen to stay on the island. Normally, they would have been rounded up and dealt with harshly, but the citizens were backed by a local *milicia* and the support of the Island's *Adelantado,* Alonso de Zuazo, who had the support of Hernan De Soto…a man not to trifle with. Andre complained to Narvaez, who was sympathetic but told him to accept the loss. The expedition needed the support of the *ciudadanos* to re-supply and refit.

In *Santo Domingo* and later when the expedition reached *Cuba,* re-placement conscripts were taken in, but these were not the same. Most of Dorante's men lost in *Santo Domingo* had fought with him in the *Revolt* and other skirmishes in *Spain.* They were skilled and experienced warriors.

"These new men are inexperienced in almost everything…almost everything except consuming supplies and complaining," Andre thought to himself.

Still, they were his responsibility. He had to see how badly this man was hurt.

Andre carefully made his way across the small enclosure, timing his moves to the brief lulls between waves. The ship's movement slid the body back and forth across the floor, alternately slamming it into hull timbers and deck stanchions. It had to be secured.

Another roll of the ship and the body began another slide across the wet wooden floor. Seeing an opportunity, Andre jumped onto the man and wedged his leg against a stanchion. Looking down Andre immediately knew there was nothing else he could do for this man. His neck had been broken and the man's lifeless eyes had a strange surprised look.

Spread-eagled on the floor, Andre raised his voice to be heard above the din of the storm. "Estevan, I need you!"

In the darkness, Estevan felt his way along the inner hull, stumbling over other bodies lying on the fetid floor. The storm was still raging and he wouldn't have heard the call at all except that he had left the forward compartments area and was relieving himself in a part of the deck amidships. Estevan moved from stanchion to stanchion, stopping at each one until the swaying deck stabilized between swells. With only one storm lantern lit, his progress was slow. Only vague shadows were visible in the poor light. His bare foot crunched into an object and he fell heavily to the floor.

"*Mierda…hijo de puta,*" he swore.

"Estevan, where are you?"

"I am coming *mi capitan!*" Estevan struggled to be heard over the noise of the storm.

Mustafa Zemmouri was born in *Azammour, Morocco*, his father, a *Berber* trader (some would say a pirate), and his mother, was a very black *African* woman of some nobility. Mustafa was almost as black as his mother, but his facial features were somewhat softened by his paternal genes. His mother had been compelled to convert to *Islam* but did not push it on young Mustafa because the father had been largely absent, spending months at sea in the lucrative trade between the *Iberian Peninsula* and *North Africa.* He only provided marginal support, and Mustafa's mother did cleaning and cooking for the local constable's wife.

At age 12 his mother allowed him to work at the docks helping local fishermen clean and distribute their catch. Life on the docks was tough and he learned early how to take care of himself. At 14 Mustafa began working on the fishing boats as they plied the waters off *Azammour.* It was during this time he realized he had a gift for languages. Cultures from all over *Africa* and the *Mediterranean* basin could be found at the docks. Besides his home dialect of *Tarifit Berber*, Mustafa understood and could speak *Tashelhit* and *Tamazight Berber.* He also conversed in *Arabic* and slipped easily into *Spanish, Portuguese, Greek,* and several black *African* and *Bedouin* languages. This ability made him valued among the ship's captains.

Mustafa was a polyglot.

As he slipped into puberty Mustafa discovered something else. He had an insatiable sexual appetite for women. Life on a fishing carrack had opened another avenue in his life…he was introduced at an early age to the brothels that lined the seaports of the *Mediterranean.*

When 16, Mustafa stood on the dock and watched in puzzlement as a fleet of warships appeared on the horizon. It was 1513 and Manual I of *Portugal* would extract the taxes refused to him by *Azemmour's* governor, Moulay Zayan. *Portuguese* soldiers rapidly defeated Zayan's small army and conquered the city.

After the battle, squads of armed men roamed the streets and collected many of the town's young men and women for slaves. Mustafa was dragged from his home and thrown into the dirt as men bound his wrists. As he looked up, his mother was pleading in the doorway; while several *Portuguese* soldiers restrained her. Mustafa was jerked to his feet and thrown into line with other youths, some as young as 5 years old. Looking back, his mother was being dragged back into the house. That was the last time he saw her.

Mustafa and the other captives were loaded onto a filthy cog for the trip back to *Portugal*. Arriving in *Lagos*, the captives were deposited in a guarded enclosure. It was here that the middlemen of the slave trade, the brokers, made their purchases. All the captives were stripped. With a guard of one or two men, the broker moved through the shackled crowd checking teeth, squeezing arms and legs, and looking for abnormalities. The younger more attractive women were separated from older women, their breasts were repeatedly squeezed and genitalia fingered, usually accompanied by the lewd comments of the broker. After the inspection a lot price was agreed upon and the broker moved his wares to a location that would bring the best price at auction.

Mustafa's group was carted to *Spain* where it was rumored that able slaves were going for particularly high prices. At the auction house in *Cadiz,* Andres Dorantes bought Mustafa. The captain had turned out to be a benevolent master. The work was easy and Dorantes made sure he was well fed and clothed. From the beginning, however, captain Dorantes would not address him by his *Moorish* name. Named after a favorite nephew of the captain, Mustafa became Estevan.

The light was bad and at first, Estevan thought that Dorantes was injured. "*Capitan*, are you all right?"

"Estevan, this man is dead. We need to remove him from here. Help me carry him up the ladder."

It was not easy. The ship continued to pitch and roll. More than once they lost their grip on the lifeless body. Finally reaching the ladder, Andre went ahead and carefully opened the hatch. A flood of water poured down on them. The storm outside was severe. Great, gray sprays of seawater coursed across the deck. The continuous discharges of electricity irradiated the sea and ships in a strobe-like illumination.

Reaching topside, Andre reached down and tried to grab an arm while Estevan pushed from below. The body was wet and all attempts to lift it failed. Finally, in desperation, Andre grabbed the corpse's hair and wrapped it around his hand. Leaning backward he pulled as hard as he could. The body slid out of the hatch, arms flailing upward as it cleared the opening.

It had been Andre's intention to lash the body to a mast until such a time it could be given a Christian burial at sea, but a tremendous roll of the ship caused him to release his grip to find a handhold. Another wave crashed down and Andre watched as the dead soldier slithered across the wet deck and over the side, its foot catching briefly in the rail before disappearing from view.

Andre looked back at the hatch. Estevan, with only head and shoulders showing, shared a look and then simply shrugged and held out his hand. Dorantes rapidly made the sign of the cross and grabbed Estevan's hand. Both men clamored below deck pulling the hatch shut behind them.

12 March, 1528

Aboard the Caravel Maria De La Meridionales Mares

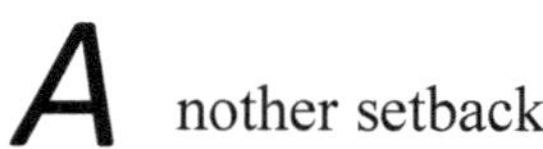 nother setback!

Narvaez was not in the best of humor. Even Campo tried to avoid him. The storm had abated as fast as it had come on, by morning the air was clear and the sea had settled. There was no sight of land.

The fleet had been scattered in the darkness. At first light, the look-outs were aloft hoping to sight the other ships, but only one sail was visible far to the north. It was *La Doncella de Plata* under full sail and moving west. Janero Flores had also set a westerly course for the *Maria,* as he knew all of the ship's pilots would do. The standing order was always to proceed to the original destination if, for some reason, the ships became separated.

"But what of the others?"

Narvaez had isolated himself on the foredeck scanning the horizon. On the aft deck, Flores worked his cross-staff and hoped to get a better idea of just how far they had been blown into the *Caribbean Sea.*

"At least here there is no danger of running aground," Flores spoke to no one in particular.

It wasn't untilmid-morning that another sail was sighted, this one the caravel *El Delfin* appearing to the south of the *Maria.*

At the noon hour *La Doncella,* still to the north of the *Maria,* fired its deck gun as a signal.

Another sail had been spotted, still not visible to those on board *Maria.*

It wasn't until another half hour had passed before the tell tale lines of *Reina de Napoles* hove into view.

Narvaez's dark mood seemed to be passing but he was still clearly worried about the little brigantine. He joined Flores on the aft castle.

"We should be seeing *La Estrella* by now. I fear for the worse!" Narvaez was shaking his head. He was genuinely worried, not only for the members of the expedition but Miruello, his pilot who would guide them to *Panuco,* was still on the brigantine.

"*Adelantado*, I am also worried, but remember, it is a much lighter vessel. If by God's grace, it survived the storm it was probably blown further to sea then us."

Narvaez seemed to brighten somewhat and finally sat down. Campo, as always, was by his side.

"*Tierra, Tierra!* From above, a seaman announced the coast of *Cuba* directly ahead.

The sharp ridges of the *Condillero de Guanaguanico* seemed to rise up out of the water in a line that extended far to the northeast before disappearing into the distance.

12 March, 1528

Aboard the Brigantine La Estrella

They floated alone. Alvar had strained to find any distinguishing mark on the watery landscape, but there was none. In fact, the sea seemed oblivious to last night's tempest. Now, there was a freshening breeze out of the south and Miruello had *La Estrella* on a beam reach with the morning sun at their stern. The brigantine was heeled to starboard and moving crisply through the water, the sun already warm on the deck. Alvar stopped and talked to the groups of soldiers and colonists gathered, assuring each that the other vessels of the expedition would show up soon. Walking carefully on the slanted deck he was startled to see Fray Velazquesz dressed only in a loose tunic while busily scrubbing his vestments. How different he looked, his white arms and legs so in contrast to the deeply tanned *marineros* that hurried about the ship.

Velazquesz looked up at him sheepishly.

"Father Velazquesz, God has provided us with a beautiful morning!"

"Senor De Vaca, it was not a good night for me. I suffered terribly in the storm."

For a moment the priest stopped what he was doing and closed his eyes.

He continued, "For a time I prayed that God would end my suffering and take my life."

Alvar countered. "Father Velazquesz, sometimes even the strongest of souls succumb to the sickness of the sea. It is nothing to be ashamed of."

Velazquesz's mood seemed to lift and he pointed at his priestly attire laid out on the deck. "For sure I could not give consul or take communion smelling of *vomito*."

Alvar laughed and clapped the kneeling priest on the shoulder, "A good morning to you."

As he moved on the friar answered, "and to you".

12 March, 1528

Aboard the Caravel Reina De Napoles

The sails had been dropped. Only the lateen remained for directional control. Just to the northwest, a broad point of land jutted out into the *Caribbean* sea. further on the coastline rapidly receded back to the west and then to the southwest. This point had been called *Punto del Estimulo*...Spur Point, because it resembled a spur sticking out from a cavalry man's boot. The boot itself, reminiscent of *Italy*, was formed by *Cape Corrientes* (heel), *Corrientes Bay* (arch), and *Cabo San Anton* (toe).

Each of the caravels coasted along at a slow pace. High in the main mast, lookouts scanned the open ocean looking for any sign of *La Estrella*. When darkness was no more than an hour away the ships turned inland to anchor. The sea bottom fell off rapidly here. Even a short distance from shore the water was extraordinarily deep. All four vessels hoved-to within 1,000 *vara* of the beach and dropped anchor.

In the fading light, the coastline faded and only the whiteness of the surf impacting on the beach could be seen. In the west, the final glow of the day disappeared. Narvaez had instructed each of the captains to display a storm lantern from the highest point of the mainmast.

On *Reina* the military captain, Andre Dorantes, ordered the *marineros* to hang, not one, but two storm lanterns. On a clear night, even a small light can be seen for more than three leagues on the dark ocean. So, the more lights the better.

The darkness was complete. The dancing shadows from the lanterns played across the waters, eerily moving to the rhythm of the waves. Beneath the water the shinning eyes of sea creatures rose to the surface, attracted by the light. Shrimp, thousands of them! On board the ships the Spaniards looked in amazement as the waters around them came alive.

Beneath the shrimp, other shadows were lurking. In a quick splash, the surface erupted with a lightning-like strike from below. The mass of shrimp separated in terror but, just as quickly, returned to the light. The attacks continued, the marauding carnivores feeding at will on the mesmerized crustaceans.

It was a hot evening and many of the passengers made plans to sleep on deck. Already several had claimed their place and had stretched out. Andre stepped with difficulty on his way to the aft-castle. Climbing the stairs he noticed the pilot, Dario Quiroz, sitting on the rail carving a piece of wood.

"Dario! Have you ever seen anything so strange?"

"Many times *capitan*, but never of such an intensity."

Andre joined him on the rail relaxing from the long day. Tonight a soft wind was blowing on shore. The vessels had swung on their anchor lines such that their bows were pointed seaward.

Andre noticed a flash of light in the darkness. It seemed far away, but very distinct.

"Dario, did you see that?"

Dario reached over and put his hand on Andre's shoulder, "Quiet!"

For a moment only the sound of the waves and murmurs of the people on deck could be heard, but then, very faint, the report of an artillery piece.

"Dario, that was a cannon!"

"Yes, *capitan*, I think *La Estrella* is announcing her arrival."

Both men jumped as the *Maria*, anchored next to *Reina* fired off an answering shot, the smoke hanging low in the evening air and slowly moving off toward the distant beach.

13 March, 1528

Aboard the Brigantine La Estrella

They had spent most of the day filling water casks, for the delay on the shoals had seriously depleted their supply. It had been simple enough. A few leagues from *Punto del Estimulo* was a small fresh water stream that emptied into the sea. All of the ships had anchored just offshore in a lazy semi-circle.

Alvar had accompanied one of the boat crews ashore. Drinking heavily of the clear, sweet liquid, he thought of how he had grown used to the pungent staleness of the water contained in the ship's casks. During the voyage, they had replenished the supply several times when short afternoon thunder showers, typical of the tropics, had come upon them. Unfortunately, the salt-embedded sails used to capture and funnel the rainwater left a taste all its own. Also, water collected in this manner tended to grow algae more easily and the casks had to be periodically cleaned. At the stream, Alvar ordered the casks thoroughly scrubbed with sand before being refilled.

During the water operation, Narvaez himself had visited *La Estrella* to welcome the brigantine back to the fleet. Alvar had talked with him about the storm and the remainder of the voyage. It was obvious that the *Adelantado* was frustrated with the delays and anxious to dock in *Habana.* The horses were growing weak and desperately needed to be exercised. At *Jugua* they had stocked the ships for a two-week voyage. Now, with the debacle in the shoals, they had been at sea for almost a month. Supplies of every sort were in short supply. The water supply was replenished, and they traveled only a short distance along the coast before finding anchorage for the night.

14 March, 1528

Aboard the Brigantine La Estrella

All of the vessels had remained at anchor. The wind was contrary, blowing steadily out of the southwest. By afternoon the direction had shifted further south and dropped significantly. Once underway, only the lightest of breezes filled the sails as the fleet stayed close in. Coasting slowly, they observed *Indianos* on shore or fishing in their long canoes. The water was deep and there was little danger of encountering the hazards that were so prevalent during the first part of the journey.

Now, at the end of the day pilot Angel Jimenez estimated their travel had only been six leagues, but just ahead was the Cape of Currents...*Cabo Corrientas.* Beyond the cape was the huge *Bahia de Corriente.* Many a pilot had mistaken this for the western terminus of the island, only to run aground in the shallow bay. Five leagues across the bay was *Cabo San Anton,* the westernmost extent of *Cuba,* its projection extending far out into what is called the *Yucatan Channel.* Here, they would turn northeast for *Habana.* Tonight, however, they would anchor and begin their run at first light.

15 March, 1528

Aboard the Caravel Maria De La Meridionales Mares

Even before the sun had risen above the *Caribbean Sea*, Panfilo Narvaez had ordered the deck gun fired. He was anxious to get underway.

The morning broke clear but with a heaviness in the air. With sails catching the off shore morning breeze the five ships moved into deeper water. The currents off *Cabo Corrientas* are unpredictable. Here, the broad *North Equatorial Current* accelerates as it passes through the narrow *Yucatan Channel* and into the *Gulf of Mexico*.

The vessels picked up speed as they encountered the strong current in the channel.

Narvaez was leaning against the aft castle rail, his gaze taking in the passing shoreline…he was lost in thought. Most of his last three decades had been spent in this land. It was close to here at the two *cabos*…*Corrientas* and *San Antonio,* that the final resistance of the native population was crushed. He had no remorse, for they were heathen non-believers…but he did remember the excitement, the anguish, the blood, and the smell of death.

The ships followed the coast but at a distance. Cliffs lined the ragged shoreline, so much so that it reminded Narvaez of *las escalas de un dragon…*the scales of a dragon.

A tmid-morning *Cabo Corrientas* was directly abeam. The point of land was marked by a glistening white beach. Years ago the *Adelantado* remembered standing on that very beach gazing seaward. Now, that gaze from memory met his…from the deck of the *Maria*.

Beyond the point extended the broad bay, *Bahia de Corrientas,* its western terminus not visible in the haze.

Narvaez's reverie was broken as Janero Flores lightly touched his arm. He turned and saw Flores studying the southern sky. Looking in that direction the dark horizon contrasted with everything in front of it. Three pelicans flying abreast seemed to glow as they passed in front of the gathering squall. Further out, shafts of sunlight found their way through the cloud buildup and exploded on the sea below. The white sails of *El Delfin*, sailing off their port side, radiated against the darkening background.

Flores had been studying the gathering threat trying to determine its direction. Faint electrical discharges were just becoming visible...a subtle momentary brightening far out to sea. Yet, all around them the sky was clear and warm and the sea tranquil.

"*Adelantado,* this storm grows with every minute. At first, I thought it but a small squall but now it begins to show itself."

Panfilo watched as Flores' finger traced a path across the southern sky. There was a sharp storm vanguard extended towards them, but behind it, the sky discoloration indicated it was something bigger. Much bigger.

Under Flores' direction, the *Maria* turned toward the storm. In unison, the other vessels responded in kind. They needed to move away from the coast. For the moment the winds were holding off shore...blowing from the northwest. It was as if the gathering maelstrom was sucking everything toward it. This was a bad sign.

From years at sea Flores knew that the most severe storms took on weather characteristics of their own, altering the natural patterns of wind direction. As the storm neared, the northwesterly breeze would probably intensify and then abruptly calm. What would follow would be an intense blast of wind emanating from the heart of the storm, a *derecho*.

Flores ordered the red flag hoisted. This was a sign to the other vessels to prepare for a powerful storm and, more specifically, to deploy anchors if Flores followed up with two red flags. They were in extremely deep water. Once deployed, the anchors would never touch the bottom but hang in the abyss, holding the bow of each vessel into the wind. In this configuration, the ships would be blown backward. As such, it was imperative to move as far from shore as possible.

Soldiers and colonists on deck were ordered below. There was a look of disbelief in their eyes as they took furtive glances at the gathering storm before moving down the ladder.

"Not again!"

The offshore breeze carried them ever seaward. Blowing due north, Flores, as lead, quartered the tailwind in a beam reach and pointed the ships on a southwest heading. This not only lessened the chance of being blown against the shoreline but would move them further westward. Flores knew that the terminus of the Island extended only 10 leagues from *Cabo's Corientas* to *San Anton*. After this, the coastline moved abruptly northeast. He was hoping they could clear *San Anton* before the *derecho* hit. If blown backward they would only drift into the open ocean.

Ahead, the sky was an angry cauldron of deep purple accentuated with a *nube gris del rodillo*, an angry, gray wall cloud that extended across the front. The electrical discharges filled the air, still not distinct, but a broad eruption of light that consumed the sky.

For a time the off shore breeze held, propelling the vessels further seaward. All possible canvas had been hung and the ships accelerated through the waves. *Marineros,* clinging to the rigging, were poised to quickly drop the billowing sails. Looking back, Flores was startled by the contrast: the sky was clear and, in the distance, both capes were visible, the low profile of *Cabo San Antone* just rising above the horizon. The sun reflected off the water, back lighting the fleet in an eerie glow as they sailed into the darkness.

They were moving rapidly, the faster ships outdistancing the heavier *Maria*. A light rain had started and the wind offshore was becoming gusty. The pleasing sight of the two capes began to fade in the graying sky. Still, they continued on, the waves rising in front of them, impacting the bows in a loud staccato beat.

The rain became stronger, lashing across the seascape in broad diagonal bands. Rolling thunder, still not close, vibrated its ominous warning. Flores wiped the accumulated water from his forehead, shielding his eyes as he scanned the sails. Winds were becoming non-directional. Flapping loudly, sails luffed in the turbulent air. The ships, still moving forward, began to slow. The boatswain looked questionably at him.

Abruptly the wind died to nothing and the sails hung limp. Strangely, the frequency of lightning bursts dropped. Large, cold drops of rain began to splat on the deck. Turning to his boatswain Flores nodded, "*Senor* Miguel, do it now please...and rapidly!"

Miguel Alvarez was a twenty-year seaman with a rough countenance that intimidated the other *marineros*. He openly bragged that he had been in more fights than the rest of the crew combined. He had slain more than one man. Alvarez's face and torso bore the evidence. Going shirtless even on the coolest of days the multitude of scars testified to a brutal lifestyle. Still, he served the ship's masters with dedication and skill. As boatswain, it was his job to insure that the orders of the ship's officers were carried out. In a word, he insulated the command hierarchy.

Alvarez jumped to the rat line and clambered half way to the top, his orders carrying above the rising sound of the wind. "Pull them down...be quick about it...watch that line!" He was everywhere, both fore and aft.

The *Maria* was no longer moving forward. The second red flag was hoisted. This was the sign to release anchors. The coils of rope unwound rapidly as both starboard and port anchors dropped. Arrayed in a rough semi-circle, the 5 vessels rolled in the turbulent surf, now completely dependent on the elements.

Shielding his eyes and looking into the dark maelstrom Alvarez turned and called out, "Brace yourselves!"

On the aft deck, Florez and Narvaez knelt behind the handrails. Ahead, a convulsion of wind, rain, and waves descended on the fleet. The sea seemed to boil. The *derecho* hit the fleet like a sledge hammer, the ship's bow actually lifting in the water. Both *El Delfin* and *Reina de Napoles*, their bows not in line with the wind, heeled dangerously hard to starboard before coming about. Aboard *Maria,* fittings groaned and a yard arm cracked, the noise sounding like a rifle shot. The wind was tremendous. Below decks, women screamed...battle-hardened soldiers shook with fear.

Behind them, the clear view of the Capes disappeared in the darkness. The lines snapped taunt as the wind pressure on the ships pulled the hanging sea anchors along. Most importantly, the ships remained pointed into the wind, deflecting the onslaught of wind and waves against the bow.

They were being blown backward.

In the raging gale, Florez strained to see, but the elements had closed around them making the day like night.

The lightning had come again. Each flash was accompanied by a simultaneous blast of noise that seemed continuous. To starboard the *Reina* materialized out of the gloom. Florez watched in fascination as geysers of seawater exploded off her bow, temporarily fading the caravel from view. The wind was relentless.

It seemed like an eternity, the noise so loud that men could not talk to each other. Anything loose on deck was blown overboard. On the mainmast, the flag of *Spanish Castille*, overlooked in the rush to lower sails, tore from its hoist and disappeared into the fury. The lacerated red signal flags, still attached, held fast, their force lifting the mizzen halyard high into the air.

To his left Narvaez sat on the deck, his long legs splayed out, one hand gripping the hand rail. They exchanged a look.

"I grow weary of this!"

To his amazement the *Adelentado* jumped to his feet, faced into the wind, and began shaking his fist at the elements. The bandana covering the injured eye had blown off, his long red hair wet with rain and seawater, swirled in the wind.

"Enough! Have you not tested me sufficiently?" Narvaez's voice bellowed into the maelstrom.

A flash of lightning illuminated the moment. To Flores, the crazed Narvaez looked like Moses atop *Mt Sinai*.

Amid a tremendous roar of thunder, the wind suddenly abated and the rain lessened to a light drizzle. Flores stood up. Around them, other seaman arose from their secure places. All were looking at Narvaez with awe.

Fist still raised Narvaez looked over at Flores and slowly brought his arm down. Looking around at the other questioning looks, he laughed aloud.

"I was tired of sitting on deck with a wet ass!"

With the release of tension, their laughter was infectious. Flores got caught up in the moment as well. He had not laughed that hard in years.

But the storm was not over. After a few moments of relative calm, a smattering of hail began to rattle on the deck. The moment of levity passed. A cold rain began to fall, further chilling the already-soaked seaman. The wind returned, not as before, but a gusty collection of squalls that lashed the air.

17 March, 1528

Aboard the Caravel Maria De La Meridionales

Mares

Throughout the previous two days and into the night the conditions had remained the same. The electrical discharges moderated into an occasional rattle of thunder, but the heavy rain and wind continued.

In the vile atmosphere below decks, water trickled through openings in the planking. Storm lanterns hanging from the oak stanchions swung with the movement of the ship, their weak light reflecting eerily off the moisture-laden surfaces. The burning whale oil on untrimmed wicks smelled noxious in the greasy air. Groans and curses continued through the night. The sounds of water cascading down to the bilges mixed with the racket of the pumps obviated any sleep. Pumps were manned by an exhausted collection of slaves and *marineros* too tired to even talk. Each took his turn before collapsing on a rough plank supported between two barrels standing upright in a foot of water. Fighting for air in the oxygen--deprived confinement, some would make their way topside for a breath before returning. Still, the pumps were manned. To ignore the pumps was to invite catastrophe.

Now, the first tinges of morning light struggled to penetrate the overcast. The rain fell unabated. Flores had noticed a continuing shift in the wind direction throughout the night. Now, an easterly blow was pushing the *Maria,* and the fleet, further into the Gulf and away from Cuba.

It was impossible to determine their location. West of *Cuba*, of that he was certain...but, how far west? And what of the northerly current that funneled through these straits?

By mid-morning the wind had abated enough to gather in the sea anchor and hoist a small contingent of sail. The going was very rough, for the seas were still running high. He pointed the bow as far to the northeast as it would hold.

In this starboard tack the monumental waves the *marineros* called "White Horses"...*caballos blancos* broke across the deck from right to left. These ridges of water moved across the seascape in long columns, the crests and troughs alternately rolling and plunging the ship. The wind, blowing along the surface, would shear the wave crests off into frothy wisps of foam, appearing like the white mane and tail of a horse at full gallop.

In the darkening skies just before sunset, the rain fell off to a drizzle and a much reduced wind shifted further to the south. The seas remained rough, however, and Flores called for the sails to be hauled in. Once again the anchors were lowered. They would weather the night, bow windward, but at the mercy of the wind.

At morning's first light, the seas were still running rough with winds moderately steady from the southwest. The sky was clearing, however, and overhead wispy rain clouds scudded across the sky. Low on the eastern horizon the intensely pink glow of sunrise burned through the mist. Flores looked astern. There in the clearing weather was the shoreline, no more than two leagues away. It was *Cabo San Anton* for sure. The storm had blown them around the cape.

They were clear!

CHAPTER 07

Almost Havana

Casi La Habana

Growing stronger still, the wind moved evermore southward. A direct course to Havana was now out of the question, they were sailing into the Gulf of Mexico.

16 March, 1528

Aboard the Caravel Maria De La Meridionales

Mares

The storm had blown them around and north of *Cabo San Anton*. As evening approached, only the barest visages of the tumult remained. Far to the east, and shore ward, all that remained was a dark cast of the sky and an occasional flash that highlighted the peaks of the *Cordillera Guaniguanico*. A north wind had returned, still somewhat gusty but moving the vessels to the northeast in a closely hauled reach of sail. The air had been washed clean and was wonderfully clear. The sweet smells of fresh water wafted through the air; the decks, timbers, and sails only now beginning to dry after the driving rain of just hours previous.

Narvaez and Pilot Janero Flores were conferring with Diego Miruelo. Although the chief pilot for the expedition, Flores had to defer to Miruelo, for he had never been in these waters. A veteran of many trips across the *Atlantic* and to *Cuba*, Flores had always approached *Habana* from the east.

Miruelo explained. "There is an offshore reef. The local fishermen call it *Arrecifes Colorados* for its red color. It follows the coast for 50 leagues. There is a passage between the reef and the coast but it can be narrow and filled with islands, keys, and shallow water. It is well protected from the weather, but progress will be slow. At night we anchor and, if the wind is contrary, we wait for a change. Further up the coast, the passage narrows."

He paused.

Narvaez shook his head. "We have had enough delays. What if we sail out here beyond this red reef?"

Miruelo shrugged, "beyond the reef, the water is very deep. If the weather is fair and the winds favorable we will be in *Habana* in three..." He thought a moment... "Maybe two days, with favorable winds and sailing all night."

Narvaez's good eye looked hard at the pilot. "What are the risks of sailing beyond the reef?"

"*Adelentado*, beyond the reef there is endless water until the shores of *Amichel*. This great sea, this *Seno Mexicano,* is like a woman. It can be calm and well-mannered or violent beyond belief...in only a moment."

He snapped his fingers for emphasis.

Narvaez seemed annoyed with the geography lesson. "Pilot Miruelo set us a course beyond the reef. Our food stores are running low, what hay is left for the horses is moldy and I long to walk on solid ground."

17 March, 1528

Aboard the Brigantine La Estrella

Fair skies abounded. Everywhere Alvar looked, the sky was clear. Far behind now was *Cabo Sant Anton,* the southern most point of the *Peninsula de Guanacabibes* and the western most extent of *Cuba.*

Alvar had thought about the Indio name of *"Guanacabibe"*. It was strange to him and somewhat haunting in its pronunciation. He had sought out one of the *Tiano* seamen who was aboard. The seaman's name was Hanico and he had been recruited in *Santo Domingo*. Although he had taken the Christian name, Alejo Sosa, all still called him Hanico. A pleasant man with an even disposition, he worked hard on *La Estrella*.

At De Vaca's approach, Hanico stiffened somewhat, for it was unusual for a man in Alvar's position to fraternize with the common seaman unless there was work or punishment involved.

"Hanico, a word with you", Alvar cried out.

"*Senor* De Vaca how can I be of service." Hanico's voice still had the lilting accent of his mother tongue.

"Hanico, the land there is called *Guanacabibes*, what does it mean?"

Hanico thought a moment, for this, was the first white man who ever asked him such a question. "*Senor* De Vaca, we say the name somewhat differently than you." And with that Hanico repeated the name *Guanacabibes*, but with the correct *Tiano* language inflection.

Alvar struggled to repeat the name correctly but finally gave up. "But what does it mean"?

With a slight laugh, Hanico replied, *Senor* De Vaca, there is no mystery in this name. It simply means, the place where the iguanas live".

Alvar had not expected something so mundane and was caught off guard. He looked at Hanico and then they both started laughing.

It was no laughing matter, however, that over a month had passed since leaving *Xuaga*. They had prepared for a journey of no more than 15 days. The horses and other livestock had suffered the most.

Just about everything was used up. The upcoming stop in *La Habana* would be most welcome.

A contrary breeze was blowing from the north. Each vessel was forced to sail very close to the wind to follow a straight line. The larger vessels, *Maria* and El *Delfin,* occasionally would fall off the wind, their sails fluttering in a raucousness of noise. Turning inland would again fill the sails. As a result, the brigantine, better able to sail close hauled, moved ahead. To compensate, *La Estrella* reduced sail and let the others pass.

The day had been clear and the sea was calm. On a port tack, an occasional swell would roll the little ship further to starboard, but it wasn't unpleasant. Alvar sat on the aft castle fence and let a leg hang over the side. Below him, there was activity on the main deck. The hold doors had been thrown open to air the fetid smell emanating from the bilge. Being aft Alvar couldn't smell the odor but noticed the soldiers and colonists were congregating on the port side of the ship. A black slave appeared through one of the hold doors carrying two buckets of the foul material. He seemed not to be troubled at all by the smell. All avoided him as he stepped to the starboard rail and emptied the contents over the side. Behind the ship, theever-present company of gulls swooped down to pick up any floating morsels. Where before Alvar's growling stomach had indicated hunger, all thought of food departed him.

In the west, the sun approached the horizon, the sky full and clear around it. Tonight they would sail through the darkness. Even now the *marineros* were preparing the storm lanterns that would be tended by the pages, one hung aft on the mizzen, the other on the main sail mast. The bow was left unlighted, for it was here that a lookout would keep watch. A collision in the darkness was always a real danger. The five vessels began to pull apart from each other, falling into a single-line formation. Finally, each would reduce sail for night running. This, of course, depended on the wind and the vessel. *La Estrella* being the lightest and fastest would run only with the mainsail and the jib.

Pilot Angel Jimenez joined Alvar on the aft deck just as the sun disappeared below the horizon. The afterglow spread across the sky in a dazzling display, vertical shafts of sunlight highlighting the few clouds suspended far to the west. To the east, the inky darkness of the coming evening approached.

It was a magnificent moment. Both men remained silent as the light faded and the darkness overwhelmed them. Finally, Jimenez broke the silence. "Tonight we will have very little moon to guide us but the sky is clear and the wind has shifted somewhat to the west. We should make good time."

La Estrella, last behind *Maria, El Delfin, Reina de Napoles,* and *La Doncella,* glided easily through the water. Ahead, the light from the storm lanterns, all in a line, reminded Alvar of a candle-lit parade in his hometown. He thought of Maria, his wife.

"Ah, if I just had her with me tonight". He threw back his head and closed his eyes. "Her touch, her voice, the smell of her hair...it is as if I had just left her. What about you, young Jimenez, is their a *senorita* at home that longs for your return?"

Angel seemed embarrassed, "Senor De Vaca, in my small town there were but few that were even worthy to look upon...there, however, was one".

"Ah, you must tell me about her.

"Her skin was like fine porcelain, with long auburn hair and eyes as big as saucers", his voice trailed off, and the conversation hung in the air.

"So, what of this porcelain woman...this...what is her name?"

"Senor De Vaca, there is not much to tell... it is Alecia...her name is Alecia Maria."

"And?"

"I only saw her from afar. In our small town, she was the daughter of our *Magistrado,* Marcos Cristian Guyon."

"You mean...you were never...ah, with her?"

"No, never...but I think she looked at me once!"

Alvar could not hold back any longer. Laughing heartily he said, "Hah, I was ready for a saucy story here in the middle of the *Indies* on my way to nowhere, and now I have nothing! It is going to be a long night."

19 March 1528

Aboard the Caravel El Delfin

There was a commotion on board.

"*Rata, rata!*"

On the main deck, a very agitated rat had scampered to a position beneath the main mast. Surrounding the rodent were three *marineros* armed with various shipboard implements. Back arched, the rat hissed and lunged at its attackers. The attackers, bare footed, nimbly jumped out of the way, showing respect for the teeth and the massive infection that could result from a bite.

The rat darted toward the rail but was blocked by another sailor just arriving on the scene. More joined the antagonists until a complete circle surrounded the animal. Others on board, hearing the commotion, clamored closer to see what was going on.

Seated on the foredeck steps, a bored Juan Ortiz had been sharpening his sword. It didn't really need it, but there wasn't much else to do. Other soldiers such as himself were also lounging around, some talking, some gambling. This was a unique diversion and many were cheering the efforts of the seamen...others, the rat.

Ortiz set down the sword and whetstone on the steps and rose to improve his view.

While cohorts kept the rat's attention, one intrepid seaman attempted to grab its tail. Keeping the mast between him and the rat, he slowly inched forward and at the last moment gingerly reached forward. Somehow feeling a threat, the rat turned and struck, narrowly missing the extended fingers. The terrified *marinero* jumped higher than Ortiz had ever seen anyone jump and the whole boat erupted in laughter.

But then the rat made a mistake. It attempted to climb the mast. A sailor with a belaying pin struck the rat with a solid blow and it fell to the deck injured but still dangerous. Now unable to escape, the circle of men moved closer, each trying for the tail. After several thwarted attempts a sailor finally raised the squirming animal victoriously.

Cheers erupted and the sailor walked the deck displaying his prize.

Finally, climbing the stairs to the aft deck the sailor launched the rodent over the stern and all rushed to the rails to see it hit the water. The show was over, the *marineros* dispersed back to their stations and the passengers resumed whatever they were doing. Ortiz picked up his sword and whetstone and resumed the slow methodical swipes along the cutting edge.

Ortiz was from *Seville*. He had been enthralled with Panfilo Narvaez's description of the New World when he visited the city in 1527. A week before, criers had announced that Narvaez would be speaking in the town square seeking "men of adventure" for the upcoming voyage. It was the talk of the community. Located on the *Rio Guadalquivir, Seville* had become a hub of activity since the voyages of Columbus. The river was navigable all the way to the sea, and the docks swarmed with merchants, finance houses, seaman, taverns, prostitutes, travelers and craftsman. From *Seville* the fleets would travel down the *Guadalquivir* to the seaport town of *San Lucar de Barrameda*. After a cursory stop for supplies or repairs the caravels, carracks, brigantines and naos would pass by the great salt marsh at the mouth of the river, *Las Marismas*, and into the Atlantic Ocean.

Although the son of a minor official in *Seville*, Ortiz shared the fate of many young men of noble bearing with warrior skills. These "*hidalgos*" were at a surplus and an adventure, such as offered by Narvaez, represented a way out. Ortiz signed with Narvaez and was put in charge of a squad of swordsmen.

Satisfied that the blade was as sharp as it could ever be, Ortiz carefully folded the stone into its leather pouch and sheathed the blade. Looking up, he was distracted by a small fishing vessel sailing in the opposite direction. Behind it was *Cuba*. The coast line was opening up. The heavy infusion of shoals and mangrove-infested islands was giving way to an open shoreline punctuated with clear beaches and an occasional inland bay.

"Tonight we will be in *Habana*," he had overheard the pilot talking with his captain.

Some of the older seamen, recognizing landmarks, knew that *Habana* wasn't far off and had passed the word. Everyone was anxious. The mood on board was soaring.

19 March 1528

Aboard the Caravel Maria De La Meridionales

Mares

At mid-afternoon, the wind changed. For the last two days, the strong northerlies had persisted, but now they had shifted directly over the bow. Forward progress was almost impossible. The decision was whether to begin a long night of contrary tacking. The northern leg would take them far out to sea before they could come about. The southern leg would put them uncomfortably close to shore. The hour was already growing late and the directions would have to be established in the dark. No problem if the sky was clear, but who was to say?

The other option was to turn inland, ride a port tack toward the shore, and set anchor for the night. They would wait for a wind change in the morning.

There, in the distance, they could see structures along the coast. They were very close. Narvaez had made up his mind.

"We will wait until morning, fire the signal cannon!"

With that the *Maria* came about and headed slowly toward the shore, the other vessels following in kind. At about 1000 *yara* offshore, the order was given to drop the anchor. All glided to a stop and then swung shoreward on their anchor lines. By nightfall the galleys had their cook stoves lit.

Beyond the shoreline, points of light indicated the location of a *hacienda* or even a small campfire. Further east an almost indiscernible glow leaked into the sky. These were the lights of *Habana*,

20 March, 1528

Aboard the Brigantine La Estrella

It was early. The signal cannon had fired before dawn. Narvaez and, indeed, the whole expedition was anxious to make port in *Habana*. During the night the winds had indeed turned westerly. It would be an easy sail into the port city. The deck of *La Estrella* was already crowded. The sun was not yet up and in the east and the glow was just spreading across the horizon. Looking up, Alvar noticed that no stars were visible. A thin haze seemed to cover the sky.

To the west, the inky blackness of the night highlighted *El Delfin* running just behind them, its lanterns ablaze in the morning darkness.

They moved away from shore and turned to the east, setting up to run in a broad reach. However, no sooner had they trimmed sails and settled in when the wind dropped to nothing.

They were becalmed.

They drifted. The sails hung limply,and the sounds of water lapped against the hull. There was little current and the tide effects were nil. In the direction of *Habana,* the sky lightened perceptibly, as a gray overcast hid the sun. Not a breath of air moved.

Pilot Jimenez sighed. There was nothing they could do but wait.

The morning wore on. On deck, crewman and passengers alike lay or sat idly looking out to sea. At mid-morning the temperature began to climb and with it the humidity. The air was becoming close and stifling. Alvar sat on the aft deck his legs splayed out in front. On the stairway, Elcano was repairing a rope. Below them, Jimenez paced the deck seeking idle chatter with the seaman and just about anyone who would talk with him.

Alvar felt it before he heard it, a low-frequency rumble just barely discernible above the noise around him. Raising up, his first instinct was to look to the west, but the gray sky that had persisted all morning didn't look any different. Others had heard it as well. Alvar moved to the steps and took a seat next to Elcano.

"Boatswain Elcano, do my ears deceive me or did I hear the sound of thunder?"

"Senor De Vaca, I heard it as well."

"Yet the sky shows no sign."

Elcano set down the rope. "Once, on a voyage from *Borinquen,* I heard thunder for a whole day and never saw a cloud. On that night a storm of such intensity caused one of our ships to smash against the rocks. Sounds on the sea carry great distance, Senor De Vaca. Somewhere out there..."

Elcano gestured with a broad sweep. "Somewhere out there a storm approaches. Let us hope we will be in the harbor before it arrives".

Another, almost sub-audible disturbance carried across the water.

20 March 1528

Aboard the Caravel Maria De La Meridionales Mares

Narv'ez's considerable temper had reached its breaking point.

"I can almost see *Habana* in the distance and here we float like a whale turd...*cagada de la ballena!*" With that, he picked up a small barrel and tossed it over the side.

Miruello distanced himself from the raging giant, moving to the other side of the aft deck. Flores held his ground. Campo, always nearby, seemed not to be troubled.

"...And now," he looked to the southwest, "another storm approaches"!

"*Adelentado*", it was Flores.

Narvaez turned angrily, "What is it pilot Flores?"

"We should consider moving the ships closer to shore where we could seek anchorage. We are becalmed and in deep water, but the seafloor rises rapidly after only a few thousand *yara*. Should this storm strike we could be in some jeopardy."

This request would require all of the vessels to release their boats and physically tow the vessels shoreward.

"No! We are too close to lay at anchor for even one more day. We will use the winds from this *tormenta* to take us into port!"

Flores looked shore-ward, the sky above was now showing the unmistakable discoloration of an approaching storm. He exchanged looks with Miruello who only threw up his hands and looked away.

A puff of air moved the sails ever so slightly.

Narvaez looked up, "You see, the winds are returning; tonight I will be drinking good Madeire in *Habana*."

Indeed, a few weak breezes began to bring the sails to life. Yardarms creaked, canvas fluttered and the stays became taunt, but just as the bows of the vessels began to respond to the pressure, the wind died once again.

To the south and southwest the overcast was becoming more sullen...a heaviness that seemed to hang in the air. The thunder was coming in regular intervals now, some in long rolling discharges.

Again, the wind came up in short swirling bursts and then disappeared.

A long trailer of lightning crackled across the sky. The report of thunder was immediate and deafening. Two *marineros*, working above, scurried down the ratlines. Flores could smell a strange pungent odor in the air; an odor that all sailors were familiar with after a particularly close discharge.

Almost imperceptible at first, a distant roaring sound began to fill the air.

Muruelo was pointing shoreward, "There!"

Narvaez and Flores rushed to the starboard rail.

A wall of rain was advancing towards them, so massive and so broad as to block from view everything behind it. Reaching the shoreline it methodically advanced on the fleet.

The sound of the rain increased in intensity.

La Doncella, a few hundred yards shore-ward, disappeared as if a blanket had been pulled over it.

Miruelo called out, "Here it comes", and the wall of water suddenly and completely engulfed the *Maria.* Rain so hard that taking a breath was fraught with choking on the water inhaled into the lungs.

Still no wind. Flores reacted by commanding *marieros* to reduce sail.

Under Narvaez's questioning look, he explained, "We are blind in this river of rain...the wind will come, we are close to shore and I want no surprises."

Another flash of lightning and the simultaneous crack of thunder. The thick pungent smell returned. Flores refereed to it as *"olor del infierno"*...the smell of hell.

20 March, 1528

Aboard the Brigantine La Estrella

The deluge continued....without stop. For an hour only the immediate world around each individual mattered. Water pounded on the deck, it ran off the yards and sails and poured in a torrent onto everything below. In the shelter of the aft deck, Alvar, the pilot, boatswain, military captain, and several seamen huddled. Everyone else was below. All shipboard activity had ceased. Lightning crackled all around them, each flash accompanied by a strange sound...like water being thrown on a hot spit.

The weather began to change again.

At first, no one seemed to notice. The force of the rain dulled the senses. Each percussion of thunder vibrated deeply into the body. Sight was limited to no more than 10 or twenty feet and the searing lightning flashes left ephemeral light spots on the eye's retina.

It was subtle at first. The pounding rain began to take a direction. Overhead, the reduced sails came alive, gently luftingat first, and then filling. Even over the tumult of the storm the sounds and movements of the ship became unmistakable. The bow came around and *La Estrella* heeled slightly to port.

They were moving. Angel Jimenez and the seaman scurried up the ladder.

A south wind was variable but gave every indication of becoming stronger. The sea, placid during the first part of the storm began to swell. Angel set a close reach to the northeast. His immediate concern was to move away from the shoreline and the hazard of running aground. It was still raining heavily. Visibility was poor and only an occasional ghostly glimpse of the *Maria* to starboard and *Reina* astern interrupted the ethereal world that surrounded them.

Growing stronger still, the wind moved evermore eastward. A direct course to *Habana* was now out of the question, they were sailing into the *Gulf of Mexico*. The evening would come early, the thick cloud cover and driving rain absorbed the light. There were no more sightings of the other ships.

Angel ordered the storm lanterns hung. The wind continued SSE.

The escalating gusts were driving quantities of seawater across the expanse. In their starboard tack to the NNE, enormous breakers began to pound against the bow. Angel reduced sail and then after only a few minutes, reduced sail again.

The night fell hard and heavy, the blackness complete. Their tack was increasingly hard to maintain in the rising seas and Angel was forced to alter course. He would hold the compass a little east of north and hope for a wind change. Thirty leagues ahead lay the *Martyrs*, an island chain strewn across the sea like so many pebbles in a stream.

Of the *Martyrs,* Jimenez had intimate knowledge. His mind drifted back to that time.

Ten years before as a cabin boy, on the slaver *Don Diego,* they had run aground in a particularly violent night at sea. Scared witless, young Jiminez had been thrown against the rail as the *Don Diego* had its hull eviscerated by a submerged reef. Listening sharply and sinking rapidly, the frightful waves and wind began to tear the ship apart. Below, the screams of the manacled *Indians* mixed with the dying sounds of the ship. As sea water swept across the deck, he was swept off the ship and into the churning water. A good swimmer, he treaded water as best as he could but the breaking waves tossed him about and repeatedly forced him under. He swallowed seawater. Somehow in the darkness, a barrel came to him and he desperately clung to it.

The storm had continued and he struggled to stay upright as the barrel rolled in the surging waves. At this moment he thought of his home, his mother, his young life.

Suddenly, and without warning, he was thrust into a mangrove thicket. In the darkness it was confusing...one moment cast about in a driving ocean, now surrounded by a profusion of twisted trunks, limbs, and leaves. Releasing the barrel, he crawled deeper into the thicket, making his way to the highest limbs. Finally exhausted, there he spent the remainder of the night.

In the morning, a glorious sunrise showed a spit of land no more than a bow-shot from where he was perched, and there on the sand were Spaniards...survivors and fellow shipmates from the night before.

By the grace of God, he had survived.

After only two days they had been picked up by a shallow-drafted fishing vessel and returned to *Cuba*.

The light of the lantern danced around the aft enclosure with the swaying of the ship. Angel stared at the compass, he thought of his mentor Bartolome Valdez, now dead for many months.

"What would he have done?"

The winds were growing stronger and the blinding rain continued. Overhead the lightning danced across the sky in magnificent displays. The air seemed alive. Joined now by Elcano, both men were startled when they looked upon one another. Elcano's hair, normally straight and black, was standing out from his head...it seemed to glow. Likewise, Elcano gazed at Jiminez, and although his head was covered with a seaman's cap his slight beard seemed alive on his face.

But, it wasn't just them. Looking around, the whole ship was bathed in an unearthly blue light. At the tips of the masts and yardarms, the light seemed to concentrate, trickling off into the atmosphere in thin blue fingers of energy.

Both men watched in awe as a ball of light advanced down a rope, stopped, and then moved in the opposite direction.

"*Cuerpos Santos*", Elcano spoke to no one in particular and quickly crossed himself.

Without turning Jiminez spoke, "Bartalome spoke of these holy bodies, but I have never experienced them...it is like the hand of God."

"I have seen this twice before...always during storms. It is thought to be a sign." Elcano's eyes intently followed the ball of luminescence as it traveled along the rigging.

Word quickly spread and all manner of inhabitants came upon the deck to gaze at the marvel. For a period, all working of the ship, its steerage, sails, and general duties came to a stop as *marineros* and officers alike stood transfixed. And then it was gone..the lights faded and passed into the night.

The storm continued.

CHAPTER 08

One Day Same As The Next

Un Dia Mismo Que el Siguiente

*"Señor Pantoja, how is it that you are up at this early hour?"
"I was about to ask you the same thing," replied Pantoja,
"One day same as the next, will this storm ever abate?" Rethinking
his comment, Pantoja lamented, "How long must we suffer on this
damnable ship, my men are close to mutiny and the horses are fairing badly?"*

23 March, 1528

Aboard the Caravel Reina De Napoles in the Gulf of Mexico

The storm had been raging for three days. Military captain Andres Dorantes de Crranza had commanded that all remain below. At first, the hatch had been left open allowing some air to circulate, but as the storm intensity increased it had been closed and made fast. The air became stale. The pitch and roll of the ship made the below-deck environment unbearable. Jamming himself in a corner, Estevan watched as people vomited until nothing remained in their stomachs. Some wretched with such force that the bile spewed across the decking.

All were seasick…all, but Estevan. Years of cleaning fish in the Mediterranean aboard the pitching dhows had conditioned him.

If the filth of the vomit wasn't enough, the other bodily functions had to be taken care of as well. *Potes de la mierda*…shit pots…were almost useless. Relieving oneself in this way requires balancing over the vessel. Early on, a few had tried, especially the women, but the wild gyrations of the ship made this maneuver impossible. Besides, most were so sick and dehydrated by now that they didn't even bother.

Estevan had particularly enjoyed watching the young slave girl, Margarita. Sick as she was, she managed to cover her actions with her dress, but not before Estevan caught sight of her thighs. His erection was instant. As she rose up to empty the pot into the common container she was thrown sideways and spilled the contents. The pot skittered across the floor and crashed into the wall. Margarita had crawled back to her original position.

Estevan had noticed Margarita ever since she came on board. When in *Santa Domingo* she had been bought by the bitch Dolores, the wife of physician Aaron Perez. The girl looked to be about 14 and a *media casta*…an Indian and *Africano* half-breed. Her skin was lighter than his and her dark curly hair hung below her shoulders. She carried herself well on long legs. From behind, her little *culo* beckoned to him. Estevan watched her whenever he could. He had dreamed of what he would do if given the chance. It had been a long time. His last woman had been in *San Lucar*, a whore who he'd taken the night before the expedition had left *Spain*.

The pounding of the sea against the hull and the ceaseless storm noise droned on through the night. In his corner, Estevan had managed to fall asleep...for how long he didn't know. A particularly hard jolt that banged his head against the bulkhead had awakened him. Overhead the swaying storm lantern flickered weakly, casting eerie shadows. He heard soft whimpering and felt a presence. To his amazement, Margarita was laying close by, holding weakly to the same stanchion that he was wedged behind. Somehow she had slid across the rough floor and ended up by his side. She was in terrible disarray. Her hair was matted and the thin cotton dress was filthy and torn.

Estevan reached out and extinguished the storm lantern.

In the darkness, he found her legs and slowly pushed the cotton dress over her head. Estevan explored her body and fondled her tight breasts. Her weak protests were lost in the sounds of the tumult.

The pressure in his groin was overpowering. He moved on top of her and spread her legs. Margarita weakly kicked at him but Estevan moved forward and held both of her legs against his chest. Feet in the air, she writhed and bucked, but to no avail. Finally, she ceased to resist.

Estevan reached down and entered her. He pleasured himself several times throughout the night and then, in the darkness, he slipped away, moving to another side of the hold.

Margarita, utterly and totally exhausted, lay in the darkness, not even caring anymore. It had been too dark to even identify her attacker. She just wanted to die.

24 March, 1528

Aboard the Brigantine La Estrella in the Gulf of

Mexico

Alvar had spent the night trying to sleep amid the noise and movement. Even the cabin's crude frame bed had been of little use; the violent swaying spilled him repeatedly onto the cabin floor. Giving up, he wedged himself into a corner. Even then, sleep had only been fleeting. Unable to bare it anymore Alvar rose from his corner.

He had to urinate.

The one sea lantern, tightly lashed to the support stanchion in the middle of the small cabin, had consumed all of its oil and sputtered out sometime after midnight. The blackness of the small cabin was disorienting and Alvar stumbled toward the door.

Outside a single storm lantern barely cast a dull glow over the aft deck. The dull shadows danced about as the lantern swayed with the movement of the ship. Far forward in the bow, another storm lantern was dimly visible, its light abated by the distance, fog, and sea spray. Only an occasional lightening flash illuminated the rest of the ship. The young page tending the *ampolleta* and traverse board recognized him and moved aside with a sleepy greeting. It was close to dawn.

He made his way to the stairs and took care to tightly grasp the handrail. Even in this effort, the violently swaying ship caused him to stumble several times. The wind and sea noise were overwhelming. It had been this way all night.

On the aft deck, the effects of the storm were intensified, rain and sea spray beat against his face. As Alvar made his way he noticed another presence. Alonso Pantoja, the ship's military captain, was moving toward the stairway.

His jovial mood belayed his fatigue. "Ah, De Vaca, another beautiful day!"

Alvar waved and made his way to the stern rail. He really had to go.

"De Vaca…tie up to a rope or we'll be fishing your bloated body out of the ocean with your *chorizo* still in hand." To this, Pantoja let out one of his thunderous laughs.

Alvar didn't appreciate his member being called a "little sausage" and didn't answer.

As if on cue, the ship lurched and Alvar lost his balance. Luckily, he was able to grab the rail …but not before pissing all over the front of his breeches.

Pantoja laughed again as Alvar quickly secured himself to a rope. Looking down he watched the sea frothing in angry anticipation, the phosphorus wake disappearing into the gloom. "Not today, *mar diaeblo*, not today". Feeling much relieved, Alvar followed Pantoja and made his way down the stairs.

"Senor Pantoja, how is it that you are up at this early hour?"

"I was about to ask you the same thing," replied Pantoja, "One day same as the next, will this storm ever abate?" Rethinking his comment, Pantoja lamented, "How long must we suffer on this damnable ship, my men are close to mutiny and the horses are fairing badly?"

"I wish I could answer that but it seems Providence has denied us the landing in *Habana*... at least for now. Pilot Jiminez tells me we have been blown far to the north and west ...how far, he is not sure."

Pantoja was clearly concerned, "We have three...maybe four more days of limited fodder for the horses; after that, they will begin to starve to death. Their muscles grow soft while in the restraints and it will take days before they can recover. Already I have lost a mare and thrown her overboard."

Alvar was concerned as well, "We can only hope that when this tempest subsides, the *Adelentado* will make a decision as to our future."

With that, Alvar left the stern and slowly moved forward. There was a deck path out to the bow with a "man rope" so that each seaman could tie off. Washing overboard in this weather was certain death. Several other seamen carefully moved about the vessel checking equipment and lashings. Even at this hour of the morning, the deck was a busy place. After the experience aft, Alvar was careful to secure himself to the rope as he moved forward.

At the bow, *marineros* monitored the lashing on the *ancla de capa*...the sea anchor that kept the bow of the small ship facing into the wind and waves. Without it, *La Estrella* would have broached in the mountainous waves long ago. The length of the *rode*, or rope bridle, between the ship and the sea anchor was critical and had to be constantly adjusted to the length of the swells. The bridle was necessary and played out in front of the ship to keep the bowsprit from being damaged. In the dark, the swell length had to be estimated by the ride of the ship. Adjustment required seamen to make their way to the bow and haul at the rode. For this, the experience of a seasoned mariner was critical. Alvar could see Elcano moving about, issuing orders, and assisting when needed. Overhead a sprit sail had also been loosely deployed to emphasize the effects of the sea anchor. It was exhausting and dangerous work and Alvar noticed that the *marineros* looked spent.

A gigantic column of seawater exploded over the bow and cascaded down on him. For a moment he couldn't breath. The water was all around. He held on tightly.

Finally air…he took a deep breath.

The sky was just beginning to lighten…almost imperceptibly. Only his peripheral vision picked it up at first. By the time Alvar reached the bow it was unmistakable. Daylight at last. With the rising light, the sky was angry gray. Wind gusted across the white-tipped waves in spasms that racked *La Estrella.* The haggard spritsail flapped. Ballistic sprays of water shot from the bowsprit rigging as the ropes suddenly became taut. Rain and sea spray felt like a thousand needles tearing at his face. Just as rapidly, the wind would fall off and the tortured canvas would collapse and sag. During these brief lulls, the rain fell in torrents, washing the salt off his forehead and stinging his eyes. The anguished cries of those below decks drifted through the laden air. Groans, cursing, sounds of sickness, and appeals to the *Virgin Santa* mixed with the terrified screams of horses. Just as quickly, a new blast ripped across the water and into the ship. Wind interaction with the rigging generated unearthly whistles and howls. Behind him, in the stern, the lateen yardarm was blown from its fork and crashed against the mizzenmast, the sound barely audible in the wind. He could see the captain and helmsmen scurrying to secure the loose yardarm.

Alvar tightly braced himself against the bow timbers and tried to anticipate the rolling of the ship. At once his view would be of the sea rushing up and then of the sky with its dark undulating clouds. Seawater rushed across the deck, sucking at his legs. The rolling momentum tested his grip on the wet timbers. Each time the brigantine rose up on a crest Alvar strained to see any change on the horizon. At times it was impossible to discern the boundary between the sea and sky. There was nothing. Alvar pondered his fate these last few months. The expedition had been fraught with bad luck.

A shout from amidships brought Alvar out of his lethargy and he followed the sound to a *marinero* hanging in the rigging and pointing starboard. Following the point, Alvar at first saw nothing…but then, almost imperceptibly, a caravel materialized out of the haze. It was the *Maria*, the governor's flagship. Like *La Estrella,* all the sails except for the sprint were furled. Even the governor's pennant, which normally flew from the foremast, had been taken down.

Watching the *Maria* close, Alvar became aware of a subtle change in the wind. No longer south, it was slowly turning southwest.

Across the watery chasm, Alvar could now see the *marineros* tending the *Maria.* Up on the quarterdeck, the unmistakable silhouette of Narvaez stood with two other men.

"Probably pilot's Flores and Miruelo," Alvar reasoned to himself.

Communication between ships was impossible. Even Narvaez's voice wouldn't carry in this wind. Under the previous agreement, the ships would close up and allow the *Maria* to move ahead. It was the *Maria* who had an experienced pilot and she would show the way.

Another shout from the rigging, *"Ho, El Delfin"*!

Behind the *Maria,* the brigantine *El Delfin* hove into view but just as quickly disappeared as another squall passed between them. Dark and drifting, the vertical bands of rain reached down to the sea as they moved leeward in a slow procession.

As the squall passed, the *El Delfin* materialized again…closer this time. Spray from the bow wake clearly visible, its frothy whiteness in stark contrast to the dull grayish green of the sea.

25 March, 1528

Aboard the Caravel, El Delfin in the Gulf of Mexico

Aboard *El Delfin,* the ship's bell sounded three times. The sound dissipated rapidly in the heavy air.

At his station on the stern, pilot Jose Eraso tried in vain to peer through the heaviness of the storm. He could feel subtle changes in the sea and in the air. The morning sky was heavy with a thick gray overcast that all but extinguished the light. Wisps of cloud sprinted, mast high, just above the ocean surface while pockets of rain fell. Still, the storm seemed to be blowing itself out.

Eyes tightly squinted against the rain, he thought of the frustrating days they had experienced. The expedition had been at sea for over a month. What should have been a relatively short excursion from *Xugua,* on the south coast of *Cuba,* to *La Habana,* on the north coast, became a calamity of mistakes, delays, and rogue storms. Now, they were here…God knows where…after being only a few leagues from the harbor at *Habana.*

This storm seemed without end. Each day the horses in their slings below decks had grown weaker. Several had already died and had been thrown overboard. The twenty hogs brought along were thin, but all survived. Supplies were almost depleted. Colonists packed below decks had had enough; tired, seasick, dehydrated, and now existing on quarter rations, they wanted to return to *Cuba*. The expedition was in danger of failing.

Of the other ships Eraso could only account for one. Yesterday the little brigantine, *La Estrella*, had briefly come into view off the stern. Quickly, however, it had disappeared from view. Now, only a blanket of weather and sea surrounded them.

Jose had never ventured into these waters and he had no experience with the seas of *La Florida,* but he was a learned man, and he knew of the voyages of Ponce de Leon. Besides, pilots talked amongst themselves and, like all pilots on this expedition, he had a copy of the *Espejo*, the official *Spanish* map of the *Indies* and *New Spain*. He knew of the *gran corriente*...the great current and of *Los Martyrs*, the string of islands and shoals that extended westward from the tip of *La Florida* terminating in *Las Secas Tortugas*. It was *Las Secas Tortugas* that worried him. This cluster of islands and reefs extended far out into the ocean almost due north of *Habana*. This storm had blown strongly for six days, its direction south to southeast. Almost certainly they had passed close by, it being a miracle they had not contacted them. By his chart *Las Secas Tortugas* was more than a degree in latitude north of *Habana*...about 21 leagues. Jose felt that they were now well north of that latitude, but without a view of the sun or stars, he had no way of telling. This area on his chart north of *Las Secas Tortugas* was empty...an unknown.

Another squall passed over *El Delfin,* but just as quickly moved to the northwest. Somehow the ferocity seemed to be diminishing. The morning suddenly seemed somehow brighter. The rain slowed to a drizzle.

"Barco Ho!"

Looking up to the ratlines Jose followed the pointed finger of the *marinero*. Directly astern *La Estrella* materialized in the mist.

The weather was definitely improving. The seas were still rough and the wind fierce, but, the visibility was improving rapidly.

Another "*Barco Ho!*"

Far to the east the flagship, *Maria de la Meridionales Mares,* came into view, sails deployed and underway. Behind her, the masts of another member of the fleet, too far away to be identified, lingered just above the horizon.

Eraso gave the order to haul in the sea anchor

31 March, 1528

Aboard the Caravel La Doncella De Plata in the Gulf of Mexico

Captain Alonzo del Castillo Maldonado removed his blood-soaked shirt and carefully set it on the deck beside him. His bondman, Pietro was already hauling up a bucket of seawater. The seas were still rough and Alonzo braced himself with a wide stance as he poured the contents of the bucket over his head. He could taste the saltiness. The seawater coursed over his face. In the morning air, the coolness felt good against his skin. Handing the empty bucket back, he rubbed his face, shoulders, and chest.

Pietro took the empty bucket and dropped it over the side once more. *La Doncella* was underway and the bucket skipped across the top of the water before it partially filled and dropped lower into the bow spray. Pietro hauled the bucket back up, being careful to not let it bang into the side of the ship.

Alonzo stepped out of his breeches tossing them on top of the shirt. Holding the bucket with one hand he slowly poured half the water down his abdomen and the other half down the small of his back. Alonzo felt uncomfortable as he cleaned himself and looked around to see who was watching.

Alonzo del Castillo Maldonado was born in *Salamanca, Spain* a region of *Castilla y Leon*. He was a thin man with amazing speed, quickness, and surprising strength. He was, without doubt, the best swordsman on the expedition. His father, a physician, also taught medicine at the *Universidad de Salamanca*. Both of Alonso's uncles were *letrados*…lawyers who had graduated from the University.

A family of professional men, an adolescent Alonzo had instead offered his services to *Spain* and worked harder than most to learn the warrior trade. Like Cabeza De Vaca and Andres Dorantes, he had proved his loyalty in Spain's *Cumeneros* revolt, albeit at a very young age. More than that, however, Alonzo had something else to prove. His family were *conversos*; Jews that had converted to Christianity. In the era of the *Spanish* Inquisition *conversos* were subject to ridicule, scrutiny, imprisonment, and even death. His services to the *Spanish* crown would help prove his family's loyalty.

Yesterday, the storm that had followed them since *Habana* had finally blown itself out, leaving a rough and unsettled ocean. All of the ships of the expedition had survived and regrouped. With the strong south wind, Narvaez and the flagship *Maria* had given up returning to *Cuba* and had pointed the fleet west, towards *Panuco* and the *Rio Las Palmas*. The day under sail had been difficult, however, with the continued roughness and occasional rogue squall forcing them to drop sail and turn into the wind. There was another force that acted upon them as well. It was the *Grande Corriente*…a great current that flowed west to east and then down the coast of *La Florida* to the *Atlantic*…the *Gulf Stream*. Even the traverse boards couldn't be believed. The knot line speed was being perverted by the current.

During the night one of these squalls had been particularly violent. A sling holding a mare purchased in *Hispaniola* had failed. In the ensuing mêlée, the mare had broken a foreleg and had to be dispatched. Alonzo was closest and performed the function with his dagger. Killing a man was one thing, but a horse was another. To a captain of cavalry, the horse was everything.

After cutting the jugular Alonzo had instructed Pietro to contain the blood, but in the chaos the bucket, held under the mare's neck, was upset by the thrashing animal. The stable deck floor, awash with blood, was slick and all were forced to crawl on hands and knees.

Now, in the early morning light, the storm was fading in the eastern sky and *La Doncella* appeared to be alone in the ocean. Ringing the shirt and breeches out, Pietro handed each, in turn, back to the captain. Dressing quickly, Alonzo briefly checked the sky and the horizon.

The hatch had been removed and the expired mare was being winched from the open hold. Blood on the body had coagulated and turned dark, the sightless eyes stared down into the hold as the animal was lifted clear. The hold cover was quickly slid back in place and secured. Unceremoniously, the mare was dropped over the side. Alonzo watched the carcass as it bobbed and rolled in the waves, one leg extended in rigor mortis...beckoning. Slowly it disappeared behind *La Doncella.*

Alonzo turned to Pietro, "Tell Antonio to meet me on deck".

Antonio Rodriguez was the company's *Sargento comandate*...Sergeant major...the direct line of communication between the captain and his horseman. Rodriguez was past 40 and had begun his military career as a horse handler in the battle of *Cerignola*. The *"El Gran Capitan"*, Gonzalo de Cordoba" himself had chosen him personally as an attendant. Nine years later Rodriquez fought with distinction at *Ravenna,* his horse company harassing the *French* even as *Spanish* forces were withdrawing from the field in defeat. In 1520 during the *Comunero* revolt Rodriguez had served with Captain Castillo. Both had a mutual respect for each other.

Not of noble birth, not much was known of Antonio's early life...he never spoke of it. Only 16 years old at *Cerignola* he had almost continuously served *Spain*. Tall and erect, in the saddle he became part of the horse. Weathered from years in the field his face was lined and tanned and his hair showed the first signs of gray. As a soldier, Antonio executed his duties without hesitation and without remorse. His intense blue eyes could look through a person…still…he was quick to laugh and immensely enjoyed the camaraderie of his men.

In *Spain,* captain Castillo had contacted Rodriquez. He was forming a company for the expedition and needed an experienced cavalry leader. In addition, the captain offered to cover his expenses. Anxious to participate in the New World adventure and share in the profits, Antonio had readily agreed.

As Antonio approached, Castillo shook his head and smiled, "Antonio, you look like a butcher, let Pietro help you clean yourself".

"Ah *capitan, gracias,* my skin is sticking together and the smell is becoming ripe".

Rodriquez stepped to the ship's gunwale and began removing the blood-soaked clothes. Pietro worked the bucket.

Averting his eyes and looking out to sea, Castillo continued, "Antonio, as soon as you can, bring the men on deck in small groups. They need to clean themselves and the fresh air will do them good."

"*Si capitan,* they are tending their mounts now but I will begin moving them up as soon as..." In mid-sentence, Pietro emptied the bucket over his head and Rodriquez sputtered to catch his breath.

Castillo laughed as the now-naked Rodriquez chased the bondsman around the deck. Although a bondsman, Pietro and Rodriquez shared a friendship. During his years of service with Castillo, Antonio had helped train Pietro in the arts of a cavalryman.

Laughing, Antonio called out, "Ah Pietro, come back with the bucket. I need to clean up and get my clothes on. If the *La Maria* shows up on the horizon the women will be jumping overboard to get to me."

02 April, 1528

Aboard the Caravel, Maria De La Meridionales

Mares in the Gulf of Mexico

The ships of the Narvaez expedition drifted in a becalmed sea. The storm of two days past was gone, leaving only rough seas and occasional squalls. But then, during the evening of April 1st, the strong southerlies dropped to a faint breeze and, by morning...nothing! They sat motionless in water tranquil as a mill pond.

The Captains and pilots from all five ships of the expedition met on board the flagship to determine the next course of action. Narvaez spoke briefly, but Flores and Miruelo led the conversation.

Quadrant and sextant readings put them at 28° of latitude...far north of the Latitudes for *Rio de Las Palmas* according to *Spain's* official map of the *Indies*, the *Padron Real*. However, their present location was still, south of the charted latitude for *Bahia Honda*, the Great Bay, an immense natural harbor on *La Florida's* west shore. Reluctantly, and after much discussion, it was determined to alter course and make for *La Florida*, the eastern most extreme of the land grant. Their supplies were gone and the horses were growing weaker by the hour. They desperately needed to make a landfall...somewhere!

Head pilot Jenaro Flores summarized, "When the winds return we will follow a course a little north of due east. At landfall, we should be close to the great bay."

Miruelo stepped to the front of the group. "There are two large bays on this coast of *La Florida*...the great bay...at 29° and one further to the south. We, of course, desire the more northerly of the two, for it is closer to the great arc of *Amichel* and *Panuco's Rio de Las Palmas.*"

What was uncertain, however, was where they lay in relation to longitude and how far to the coast of *La Florida*. The traverse boards could no longer be believed, for they had been at the mercy of the winds and current for a week. There was no solid point of reference on which to base a location. When asked their opinions, each ship's pilot had a different idea as to their whereabouts, but all agreed that they were much closer to *La Florida* than the *Rio de Las Palmas*.

It wasn't until late afternoon that the meeting broke up. Tied off around *Maria,* the four boats of the other vessels bobbed lazily. On board, their crews, consisting of four lounging oarsmen and a guardian, each got up and made ready for the return trip.

As night fell over the cluster of vessels the moonless sky was unusually clear. The stars seemed to hang just above the masts. All on board watched in awe as meteors coursed across the heavens in astonishing numbers. Janero Flores looked at the display with some trepidation. He wasn't a superstitious man...still...some might say this was a bad sign. One particularly bright *meteorito* glowed so bright he could have read a book in its light. For a brief moment it cast a shimmering green glow, and then...it abruptly disappeared.

Below him, on the main deck, his attention was taken by the three women leaning against the rail. One was talking loudly.

"You see, it is a sign. This expedition is cursed. I didn't believe the *Moor* woman at first, but now I am certain...bad things are about to happen."

It was dark and Janero couldn't see, but he recognized the voice. It was that bitch Rita la Salvaje...the wife of carpenter apprentice Bonito Pina. Actually, she was no wife at all. She had tricked Bonito into marrying her while he was blind drunk in *Cadiz*. Her escape from that harbor town now insured, she traveled to the New World...spreading her legs for anyone who would pay. Since she was his responsibility, Bonito had to suffer for her actions. He thought seriously about hitting her over the head with one of his mallets but didn't have the courage.

Even Narvaez had been subject to her sharp tongue. Being approached repeatedly to protest every discomfort, Narvaez had finally instructed his military captain, Alejandro Tellez, to do whatever it took to keep her away from him. Rita was no small woman, and in truth, could probably have held her own with most men in a struggle...but not Tellez.

Alejandro Tellez was a bull of a man and fearsome in appearance. A long scar crossed his face from forehead to the left ear...or, what used to be an ear. Another scar began just under the nose and terminated at his chin, giving his mouth a permanent drooping scowl. Fiercely loyal, his courage was beyond question.

His one confrontation with Rita had been brief. Finding her alone, he had seized her around the neck, partially lifting her body off the deck.

As she struggled, bug-eyed and gasping for breath Tellez had stated matter-of-factually, "The *Adelentado* wishes never to be disturbed by you again and if you persist I will personally throw you overboard."

He had dropped her then. She fell in a heap clutching her throat. Tellez turned abruptly and left the area.

From that moment Rita La Salvaje made a point of avoiding Narvaez...and...Tellez whenever she could.

03 April, 1528

Aboard the Brigantine La Estrella, in the Gulf of Mexico

Friar Juan Velazquesz de Salazar had just completed his readings for the mid-morning *Tierce*. He had chosen Psalm 119, Verse 105...” Thy word is a lamp unto my feet”. He felt it particularly applicable to their situation.

“And praise be to God...Amen.” He kissed the bible he was holding and looked around. The *marineros* were lounging around, some sitting on the deck others propped up against the gunnels. A few hung loosely to the ratlines and yards. Behind, soldiers and colonists were standing on the main deck. Above, on the aft castle, *Alguacil* De Vaca and pilot Jimenez were looking down at the proceedings. Further out, the other ships of the expedition drifted haphazardly in the placid sea.

As the good father collected his vestments, the hint of a breeze brushed his cheek. A page of the bible, still open in his hands, fluttered and turned. Immediately, everyone looked to the sails. The canvas hanging from the yards stiffened from disuse, began to move ever so slightly.

Velazquesz crossed himself, “praise God.” Many around him did the same.

Over the next hour a light south breeze developed. Under full sail the *Maria* was allowed to move to the lead. The *Estrella* took a position 1000 *vara* to starboard. Pilot Murielo, aboard the flagship, would guide them through these waters. Their course was now northeast. If the wind held they should contact *La Florida* somewhere south of the *Bahia Honda*, but no problem, they would simply coast north until they came upon the bay.

For the rest of the day, the expedition's hopes lifted. The south wind, although light, remained constant. The skies were clear and they proceeded under full sail.

That night the storms returned.

04 April, 1528

Aboard the Caravel, Maria De La Meridionales

Mares

The night previous, a storm had descended with unrelenting fury. It had appeared unexpectedly with no harbinger of lightning to announce its arrival. The sky had been clear. From the poop, Janero Flores had been working the astrolabe when the first blast of misture-laden air blew across him. Turning to the southwest, there was only blackness...too much blackness! No stars shown and early in the evening as it was, there was no residual after-glow in the west. The smell and feel of the air was unmistakable and he had quickly ordered a reduction in sail.

It came upon them then, scattering the ships and forcing all to heave-to, great towers of sea spray exploding into the air as wind-blown waves collided with the bows. That night many believed they would not see the light of morning. Dropping into cavernous valleys the big caravel's masts seemed only a few feet from the mountain of water crashing towards them. Unrelenting, the gale continued through the night and into the next day.

Two more horses died.

Now, it was the evening after the storm had come upon them. The light was fading and Janero braced himself as he walked the stairs to the poop. The rain only came in spurts now, and the wind had noticeably dropped. He looked to the top of the mizzen mast where a tattered pendent still flew. Still strong and steady, the wind had shifted to the east. He stepped onto the top deck and made his way to the rail. The ocean was aglow. To the west, the overcast had lifted and shafts of light from the setting sun stabbed through the clouds and across the water. He looked around him. Everything was bathed in the reddish glow of sunset. Against the dark background to the east a string of puffy white clouds, hi-lighted by the sun, trailed just above the water. When but just a boy in *Extremedura*, he remembered his mother talking of such clouds after a storm. She called them *nubes de dios*, God clouds. She would tell him they were good luck and always marked the worst of storms going to another place.

Janero smiled as he thought of home.

Diego Miruelo joined him on deck. "Senor Flores, I think this one has about blown itself out."

"Ah, Diego, I agree. With God's blessing, we should see clear skies later tonight. I would hope for a look at the stars."

Miruelo considered before speaking, "A long time to suffer these strong winds and frightful seas...and now this east wind. I would think we are at least 20 leagues north and..." He thought for a moment, "who knows how far to the west."

Another pause, "Our last latitude...before the storm, was 28°."

Janero continued, "A degree of latitude is 23 leagues...more or less. If what you are saying is true we could be directly west of *Bahia Hona*."

Miruelo looked to the east, "But, how far west?"

"Friend Miruelo, I've thought long and hard on this matter. I think it wouldn't be unusual if we were 60 to 70 leagues from *La Florida*. With a good wind...two days."

"Then let us hope that this easterly subsides or we will drift another 10 leagues by morning."

As darkness enveloped them the east wind continued. There was a moon, but it periodically disappeared behind fast-moving clouds that scudded across the sky. Just before midnight, there was a noticeable lull and the wind turned southerly.

Janero called to the boatswain for sails.

"Senor Alvarez, as the wind allows I suggest we begin hoisting our sheets and set the course northeast."

Miguel Alvarez thoughtfully nodded in agreement. Although subsiding, the winds were still volatile and unpredictable, shifting, gusting, and not well-established. In these conditions setting too much sail would be dangerous. Any extreme movement of the ship could sling men out of the rigging.

Under sail, however, there would be some degree of control that they didn't have now.

Turning to a group of *marineros* Alvarez commanded, "Make ready to set the yards and drop the mainsail…wait for my signal."

To another group he called, "Prepare to set the fore and spritsail and make ready the lateen."

Calling to his helmsman, "Stand ready by the rudder". They would bring the bow directly into the wind, briefly luffing the sails and giving the crew the best possible conditions to finish their work in the rigging.

"Rudder to starboard"

Moments passed while up above the *marineros* completed their tasks.

Finally, "Rudder to port. Set the mainsail. Helmsman, continue to come about and hold to course northeast."

The *Maria* came about and began picking up speed, its bow pointed east northeast in a broad reach. Narvaez, just coming on deck, ordered two cannon shots fired, at intervals, every 30 minutes. This was the prearranged signal for "follow me" and was to be answered by a single shot from the other ships in the expedition until all had responded. One of the ships answered immediately from the port side, its muzzle flash visible in the dark. From astern, another flash and then, after a brief delay, the sound...this ship much further distant.

Marineros lit additional *farols* and placed them fore and aft. To port, about a thousand *vara* out, the other ship, probably *Reina*, was also showing its lanterns.

Thirty minutes later the *Maria* discharged its cannon again. From the port side came an immediate response. From astern, now much closer, another answering shot. Further astern, a faint flash followed by an audible but very weak discharge indicated a third ship. The signal shots continued into the night.

Two hours passed before the final ship answered the call from far to starboard...probably *La Estrella*.

From his position in the aft castle, Janero put down the astrolabe. Both he and Miruello had come up with similar latitudes in their calculations. Janero calculated 29°, 06 minutes North, Miruello 29°, 07 minutes North. Unrolling the *Padron Real* they scanned the map, moving the lantern closer to make out land mass and lines of latitude.

Narvaez hovered over them. The peninsula of *La Florida* projected across the map like a pointed finger...below it the island marked *Juana*, now *Cuba*.

"There!" Miruello stabbed at *La Florida* with his little finger. "There!" He moved his finger back and forth. "There are the two great bays".

Flores and Narvaez almost bumped heads as they leaned closer to see the small details.

Following the line of latitude from the more north of the two bays, Flores stopped at the number 29 clearly marked on the map.

"If we can steer a straight line, we should arrive exactly where we want to be".

"How long?" Narvaez did not look up.

Miruello and Flores looked at each other. Finally, Flores answered.

"Adelentado, the storm blew us north and west...how far I'm...we...are not certain. My guess...and it is only a guess...we are two days sail from *La Florida*."

Narvaez turned and focused his one eye on Miruello.

"And you, what are your thoughts?"

Miruello seemed to wilt. "Your excellency, Senor Flores and I are in agreement...two days...maybe more, maybe less, depending on the wind."

05 April, 1528

Aboard the Brigantine, La Estrella

Page Lucio Haro was coming down. Around his neck hung a length of rigging attached to a wooden block and tackle...or what was left of it. The wooden block was split and the metal shaft and pulley within had separated. It was a critical component of the mainsail and had to be replaced. Boatswain El Cano had taken the job himself, balancing precariously on the yard while he cut away the ropes and made the necessary splices. He had called down to Lucio for help.

When El Cano had made it clear he wanted him "up here", Lucio gulped and started climbing. He hated high places. So far he was able to hide his fear. To compensate he would climb rapidly, look straight ahead...not giving himself time to think about it. At elevation he would concentrate hard on the job at hand, working as quickly as possible to complete it, hoping no one would notice the tenseness. Coming down was even harder because now, he had to look down. His peripheral vision would pick up the dizzying movement of water past the ship, the miniature men on the deck far below, and the shifting horizon as the swaying mast accentuated the movements of the ship.

He marveled at men like El Cano who seemed just as relaxed balanced on the yard's foot ropes as if he was sitting in a chair. Watching the boatswain gave him a queasy feeling in his stomach.

Lucio stopped. Now fifteen feet from the deck, he was finally comfortable. Turning, he scanned the horizon. Nothing. In all directions the sea trailed off into the distance, its flat surface unaltered. The wind was light and out of the south, the movement of *La Estrella* was marked by the light-colored wake on the ocean's surface. Ahead, the sky was bright and clear, the sun already a blazing ball just above the water's surface. The other ships of the expedition were all around. Up ahead was the *Adelentado's* flagship.

Lucio's uncle had been a childhood friend of Narvaez. Both families were close and, although Panfilo lived in *Valladolid,* it was but an afternoon ride to the family farm in *Cuellar.* Lucio's father had heard of the great expedition and had asked his brother to talk with Narvaez. Although only 13, he felt it was time that Lucio got out into the world, and what better opportunity than with "*Tio* Panfilo" in a great expedition to the new world.

At first, he had worked on the *Maria,* sharing many of the responsibilities with Campo, Narvaez's personal page. In fact, they had become good friends using what little free time they had to talk and play shipboard games. The great hurricane had changed everything, however, and Narvaez had reassigned him to *La Estrella*.

Aboard *La Estrella, aguacil* De Vaca was a much different man than Narvaez. He was quiet and thoughtful. As to the operation of *La Estrella,* De Vaca seemed to have total confidence in the pilot Angel Jimenez and shared a close relationship with boatswain El Cano. He knew, of course, about the loss of the two ships in *Trinidad* and sensed that De Vaca felt a deep responsibility. But...life on the little brigantine was easy and he got along with everyone.

Aboard ship the excitement seemed to be growing as they neared the mainland of *La Florida.* The expedition, to date, had been fraught with hardships and disappointment, and now...finally...they were close to their goal.

Lucio looked again to the east, shielding his eyes from the rising sun. Still nothing!

06 April, 1528

Aboard the Caravel, Reina De Napoles

A tranquil day had passed. Too tranquil! Yesterday the wind had been slight or not at all. The hours under sail had passed slowly, the traverse boards accumulating their data in a virtual straight line. Pilot Dario Quroz estimated they had traveled no more than 5 leagues, a modest distance for a day's sailing. Late in the evening, however, what small wind they had been enjoying fell away to nothing. Now, at this early hour, they sat motionless, drifting in a stifling fog bank that covered everything like a blanket. Just ahead, and too close, was the *Maria*.

In the stillness, only the current and wave actions had any effect on the ships. During the night both ships had closed on each other. A collision was a real possibility. Even drifting, two ships coming together could break spars and entangle rigging. Already two boats had been lowered. Together they would attempt to pull the *Reina* off to one side. At 110 *toneladas*, it was the lighter of the two ships.

Walking to the prow Quroz watched as two tow ropes were attached, one starboard and one to port. Pulling out the slack, both boat crews rowed ahead, fading into the thick humid air. Even the *Maria*, now very close, was no more than a looming dark shadow.

"Friend Dario Quroz, I know you are out there!" Came the call from across the water.

Dario laughed, it was his friend for many years, Janero Flores, pilot of the *Maria* calling out to him.

"I am here, Janero wondering how it is that you have maneuvered your ship directly into our path."

He heard laughter. The air was so still, it was as if they were standing close to each other.

Janero ignored the gibe. "Friend, how are you?"

"I am fine, and you?"

"I am doing well, but more than ready to land these tubs and sit down to a fine meal with a large cut of beef."

The thought of food was almost overpowering. They had been on half rations now for weeks. What they did have was moldy and even the water casks smelled badly.

"Don't forget the wine and cheese." Dario could feel his mouth watering.

From across the water, "and bread...a freshly baked loaf of bread."

"Enough Janero!" Dario laughed, "...or else I will jump overboard and swim back to *Habana*."

The bow of *Reina* was beginning to turn. Further out, he could just see the men straining at their oars. The ship was moving...slowly, but it was moving.

After an hour had passed, and the two ships were out of danger. The boats had returned and were being hoisted back aboard. The oarsmen lay on the deck exhausted. *Capitan* Dorantes had allotted a ration of rum to the boat crews...much appreciated.

The morning dragged on without change. They fog remained, the air was still with only the sound of the waves lapping against the hull. Nothing was happening. At several locations on deck, *marineros* played cards while other groups of soldiers and colonists talked or just stared out into the distance. Friar Alaniz moved among the people, stopping for a moment at each gathering. He discussed pleasantries, laughed at jokes, and then offered up a prayer. Estevan, idly whittling on a piece of wood, straddled the bowsprit, his feet dangling in the air.

As noon approached, the sky at last began to brighten. In no more than15 minutes the fog had disappeared as if it never had been there. A slight breeze had picked up, but now contrary to their destination...from the east. The M*aria,* firing a signal shot, led the way with a close-hauled tack to the north-northeast. If the wind direction persisted, this point of sail would take them far north of their objective...they would be forced to run for a few hours and then tack back to the southeast. Today's progress would be slow.

06 April, 1528

Aboard the Caravel, Maria De La Meridionales

Mares

Two hours this way, two hours that way. Rita didn't understand any of it. They didn't seem to be getting anywhere. The turnarounds, as they appeared to Rita, seemed only to reverse direction.

She was tempted to march up the stairs and confront the pilot...pilots! Today, however, Narvaez had joined the pilots with Alejandro Tellez, the one man on the expedition she avoided. But...the day was fair and she was just glad to be on the deck, free from the stinking existence below. She and most of the inhabitants quartered there now milled around in the open air. Narvaez had crews working below, manning the pumps and carrying buckets of sludge to be thrown over the side. A fuscous streak of waste, from the pump's discharge, trailed behind the ship.

Even with all the hatches thrown wide open, the air emanating out of the openings was stale and vile. Bad smelling at any time, the collection of liquid in the *pantoque*, the bilge, is exacerbated once the surface "crust" is broken in a cleaning operation. The smell drifted across the deck. Now, on a port tack, everyone avoided the starboard side of the ship.

Her attention was distracted by a pair of dolphins frolicking in the water, and Rita was startled by a leering *marinero* grabbing a fist full of her buttocks from behind.

"Que culo!"

Her reaction was quick. A robust woman with arms strengthened by years of toting trays of ale in the waterfront taverns, Rita caught her assailant with a roundhouse right. It caught the surprised seaman full in the nose, a spray of red mist enveloping his head as he collapsed to the deck.

She recognized him now. It was just two nights ago that she had lifted her dress for him. For a copper *maravedi,* she had allowed him to pleasure himself, both hidden from view behind a bulkhead.

Laughter erupted from around the ship as the stunned *marinero* slowly regained his feet and slunk off muttering to himself, *"Puto loca*...crazy bitch!"

The five other women on board had joined her, passing the bleeding *marinero* as they approached. The youngest of the women, Consuelo Salvador, looked wide-eyed at Rita, who was rubbing her bruised knuckles, and then back at the retreating seaman. Consuelo, only 17, was accompanying her new husband, one Andres Zapata, a lieutenant of a group of 20 crossbowmen.

There were sisters Felicia and Maria. Felicia was married to a cavalry officer, Cristobal de Veresa and unmarried Maria was accompanying Felicia as her consort. Maria, strikingly beautiful, had been highly sought after by most of the men on board but sister Felicia and husband had guarded her closely.

Another woman, Antonia, had been widowed when the two ships of the expedition were lost in *Trinidad*. Both she and her husband, *Capitan* Pasqual Aguayo had been traveling on *El Viento del Sur.* Antonia had been displaced to the flagship to facilitate the loading operation. It had saved her life. Rather than stay in *Cuba* or take passage back to *Spain* she had decided to stay with the expedition in memory of her beloved Pasqual.

Finally, Dolores was the plump wife of physician Aaron Perez. Perez was a member of the *latrado* class. These educated professionals were of a higher social order and Dolores had tried hard to maintain her elevated status in the flagship's cramped confines. Months at sea under extremely trying conditions, however, had been a great equalizer. She had grown close to these five women, and surprisingly, Rita Salvage was her closest confidant. Still, Dolores maintained a slight air of superiority. She was always the last to arrive and refused to enter into petty arguments or disagreements of any kind.

From above, Narvaez looked down at the six women now embroiled in lively chatter. He had watched the whole incident with Rita and the *marinero* with interest. This woman was a troublemaker...still, he had to turn away in his amusement when she had dropped the sailor to the deck.

He was frustrated with their progress. Continually tacking in this contrary wind had slowed them down considerably. Today, progress would be 10, maybe 12 leagues and there was still no way of knowing how much further they had to go. Panfilo hoped that a successful landfall could be made sometime during *Sementa Santa*...Holy Week.

Surely they were getting close.

06 April, 1528

Aboard the Caravel, La Doncella De Plata

It was almost dark. The ships of the expedition had reduced sail. Overhead, thin wispy clouds, barely visible, moved across the sky. The stars dimmed or blinked out as the clouds passed, only to reappear a few moments later. Just above the horizon, the full moon was rising, and a ribbon of moonlight highlighted the waves. Sea lanterns of the five expedition ships winked on as the last streaks of sunset faded.

Pilot Amando Lucero studied the sky intently. Cloud cover was moving in. The wind was changing. Variable at the moment, it appeared to be shifting out of the west. This was good news. It meant they could forgo the time-consuming process of tacking and run in a broad reach to *La Florida*. Lucero's last astrolabe reading had placed them at 28° 60' North latitude, just south of their target latitude of 29° for *Bahia Honda*.

The flagship *Maria* fired off its first signal cannon of the evening. A single report to show everyone, *"I am here"*. To Lucero it looked like *Maria* was moving to a new heading that was a little north of east. This made sense if they were going to find the bay. He called for a change in direction and positioned *Doncella* such that *Maria's* lights were just off the starboard bow. Looking around, it appeared all of the other ships were making a similar correction.

Earlier, Fray de Palos had given a short mass. There had been no service during the day, but with the darkness, he had talked of Holy Week and the last days of the Savior. Lucero chuckled to himself. He thought of the frustrated Fray trying to light a candle on the windy deck. Fray Palos had finally given up and promised to try again, below deck.

The mass broke up early.

Throughout the night the wind increased; not a steady blow, but gusty, primarily westerly and moving in a broad spectrum from south to northwest. It was a busy night for Lucero. Before midnight the stars disappeared. The moon, now high in the sky, had been swallowed up as well, its once bright glow hidden from view with only a faint back light behind the clouds. He was forced to guide the ship by compass alone...and by their relative position next to the flagship.

07 April, 1528

Aboard the Caravel, Maria De La Meridionales

Mares

Janero Flores yawned. He had been up all night. The wind was now directly astern and their heading was fixed to the northeast. The breeze had settled down sometime in the early morning, allowing the exhausted crew to set the sails and get some sleep. The morning light was slow in coming, a gray pall of overcast hung over them; a lingering haze washed out the horizon.

Looking around, there were only two other ships in view. On the starboard side, *Reina de Napoles* was almost within hailing distance. Janero could see pilot Quiroz on the poop deck looking back at him.

Both pilots waved a greeting.

Directly astern and just visible in the haze was the caravel *La Doncella de Plata* moving steadily through the waves, its bow spray turning to mist before settling back on the surface. Janero turned, Diego Miruello had moved up next to him.

"The wind has dropped considerably but we have a good heading pilot Flores".

"Ah, *buenos dias* Diego, I would like to see a clear sky today."

The overcast had begun to lighten. Overhead, wisps of blue would appear, but at sea level visibility was restricted. They continued on, following a northeast compass heading, a slight breeze holding steady from astern. These conditions persisted for only an hour. At mid-morning the breeze slackened once again. Ahead of them the horizon seemed to terminate in a wall of fog, a great towering cloud that extended out of sight in both directions. Janero had never seen fog such as this where the terminus was so well defined.

The ships entered into it as if passing through a curtain. Once inside, the visibility dropped to nothing. From the poop deck Janero could not even see amidships.

"This is very strange indeed!"

The slightest of wind continued to propel them forward, but there was no feeling of movement. The air was heavy with moisture and it soaked everything. Even taking a deep breath would cause one to begin coughing from the amount of water taken into the lungs. Even the ship board sounds were muted. For an hour they moved through this netherworld of mist.

Then it happened. Quite unexpectedly the *Maria* sailed out of the enormous fog bank. Sunlight exploded onto the decks. Turning to his right Janero saw *Reina* emerge from the mist like a ghost ship, its white sails in contrast to the fog line that extended into the distance. He spun around and caught *Doncella* as she also emerged from the wall of white.

Looking forward there was more haze...and on both sides...it was as if they were in a giant amphitheater surrounded by white walls that extended high above, only to disappear in a dazzling blue sky.

No other ships were visible.

Janero turned to his boatswain, "*Senor* Alvarez. I need someone above keeping a sharp eye."

The boatswain, Manuel Alvarez, ever anticipating Janero's commands already had a *marinero* scampering up the ratlines. "Pilot Flores, Pasquel will be in position very shortly."

"Let me know as soon as he sees anything...this is very unusual." Pausing, he looked at Miruello, "Have you ever seen anything like this?"

"I have been between fog banks, but never surrounded by one...and this clearing...look, how the sun is warming the deck."

The deck, wet with mist, was heating up in the direct sunlight, faint wisps of steam rising into the air.

From above. "Ho! I see a ship."

Boatswain Alvarez backed up to better see the seaman high above. He cupped his hand,

"Can you tell who it is?"

There was a pause.

Impatiently Alvarez called up again, "Pasquel, who is it...where is it?"

"I can only see the masts and a bit of the topsail. It lays ahead, out from the port bow."

He was pointing.

Flores and Miruello moved to the port side of the ship, but could see nothing.

As *Maria* approached the far wall of fog, Pasquel sounded out from above, "The fog is lifting...I see her clearly now...it is *La Estrella*...and I see..."

Narvaez had joined them at the bottom of the stairs, his booming voice easily carrying to the top of the mast. "What is it you see Pasquel, come on man, tell us!"

"It is land *Adelentado*, I see land!"

The fog began to dissipate as if a giant hand had suddenly wiped it away. Where before a solid wall of fog existed, now only wisps rapidly disappeared into the air.

From the deck, *La Estrella* came into view, but it was very far out and only the tops of the mast shown to those on deck. Strain as he might, beyond *La Estrella,* only the watery horizon appeared to Flores. He yelled up to Pasquel, "Are you sure it's land?"

The seaman could hardly contain himself, "*Si* pilot Flores, it stretches out of sight in both directions".

Narvaez bounded up the steps, a broad smile on his face, "*La Florida*!"

Turning to the boatswain, "Mr. Alvarez let us announce our arrival."

The smiling boatswain issued a series of commands and two of the ship's cannons fired simultaneously. From across the water the deck guns of *Reina* and *Doncella* answered in reply. Again, the *Maria* discharged her cannon.

Narvaez laughed aloud and called out, "Mr Alvarez that should be enough. Any more and we will deplete our powder."

The deck was flooded with soldiers and colonists vying for their first view of *La Florida*. They shook hands, congratulated each other and laughed. They had finally arrived.

Flores was less elated. Once again he yelled up to the lookout, "Pasquel, do you see *El Delfin*?"

There was a moments pause as the seaman extracted himself from viewing the approaching landmass and scanned about in all directions.

Now, with shared concern Pasquel answered, "There are no other sails in sight."

CHAPTER 09

Florida

La Florida

From his vantage point the changing sea color indicated shallows, shoals and sandbars. Eraso looked up and followed the lookout's points both to port and starboard. Breakwaters were all around them. The fog was clearing rapidly now. A small island to port...and beyond...the unmistakable coastline of La Florida emerged, its green presence continuing in both directions.

07 April, 1528

Aboard the Caravel El Delfin, off the Coast of Florida

From above came the call, *"Rompeolas al Puerto"*…breakwater to the port.

The lookout's warning passed through the ship like electricity.

Pilot Jose Eraso rushed to the side. Even from the deck, the unmistakable sign of breaking waves was clear.

His commands were instant, "Boatswain, lower the fore and mainsail, tighten the lateen and employ the sounding line!" He yelled to the Helmsman to bring the rudder hard around.

Another call from the mast, *"Tierra al Puerto"*…land off the port side. Behind the breakwater the unmistakable silhouette of trees and shoreline emerged from the mist. It looked to be an island or narrow peninsula less than a league distant.

El Delfin heeled to the left as the rudder came about. *Marineros* in the rigging scrambled to lower the fore and mainsails.

"*Amo, cuatro braza*", the guardian called out 4 fathoms.

"*Bajios, Bajios*", the lookout was fairly frantic. From his vantage point the changing sea color indicated shallows, shoals and sand-bars. Eraso looked up and followed the lookout's points both to port and starboard. Breakwaters were all around them. The fog was clearing rapidly now. A small island to port...and beyond...the un-mistakable coastline of *La Florida* emerged, its green presence con-tinuing in both directions.

El Delfin had passed rapidly from deep water to shallows, masked by the fog, the telltale signs had been hidden until it was too late. The forward speed carried the caravel deep into the dangerous water.

Eraso called out, "Boatswain, lower the anchors". At least if they could get *El Delfin* stabilized they could evaluate the situation be-fore the ship ran aground.

"*Amo, Tres braza*", the guardian called out 3 fathoms.

Jose Eraso faintly felt the first hints of sea floor scrapping the keel. Instinctively he grabbed for a handhold. It was at this moment that *El Delphin* hit the shoal. Already under stress from the hard turn to starboard, momentum was transferred laterally and the large vessel heeled heavily to port but not before carrying itself well onto the rocks and sand below. A grinding roar filled the air as the forward energy rapidly dissipated. Hull planking cracked and anything loose became a projectile. Catapulted from their positions in the rigging, *marineros* flailed through the air landing heavily in the sea on the leeward side of the ship. Others, fouled in the ropes, swung in arcs dashing against the masts and spars. Below decks soldiers and col-onists alike were thrown against the hull and decking with great force. Horses in their transport slings and hobbles flailed about. One mare broke its neck, one gelding suffered a broken leg. The west wind pushing on the half-lowered sails completed the disaster as *El Delphin* heeled further over, finally rested on its side, the main mast severed at the base.

On the quarterdeck Eraso had been thrown into the port side mizzenmast shrouds, now partially submerged. His head was underwater and his legs flailed about above him. Twisting about, he freed himself from the entanglement and surfaced. He was dazed. Little fireflies of light danced in front of his eyes. His left arm and side hurt. Holding tightly to the shroud lines and partially submerged, Jose struggled to clear his head.

The sounds of the moment slowly began to register. Men were cursing, horses banged about, their muffled screams rising from the holds. Looking about, *El Delfin* rested on her port side, wave action now rocking the hull. The mainmast was broken at its base, the mizzenmast cracked halfway up. The mizzenmast boom had disconnected and it and the sail floated in the water next to him. Turning to his side he could now clearly see a small island in the distance. Movement caught his eye. Watching in amazement, a *marinero* seemed to walk across the water toward him. He blinked. Jose recognized the man; it was Pepe Mallaina one of the *marineros* assigned to lower the mainsail.

"Pilot Eraso, are you hurt?"

Using his right arm to raise himself he could now see that Pepe was walking toward him on a *banco de arena*…a sandbar, the water only slightly above his knees. The collision had thrown Pepe completely clear of *El Delfin* landing in the deeper water just on the other side of the sandbar. Unhurt, he was able to swim to the shallow water and walk towards the now floundering vessel.

Jose Eraso extracted himself from the tangled ropes and clambered back towards the now slanted quarterdeck.

"Mallaina, help me to get the hatch open, there are still people below."

There was already a multitude of people clambering along the now almost horizontal stairs. Most were uninjured, but a few had cuts and abrasions. There was a bottleneck at the door as people tried to negotiate the steeply slanted deck.

Mallaina and Eraso made their way along the gunnels until they reached the area of the deck amidships where the hatch was located. This had been dogged down and required considerable effort to release. Four turnbuckles had to be loosened. The last one fell away and the heavy cover slid down the deck and into the water.

The sight inside the hold was complete chaos. Cargo, and animals were displaced and thrown about. Several pigs had been liberated from their wooden cages and were running about, their squeals adding to the mayhem. More colonists, soldiers and crew members made their way out and balanced themselves on the rocking hull. The commander of the military group, Captain Juan Sarrano, dropped out of the hold. Carefully using the shroud lines for support he moved up next to Eraso and Mallaina.

Wind, wave action and rising tide was slowly pushing *El Delfin* higher onto the sandbar.

Looking to the stern Eraso saw that the boatswain and three *marineros* had freed the ship's boat and were bringing it around to the leeward side.

Boatswain Diego Mendosa called out, "Senor Eraso, I fear the tide is rising and we need to move these people off the ship". He stood in the bow and threw a line. Jumping into the shallow water he guided the boat up against the overturned hull.

Knowing that the ships boat would only hold ten including the four oarsmen, Eraso called out directions, "Boatswain, take six soldiers to secure that island". He pointed to the small island just to the north. He turned to Captain Sarrano for confirmation and got a nod of agreement.

Quickly, Sarrano chose three crossbowman and two pikes men for the journey…he would accompany them. There was a slight delay as the necessary equipment was gathered from the ship. The soldiers would don their armor while underway. As soon as all was loaded, the boatswain, walking beside, guided the boat into deeper water. The oarsmen began their pull to the island.

07 April, 1528

Aboard the Brigantine La Estrella, off the Coast of Florida

De Vaca and Jimenez were startled by the boom of the guns behind them. In the fog they had unknowingly outdistanced their flagship. They had been following *El Delfin* who, in turn, was well ahead of them.

Aboard *La Estrella* the distant sail had suddenly disappeared. At first this wasn't a concern because *El Delfin* had been fading in and out of the fog all morning. Alvar climbed into the shrouds for a better look. The sky was clearing and large patches of blue were now overhead. The soft green on the horizon was a welcome sight…finally, the coast of *La Florida*.

The hold doors were thrown open and small groups of soldiers and colonists were moving about the deck. Trailing to starboard, Alvar could see *Maria*…behind her *La Doncella*. Off *Maria's* starboard bow was *Reina*. The wind, now due west, was hurrying them along. To the east a line of gray haze still hung in the air, made all the more foreboding by the brightness of the sky now overhead.

From above, the lookout called, "*Vela avistada al puerto!*" The lookout had spotted *El Delfin's* sail. Following his point, Alvar strained to make it out but could see nothing from the quarterdeck.

Again, partially climbing the mizzenmast shrouds Alvar called to the lookout, "Where is she?"

"Si Alguacil, two points off the port bow. I can see her sails...but something is different, it's very low in the water...!"

Alvar continued further up the shrouds. As he climbed, a patch of white came into view, it appeared to be the topsail but there was still mist in the area and he couldn't get a clear view. Before regaining the deck Alvar lingered, taking in the expanse before him. The earlier grayness of the sea was gone. Looking to the horizon, the ocean before him was a patchwork of blue and green. Shafts of sunlight shone through the rapidly dissipating clouds. Below he watched the dolphins chasing the bow wave. Further out, a giant sea turtle languished on the surface.

Again, the voice of the lookout called from above...*rompeolas*...I see breakwater...there are shoals ahead!

Jimenez was quick to react. "Lower sails, man the sounding line." *Marineros* quickly clambered into the rigging. The boatswain and *guardian* busily oversaw each operation. The rapid disappearance of *El Delphin's* sail and the sighting of breakwater could only mean that the caravel was in trouble.

"What of *El Delfin*?" Alvar called to the lookout.

"Alguacil, the fog is still heavy ahead but she appears to be broached...I see waves breaking around her..." the distance was still too great. "There looks to be an island to her port side".

The morning sun began to show brightly as the last visages of the early morning fog bank burned off. The moderate morning winds were beginning to pick up. Still from the west, the breeze was steady but not uncomfortable.

Movement on the deck...

Marineros were preparing the ships boat. During normal operation it was overturned and lashed down to the deck. Freeing up the retaining ropes, the boat was quickly righted. Oars that were tied together and stored underneath were freed up and placed inside. Four oarsmen were standing by.

Alvar ambled over to where military captain Alonso Pantoja was in a discussion with the pilot.

Jimenez nodded to De Vaca, "Capitan Pantoja, we will approach *El Delfin* cautiously. It appears she may have run aground. I am not familiar with the coast of *La Florida*. Pilot Miruelo aboard *Maria* will have to address this when he comes up. They look to be a half hour behind us."

Years before Jimenez explained he had accompanied a slave expedition to *La Florida* as a cabin boy, but only in the area below latitude 26°. Even so he had been much too young to remember much of the voyage.

Addressing Alvar he continued, "*Alguacil, m*y readings indicate we are at a latitude of 29°. This is the correct latitude given to us by pilot Miruelo for the great bay."

07 April, 1528

Aboard the Caravel Maria De La Meridionales

Mares, in the Gulf of Mexico

Aboard *Maria,* Narvaez paced the deck. The initial euphoria over the appearance of land had evaporated as the *Maria* closed on *El Delfin* and *La Estrella.* The little brigantine was moving slowly forward into the area of the breakwater.

"Delays in the *Islas Canarias*, delays in *La Espaniola*, delays in *Cuba*!" Narvaez was talking to no one in particular.

He had already lost two ships in *Cuba*. Now, it appeared as if he was to lose another. It would be another half hour before they were close enough to access the damage, but any shipwreck in these waters was not good. Supplies would be lost; horses would be injured or dead. Soldiers and colonists, if not injured, would be dispirited. Transferring people and materials was time consuming and dangerous. Worse, the men, animals and recovered supplies would put a burden on the already overloaded ships.

Narvaez bellowed up to the lookout, "*Que esta sucediendo…*what is happening, can you see anything more?"

"Governor, *La Estrella* is very close to *El Delfin*. I can see a ship's boat in the water moving toward the ship."

Impatiently Narvaez asked, "And what of the condition of *El Delfin*"?

"Governor, she is broached. She is lying on her port side and the main mast seems to be broken."

The sun was visible now and the seas had quieted. Below him a *marinero* was heaving out the sounding line. With most sails lowered the *Maria* slowly moved toward *El Delfin*. Off the starboard stern the *Reina de Napoles* and *La Doncella* had also reduced sail.

Frustrated, Panfillo looked for the pilot Miruelo but he was at the bow busily adjusting the astrolabe.

"Pilot Miruelo!"

Navarez's voice literally shook the deck. All those aboard turned toward the governor. When the governor was in this kind of mood, one paid attention.

"Pilot Miruelo, I need your council, join me on the quarterdeck."

Diego Miruelo scurried across the deck. Panfillo watched him with growing disdain. The pilot had been added to the expedition during the winter while Narvaez was in *Habana*. Pilots familiar with the cost of *La Florida* were hard to find…those that were available, charged high prices for their service. The expedition was costing Narvaez more than he expected, and the loss of two complete ships, crews and supplies near the port of *Trinidad* had severely curtailed his spending. Miruelo had offered himself at reasonable rate and Narvaez hired him. Now he was having second thoughts.

"Pequena mierda de la comadreja…little weasel shit", Narvaez thought out loud…a little too loud. One of the seamen, working close by, stifled a laugh. Janero Flores also heard the remark and shook his head. He didn't share the opinion of the *Adelantado*.

There was something in the man's character that made Narvaez uncomfortable. He was cowardly and without honor, of that Panfillo was sure. Supposedly, Miruelo had gained his knowledge while serving in the *naves de la esclavitud*…slave ships…that plied the coasts of the peninsula in search of *Indians*. Most slavers that Panfillo had met were despicable men who were at their best when in a position of power over the helpless.

It wasn't that Narvaez had anything against slavery…he didn't…it was necessary and profitable. The *Indians* were heathens and non-*Christians*. It was God's will that they be used for the betterment of *Spain*. Be that as it may, Narvaez held the little weasel shit responsible for the grounding just after leaving *Jagua*. It had cost them 15 days.

Miruelo sidled up to the governor, *"Si Adelantado,* how may I be of assistance?"

Flores joined them.

"Senor Miruelo, we have arrived at *La Florida*...of that I am sure." With that Narvaez swept his arm in a long arc indicating the broad expanse of land now visible to them.

"Do we have any knowledge of where in *La Florida* we are?"

"*Adelantado*, my most recent astrolabe reading positions us a little past 29° latitude. We should be very close to *Bahia Honda*. However, we are not yet close enough to recognize any identifiable landmarks."

Narvaez seemed to take this all in while he stared across the water.

"Here's what I want you to do Miruelo."

"*Si Adelantado.*"

"Depending on the damage to *El Delfin,* we may be here awhile. I want you to join A*lguacil* de Vaca on *La Estrella* and use your knowledge to find the great bay...*Bahia Honda.*

Flores could not help but hear the sarcasm in Narvaez's voice.

Narvaez continued, "The *Padron Real* specifies the Great Bay at 29° latitude. According to what Senor Flores tells me, we are there."

Flores spoke for the first time, "I have found the *Padron Real* to be in error before, and am ever suspicious of its contents."

Narvaez considered the comment. "If the search continues to the north and finds nothing it will verify that the Great Bay lies to our south."

Flores nodded, "I agree *Adelantado.*"

Turning to Miruelo, Narvaez thought for a moment, "*La Estrella* is of slight draft and the best equipped to scout the shoreline. Sail the coast northward with the object of finding *Bahia Honda.*"

Narvaez stopped and looked at Miruelo as if expecting an answer.

"I understand *Adelantado.*"

"If you find *Bahia Honda,* return as quickly as possible with the information."

"*Si Adelantado.*

Turning to Flores, Narvaez included the head pilot in the decision. "Pilot Flores, do you agree with this strategy?"

"*Si Adelantado,* but I would add that they limit their search. We are in unknown waters and shouldn't become too far separated. We will need pilot Miruelo's guidance when we have finished here.

Narvaez considered this a moment, "Good advice." He looked again at Miruelo.

"Investigate what lies to the immediate north of us, but return as soon s you are assured the bay is not in that direction. Do you understand?"

"*Si Adelantado.*"

"Good. As soon as we anchor, take the boat over to *La Estrella* and explain to Senor De Vaca my wishes. I want you to leave as soon as possible."

With that, Narvaez turned and left the poop deck. Miruelo let out a breath of air...he was clearly intimidated by Narvaez.

"The governor is a difficult man!"

Not wanting to broach this subject Flores asked, "Tell me about *Bahia Honda.*"

"It is a bay of immense size. From the sea it is somewhat hidden by a line of barrier *islas,* some of which are very long. Once inside it stretches inland 8 leagues to a peninsula that separates two smaller bays. The bay to the left is half again bigger than the one on the right and extends another five leagues inland. The main part of the bay is very large...about 3 leagues at its widest."

Flores was impressed. Nothing in the Indies and not even the bay at Cadiz could compare with this.

07 April, 1528

Aboard the Caravel El Delfin off the Coast of Florida

The ships boat had returned from the island for the third time. Jose Eraso had been busy trying to move the horses out of the ship. With *El Delfin* listing heavily on the shallow shoal, everything below was thrown about and movement was difficult. The horses, already weak from the long journey were severely stressed and laying on their sides in the canted hold. The first order was to blindfold the animals and then truss up their legs so as not to thrash about.

It took as many as eight men to drag the beasts out of the hold where they would slither down the deck and into the water...now waste deep. Once in the water two men would keep the terrified animal's head above water while others released the leg restraints. This was difficult because, even in their weakened condition, a kick could break ribs or send a man reeling. Free from restraints, with only the blindfold on, the horse would stand trembling and breathing hard. As quick as possible, two handlers would move the horse into shallower water.

The horses could almost walk to the island save for a strip of water 500 *yara* wide that was ten to fifteen feet deep. Here they would have to swim. Weakened by the journey, however, they were in no condition to swim and each had to be accompanied by two boats, one to each side. A seaman in front, holding bridle lines, kept the animal's head above water, while seaman further back would support the horses weight with a girth strap that passed under the animal from boat to boat.

It was a slow process.

On the small island, *Capitan* Sarrano and his men had found it un-inhabited and now assisted with the growing number of horses, pigs and people that were accumulating. Vegetation was limited to man-groves and a few sparse patches of sea oats growing in the open areas. This was quickly consumed by the ravenous horses.

There was no water. A boat had been dispatched to the *Maria*, now on site, to bring a barrel to the island. It would have to be rationed.

07 April, 1528

Aboard the Brigantine La Estrella off the Coast of Florida

Alvar was returning from the wreck aboard the ship's boat. Be-sides the oarsmen, five soldiers from *El Delfin* accompanied him. Earlier, when they had arrived at the shipwreck, all manner of colonists, soldiers and seaman were wading about not knowing what to do. There was an on-going effort to rescue horses and ma-terial, but so far only a few passengers and crew had made it to the island.

Alvar had quickly evaluated the scene and determined that *El Delfin* would not sail again. He called out to several men on the ship to gather their things and join him. Amongst a small pile of personal items, weapons and accouterments they had boarded the small boat. He would take them back to *La Estrella*.

Once tied up, it took a little time to unload the men and equipment. Coming on deck Alvar was surprised to see pilot Miruelo talking with Angel Jimenez on the poop deck.

"Senor Miruelo, what brings you to *La Estrella*?"

"Greetings *Alguicil* De Vaca, I bring compliments from the *Adelen-tado* and sailing orders for your ship.

07 April, 1528

Aboard the Brigantine La Estrella, off the Coast of Florida

They left the wreck site at the noon hour, leaving one of their two boats and crew to assist in the rescue effort. With a fair west wind *La Estrella* sailed easily past the shoals and *cayos* that had trapped *El Delfin*. As they moved northward, the shoreline began to gently recede to the east forming what appeared to be a shallow bay. It was marked by an endless array of inlets, cuts and waterways. At water's edge, mangroves abounded.

The water was shallow here and for a while, two parallel shoals forced *La Estrella* to lay off the shoreline a league or more. Each shoal was marked by elevated sandbars than shone bright white in the afternoon sun. There was also a subtle difference in the water, it was more turbid and of a different color. The source of this was soon discovered when the mouth of a large river was encountered after sailing no more than 5 leagues.

Coming upon the river's mouth several *marineros* threw a bucket into the water and with a rope attached drew it back onto the ship. The water was only slightly salty and they brought a cup for Alvar to taste.

"My first taste of *La Florida*!" Alvar took a sip and then handed the cup to Jimenez who agreed. As sunset was only a few hours away, Alvar ordered them to continue on.

07 April, 1528

Aboard the Brigantine La Estrella, off the Coast of Florida

La Estrella continued north, staying as close as possible to the shoreline. It was perilous going, for the water was of marginal depth. Only the shallow draft and excellent sailing characteristics of *La Estrella* allowed them to maneuver in these waters. Inland, a sea of grass waved in the wind. The grass lands were punctuated with groves of palms and hardwood trees. All aboard commented on the sweet smells that wafted across the water, as if in a flowering orchard in springtime. A large canoe was sighted gliding between two mangrove islets. The lookout called out and everyone stopped to look. At least ten *Indians* were effortlessly guiding their craft across a small bay when they, in turn, noticed *La Estrella*. Their pace abruptly quickened and just before disappearing behind the thick foliage the rearmost *Indio* picked up a bow and loosed and arrow toward them. It, of course, fell far short but reminded the *Spaniards* that they were in hostile country.

Alvar could only imagine what the *Indio* was thinking when he saw this strange aberration from another world coming upon them. He chuckled to himself.

As they continued northward, small rivers and streams continued to permeate the shoreline. At latitude 29° 26' they came upon a strange island whose protruding layout reminded Alvar of a large horseshoe. On its southern approach it was preceded by a shallow bay that teemed with water fowl. Flocks of pelicans, cormorants, ducks, egrets and all manner of gulls filled the air.

Passing the horseshoe shaped beach, the shoreline bulged to the west where a beautiful sandy beach extended into the water. Here the depth was very shallow and *La Estrella* had to put out further to sea to find even two fathoms under her keel. To the northwest an accumulation of islands thickly covered with beach grass stood just out from the mainland.

They continued northward another 3 leagues and encountered another river delta. Here, once again, the shoreline turned abruptly westward.

It was now almost evening and Miruelo approached Alvar. He motioned for pilot Jimenez to join them.

"*Algucil*, nothing during this day is recognizable to me. From my experiences I know that *La Florida* is but a large peninsula that protrudes off the mass of *Amichel*. As the line of the coast is now shifting west I feel that we are nearing that terminus. Any more travel in this direction is fruitless."

He looked to Jimenez who nodded in agreement. "My conclusion is that the latitude noted in the *Padron Real* is incorrect. We should return to the expedition and lead them to the south. In that direction I am sure we will find *Bahia Honda*."

All were in agreement and since the evening hours were close at hand *La Estrella* anchored in the bay and spent the night.

Sometime during the night a page woke Alvar to tell him that one of the sentries had seen a light on shore.

"My apologies *Agucil*, but as I was performing my duties the guard stationed aft asked me to inform you that a light was sighted."

Hurriedly dressing, he climbed to the poop deck and joined the young *Spanish* soldier who was intently peering shoreward. The night was dark and moonless with a partial cloud cover that eliminated most of the starlight. To the south an occasional flash of heat lightning briefly interrupted the darkness. Except for the lapping of water against the hull and the far away drone of waves on the shoreline there was no other sound. There it was again. They both watched as a faint light appeared. It appeared to be moving slowly along the shore. This continued for half an hour and then...it was gone. Alvar could sense the soldier's uneasiness and talked a bit about *Seville* and places familiar to both. It seemed to have a calming effect and after a time he left the aft deck and moved to the bow to check on the other sentry.

Making his way forward Alvar met Alonso Pantoja moving aft. He had also been notified of the sighting but had visited the forward sentry first. There was a brief discussion and it was determined that the crew should make the boat ready for departure. The night was clear, the moon was just rising and the wind was steady out of the northwest. They would sail further into the gulf to avoid hazards and return to the expedition.

08 April, 1528

Off the Coast of La Florida at the Wreck Site of El Delfin

Alonso de Castillo was exhausted. For two days they had labored to remove as much usable equipment from *El Delfin* as possible and distribute it amongst the three remaining ships. This had become increasingly difficult because the mild weather of only two days ago had worsened. Strong westerly winds now blew onshore pushing three foot waves that slammed against *El Delfin*. The caravel was beginning to break up and it was becoming ever more dangerous to go on board. White caps covered the ocean surface and sea spray, blown up by the wind, partially obscured the coast.

Looking east across the water, Alonso could see the small island that only yesterday served as a collection point for everything removed from the wreck. Now, it was virtually empty with only a few broken crates left to mark their presence.

They had loaded the supplies and hardware first, leaving people and animals on the island. Finally, yesterday the horses were moved onto the ships, a long and tiring process. This morning, the last of the people, seaman, colonist and soldiers, were transported by teams of oarsmen that strained against the head winds. Alonso had commanded his men to relieve the exhausted sailors and had even taken his place at the oar locks.

The *Adelantado* had been everywhere. Supervising the operation, he had pushed, prodded and forced the pampered *Spanish hildagos,* the non titled noblemen, to assist in the effort. Exasperated at one haughty dandy, a Juan Velazquez, the *Adelantado* threw him overboard. If there hadn't been a rescue boat close by, the wretch would have drowned. No one else dared argue with Narvaez. Now as Alonso looked about him, soldiers, sailors, colonists, servants and slaves alike lay prostrate on the deck, absolutely worn out from their efforts. The work was done, however, and now they waited for *La Estrella* to return before continuing the journey.

08 April, 1528

Aboard the Caravel Reina De Napoles off the Coast of Florida

Estevan sat on the aft rail, his legs dangling over the side. In his hands was a length of twine to which he had fastened a hook and a piece of salt pork. He had picked this location because it was somewhat leeward of the strong wind that was blowing. The line would drift away from the ship instead of becoming entangled by the barnacles on the hull. He lowered it about four feet into the water and was waiting for the familiar tug.

Save for the noise of the wind and the waves banging against the hull, the ship was unusually quiet. Everyone was resting. The last few days had been very busy. His back and shoulders ached from loading supplies and rowing.

Estevan thought to himself. "If I'm sore how bad must it be for these soft *gueros* with the velvet hands?" He laughed to himself.

At that moment a strong gust of wind came up and he had to steady himself on the rail. Looking up, something caught his eye on the horizon. It was a sail. To no one in particular he hollered, "Sail Ho, *La Estrella* has returned!"

CHAPTER 10

Blind Mouth Bay

Bahía de boca ciega

They would call this main bay, Boco Ciega...blind mouth...because there appeared to be no river system feeding it.

08 April, 1528

Aboard the Brigantine La Estrella, off the Coast of Florida Near Present Day Cedar Key

They sailed away from *El Delfin,* now laying completely on her port side. A bit of torn sail still attached to a yardarm on the main mast fluttered wildly in the rising wind. Breakers beat against the overturned hull, generating a mist that blew shoreward in a steamy cloud. Alvar watched as the wreck passed from sight. It had been a constant companion, a home for some, a workplace for others. Now, in a matter of months, it would be torn apart and obliterated on the shoals of *La Florida.*

The weather was worsening. Heading south southeast on a starboard tack, the remaining four ships of the expedition heeled heavily in the west wind. Almost immediately, the shoreline trailed off eastward and the ships made the necessary turn to port. Now, running in a broad reach, the decks leveled somewhat and the ride became smoother. Aboard *La Estrella,* Diego Miruelo studied the shoreline looking for a anything recognizable. So far there was nothing. Miruelo, now permanently assigned to *La Estrela* by Narvaez was in the lead, the lighter drafted brigantine the obvious ship to lead the expedition in these unknown waters.

At first the sharply receding shoreline was thought to be the entrance to the Deep Bay, but after traveling only four leagues, they encountered the mouth of a river and a broad shallow delta. It was not *Bahia Hondo*. From here the shoreline turned south again. The ships corrected their course. Again the wind blew hard on the starboard side. They stayed well out, for the shore was marked by numerous obstructions.

They continued on. The extremely strong wind forced all the ships to reduce sail. As noon approached the temperature climbed and, had it not been for the wind, the heat would have been stifling. But, the heat and wind also brought storms. A little after noon a broad squall line seemed to appear from nowhere. As it approached, the lightning split the sky. The booming of the thunder carried across the water reverberating through the little ships. Almost as quick as it appeared the storm dissolved into sunshine and blue skies again.

Just after passing the delta of another river they came upon a shallow bay marked with an uncountable number of shoals and mangrove islands. Here the larger caravels stayed well off shore while *La Estrella* investigated. Alvar was amazed by the number of birds. Vast flocks wheeled and turned in the sky, alternately landing and taking off from the water's surface.

Again, another line of squalls rapidly descended on the expedition from the west. Same as before, the lightning was fierce and the rain came in torrents. No sooner had one storm passed when another would come upon them. This lasted for almost an hour and then, miraculously, the sky cleared once again. Alvar watched as the dark signature of the storm moved inland, spectacular shafts of lightning stabbing into the land below.

The profusion of little isles and mangrove swamps continued. All the ships of the expedition stayed well offshore while *La Estrella* ventured into this maze. Exposed sand bars seemed to cross the area in all directions. Closer in, the mouth of another river was encountered...or was it many rivers? The coast line was a labyrinth of inlets and coves. *La Estrella* went forth to explore. The little brigantine threading its way through the many shallow inlets checking for any kind of suitable bay. All were shallow and unsuitable.

They moved on, actually sailing south by southwest to follow the coastline as it bulged out. The small mangrove isles that had choked the shore now gave way to long barrier islands that paralleled the coast. Now *La Estrella* entered a deep protected sound. To the west was a long barrier island, to the east the shore of La Florida. Because the hour was getting late Alvar made a decision to lead the other boats into this bay for the evening anchorage. They sailed out to rejoin the other vessels.

As *La Estrella* arrived a boat from the *Maria* had been sent out to meet them. Pulling alongside, the guardian called up to Alvar.

"Greetings *Algucil*. The *Adelentado* requests the presence of you and *senor* Miruelo aboard the flagship as soon as possible."

Just as Alvar and Miruelo boarded the boat the anchor from *La Estrella* was released with a clatter of chains and a huge spray of water that doused all the occupants. Angrily, Alvar looked up at the ship, but not a face could be seen. Apparently all were hiding behind the gunnels, undoubtedly enjoying their little joke.

As the *marineros* rowed toward the flagship Alvar's anger abated. He thought about what just happened and had to smile to himself.

08 April, 1528

Aboard the Caravel Maria De La Meridionales

Mares, off the Coast of Florida Near Present Day

Port Richey

Narvaez was dark and sullen as De Vaca and Miruelo approached. He ignored Miruelo.

"Senor De Vaca, what are your thoughts on the Deep Bay?"

Alvar thought a moment. "*Adelatado*, in our journey to the north we did not encounter the Deep Bay and although I am not a navigator, I feel certain that its presence lies to the south."

Navaez's good eye bore down on De Vaca, "Are you sure that the mouth of the bay was not passed by mistake?"

Annoyed, Alvar answered curtly, "No, your excellency, we coasted the shoreline very closely, at times in no more than two *brazas*...fathoms. If the mouth of a deep bay had been present, we would have seen it."

"And what of the *Espejo*?"

"Again, your excellency, I am no navigator but I feel the the *Espejo* is in error."

Alvar looked to Janero Flores who was standing next to Narvaez. He nodded in agreement.

Alvar continued, "Today we have encountered many bays, but they all have been shallow and fraught with obstructions. The land appears to be swampy and drained by many rivers and streams that cut the coast with inlets, coves and numerous *cayos*. It is nothing like what I have heard of the Deep Bay. Now we have come upon a deep sound that I believe would be ideal for the evening anchorage."

Narvaez turned toward Miruelo and exploded, "And just where is the Deep Bay, pilot Miruelo!"

Diego Miruelo seemed to shrink in size as he stammered, "*Adelantado*, my travels to *La Florida* were always...ah...limited to the Deep Bay and the land immediately to the south.

"I don't need excuses pilot Miruelo, I need to find the Deep Bay. Our horses grow weaker by the hour and our supplies have dwindled to nothing.

Miruelo seemed to stiffen, "My experience with the Deep Bay was but two forays out of *Habana*. I am familiar with it, the equally large bay further south and the land in between...but...respectfully, *Adelantado* my greatest area of expertise is the area of *Panuco* and *New Spain*...our original destination, and the destination for which you procured my employment."

Narvaez was about to lose control of his famous temper. It was Janero Flores who stepped forward. "From what I am hearing, it seems we were blown a considerable distance to the north and the bay of which pilot Miruelo speaks has to be further south. Tonight we should find a suitable anchorage and if there are favorable winds in the morning we should continue on as rapidly as possible. Once we have identified *Bahia Hondo*, our fleetest ship should be immediately offloaded and sent back to *Habana* for additional supplies." Flores stepped back into the group.

Looking up at the sun now dropping lower in the sky Narvaez continued, "We will finish this day and find a suitable place to anchor. Tomorrow is *Jueves Santo*; when we will pray and remember our savior. It will be the day that we go ashore and begin our royal entitlement."

There were nods of agreement all around, even Narvaez seemed satisfied with this plan. "Tonight we will anchor in the sound *Senor De Vaca* has discovered and tomorrow we will follow the coast one more day in search of the Deep Bay. If, by tomorrow night it is not found we will go ashore at the most desirous location."

At that Narvaez turned and walked off. No one except Campo accompanied him.

09 April, 1528

Aboard the Caravel La Doncella De Plata, off the Coast of Florida at the North End of St. Joseph Sound

Alonso de Castillo was awake early. The sun hadn't appeared over the mainland yet, but the sky was ablaze with dawn's promise. The order had already been given to bring in the anchor. The morning quiet was disturbed by sharp orders, curses, grunts and the sounds of the anchor chain banging against the hull.

Looking shoreward Alonso watched a pelican fold its wings and dive vertically into the calm morning water. Reappearing on the surface, the effort was rewarded by a fish tail hanging from its beak. A nod of the head backward and the tail disappeared. Quickly the pelican was airborne again in quest of another meal. Beyond the pelican, the green shoreline was just becoming distinct and except for the multitude of birds it seemed very quiet. He wondered how many eyes were looking back at him.

How he longed to go ashore. Alonso was not keen on sea travel and these months of being jammed aboard ship was wearing at him. He was not the only one. His men lay idle and bored, the perfect formula for trouble. Already, there had been more than a dozen fights and two knifings. Only two days prior, swords had been drawn. Had he not been present to hit one of the assailants over the head with a cooking pot, men may have died. Punishment for infractions such as these was severe and ranged from being tied to the mast to public floggings. He disliked punishing these men but it was necessary to maintain order. Both of the assailants had received 25 lashes.

Overhead Alonso heard the mainsail drop into place and looked up as the topsail also fell into position. *Marineros* hustled to tie off the clews and set the yards. Only a hint of a breeze was blowing, still from the south, but it was enough to get *Doncella* moving. Progress would be slow today with the contrary wind. To each side the *Maria* and *Reina* were moving as well. Further ahead, the little brigantine *La Estrella* was already under full sail and moving shoreward. All of the caravels returned to deep water while *La Estrella* investigated this area between the barrier islands.

09 April, 1528

Aboard the Caravel La Concella De Plata, off the Coast of Florida in St. Joseph Sound Near Clearwater Pass

Friar Juan de Palos was preparing for tonight's service, for Maundy Thursday was a holy day in Christendom, one of the many of holy week. Today the savior had broken bread for the last time with his band of loyal apostles. Tomorrow they would commemorate the pain and anguish the savior experienced as he died on the cross at *Calvary*, a death that Jesus had accepted for His love of all mankind. Palos was much moved by the thought of this as he moved to the front of the ship with bowed head and clasped hands. He walked carefully, for many of the seaman and passengers slept on deck, their blanketed forms contorted in all manner of positions. Usually he found the bow of the ship to be the most private. It was not to be on this day. Stretched across the open section of deck sprawled a burly seaman snoring loudly.

He stood over the seaman, hoping his presence would wake him. This not working, Palos noisily cleared his throat and was rewarded with a rasping fart as the seaman rolled over in his sleep. With that, the good friar swung a sandled foot that caught the man full in the buttocks.

"Holy Mary mother of God, who the hell kicked me!" The angry seaman jumped to his feet wiping the sleep out of his eyes. Recognizing the Friar, the seaman changed his tone, "Ah...excuse me *Padre*, I didn't know it was you." Palos made the sign of the cross as the seaman moved away.

"God be with you my son."

Here he would meditate and pray.

Before kneeling, Friar Palos scanned the horizon. Around *Doncella* the other two caravels of the expedition rested at anchor. To the southeast the sails of *La Estrella,* already underway, stood out against the shoreline as they proceeded further down the sound.

09 April, 1528

Aboard the Brigatine La Estrella, off the Coast of Florida in St. Joseph Sound Near Present Day Honeymoon Island

It was a marvelously clear day. Not a cloud could be seen. Alvar had climbed half way up the port ratlines for a better view. No mountains or hills disturbed the contour of this land, it seemed endlessly flat.

As they sailed further south into the sound Alvar straightened when he noticed a thin wisp of smoke rising into the air from one of the barrier islands. It was obviously a camp fire. He watched the island intently as it passed astern, but no other signs of habitation were visible.

After passing the island an inlet appeared leading back out to the open sea. The tide was coming in and the flow of water through this portal was swift. They determined to continue on down the sound.

To the south of the inlet the barrier islands continued unabated. Thick mangroves grew along the shorelines while further inland massive oak trees and palms towered against the oceans backdrop. Strangely, the forest abruptly ended, only to be replaced by huge tracts of grass and broad pristine beaches. The tall grass bowed to the on-shore breezes, sending long windrows undulating across its surface.

In his favorite lookout location, halfway up the ratlines on the main mast, Alvar was carried away by the grandeur of it all. He reasoned that this was the first time any *European* had gazed on such magnificent sights.

Their course continued south southwest. The shoreline seemed to be changing. Here it seemed more defined. Jimenez took an astrolabe reading and called out to Alvar.

"We are at 28 degrees and 01 minutes *Algucil*, well south of where the *Espejo* said we would find the Deep Bay."

Alvar dropped back down to the deck. "We will redraw this map when we return to *Spain.* While I'm there I will tell the royal cartographers what I think of their...*Espejo.*"

Turning to Miruelo who was standing next to him, Alvar inquired, "Pilot Miruelo, would it be possible to unknowingly pass by this Deep Bay as the *Adelentado* questioned when we were aboard the flagship?"

Miruelo laughed, "Senor De Vaca, this bay is enormous. From one side of the inlet one cannot see the other unless you are on the mast. To miss it, you would have to be a blind man."

The little brigantine continued down the sound, constantly altering course to avoid obstructions and to investigate the many bays and contours of the coast. Offshore, the remaining three ships of the expedition idled along, waiting for some sign from *La Estrella.* They passed another inlet and Alvar considered returning to the caravels. At noon, however, a large canoe with nine or ten men was spotted gliding close to shore. Alvar called for a change in course.

"Let us see where these *Indios* are traveling."

La Estrella entered the inlet but was forced to stay well away from the shallow, rock strewn shore. In the bow a *marinero* straddling the bow sprint, kept a sharp eye for obstructions while overhead in the *carajo* another seaman called out constant course corrections. On the starboard side a third seaman handled the sounding line, his hails sharp against the deck noise.

Alvar commanded all aboard to "proceed with as much silence as possible." Amazingly, the *Indians* in the canoe were so intent on their destination they hadn't seen the brigantine.

La Estrella cautiously moved closer. Commands on deck were whispered.

The *Indians* were entering a shallow bay when the low rumble of thunder drifted across the water. Alvar looked back to the west to see a dark line of threatening storm clouds forming on the horizon. It was a weather pattern that seemed to be common for this latitude; clear mornings followed by brief afternoon downpours.

Almost into the shallow bay, one of the *Indians* turned as another clap of thunder sounded. With a start he sighted the brigantine outlined against the upcoming storm. Standing, he called out to the other rowers who in unison turned to see this strange apparition. The change in balance almost caused the canoe to capsize and Alvar laughed as the *Indians* scrambled to set it upright. Regaining their composure, the canoe and its passengers quickly disappeared into a line of mangroves while the rowers took furtive looks over their shoulders.

"We will not see them again."

Finally, with the path ahead narrowing, Alvar ordered *La Estrella* to return to the passed inlet so as to rejoin the caravels. Once in the gulf, a signal shot from the *Maria* boomed across the water. Narvaez was requesting their presence.

09 April, 1528

Aboard the Caravel Maria De La Merdionales Mares, in the Gulf, off the Coast of Florida Near Present Day Clearwater Beach

Panfilo was seated at the edge of the poop deck, his feet resting on the rungs of the steps. Below him were assembled the military captains and pilots of the three caravels. The representatives from *La Estrella* were just arriving. The three caravels had remained well clear of the shoreline and it had taken some time for the brigantine to make its way out to them. This had been slowed somewhat by the afternoon squall that descended upon them while in route. The crew had been forced to lower sails and tack against the gust front that threatened to blow them back to shore. As it passed, the wind dropped to nil. Sheets of water fell for half an hour, "like being poured from a bucket." For this half hour the rain continued and then, abruptly, it stopped. Clear sky reappeared and the dark mass of storm had moved rapidly to the east.

Still completely soaked, De Vaca, Miruelo, Jimenez and Pantoja joined the gathering. Campo scurried about, offering water to the new arrivals.

Finally, Panfilo stood up and addressed the group. "*Senor* De Vaca do you have anything to report?" All heads turned toward Alvar.

"*Adelantado*, we have investigated many of the bays and estuaries along the coast and have, as yet, not located *Bahia Hondo*. I have seen more than a few signs of *Indio* habitation, however, and just before you summoned us, observed a large canoe making its way along the shore."

Narvaez considered that a moment and then addressed Miruelo with surprising servility. "Pilot Miruelo, what are your thoughts on *Bahia Hondo*?"

"Adelantado, as I have expressed, I am unfamiliar with the area immediately north of the *Deep Bay*. There is no doubt, however, that the bay is somewhere to the south and I have confidence that we will find it soon."

Looking to the east, Narvaez hesitated a moment and then started to talk, "Today we lost another horse. From here, I watched it's carcass float in the currents until the sharks found it. I watched them devour it, taking great bites out of the body. Soon it disappeared from view."

Narvaez stopped for effect and then began again. "Are we to end up like this horse, so weakened that we will be consumed just as the *tiburones* consumed this horse?" He looked at the group below him.

Many shook their heads, *"No, Adelantado!"*

Narvaez continued, "As soon as this meeting is concluded I will move to La Estrella and together with the pilots we will fin a suitable anchorage before the day is through.

There were nods of approval all around and many voiced their agreement. Friar Xuares nodded his head as Narvaez smiled at him.

09 April, 1528

Aboard the Brigantine La Estrella, off the Coast of Florida

Hanging on the ropes, Diego Miruelo studied the shoreline. He looked for an obvious peninsula, bay or islet, anything familiar that would guide him to *Bahia Hondo*...the Deep Bay.

Nothing.

Only once had he been north of *Bahia Hondo,* but that had been well out to sea and out of sight of shoreline particulars. He prayed that the bay would manifest itself, if for no other reason than to silence the *Adelentado*.

He climbed higher.

From Miruelo's vantage point it was easy to loose concentration, for there was so much to see from this height. One could look down into the water and see the multitudes of sea life scurrying out of the way of the advancing ship. Sea turtles dotted the surface as far as the eye could see and giant manta rays glided silently jut below the surface. Towards shore a pod of dolphin had corralled a school of mullet. The surface of the water churned, while overhead thousands of gulls circled to dine on the scraps of the mass feeding.

Below him on the aft deck, Narvaez chatted with De Vaca. The *Adelentado* had come aboard so as to choose a landing site. As always, *La Estrella*, with its shallow draft, led the expedition. This morning, however, the caravels would remain at anchor while *La Estrella* finished exploring a promising sound.

Narvaez seemed uncertain as to his choice of a landing site. He had several criteria, the first of which was a reasonable anchorage clear of obstructions. As to the ground, security was of prime importance. A clear view with open ground for the horses and, of course, drinking water were the main concerns. He asked the military captain, Alonso Pantoja, to join him.

Still protected by the coastal barrier of islands, this sound remained deep but was narrowing rapidly. Further ahead an accumulation of small islands seemed to dot their pathway. They could go no further. Narvaez called for the brigantine to reverse course and return to the caravels. The tide was running out as they passed through the inlet and into the gulf. At the anchorage Narvaez held a quick conference and briefed the pilots and captains of his intentions. They would continue south.

Now in the open sea, a brisk west wind whisked the four ships along. Even sailing close to the line of shoals and keys, the water remained deep and clear of obstructions. By noon the expedition had sailed three leagues further south. Still protected by the barrier islands, the shoreline took a decided turn to the southeast. They sailed on for another two leagues.

Narvaez had had enough. Seeing an inlet in the barrier islands approaching, he ordered *La Estrella* to turn shoreward. They passed easily through the opening and maneuvered around several small islands that blocked their way. This widened into a spacious bay with several other islands clustered about. To the north, the bay was bifurcated into two smaller bayous. *La Estrella* proceeded forward to investigate while the caravels made anchor.

Sailing cautiously up the eastern side, the small bayou quickly turned into a marshy conglomeration of mangroves and mud flats. Two smaller streams did enter this area, but neither was navigable. *La Estrella* came about and headed back out.

The bayou to the west was much larger and extended further inland. Cautiously, *La Estrella* moved up this waterway for about a league, but it also ended in mud flats and a tangle of mangroves. *La Estrella* then turned about and proceeded back down the west bayou into the main bay. They would call this main bay, *Boco Ciega*...blind mouth...because there appeared to be no river system feeding it.

La Estrella proceeded past the anchored caravels. Here the bay widened.

From above the lookout cried, "*Indios, Indios*" and all eyes turned skyward to see where the seaman was pointing.

To the larboard side, a cluster of thatch dwellings was visible on a prominent point of the mainland. As they drew nearer, several more could be seen in amongst the trees. Some of the dwellings were set atop mounds of earth and one larger structure located at the approximate center was set atop the largest of the mounds. At least three cooking fires burned the smoke from each quickly dissipated by the onshore breeze.

Along the shoreline, the curious inhabitants gawked at the strange visitors from the sea. Some moved boldly to the water's edge to get a better view, others retreated backward and peered at the *Spaniards* from behind trees.

After observing the *Indians,* Narvaez ordered *La Estrella* to set anchor. He would return to the other three ships who had held back from entering any further and were drifting serenely in the waters of the bay.

"Senor Jimenez, we will anchor here", cried out Narvaez. "Launch the boat, I need to get back to my flagship."

09 April, 1528

Aboard the Caravel Maria De La Merdionales Mares

Narvaez clamored aboard the *Maria* as soon as the boat pulled alongside. The caravels were well offshore and taking no chances of grounding with the low tide.

Narvaez turned to Janero Flores. "Bring us as close to *La Estrella* as you can. We have sounded the bay and believe it to be deep enough."

This was no port, but it would have to do. It was quite obvious that the *Adelantado* intended to offload here.

Narvaez immediately called for Alonso Enriquez, the tall, dour, comptroller of the expedition. Although a man with a sour personality and few words, he was a master arbitrator and would be the right person to lead an advance party to meet with the *Indians*. Narvaez further assigned his military captain Alejandro Tellez and two crossbowmen to accompany the comptroller. He sent his commissary and religious leader Friar Juan Xuarez along. Finally, he included the *Tiano* seaman whose Christian name was Marino Carmona. Carmona would serve as an interpreter or, at least be able to converse in sign language. With the oarsmen, the party would number 10. The oarsmen and crossbowmen would remain in the boats while Enriquez, Tellez, Xuarez, Carmona, and a flag bearer would attempt to parley with the inhabitants of the village.

Immediately across from the village was a small uninhabited island, no more than 300 *yara* from the shoreline. It represented an excellent neutral ground for a meeting.

Narvaez and Enriquez decided that this was where the party would go ashore. Narvaez himself had decided to remain on board the *Maria*, to stay aloof during the initial contact.

The boats were made ready and loaded with trade items. Supplies aboard the caravels had dwindled to almost nothing and Eniquez's first order of business would be to acquire food.

In the village, the inhabitants continued to crowd the beach watching and pointing at the new visitors. Several canoes had been launched and warily circled the expedition's ships from afar. Once the larger ships had anchored in place Enriquez and his small party pushed off from the *Maria* and began rowing toward the uninhabited island. The consternation among the natives seemed to grow; many began pulling back from the beach while others openly ran to the shelter of the trees.

On the boat, two of the four oarsmen were soldiers properly disguised as seamen. Diego Dorantes, a lieutenant and brother to Andre would accompany Tellez. Finally, Fray Juan Xuarez, at his insistence, would evaluate the spirituality of the *Indians*. And, of course, Elonso Enriquez as a representative of the king of *Spain* would be in command.

Enriquez studied the shoreline as they closed on the island. "Capitan Tellez, instruct your men to keep their weapons hidden below the gunnels, we want to appear peaceable...besides, there are many more of them than there are of us."

CHAPTER 11

Ugly Canoes

Canoas Feos

The strangers' canoe was so much different than anything Sih-la-pah had seen. It was very wide and looked hard to maneuver. Compared to the sleek craft of the Toco-ha-baho, it was ugly.

09 April, 1528

On the Beach of Boco Ciega Bay Near Present-Day Jungle Prada, Narvaez Park in St. Petersburg, Florida

Twinax-so-ha (*sunrise over the water*) had seen the "great clouds" as they first entered the bay. She had been busily digging turtle eggs in the sand. This part of the beach, untouched by mangrove trees, was a favorite nesting area for the great loggerheads that lumbered ashore in the dead of night to deposit their cache of eggs. Finding a site, she had been careful not to take all of the eggs. Her mother had taught her this.

"Always leave some and spirit turtle will return next year."

She had carefully covered the hole and then smoothed the sand. No evidence of her predation remained. She rose, picked up the basket, and, head down, continued walking the shoreline, looking for the tell-tale drag marks of the mother turtle as it returned to the sea.

She had stopped then. There was a presence...something different. Raising her head, she turned toward the bay. Suddenly, Twinax-so-ha dropped the basket of eggs and stumbled backward, falling to a sitting position on the sand. Before her, the great sails of the Nar-

vaez fleet slowly moved into the bay. Her only reference to this alien object was the great billowy clouds that frequented the sky over
her home.

Regaining her feet, Twinax-so-ha hurried off the sand and moved
back to the thick sea grass that bordered the beach. Here she
crouched down and silently watched.

The "great clouds" continued across the bay. Only then did she realize they were moving toward her village. She rose and hurriedly
began walking the return footpath, only to stop abruptly and return
for the basket of eggs. She had worked too hard to leave them lying
in the sand for the gulls.

Twinax-so-ha had lived her entire life on this bay and except for the
big winds that occasionally came upon them, hers was a quiet and
peaceful life. She really didn't know how old she was, only that her
mother had cut slash marks in the great council tree for every winter
that had passed since she was born. There was no numbering system.
Her language only had words for one to ten things or the amount of
fingers on both hands. Anything more than that was identified by
words such as *ceehi*...many, and *tahona*...more. Looking out at the
"great clouds", the word she used to quantify them was *tabo*, or the
fourth finger on her left hand, palms down, starting from the small-
est finger...*deechi*.

Stopping to catch her breath, she again peered out at the "clouds"
and studied them closer. In her excitement, she hadn't noticed the
large canoes that floated just below them. Somehow the two seemed
to be attached by large trees growing out of the canoes. What a
strange thing!

Twinax-so-ha wondered if she was having a spirit dream.

Up ahead, her sister and a group of other young girls were hiding
behind trees, their collection baskets strewn on the beach. All were
scared, some were crying. They saw them too!

A natural leader, Twinax-so-ha gathered them all into a group and proceeded down the trail, herding them along as quickly as possible. Soon the trail moved inland and they lost sight of the bay and the new visitors. The girls became less afraid, but Twinax-so-ha hurried them along.

They ran as fast as they could, having to wait for the younger girls to keep up. Everyone was breathing hard by the time they got to the clearing near the back of the village. *Twinax-so-ha* moved up next to her sister who was bent over, with her hands on her knees.

Her sister, Lahatoni *(sleeps with the butterflies)* had been born four...*tabo* summers after Twinax-so-ha. Her age was still countable by the last digit of the right hand...*deechi di.*

"It was a long run sister."

"Twinax-so-ha, what sort of monsters have invaded our bay...I am afraid!"

Twinax-so-ha patted her sister on the back, "We should find father and mother, they will know what to do."

The girls moved forward into the area between the huts. There was no one around. Cooking fires were untended and none of the children were running about playing games. It was strangely silent. Nearing the beach they found out why...all of the people were standing on the shoreline watching the strange crafts.

Her mother separated from the crowd and ran toward her. "Twinax-so-ha, Lahatoni, your father and I have been worried!"

Twinax-so-ha's father turned to look at them but stayed on the beach. She noted that he was holding his long hunting bow and a handful of arrows. At his side was her younger brother Tocobaga holding a handful of arrows. In fact, all of the men of the village had armed themselves.

The "great clouds" had stopped moving and Twinax-so-ha watched in amazement as the "clouds" above the canoes began to disappear. She moved closer to the beach, closer to her father. Sounds were drifting across the water, the clanking of the anchor chains and something else.

Voices!

Looking hard, Twinax-so-ha could now see the figures of men moving about the large canoes. A few were even climbing in the trees above the canoes.

The strange voices drifted across the water, a language she had never heard.

"Father, who are these people?"

Sih-la-pah (Flying Heron) was the headman of this village. It was he whom the other inhabitants would look to for guidance. He looked down at his daughter and then back at the bay.

"These people and their strange crafts are nothing like I have ever seen. We need to be very careful until we know why they are here and what is in their hearts."

Sih-la-pah had been head man of this village for six winters. Their last leader had been killed when a rival band ambushed a hunting party that had strayed too far inland. Sih-la-pah had been part of that hunting party and in the ensuing fight had fought bravely, single handedly killing two enemies before joining with the other survivors to drive the enemy off.

Based on this performance the village had chosen him to lead. In truth, however, his only power was in times of conflict and leading the hunt. In councils, his words were perhaps considered more than others, but the day-to-day decisions were made by the will of all the people. His village...his people...were part of a larger group, a diversity of villages that spread in all directions and related by marriage and custom.

They were the *Toco-ha-baho (those that live on the water's edge)*

As Twinax-so-ha and her father watched, a smaller canoe disgorged from one of the larger canoes. It traveled amongst the large canoes and then returned from where it had started. The people of the village were becoming anxious, they looked to Sih-la-pah for guidance. He indicated that they should wait and see what happened.

Soon another small canoe set out and this one moved toward them, or rather to a small island just a few hundred feet offshore. Sih-la-pah commanded the women and children back to the tree line. The men should arm themselves and gather around him.

As the visitor's canoe drew closer, Sih-la-pah could see how it was propelled. Men sitting in rows pulled on long paddles that stuck far out from the craft. There were eight men on board. He indicated this by holding up both hands and displaying all five fingers on his left and three on his right. The strangers' canoe was so much different than anything Sih-la-pah had seen. It was very wide and looked hard to maneuver. Compared to the sleek craft of the *Toco-ha-baho,* it was ugly.

The man in front carried a long stick with a white banner that fluttered in the wind. On the banner was a large red cross. As the ugly canoe skidded to a stop on the island's shore, the man in front jumped down and strode onto the beach. Here he jammed the long stick into the sand and turned to signal the others. Three of them advanced across the island.

These men were dressed like no one Sih-la-pah had ever seen. Two wore metal on their heads and upper bodies...it glinted in the sun. The day was very warm and yet the third was wrapped in a heavy white blanket. Most astonishing was the hair growing on their faces and the whiteness of the exposed skin.

The "hairy faces" stopped at the beach separating the island from the mainland. For a time both sides stared at one another. Finally, one of them gestured to the people of the village in a welcoming manner. It appeared he was inviting Sih-la-pah and his people to join them.

09 April, 1528

A Small Island Just off the Beach Near Present-Day Jungle Prada, Narvaez Park in St. Petersburg, Florida

Diego Dorantes was uncomfortable. He counted at least forty armed *Indians* and more were arriving all the time. There was only a hundred yara or so of shallow water between them and the village. Several canoes were cruising in the immediate area, each with three or four armed warriors.

They were vulnerable...very vulnerable.

Captain Tellez had stayed at the boat with the four oarsmen. They would be of some help if attacked, but they were still vastly out-numbered. He knew that Narvaez had several boats ready to load with armed men, but by the time they got here, he would be long dead. Three *Spaniards*, Alonso Enriquez, Friar Xuraez, and Andres Dorantes moved away from the boat. With his left hand holding the flag, Andres Dorantes slowly reached down and felt the hilt of his sword. If they attacked he'd take a few of them with him.

Alonso Enriquez stepped forward, "Greetings from the King of *Spain*, we come here in peace and bring many gifts." With that Enriquez held out a bag of brightly colored glass beads and then laid them in the sand and then made a gesture as if to say, "come over!"

The *Indians'* demeanor didn't change, they continued to stare intently.

Enriquez, frustrated, turned around, "Let's try spreading the trade goods on the sand and then sitting down as if we are expecting them to come over and parley."

"Try to act relaxed."

Dorantes took his hand off the sword, backed up, and knelt in the sand. Friar Xuraez who had been carrying the trade items stepped forward and spread the items in a rough semicircle. This completed, he joined Enriquez and Dorantes in a relaxed position.

For a while, the *Indians* continued to stare, but finally, there was movement. A single man stepped forward and walked to the water's edge. He was holding a very long bow while his other hand grasped several arrows. He turned to his people and said something that was unintelligible to Dorantes. Then turning back towards the *Spaniards*, he spoke again.

"*Twanakeeno sia la mano.*"

With that, he made gestures as if his people should come over and join him.

"All of you stay seated!" Enriquez rose to his feet and also walked to the water's edge.

He repeated his gestures to come over.

With that, the *Indian* nodded and turned. He apparently called for canoes because four showed up almost immediately.

Dorantes watched the canoes slide into the water and move toward them. "Four canoes each with four men. Sixteen against eight."

Enriquez looked back, "Capitan Dorantes, I don't think they intend to fight...but be ready."

Dorantes thought to himself. "Of course I'm ready to fight, I was ready to fight when I got in the boat!"

As soon as the lead canoe touched the sand the *Indian* with the long bow jumped effortlessly onto the beach. He gave a series of quick orders and two *Indians* joined him. Dorantes couldn't help but admire these men. They were all very tall, much taller than he, and built like conditioned athletes. Each was only wearing a loin cloth and the musculature of their upper bodies was well defined. Together they moved towards the *Spaniards*.

Enriquez turned and motioned for Dorantes and Friar Xuraez to rise. "Try to look friendly."

09 April, 1528

A Small Island Just off the Beach Near Present-Day Jungle Prada, Narvaez Park in St. Petersburg, Florida

Sih-la-pah approached the "hairy faces" cautiously, although he tried to walk strong. Next to him were his brothers Seo-ah-ton (*Angry face*) and Wa-so-bani (*Walks in the night*). He looked around. The other strangers who had come over in the ugly canoe were still far down the beach and posed no immediate threat.

This was no ambush.

As he got closer, the three men in front of him didn't appear to be holding any weapons. He noted, however, what appeared to be very long knives hanging from their waists. Most amazing was the shiny metal they were wearing. Metal hats covered most of their head while their upper bodies were protected as well. Their arms and upper legs were covered by strange-colored material that fluttered in the wind. Their footwear was like nothing he had ever seen.

How very strange.

Sih-la-pah stopped ten feet in front of the *Spaniards* and for a moment both sides just looked at one another. Their smell was very strong, Sih-la-pah thought like a wet raccoon. Seo-ah-ton made a noise and then wiggled his nose in a most disagreeable manner. Sih-la-pah turned and gave him an angry look.

One of the strangers stepped forward with his hand outstretched, "*Bueos dios*!"

Sih-la-pah looked down at the hand and didn't know what to do. The stranger took one more step forward and stuck his hand out further. Sih-la-pah was confused.

Suddenly, the man in the long blanket stepped forward, grabbing the man's hand and shaking it while looking at Sih-la-pah. Then "*Long Blanket*" talked to "*Man with hand out.*"

"Senor Enriquez, they don't understand our greeting customs."

They unclasped hands and pantomimed meeting anew, again clasping hands. Shaking hands for a few seconds they stopped and looked at Sih-la-pah.

His blank stare gave them their answer.

The two *Spaniards* separated and walked away from each other. Turning, they play acted again.

"Ah Friar Xuraez, so nice to see you!"

Senor Enriquez, I have thought of you often!"

With this, they again clasped hands and patted each other on the back.

It came to Sih-la-pah then. He turned to Seo-ah-ton. "I think the "*hairy faces*" greet each other in this manner."

Not waiting for a response, he shifted the bow to his left hand and slowly extended his right hand, thumb up, just like *"Long Blanket"* did.

Immensely relieved, Enriquez stepped over and grasped Sih-la-pah's hand. He shook it up and down for several seconds and then let go. Turning to Seo-ah-ton he extended his hand. Seo-ah-ton backed up.

Sih-la-pah turned and commanded, "Seo-ah-ton, shake this fool's hand, as I did."

That completed, Enriquez turned to Wa-so-bani who was waiting with his outstretched hand.

"Man with hand out" then began banging on his chest and saying "Enriquez". He turned to *"Long Blanket"* and said "Xuraez" and finally to the silent bearded one and said "Dorantes".

These were very strange sounds, but Sih-la-pah understood. He, in turn, spoke his name and those who were with him.

"Long Blanket" then came forward with gifts. To Sih-la-pah he handed a copper bell, to Seo-ah-ton, a string of beads, and to Wa-so-bani, strips of brightly colored fabric.

All were invited to sit. After much talk and gestures, Sih-la-pah came to understand that the newcomers wanted to trade for food. Turning to Wa-so-bami he instructed him to have the village collect as much food as they could and bring it to the island.

10 April, 1528

At Anchor Aboard the Caravel Maria De La Meridionales Mares in Boca Ciega Bay

Yesterday's foray with the *Indians* had been very successful. That night the crews, settlers, and soldiers had feasted on fresh venison, turkey, and fish. The mood was upbeat.

Panfilo Narvaez had called for an early morning meeting. He was relaxed, half sitting on the deck railing. Below him, on the main deck, were all of the military captains and royal officials of the expedition. In the background, the colonists and crew aboard *Maria* congregated. Narvaez noted the clutch of women amongst the colonists. Rita La Salvaje, as usual, was eyeing him suspiciously.

Narvaez looked up and scanned the bay. It was a fine morning. The wind was light, blowing to shore. At the Indian village, the smoke from several cooking fires rose in the air and then trailed off to the east. There were already several canoes in the water keeping a wary eye on the newcomers.

Panfilo cleared his throat and asked Fray Xuraez to lead them in a prayer of thankfulness for this marked the day that Jesus Christ was crucified and died on the cross for their sins. This he did, taking too much time in Panfilo's opinion. Thanking the Holy Father for the bounty of food received was one thing, but recognizing the fishes in the sea, the stars in the sky, and a multitude of other unrelated platitudes was another. Narvaez was growing impatient.

The "Amen" was hardly out of Fray Xuraez's mouth before Narvaez began speaking.

"We are beholding to the brave efforts of Senor Enriquez and his party who yesterday ventured forth to make contact with the *Indios*. As a result, we will, today, proceed directly to the village and make arrangements for unloading of the horses."

Narvaez continued, outlining the operational plans. He would begin by landing a moderate force at the *Indian's* village and securing the area. If successful, he would begin offloading the horses, settlers, and equipment. On the following day, an official ceremony would read the *Requerimiento* and claim the land for *Spain*. Narvaez stressed that this would be a peaceful mission, but that each man should be ready to defend himself. Swords should be sheathed while crossbows and arquebuses should be covered. All but one Friar would accompany the mission. The *Indians* of this village were definitely not *Christian* and every effort should be made to introduce them to the ways of the Holy Savior.

The initial force would set out within the hour. Since the six boats of the expedition (*Maria* and *Reina* each had two) were not sufficient to transport all in one trip, several relays would ferry the landing party. The laborious task of unloading the horses would begin immediately. As soon as arrangements with the villagers could be made, Narvaez would call for their transport. He hoped that all horses could be offloaded by nightfall.

And so it was. The meeting broke up and each group returned to the ship to assemble their landing party. All would cue on the *Adelentado's* departure.

With help from Campo, Panfilo donned his body armor. Campo had spent all morning bringing the metal to a high sheen. Narvaez was one of only a few on the expedition whose height equaled that of the *Indians*. The breadth of his chest, huge biceps, and sinister eye patch made the *Adelantado*, even at age 52, an imposing figure.

Walking across the deck Narvaez hoisted himself over the gunnel and climbed down into the boat waiting below. Once in place, Campo handed down his sheathed *montante*, the same broadsword lost at *Cempoalla* on that terrible night. Cortes had returned it to him. Strapping on the sword, Narvaez turned to Jeronimo de Alaniz, the expedition scribe, who was in the same boat. "*Senor* Alaniz, are you prepared to record everything that happens this day?"

"Yes, Your Excellency." Enriquez lifted his writing material contained in an oiled pouch.

Looking back at the flagship Narvaez commanded, "Let us be underway then."

Panfilo Narvaez would never board *Maria de la Meridionales Mares* again.

10 April, 1528

Indian Village on the Beach of Boco Ciega Bay Near Present-Day Jungle Prada, Narvaez Park in St. Petersburg, Florida

For the last 200 feet or so, Narvaez stood at the bow of the boat as it neared the shore. When the keel crunched into the soft sand of the shoreline he nimbly jumped off and strode through ankle-deep water onto the beach. He was accompanied by Comptroller Alonso Enriquez. Behind them, cousins Andre and Diego Dorantes carried the flags of *Spain* and *Castille*. At a distance, the black slave Estevan followed with the large oilskin pouch of documents, and finally seaman Marino Carmona who, as a full-blooded *Tiano Indian*, might be able to assist with translation.

To the right and left of Narvaez, two other boats had timed their landing to coincide with his. From each, six swordsmen had formed up rapidly and converged on their leader. These were led by military capitan's Alejandro Tellez and Alonso del Castillo. The boats immediately pushed off and returned to the ships at anchor. The next two boats contained the crossbowmen and *musketeers*. These men offloaded but stayed close to the boats which contained their weapons.

Finally, the last boat came ashore and deposited the remainder of the expedition's royal contingent. This included *Alguacil* Cabeza de

Vaca, *Factor* Alonso de Solis, *Scribe* Jeronimo de Alaniz, *Commisary* Fray Juan Xuraez, and three monks, fathers Pietre de Asturiano, Augusto Alaniz and Juan de Palos.

Climbing out of his boat, Alvar Nunez Cabeza de Vaca scanned the beach. To him, it looked like a military invasion rather than a peaceful entree. Apparently, the *Indians* felt the same, for, as he looked toward the village, it was completely deserted. Cooking fires burned but evidence of normal activity was absent. The inhabitants had fled to the forest.

Panfilo Narvaez believed in making a strong showing. He had spent the previous night forming contingency plans with his *capitans*. If attacked they would fall back to the island which would screen their retreat if it became necessary. All of those coming ashore were to have their armor, weapons, and dress in the best condition. It was no coincidence that he had chosen Dorante's slave, Estevan to accompany the initial landing. His experience in *Cuba* had shown that the *Indians* were in awe of a black man, especially one as well put together as Estevan. He didn't have the time for long negotiations with these people. His horses had to be offloaded as soon as possible. An overwhelming show of strength was the only way to get this done.

Narvaez, surrounded by his contingent, scanned the village. He hesitated. The wind was blowing onshore and, for a moment, the surf and the flapping of the two flags were the only sounds on the beach.

The booming voice of the *Adelantado* broke the reverie.

"Since the inhabitants of this village have chosen not to honor our presence, let us advance and set up a perimeter. I don't want to be surprised on this beach."

Signals were given and the two outside flanks advanced slowly on the village. The mood was tense but it soon became apparent that the *Indians* were nowhere around. The *Spaniards* moved cautiously between the structures, entering each one and laying anything of importance outside.

Narvaez's group approached the central courtyard where an enormous structure, situated on a high mound, seemed to command the entire village. Standing in the doorway, Alvar Nunez Cabeza de Vaca studied the construction. The perimeter walls were supported by poles dug into the ground. At each end, a longer spar supported a spliced ridge pole that was further supported by a massive spar at the center of the structure. The slope of the rafters from the ridge pole to the walls was fairly severe. Between the rafters, small saplings spaced no more than a hand width apart supported a final layer of palm leaves. All were lashed together with strips of palmetto braided together to form a strong and resilient lashing. Looking up, Alvar could see no light coming through the roof. This was obviously a meeting house and he estimated that 300 people could be seated comfortably inside its walls.

Within the smaller structures were the things of everyday life. All around were signs that the *Indians* had left their village in a hurry. Fire pits still burned, many with food still roasting on the spits. To these, the *Spaniards* helped themselves. Outside the houses, the invaders piled whatever they found of interest. Nets, blankets, tools, and weapons were spread about on the ground.

"*Adelentado*...over here!" It was *Capitan* Alejandro Tellez. The *capitan* was standing next to one of the small houses holding an object in his hand.

Narvaez strode across the courtyard his retinue close behind. "What have you found *Senor* Tellez."

"I think it is gold, Your Excellency."

He handed what looked to be a small rattle to Narvaez. The mere mention of "gold" sent a shock of excitement through the *Spaniards*. Many hurried over to Narvaez. His head oddly cocked to one side, he studied the piece intently with his single eye. Finally, raising it up to his mouth he felt the softness of the metal as it yielded to his bite. Raising the piece above his head he shook it back and forth. Within, the smooth stone clapper made an audible rattle.

"It is gold! There has to be more from whence this came from. This ensures that our journey to *La Florida* will be a success."

All around the *Spaniards* cheered and slapped each other on the back. Finally, a good sign had presented itself to the Narvaez Expedition.

CHAPTER 12

The Requirement

El Requerimiento

Panfilo shook his head. He had done this many times before and each time he was struck by the absurdity of it. He would read this "requerimiento," a lengthy decree in Spanish to primitive, uncivilized people who didn't understand a word. All this to satisfy the amantes de los Indios...Indian lovers who constantly sought to influence the King.

10 April, 1528

Boca Ciega Bay

From the front of the four-man canoe, Sih-la-pah watched as the onslaught of "hairy faces" spread throughout his village. He kept well away from shore, at least two bow shots, where he knew that the invaders couldn't reach them with the strange little bows that they carried on a stick. The "hairy faces" were aware of his presence, however, and he could see the guards on shore keeping a wary eye on him.

The three other warriors on board talked quietly among themselves. His brother, Seo-ah-ton was the most vocal.

"I will kill the hairy faces and eat their hearts. Yesterday we brought them food and today they repay us by disrespecting our village. Let us attack now and drive them back into the bay."

Sih-la-pah kept his eyes forward. "Patience brother, we know nothing of these people or their weapons. We will watch them and see what it is that they want. Let us move closer, for I wish to observe the large man whose hair is as red as fire. I think he is their chief."

The canoe glided closer and Sih-la-pah watched intently as "hair like fire" directed the takeover of his village. He studied the weapons and their armor. For the first time, he saw from afar men carrying strange sticks that smoked at one end. "Were these weapons"?

Seo-ah-ton tapped him on the shoulder and pointed towards the bay. Three more "ugly canoes" were moving toward shore, only these were carrying what looked to be large bundles.

The warriors continued to keep the canoe at a safe distance but now the object of their attention had changed.

"What could this be, what were they bringing to the village?"

As the "ugly canoes" reached the shoreline, a group of men rushed to them, each grabbing part of the bundle and rolling it gently onto the sand.

It was then that Sih-la-pah and the warriors stopped rowing and stared in terror and amazement at the activity on the beach.

The bundles were alive! Assisted by the "hairy faces" a huge beast rose up from the sand. It resembled a deer but much, much bigger with a tail that almost reached the ground. It stood for a time on wobbly legs before being slowly led to the village.

The *Indians* had never seen anything like it and were transfixed watching the strange animals being unloaded from the ship's boats. Finally, it was Sih-la-pah who realized they had drifted uncomfortably close and called for his companions to back away. He would return to his people, now staying with another village, and tell of what they'd seen; how these strange men from the sea had invaded their village and seemed to have command of great and powerful beasts.

Sih-la-pah was greatly troubled as they rowed silently across the bay.

10 April, 1528

Boca Ciega Bay

Throughout the day the influx of men, horses, and materials to the shore continued. Moving the horses was particularly time-consuming. The animals were in such a state of stress that they had to be handled with unusual care. Blindfolded and trussed like mummies they were slowly winched up from the holds below. Swung over the side of the ship, they were lowered, head towards the bow, into the waiting boats where planks had been placed for them to lay on. Tied securely, a handler accompanied each one to the shore, trying his best to keep the terrified animal calm.

Ashore, a special group of laborers would descend on the boat. Untied, the horse was moved to the extreme side of the craft, then, eight or ten men would lift and roll the boat as other laborers gently slid the trussed-up animal onto the sand. Handlers were careful to keep their head out of the water and sand. The boat was quickly moved away while the straps, blankets, and restraints were removed. Once free, the horses had to be physically helped to their feet, many so weak and muscles so atrophied that three or four laborers would have to accompany and support the animals as they made their slow trek up the beach to a flat stand of seagrass that temporarily served as a makeshift corral.

For a time the exhausted animals would stand, trembling, head down and breathing hard, their ribs and pelvis bones starkly visible under the loose and discolored skin. The handlers moved among them offering water and fist fulls of grass. Slowly, each animal would take the offering and begin to eat, the fresh grass like an elixir that pumped energy throughout their bodies.

Andres Dorante's favorite mount, *Medianoche*, had been one of the first to be offloaded onto the shore. Estevan stayed with the animal continually, vigorously brushing and kneading the long leg muscles. Slowly, the dappled gray stallion began to respond, moving under its own power among the clumps of grass. Estevan and *Medianoche* had long ago formed a relationship, Estevan jealously caring for the stallion at the exclusion of all others.

"Ah, my friend, you are looking much better. Regain your strength, our *capitan* will soon need your help in this strange land."

Around the ever-growing number of horses, a strong ring of crossbowmen stood guard. The horses were the *Spaniards'* most prized possessions. Their loss would be of catastrophic significance. Above all, Narvaez would protect them with every means at his disposal.

By nightfall, all but ten of the horses had been transferred to shore. Now, with the light fading, Alvar Nunez Cabeza de Vaca stood by the makeshift corral and was appalled at the sight of the animals. His companion, Captain Alonso Castille, could only remark, "They will not be able to hold the weight of a rider for at least two weeks."

Darkness came early. To the west, a developing thunderstorm promised rain. All transfer operations from the ships had been halted until morning. Around the horse corral, bonfires were maintained every fifty feet. Each horse was hobbled and assigned an armed handler to remain with it throughout the night. The crossbowmen surrounding the corral closed ranks and stared uneasily past the ring of light provided by the fires. Out there somewhere were the *Indians* of this village. Everyone was sure they wanted their village back.

10 April, 1528

Aboard the Caravel Maria De La Meridionales

Mares

Rita La Salvaje addressed the small group of women. They had all come together here on the *Maria*, a gathering of women folk from all four ships.

"It was there in *San Lucar* that the old *Moor* woman came upon me quite unexpectedly. At first, I thought her nothing more than a poor beggar for whom I took compassion."

Those around Rita leaned closer to hear the words. Some of the tradesmen on board and even a few *marineros* shuffled over to hear what she had to say. The darkness had come early as the approaching storm shielded the sunset. Lightening played across the sky and the sound of thunder rolled over the bay. On board, the sea lanterns had been lit.

"She looked at me...and yet, she didn't look at me, but rather, through me...Like I wasn't there. She talked of our journey as if it had already happened."

A lightning bolt split the air and the thunder followed almost instantaneously. In the ever-growing circle of listeners, many jumped at the sound. Rita hesitated in her story and briefly turned to look at the storm. Again facing the crowd, her eyes were wide and a slight smile played upon her lips. Rita La Salvaje was a master storyteller.

"The *Moor* woman said she had dreamed of our *Adelantado* many times. She called him 'the great red-bearded one'. She talked of his great strength, his fearlessness in battle, his cruelty, and his greed."

Above the circle of listeners, Alejandro Tellez, sitting on the aftcastle rail, stiffened at the description of the *Adelantado*. As the ranking military captain, he was now in command of the *Maria* while Narvaez was ashore. It was not good to instill descent and negative talk of the *Adelantado*. He stood and looked down at Rita. Rita, in turn, hesitating ever so briefly, cast a hard look at the captain. Tellez remained standing but said nothing.

"The *Moor* woman's name was Talibah and she spoke of a life heavy with loss. Her sons and her husband all died in the *reconquista* and she was forced to a life of poverty."

"But!" Rita pointed at the crowd. "Talibah had a gift. Even as a child, she would know of things before they happened. In her time of hardship, this gift became more pronounced. Many in *San Lucar* would seek guidance as her reputation grew."

A wind generated by the storm front began to blow, the sounds and the cool air added an air of mystery and foreboding. On the aft castle, Tellez reclaimed his seat. Even he was captivated by the story unfolding below him.

"The *Moor* related that we would have an uneventful trip across the ocean sea. Once in the Indies, however, our fate will take a turn. She spoke of many desertions and a terrible storm that would claim the lives of many and the loss of ships."

Rita paused for effect and then quietly hung her head. Her voice was so soft that the onlookers leaned forward to better hear.

"Of course, I couldn't have known it then, but she spoke of that terrible *hurican* that destroyed our ships sent to *Trinidad.*"

Several voices from the crowd cried in unison, "What other predictions did she make?"

Rita continued, "She spoke of a voyage fraught with storms, delays, and hardships before we reached the land of *Amichel.*

Many shook their heads in disbelief, "How could she know all of this?" A voice from the back shouted, "And what will happen to us now that we are here?"

Rita spread her hands in supplication. The crowd quieted. "That is the most frightening of all."

There was stone silence aboard the ship.

"The *Moor* woman spoke of a great split in the expedition where some would continue on and others would return to the ships. Those that continued would experience death and deprivation and would vanish from the face of the earth, save for a few who, alone, would tell the horrible story."

A collective gasp arose from the group. Some talked among themselves, others quietly contemplated what had been said, and many, like Alejandro Tellez, scoffed at the story.

He called down to Rita, "And what else did this so-called, *Moorish* fortune teller have to say?"

Rita threw a sharp look at Tellez before turning back to the crowd, now quietly waiting for her to continue.

"Talibah gave no particulars, only that a very small number would survive. She beseeched me to tell all who would listen of the perils that awaited them. I questioned her more but the old woman held up her hand and quietly said that this was all she could tell me."

"The next day, the day of our departure, I saw her again, but only for a moment. "She grasped my arm and warned me again of the dangers...but then she began talking of something else."

"What were her words?" A young seaman asked who was sitting cross-legged on the deck next to Rita.

"The old woman became distant and I had trouble hearing her. She seemed confused. She talked of a great harbor, of things she didn't understand. A land populated by people beyond counting. Roads, bridges, carriages without horses, and even..."

Rita hesitated and then cleared her throat, "She talked of machines that flew through the air."

"Ha! I have heard enough." Tellez was standing now. "Machines that fly...did she speak of also of dragons and leprechauns?"

Tellez bent over and looked directly into Rita's eyes. "She is crazy, just like any of you who believe this story!"

11 April, 1528

Ashore off Boco Ciega, at the Site of the Indian Village

Pnfilo stood on the shore surveying the bay that spread out before him. The morning's calm belied the fierce storm that had raged throughout the night. Now, the waves gently lapped the shoreline and the clear sky, washed clean from the storm, promised a hot day.

Two boats approached the village. These contained the remainder of the expedition's

dignitaries, soldiers, and royal appointees alike. This morning, Holy Saturday, Panfilo would assemble his people to read the *Requeremento*, the royal document that spelled out *Spain's* right to take possession of territory and what powers he had over the indigenous people.

Meeting the boats at the beach Narvaez again questioned the expedition's scribe and notary.

"*Senor* Alaniz, do you have the copy of *El Requerimiento?*"

"Yes, Your Excellency."

Panfilo shook his head. He had done this many times before and each time he was struck by the absurdity of it. He would read this *"requerimiento,"* a lengthy decree in *Spanish* to primitive, uncivilized people who didn't understand a word. All this to satisfy the *amantes de los Indios...Indian* lovers who constantly sought to influence the King.

Turning to the other man on the beach with him, he said, "Senor Enriquez, since the *Indios* have decided not to be present, let us conclude these proceedings as quickly as possible."

The boats skidded to a stop on the shore and the occupants quickly piled out. Enriquez rushed forward and directed them to a position about halfway up the beach where flag poles had been set into the sand.

Notary Jeronimo de Alaniz carried the large oilskin pouch containing the royal documents. Jorge Tostado, a cavalryman...*Jinete*...had the honor of carrying the official flags of the expedition. These were rapidly unfurled and affixed to the flagpoles set in the sand. There was the *Cruz de San Andres* or the *Burgundy cross* of *Spain. Spain's* Charles I was represented by the double-headed Imperial Eagle set against a yellow field. Narvaez's personal coat of arms and the standard of *Castile* were also set in place, both within a blazing field of red.

All of the royal officials were assembled and each carried his credentials and titles. These were read in turn, beginning with Narvaez and moving down through the assembly. Finally, when this was completed, the notary stepped to the front and began to read the *Requiremento*.

Alaniz, facing the *Indio* village, read loudly as he began to plod through the document,

"On the part of our King and Holy Roman Emperor..."

Narvaez tried to settle into a relaxed stance while the notary droned on.

"Of all these nations God our Lord gave charge to one man, called St Peter, that he should be lord and superior of all the men in the world..."

A sudden breeze coming off the bay caused the flags to strain against their poles, so much so that the Royal standard loosened and began to fall over. Tostado, standing the closest, broke ranks and caught the wayward banner. His movement caused Alaniz to hesitate, and all eyes watched Tostado as he placed the pole back into the sand.

Narvaez rolled his eyes but said nothing.

Alaniz continued, "Wherefore as best we can, we ask and require you that you consider what we have said to you..."

For another 5 minutes the reading continued until finally, blessedly, it came to an end.

Narvaez now straightened and moved to the center. Taking his sword from his sheath he held it before him and announced to the crowd, "I now claim this land in the name of our most gracious sovereign and Holy Roman Emperor, His Majesty Charles V under the directions and stipulations of his Royal decree."

With that Narvaez dropped to one knee and was followed by the rest of the throng as Fray Palos offered a prayer to the proceedings.

With that, the ceremony was over. The official flags were taken down, refolded, and returned to the ships. Out in the bay, the last of the horses were being brought to shore.

12 April, 1528

Ashore off Boco Ciega, at the Site of the Indian Village

It was early morning and Sih-la-pah sat in the front of the five-man canoe. Two other canoes accompanied him, his brothers Seo-ah-ton just to the right and Wa-so-bani trailing slightly behind to the left. Around his neck hung the symbol of authority, a necklace of brilliant white Egret feathers. In his right hand, he held the ceremonial council spear, the tip of its shaft adorned with the flight feathers of an Osprey.

The oarsmen had been carefully chosen, each for his height, strength, and bravery. Sih-la-pah wanted to make an impression. Except for the fire-haired giant and a few others, the bearded ones were mostly little men, short in stature. He, his brothers, and all the men that accompanied him were easily over six feet.

Today they would confront the bearded ones and find out why they were here and what they wanted. Sih-la-pah had watched yesterday's proceedings from a distance and knew that the great gathering under the colored flags meant something, but he had no idea what it was.

The canoes pulled up a long bow shot from the beach. Ashore, a well-armed crowd of men watched them intently. For several minutes nothing changed, each side watching the other. Sih-la-pah took notice of the weapons. Many carried the long knife attached to their waists, while others held the small bow on a stick. Most intriguing, however, were the men who held the smoking stick. He had no idea what it was, but instinctively knew it was a weapon of some sort.

Finally, the fire-haired giant emerged from one of the huts and approached the shore. He quickly dispersed the crowd of men, moving them back from the beach. Then, with a gathering of only five other men, he walked to the water's edge and motioned for them to come in. Sih-la-pah directed his brothers to join him and then motioned for the oarsmen to paddle slowly ahead.

As the bow of the canoe lightly ground into the sand, Sih-la-pah lightly jumped out and waited for his men to assemble around him. Except for his own canoe, which was to remain on the beach, he directed the others to remain offshore.

Together the brothers closed the short distance to where the fire-haired giant was standing. As they stood facing each other Sih-la-pah immediately recognized the one called En-ri-quez whom he had met two days before. He nodded slightly. His gaze fell on *Fire Hair*. He was of equal height but much heavier in stature. His upper arms were the size of Sih-la-pah's thighs. Sih-la-pah took in the multitude of scars and the eye patch that didn't completely cover the disfigured eye. This was truly a very powerful warrior who had seen many battles.

There were three other men behind *Fire Hair* and En-ri-quez. *Long Blanket* was there, smiling broadly as Sih-la-pah took in his gaze and nodded. Next to Long Blanket was the silent one who called himself *Dor-an-tes*. Even now, Sih-la-pah smiled to himself, for the words *Dor-an-tes* in his language roughly meant, *"shits in the trees"*.

It was the other man who most intrigued Sih-la-pah. Except for a single knife shoved into his waistband, he was unarmed and dressed much differently than the others. Beardless with dark black hair, Sih-la-pah immediately recognized him as one of his own race. Their eyes met and the look that passed between them confirmed his thoughts.

Fire Hair turned to this man and said something unintelligible to Sih-la-pah. The man stepped forward.

Marino Carmona welcomed Sih-la-pah in his native *Tiano* and asked if he understood.

Sih-la-pah had heard the language of the *Tianosa-la-na* before. They were a seafaring people and had visited his village many times on trading runs. He understood a few words but used hand talk to answer Carmona's inquiry.

 "Brother, you are one of us, tell me why it is that these *bearded ones* have taken our village after we treated them as friends?"

The question was relayed to Narvaez who thought for a moment before passing his answer to Carmona. With the hand talk and a few common words, Carmona managed to paraphrase the answer.

"Brother, it is not the *Bearded One's* intention to take your village. They only came to visit and bring gifts. It was then that they found you gone."

Sih-la-pah took notice that Carmona spoke of the *Bearded Ones* as "they." He still had the heart of his ancestors. Sih-la-pah became more forceful,

"Their warriors have moved into our houses and taken things of value, they eat our food and defile our village. I do not want them here."

Carmona dutifully repeated the words to Narvaez who thought a moment before answering.

"First things first, who is this *Indio*? I need to know his name and if he represents all the people here. We will not be leaving this village for a while, so tell him that we would be most appreciative if he would allow us to remain a few days."

Carmona struggled with the translation. He tried to find the right meaning with hand talk and common words. As Carmona labored,

Narvaez nodded to Dorantes who in turn signaled to his slave, Estevan, to bring his stallion up.

Sih-la-pah noticed the exchange as he received the message from Narvaez. It was obvious that the *Bearded Ones* had no intention of lea a ving. He could feel his anger growing. Before Carmona had completed his efforts, Sih-la-pah cut him off with a swipe of his hand.

"I am Sih-la-pah and this is my village. Who is this *fire-haired* giant that I speak with and why is he here? I speak for all my people when I say we want our village back. We at first welcomed you with food, but now you are no longer welcome and we ask that you leave."

As Carmona was relating his answer to Narvaez, Sih-la-pah was aware of movement to his right. From behind a structure, one of the beasts emerged that Sih-la-pah had seen from his canoe the day before. The beast was being led by a man whose skin was as black as charcoal. The beast was agitated and pawing the ground with his front feet. Its nostrils flared as it inhaled and exhaled great quantities of air. Sih-la-pah felt himself step backward as the great beast was led toward them.

Narvaez was no fool. Long experience with *Indians* had taught him that they had no knowledge of horses. As they had approached in their canoe, he had given instructions to saddle a stallion and to excite it with one of the mares that was in heat. Even as emaciated as the stallion was from the long journey, it was tremendously imposing to these *Toco-ha-baho* who had never experienced an animal of this size before.

Estevan led the animal to within ten feet of the assembly of *Spaniards* and *Indians* and then held the bridle as Dorantes mounted the agitated stallion.

Sih-la-pah tried hard to maintain his composure. The sight of a man astride of this beast, and apparently in control, riveted his attention.

Dorantes, now holding a lance in one hand circled the group. The saddle and reins had been festooned with small bells that rang and rattled with each step. This cacophony of sound and movement further intimidated Sih-la-pah and his brothers. Even the warriors that had remained with the canoe moved back into the water as they watched the proceedings from afar.

Finally, Dorantes brought the stallion to a halt a short distance behind Narvaez. He remained astride of it, with the effect of accentuating the power of the *Adelentado*.

Once more Carmona spoke to Sih-la-pah, "The *fire-haired* one is known as Narvaez. He is our leader and a great warrior. He only asks that you allow us to remain here for a short while. For this, we will give you many gifts."

Sih-la-pah was still somewhat shaken by the huge beast that, even now, looked down on them from behind this...*Nah-ves, the fire hair*, but he was no less adamant in wanting these invaders gone from his village. This time as he spoke, and used the hand language, he looked directly at Narvaez and spoke in his most commanding voice.

"We want you to leave at once, this village is not yours and we care not for your gifts!" He accompanied this with the hand talk and when finished pointed directly at Narvaez and shook his fist.

Narvaez waited for the translation and then turned and directed Dorantes to bring up three arquebusiers and wait for his signal to fire their weapons.

"*Si Adelentado*, but what shall I have them use as a target?"

Narvaez smiled deviously and then answered, "The *Idios* canoe, but have them hit it above the water line."

With this Narvaez turned back to Carmona. "Tell this chief that we are staying. I would prefer a peaceful relationship and hope he would see it in his heart to join us. Also, tell him that our power is great and we have a demonstration for him."

As Carmona translated Sih-la-pah grew increasingly angry. Beside him, his brother Seo-ah-ton began to mutter curses and make threatening gestures towards *Fire Hair.*

Si-la-pah had had enough. He turned abruptly on his heel and began to move back towards the canoe. Carmona, however, grabbed his arm. Si-la-pah spun around and in one motion brought his spear to bear against Carmona's throat. Around them, swords were drawn and the crossbowman moved closer.

Narvaez began waving his hands in the air, "No, No, put your swords away. He spread his arms in appeal and looked at Sih-la-pah. who slowly lowered his spear. The *Spaniards* moved back.

Carmona hurriedly tried to communicate. "Brother, I meant no disrespect only to tell you to beware of the white man's power, they have fearful weapons.

With that, the three arquebusiers moved to within fifty feet of where Sih-la-pah's canoe was beached. Other *Spaniards* signaled the oarsmen to move back.

Narvaez stepped in front of Si-la-pah and began to talk. When he had finished Carmona began to translate, a grave look on his face.

"Brother, our leader Narvaez wants to live in peace and only asks for the use of your village for a short time. For this, you will be well rewarded." With the combination of language and hand talk, Carmona wasn't sure he had gotten the meaning across, but finally, Sih-la-pah nodded in understanding.

Carmona continued, "If you, instead, choose to resist him, he has powers of which you are unaware."

With this, Carmona looked to Narvaez who nodded to Dorantes.

Sih-la-pah had no idea what was to happen. He saw three men with the firesticks stand in a line and point them toward his canoe. The bearded one called *Dor-an-tes* raised his arm and then quickly lowered it. From the fire sticks came a great noise that so stunned Sih-la-pah, Seo-ah-ton, and Wa-so-bani that they stumbled backward in the sand grasping their ears. The bow of their canoe exploded in a profusion of wood splinters while a pall of gray smoke drifted across the beach.

Sih-la-pah had dropped to a crouch not knowing what to expect. His brothers looked at the canoe in stunned disbelief. Many of the *Indio* oarsmen fled into the water and were swimming away, their heads bobbing in the surf.

From behind him, Sih-la-pah could hear the hoots and laughter coming from the *Spaniards* as they watched the *Indio* reaction to gunpowder. Slowly rising, he walked toward the canoe and inspected the damage while the oarsmen slowly returned. Not saying a word, Sih-la-pah and his party pushed the canoe into deeper water and slowly paddled away.

CHAPTER 13

Signal Fires

Senales De Fuego

From the shoreline, Alvar De Vaca surveyed the bay. It was a clear night and the vastness of the scene was overwhelming. Small clouds skudded through the sky, their shadows tracing across the bay. The collection of colors on the water's surface revealed the depth below, the dark blues being deep water, the lighter hues indicating shallows, sand bars, and beds of sea grass. Along the shore, thick collections of mangroves extended in both directions. Further down the beach, the light from the signal fire reflected off the waves and the vegetation on the shore. It was a surreal moment.

12 April, 1528

Indian Village on Boca Ciega Bay

After the *Indian* visit, those still on board the ships were allowed to come ashore and walk around. They had been aboard the ships ever since leaving *Jagua*, 54 days previous. This was Easter Sunday and their joy at being able to step back onto dry land was indescribable. Many splashed around in the clear shallow bay. The women requested an escort of soldiers so that they could bathe further down the beach unobserved. Narvaez sent five men and then ordered Fray Palos to watch over the soldiers to ensure the women's privacy was not compromised. Later all laughed aloud when it was related that several of the soldiers had seen the good Fray sneaking a look through the tall grass as the women giggled and splashed in the water.

Narvaez had increased the size of the guarded perimeter around the village, but throughout the day not a single *Indian* was to be seen. Toward evening the bonfires were relit and the perimeter guards were called back in. All of the colonists were returned to the ships. A central core of 25 soldiers was kept at the ready throughout the night. Their job was to act as the initial shock troops should an attack come. They would hold off the enemy long enough so that the others, sleeping beside their weapons, could organize and join the fight. But an attack never came and the night passed uneventfully.

The morning was clear and calm as Alvar ambled down to the beach. He had not slept well, clouds of sand fleas had pestered him throughout the night, buzzing in his ears, flying up his nose, and biting any exposed skin. Now, his whole body itched and all he wanted to do was rid himself of the feeling. At the water's edge, Alvar hesitated and looked around. Out in the bay, the four ships swayed serenely at anchor. Further to the south, a lone *Indio* canoe watched them from afar but seemed non-threatening. Closer in, the fins of two dolphins patrolled close to shore. Stepping out of his pantaloons, Alvar waded out into the clear warm water. The saltwater felt good on the skin. He submerged his head and vigorously rubbed his hair and beard. The many stings stung slightly in the salt water. Further out the water was waist-deep and he lay back and just floated. After the long night, this was most relaxing.

He drifted off in a half sleep staying just alert enough to keep his head above water.

13 April, 1528

Indian Village on Boca Ciega Bay

Andres Dorantes walked among the horses, taking mental note of the condition of each. He shook his head, all had improved, but they were still terribly undernourished, with ribs and pelvic bones pushing against loose skin. The good news was that all 40 were moving well and eating heartily. Armed parties had ranged inland to gather fodder which had been heaped in piles around the improvised corral.

Ahead of him, Estevan was holding the reins of one of the mares while the expedition *herrador* tested the fit of an iron shoe against the animal's left rear hoof. Using long tongs to hold the shoe, it sizzled and gave off a puff of smoke as it touched the hoof. Pulling it away, the blacksmith squinted at the burn mark. Satisfied that he had a good fit he thrust the hot shoe into a waiting pail of water. The loud "p-f-f-f-f-t" momentarily startled the horse and it skittered sideways away from the noise.

"Hoa!" Estevan used the bridle to maneuver the animal back into position. Grabbing the left rear leg, the blacksmith lifted and braced the hoof on his knee. The action caused the horse to lose its balance somewhat, and it struggled to stay upright on three legs. Estevan moved to the side to support the animal. Grabbing the now cool shoe from the pail, the blacksmith carefully placed it onto the hoof. With deft strokes of the hammer, he drove the iron nails that he held in his mouth through the hoof wall.

Dorantes stood to the side and watched the operation with interest. He had always been fascinated by the *herrador's* trade, and although he had never done the labor, he knew each step of the process.

After clinching the exposed nails, the blacksmith carefully set the hoof back on the ground. Straightening, he calmed and stroked the horse's flank.

He noticed the captain. "*Capitan* Dorates, how are you this morning"?

"*Senor* Nazario, I am well thank you, and I see you are doing your usual good work."

"You are most kind *Capitan.*" Nodding toward the village he continued, "It looks like the *Adelantado* will be joining us.*"

Panfilo Narvaez and Alonso Enriquez made their way across the makeshift corral, stopping here and there to look at a horse and talk with its handler.

Narvaez was first to speak, "Ahhhh, *Senor* Nazario, are you ready for another contest?"

The *herrador* and Narvaez had known each other for years. Although not as tall as Narvaez, Nazario was his equal in strength. On many occasions, the two of them would enter into arm wrestling competitions aboard ship, much to the delight of the soldiers, sailors, and colonists. The outcomes were usually equal, with Narvaez winning one and then Nazario taking the next.

"*Si, Adelantado*, but next time I think I will use my left arm to give you more of a chance."

Narvaez roared with laughter as he crooked his arm around Nazario's neck and pulled him close. "Tell me, friend, can any of these horses be ridden?"

Nazario swept his arm around the makeshift corral. "A*delantado*, most are in very poor shape. They will need at least two weeks before they can be ridden, and even then, not that much. There are maybe six that can be ridden for short distances, one of which is your *Santiago*."

Narvaez had brought back his prized stallion, *Santiago,* on returning to *Xugua* just before the expedition had left *Cuba*. It and a few of the other mounts had received special attention during the voyage with daily rubdowns and additional feed. Dorante's stallion, *Medianoche,* was also one of the six.

"*Capitan Dorantes*, it is time we see where we are. Have those six horses lightly saddled and instruct the riders that we will be infantrymen for most of the trip. Also, assemble 40 men with full armor to leave within the hour."

Turning to Enriquez, Narvaez continued, "*Seno*r Enriquez, you will be the King's representative in my absence."

"But, *Adelantado*, *Senor* de Vaca is next senior to you, why..." Enriquez was cut off by Narvaez.

"*Senor* de Vaca will be going with us. As royal treasurer I want him close at hand should we find anything. I will also ask *Senor* de Solis and Fray Xuarez to accompany us. I will need his expertise in evaluating the land that we will be passing through. Further, you will have the assistance of *Senor* Alaniz who, unfortunately, is suffering from problems of the bowels and will not be able to march with us." Narvaez's tone made it clear that there would be no more arguments.

"Yes, *Adadentado*."

Immediately the village came to life. Soldiers donned armor and collected their weapons. One by one the saddled horses were brought to the central square which had been designated the assembly point. In a little over an hour the 40 men had assembled and were milling around waiting for orders. At center the six saddled horses stood riderless, their handlers fussing over them. Of the 36 infantrymen, six were *arquebusiers*, ten pikesmen, eight swordsmen, and a squad of ten *arbalesteros*. Two *perros*, the slang name given to the *soldados de Perro,* or dog soldiers, were also included. The infantry was under the direct control of Captain Alonso del Castillo. The six horsemen consisted of Narvaez himself, Treasurer and Legal Officer, Cabeza de Vaca, Captain of Cavalry, Andre Dorantes, and three riders picked by Dorantes. All of the horsemen, however, were no better than swordsmen for they would walk their animals and only mount them should the situation require it.

Since Narvaez had decided that this would be no more than an overnight excursion, each *arbalestero* carried only ten bolts for his crossbow, and each *arquebusier* carried a minimum of shot and ball. All of the *Spaniards,* save Fray Xuarez, also carried their personal swords and a small shield called a *buckler.*

Fray Xuarez would accompany the group to evaluate the worthiness of the *Indians* for conversion to *Christianity*. This was a stipulation handed down in the original agreement between Narvaez and Charles I.

It was late morning before the party marched north out of the village. It was Narvaez's belief that the expedition had missed the entrance to the great bay and that in exploring in this direction they may come upon it. Narvaez led the procession as it moved out of the village, followed closely by de Vaca and Inspector De Solis. Behind them, two soldiers of the color guard carried the national flag of *Esapana* and the personal flag of Narvaez. Trailing the color guard, Captain Alonso del Castillo and Fray Xuarez walked together at the front of the infantry unit of 38 men. Following the foot soldiers, Capitan Andres Dorantes, accompanied by Estevan, led the small procession of cavalry, each man leading his mount. Narvaez's mount, *Santiago*, was being led by Campo who took great pride in this, his first military foray. Narvaez had provided him with a dagger and sheath which he proudly wore strapped to his waist.

Finally, in the rear marched a contingent of 15 personal servants and slaves carrying additional supplies.

Once on the move, Narvaez called the two *Perros* to the front with their war dogs. These animals, trained since birth, could smell or hear an enemy long before anyone else.

For a league, the procession moved to the northeast. Passing through stands of sea grass, the sandy footing made walking a chore, and it was with relief that they came to the terminus of the bay and began their trek inland. Here the land changed considerably. Gone was the coarse sea grass, now replaced by endless stands of sparse pine that towered over a green carpet of saw palmettos. The footing was better and they easily followed the maze of footpaths already established by millenniums of *Indian* habitation. Alvar noted with interest that the bases of all the trees seemed scorched. Just by touching the bark, his hand came back covered with soot. This was a land where fire must be common.

Many felt that it was only a matter of time before the *Indians* would fall upon them. The procession was unusually quiet as they moved along. Capitan Castello dropped to the back and urged the line to tighten up. He didn't want the rear of the column exposed to intermittent attack. Finally, he pulled ten swordsmen from the center to trail in a kind of rear guard. Mostly, they were there to prod the stragglers.

At mid-afternoon the worn footpath they were following expanded in size. Other paths intersected with it until it appeared to be a major thoroughfare. They stopped here in a small clearing and rested. Overhead birds of every type crowded the trees and the skies. Alvar marveled at the diversity.

So far the group had seen but one *Indio,* and he had seemed as surprised as them at the encounter before he disappeared into the woods. Even so, a strong guard was stationed about the clearing. Alvar drank deeply from the water gourd he carried about his neck. The day was warm and the confinement of his body armor was becoming irritating in the humidity. He thought of removing it but decided against it, at least for the time being.

After resting for about a half hour, the group reassembled and continued along the wide path. Narvaez seemed almost exuberant and walked tirelessly, talking easily with Alvar and de Solis. By late afternoon Narvaez estimated that they had come about three leagues. The land became more open with grasses and other plants, replacing the endless pines. The lower areas had standing water in them. Frogs, lizards, snakes, and a whole manner of wildlife scrambled to get out of the way of the *Spaniards* as they passed through. The last of the pines finally gave way to a marshland with only occasional clumps of trees and shrubs looking like islands in a sea of grass.

Looking back, Alvar could see the terminus of the pine forest behind them.

Finally, at about the hour of Vespers, open water was sighted just ahead. It seemed to be an enormous bay. Upon reaching it, Narvaez scooped up a handful of the water into his mouth and immediately spat it out.

"*Aqua salada!*" It was salt water. This must be the bay that they were seeking. The shore was ill-defined, and what extended out before them was an endless expanse of sea-grass and reeds, sparsely spotted with an occasional mangrove cluster. Narvaez called upon several of the *Moor* handlers to wade into the water to check the depth.

Using pikes to probe the muddy bottom, the three *Moors* slowly moved out into the marshy expanse. Little by little their forms grew smaller as they waded ever further into the bay. After a half hour, it was difficult to differentiate their silhouettes from the swaying reeds. What was obvious, however, was the shallowness of the water. Narvaez finally ordered an *arquebusier* to fire a charge into the air, a prearranged signal for the *Moors* to return.

The loud report of the firearm crashed across the bay. Clouds of waterfowl hurtled into the air in circles of confused flight. Alvar had never seen such a profusion of birds. The *Moors* disappeared, blocked momentarily from view. After several minutes had passed, the conflagration of feathers began to settle once again. Far out in the bay, the three figures had slowly begun their return trip.

Seeing the sun settling in the west, Narvaez called for camp, and on a raised section of ground the assemblage formed a rough circle. Weapons were stacked and the heavy armor was removed. Guards were posted at regular intervals. The horses were tethered and allowed to graze on the profusion of grass that surrounded them. It wasn't until dusk that the three *Moors*, exhausted, scratched, and mud-spattered, returned to the camp. From their furthest point, they related to the *Adelantado* that the sea of grass extended far out into the bay. Seldom did the water depth extend above their knees, and only once were they forced to swim in water that was chest deep. However, just before they were called back the depth of the bay increased dramatically, so much so that they feared to go further. They talked of schools of mullet so thick that they were forced to stop until the water cleared. Dolphins were everywhere and they had even seen several of the cows of the sea, *el manati*, looking back at them with their strange whiskered faces.

Panfilo sighed. This must be the Deep Bay...this *Bahia Honda*...of which they were seeking. But, where was the inlet? A meeting was called.

Narvaez, seated on a huge section of bleached driftwood, addressed the small gathering around him.

"From the point of our first sighting of *La Florida,* we have seen no evidence of an inlet to the great *Bahia Honda* shown on our maps. Today we have found this *Bahia Honda,* but its entrance still eludes us."

The small group, seated haphazardly around Narvaez, nodded in agreement.

"*Adelantado.*" It was Alonso de Solis. "This can only mean that the entrance is further to the south."

Fray Xuarez was standing just behind de Solis. "I agree, perhaps we should return to the village and scout further to the south."

Narvaez remained silent as he tore off a piece of salted pork and stuffed it into his mouth.

Cabeza de Vaca was next to comment. "There is always the possibility that we sailed past the entrance without seeing it. The coastline is extremely flat and at times shielded by cays and mangrove forests. We also encountered several squalls on our voyage that may have further masked the entrance to the Bay."

The two captains, Castello and Dorantes, had moved behind de Vaca but remained silent.

It was Fray Xuarez again. "I am but a simple man of God, explain to me why we cannot stay at the *Indio* village and use it as our base."

Narvaez spoke up. "Fray Xuarez it is your job to save our souls from the fires of hell. We cannot expect you to understand the advantages of a well-placed base of operations."

Everyone laughed including the Fray. "*Adelantado*, you are correct. Seeing what I have to work with..." He spread his arms to encompass the circle of men. "I have more than enough challenge before me."

Again, laughter.

Narvaez continued. "The *Indio* village is a poor location. First, the Bay...this *Boca Ciego,* is shallow and unprotected. After what happened in *Trinidad,* I don't want to lose any more ships to the *huracans*. Second, the land around the village is sparse, dry, and not suited for farming. Finally, it is an indefensible location militarily. The *Bahia Honda* of which our pilot Miruello speaks so highly is deep and well protected. The shoreline around the bay is marked by streams and rivers."

With that, the meeting grew silent with only an occasional slap of an insect. Overhead the sky was clear and moonless. The stars seemed to be no more than a good reach away. Out in the grasslands, an owl voiced its mournful call, just audible over the cacophony of frogs and insects calling into the night.

Finally, Narvaez spoke again. "Here's what I propose to do. We will return to the village on *Boca Ciega* and send the brigantine to the south in search of the Bay's entrance. As soon as they sail we will return to this place and see if we can make contact with them. It was settled. They would leave in the morning.

14 April, 1528

Overnight Camp at Old Tampa Bay

Leaving just after daybreak, the party moved rapidly back down the trail. Except for a brief rain squall that thoroughly soaked everyone, nothing unusual was encountered and everyone had returned to the village at *Boca Ciego* by late morning.

Narvaez quickly called for Miruello who shortly reported to the *Adelantado*.

"*Senor* Miruello, we have found what I believe to be the *Bahia Honda*. The shore that we encountered lies about three leagues to the northeast and extends out as far as the eye can see."

Miruello's mood seemed to brighten, "that is good news, *Adelantado!*"

"We feel that the mouth of this great bay is southward down the coast and probably not far."

Miruello considered this but said nothing.

"As soon as it can be made ready, I want you to take the brigantine south and closely follow the coast until you find this inlet. I will lead another scouting party out and return to our camp of last night. When you have found this inlet, proceed along the western shore of the bay until you encounter our party. We will light fires as a signal."

"*Si, Adelantado.*"

"Once we have met up, I will join you aboard the brigantine and we will search for a proper landing site for the expedition. The rest of the scouting party will return to *Boca Ciega*."

"I have a question *Adelantado*."

Narvaez looked uncomfortable, "What is this question...*Senor* Miruello?"

"If the inlet is out there...by God's Holy grace...I will find it. But, if the inlet is not to our south or we fail to make contact, what are my instructions?"

So sure was Narvaez that the inlet was to the south, he hadn't considered it not being there. He unbuckled his heavy *montante* and leaned it against a tree. He sat down in the sand and stroked his beard.

"Your question is a good one, *Senor* Miruello, and something that I will have to consider." He paused.

Narvaez looked about him. The six horses that had been with the scouting party were being led back to the corral while the remainder of the soldiers, slaves, and servants were walking back to their campsites. To his right Fray Xuarez and de Vaca were having some kind of a discussion. In the bay, one of the ship's boats was returning with a load of colonists. He looked back at Miruello.

"It would be most disappointing if the inlet cannot be located to the south, but if that happens, I would have you continue on to *Havana* and rendezvous with Alvaro de la Cerda who waits with a ship and fresh supplies. Return as quickly as possible, for our situation here will soon become most critical."

"*Si, Adelantado.* With your permission, I will transfer the supplies, gather the necessary personnel, and be ready to sail with the tide tomorrow morning.

Narvaez grabbed his *montante,* and using it as a support, rose again to his feet. "Good, good, keep a sharp eye for our signal fires. We will leave again for the campsite as soon as you set sail."

With this, Miruello was off, commandeering the colonist boat just after it skidded ashore.

"*Capitan* Dorantes!" Narvaez called out, his booming voice reaching every corner of the village. "Have the men rest up today. Tomorrow we will return to our campsite as soon as pilot Miruelo and *La Estrella* set sail."

15 April, 1528

Aboard the Brigantine *La Estrella,* off the Coast of Florida

People were quickly transferred to other ships, a new crew was pulled together and provisions were loaded in record time. The anchors were hoisted and the brigantine *La Estrella* was underway at first light. The wind was blowing offshore and they had no trouble in reaching the inlet to *Boca Ciega* with only a minimum of sail. The trip through the inlet, however, was treacherous. In the rising tide, the swirling water and eddy currents made travel perilous. For a time there was concern of floundering against the heavy shoals that extended far out from the entrance. Caught in the swift moving current, it reminded the ship's pilot, Angel Jimenez, of his times as a boy sledding on the ice with no control.

Soon, however, the brigantine was in deep water, and Miruello called for a course change to the south-southeast. They would hug the shore as close as possible in search of the entrance to the Great Bay. The inlet to Boca *Ciega* was only a league astern when everything changed. It was at this moment that the brisk offshore winds died completely. In only a matter of minutes, not even a breeze rippled the canvas of *La Estrella.* It sat like a cork in a mill pond, subject only to the current that pulled it to the southwest and away from the coast.

Miruello and Jimenez were incredulous. Just at the moment they most needed it, the wind had dropped to nothing. It was as if a divine hand had swept the wind away in one deft stroke. They were becalmed. Miruello considered using the oars, but decided, instead, to drift and wait for the wind. It was still a long way to *Cuba*.

15 April, 1528

On the Trail to Old Tampa Bay

Now, once again Narvaez and the same group as before trudged back to the campsite by the great bay. The party had waited until Miruello had hoisted sail and cleared the inlet before starting their march.

"It is our third journey on this damned trail!" Santo Corral hissed to the man next to him. "Couldn't it have waited until we rested a bit and got something to eat?"

It was mid-afternoon and the temperature was climbing. A thunderstorm had just passed through the area and everyone was soaked. Around them water vapor seemed to rise like steam from the ground, grass, and palmetto leaves. Santo removed the *morion* from his head and tried to wipe the sweat from his eyes. The helmet seemed to concentrate the sun's heat and his head felt like it was going to explode. Under his long sleeve *camisa,* the sweat and rainwater combined with dust as it ran down the crack of his ass. Even itching the irritation was impossible without first taking off the bulky *escuapil* padding. He was getting chaffed and had to walk with his legs wider apart in an effort to relieve the discomfort. Periodically he reached down and readjusted himself for some relief.

From the line behind him, someone yelled. "*Soldado* Corral you walk like you made love to a stallion last night!"

Everyone laughed. Everyone but Santo.

Each soldier wore a variety of armor depending on what they could personally afford. The Camisa was a long sleeved shirt or undergarment that gave protection from the chaffing effect of the armor. Over this, most of the soldiers wore the *escuapil* padding that had been introduced by the *Aztecs*. Some wore a *brigandine* or heavy cloth coat embedded with numerous metal plates sewn into the material. Only Narvaez, the royal officials, and the captains wore the fitted metal *coraza.*

On this trip, ten additional soldiers had been ordered by the *Adelantado*. Once Narvaez met up with the brigantine, he planned to take these men and possibly more with him on the brigantine. Together they would look for a permanent site in the Great Bay and he would need their support and protection. Two more friars had also asked to come along. Both *Franciscans.* Frays Pietre de Asturiano and Augusto Alaniz would join the commissary, Fray Xuarez, as the religious representatives.

Even with the heat and humidity, they moved quickly on the now well-beaten trail. There was now little fear of an *Indio* attack. By late afternoon yesterday's campsite finally came into view. Immediately men and slaves were assigned to gather anything burnable to light the signal fires that Narvaez had promised. A special detachment of men and two horses was sent back to the pine forest to gather wood.

A space had been cleared and small fires started by the time the special detachment had returned. Both horses were loaded with wood, and the six slaves that had accompanied the group offloaded the material onto a common pile.

Fray Xuarez joined Narvaez. "God be with you, *Adelantado*."

"And to you, Fray Xuarez."

"I have prayed that *Senor* Miruello finds the entrance and appears to us this day."

"Let us hope that your prayers are answered, Good Fray, but I fear this location will be difficult to find from the bay. I am considering moving further to the north in search of a better landing site, one of deeper draft and not inhibited by vegetation. Just sighting a mast in this..." Narvaez waved his hand to encompass the marshland before him and didn't finish the statement.

Narvaez kept one signal fire burning throughout the night.

16 April, 1528

On the Trail to Old Tampa Bay

After a long and busy night, the sun rose clear and bright over the water. Even as the sun was rising, Narvaez was standing on the shore scanning the horizon. In this sea of endless grasses, however, just sighting a distant ship would be a challenge. He ordered that two more fires be lit and to these they would burn green palmetto leaves, hoping to make as much smoke as possible.

By mid-morning the second fire had been started, and the green palmetto leaves were producing the desired result. Dark clouds of smoke rose and drifted eastward in the morning air. The smoke was beginning to draw attention, and out in the bay, canoes were becoming a common sight.

A little before noon Narvaez decided to assemble the men and proceed further around the bay. Again they followed the well-defined *Indio* trails that skirted the bay in all directions. Staying close they marched northwest and then, abruptly, the shoreline turned northward. Here the trail moved further inland to avoid a vast impassable salt marsh. On this higher ground, the countryside was dominated by hammocks of deciduous trees with only an occasional pine grove interspersed among the vegetation. For a while, they lost sight of the bay entirely. They rested by a stream that flowed slowly toward the bay. The water was clear and sweet. All of the men and horses drank their fill.

Captain Alonso del Castello had separated himself from the group to find a location that, at this moment, was of high importance to him. Behind a large live oak, he kicked away the brush, leaned his sword against the tree, and removed his pantaloons. His stomach had been growling for the last two hours and now that familiar pressure in his bowels told him the time was imminently near. Squatting down, he reached out and grasped a sapling to support himself. The relief was overwhelming and he paused a moment just to take in the feeling of contentment that cursed through his body.

Just on the other side of the tree two figures silently passed by him. They were not *Spaniards*.

His partial view showed naked bodies, dark black hair, and feathers Now, with only one purpose, Castello grasped his sword and thrust himself through the bushes. Four *Indio* boys, no more than teenagers, turned in terror as this strange bearded man, naked from the waist down and smelling of feces, thrust a sword in their faces while screaming strange words at them.

"Ceder, Ceder!"

Not understanding his demand to submit, they stood, wide-eyed, and stared. Each of the boys was holding a light bow and several arrows, the type used for hunting birds. Castello used the flat of his sword to knock the weapons from their grasp.

By this time several soldiers had heard the commotion and had rushed to the aid of their *capitan*. They were taken aback almost as much as the young *Indio* boys at the scene that greeted them. They immediately bound the captives' hands and led them back to the main camp. Walking away, several of the soldiers looked back and laughed. Castello, still standing in the middle of the trail with his sword in hand, looked down and suddenly felt foolish. He had to clean himself. He gathered up his pantaloons and trudged toward the stream but, unfortunately, he had to pass by the bulk of his men.

At first, not a word was said, head held high and eyes straight ahead he walked as regally as the situation would allow. But then, someone whistled derisively and the collection of men, who had been busting to let it out, exploded in laughter. Even Narvaez, who had been talking with de Vaca and Fray Xuarez, joined in, his guffaws sounding above the rest. Castello, good commander that he was, although embarrassed, was appreciative of the moment and good-naturedly waved.

At the stream, the captain waded into the cool water until he was crotch deep and began scrubbing the foulness off his body. The day was warm and the cool water felt good. In the background, the laughter had died away and he could hear Narvaez and some of the men trying to communicate with the young *Indio* boys that he had captured. Feeling that he had cleaned himself sufficiently, Castello started his return to shore when an explosion of water and spray erupted next to him. Startled, he turned and saw the gaping, tooth-filled maw of an enormous *lagarto*...alligator rising from the water. To the onlookers who turned at the sound of the commotion, it looked like Captain Alonso del Castello rose out of the water by divine intervention in his effort to escape the massive reptile. Even when on dry land, he didn't stop until a large limb tripped him up.

"*Madre de Dios*, Mother of God" was all he could say.

Back at the water's edge a Soldado Pedro de Valdivieso, had earlier noticed the huge animal and had unknowingly accompanied Castello to the stream. As El *Lagarto* made its attack run, he plunged his long pike into the water. This was the explosion of water and spray that had startled Castello.

Now thrashing back and forth, Valdivieso was having trouble bringing the animal to land. Several other *soldados* rushed to his aid and together they hauled the writhing monster up on dry land. One stepped forward and plunged his sword deep into the *alligarto's* skull. With this, the writhing stopped.

All now stood over the animal and marveled at its size. From snout to tail it was over five paces long. Castello, still shaken, but now wearing his pantaloons, approached the crowd.

"*Senior* Valdivieso, I am in your debt. Except for you, I would have been torn to pieces."

"*Capitan*, I am just glad my first thrust found its mark."

Walking up to Valdivieso he clasped his hand, "Me too *Pedro*. Me too."

16 April, 1528

On the Northwestern Shore of Old Tampa Bay

The four *Indio* boys sat on the ground, their hands tied. Standing in front, Narvaez was the biggest and most fearful man they had ever seen. Eyes wide, the youths were shaken and baffled by the profusion of alien sights that surrounded them. One of the stallions was brought up and located only feet from where the captives were sitting, so close that its hot breath could be felt on their bare skin. Walking up to where they were sitting, Narvaez reached down and, one by one jerked them to their feet. Behind Narvaez the *Tiano* seaman, Marino Carmona, waited for the *Adelantado* to finish.

"*Senor* Carmona, I need to know where these boys are from and how far from here is their village."

Carmona began by questioning the *Indians* in his native *Tiano* tongue. There was no response. The boys knew they were being addressed, but the words had no meaning to them and they just stared.

From behind, the big stallion lowered its head and nuzzled the closest *Indio*. The reaction was immediate. The terrified boy lurched forward and tried to run. A lead rope attached to his restraints and held by a guard was solidly jerked, and the boy fell to the ground in a heap. Brought to his feet again, he began to sob silently.

Carmona resorted to sign language, and this time the boys began to respond. Communication was slow at first. Only some of the hand talk was understood by either party. At Carmona's signal, Narvaez and the stallion backed off. This seemed to settle the young *Indians*. For a time the hand talk flew back and forth. Some of the gestures were comical in appearance and, while trying to describe a sailing vessel, Carmona gave a hard look to a snickering guard.

Narvaez was becoming impatient. *"Senor* Carmona, what are these *chico's* telling you?"

"*Adelantado*, I think they come from a village not too far from here. The village is located on the bay."

Reaching into a haversack, Narvaez pulled out a fist full of maize kernels and handed them to Carmona. "And what of maize, do they have any maize?"

Carmona held out one hand with the maize and gestured with the other. All four *Indians* began to bob their heads in unison and pointed in the direction of their village.

With that Narvaez turned and gave the order to march. To the *Indian* boys, he removed the restraints and gave each bright beads to which they became quite excited. He set them at the front to lead the way but with guards on either side.

The party of *Spaniards* continued along the trail much as before. With the knowledge of *Indians* in the area, however, Narvaez increased the rear guard and once again the dogs patrolled far to the front. It was not long before the grass and mangroves cleared and the water in the bay appeared deeper. The bay was enormous, the shorelines extending far into the distance, gradually fading out of sight. To the southeast, open water with no end continued to the horizon. Many times Narvaez stepped to the beach and scanned the bay for any sight of *La Estrella*, but to no avail. Rounding a bend, the profile of huts and the telltale wisps of cooking smoke came into view. The column stopped. A contingent of about fifteen warriors approached the *Spaniards*. The dogs became unruly and Narvaez quickly ordered them to the back.

Fray Xuarez, de Solis, Carmona, and four *soldados* proceeded forward to meet the warriors.

From his position Cabeza de Vaca watched as the two parties met at the center of the trail. At first, there was no movement. Carmona then began with the hand talking, and Xuarez stepped forward to distribute glass beads and copper bells. The *Indians* seemed pleased with the gifts and began talking among themselves. At this point, Narvaez released the four captives and the boys joined the other *Indians* from the village.

Dorantes had mounted his stallion and proceeded forward. The *Indians* stopped talking and stared in amazement. At Carmona's beckoning the *Indians* approached the mounted cavalryman and stood in a circle around him, never closer than ten feet. As Dorantes reined his mount to the right and left, the *Indians* would back off in terror, but always returning to stare at this strange beast with a man atop its back.

Now, from the direction of the village, a smaller party approached the *Spaniards*. This was obviously the headman of the village.

Narvaez turned to Castello and de Vaca. "Let us see what this *cacique* has to say."

Narvaez, accompanied by Castello and de Vaca, proceeded forward. Behind them a line of *arbalesteros* stood ready, but with their crossbows resting on the ground.

As Narvaez approached, Carmona, Xuarez, de Solis, and the group of warriors all joined him. Upon reaching the *cacique,* the warriors respectfully moved behind their leader. Again, gifts were presented and the discussion between Narvaez, Carmona, and the *cacique* began. After much discussion and pantomiming, it was learned that the *cicique* was called Hirrihigua and he was the leader of all the inhabitants of this part of the Great Bay. They were called the *Ucita*. He said this word many times, motioning to all the *Indians* around him and then moving his hand in an arc around the bay.

Like the people of *Boca Ciega,* his language was soft and lilting with many inflections and a lack of conjunctions. The meanings of many words seemed to be reflected in the facial contortions of the speaker. In turn, the *Indians* had many problems pronouncing the *Spanish* names, and "Narvaez" was repeated by them as "Ne-vets." Carmona continued to struggle with the language and concentrated on the hand talk to which he was rapidly improving.

After a period of time and the distribution of more gifts, it was decided that the *cacique* would allow the *Spaniards* to enter his village to rest and barter for food. With that the warriors stepped forward and, grasping the hands of all in the greeting party, gently led them to the village. Narvaez briefly turned and signaled for the column of men to follow him.

They had marched only a short distance when the former boy captives began to jabber and point toward a location just off the trail. It finally became apparent to Carmona that they were identifying the maize field to which they had been earlier questioned. It was readily apparent, however, that the maize was not mature and the ears were small and green. They moved past the field leaving it untouched.

Narvaez, Alvar Cabeza de Vaca, and Capitan Alonso del Costello led the column as they entered the village and proceeded to a large open space or courtyard. This was dominated by a mound of considerable height. Atop the mound, a structure resembling a long house had been constructed. Other smaller mounds also surrounded the open area, each with its own unique structure. There were other mounds situated along the shoreline which, in fact, were huge piles of discarded oyster shells. Behind the main body of *Spaniards*, Andres Dorantes and two other cavalrymen rode abreast followed by the remaining three horses led by their servant handlers. Far in the rear the two war dogs had been muzzled and were under tight control of the *perros*.

The inhabitants of the village hung back and observed the entering *Spaniards* from afar. The *Indio* men all appeared tall and well built, but it was the women that the *Spaniards* concentrated on, comely and naked from the waist up with coal black hair that hung far down their smooth backs. A short, loosely woven skirt, attached at the waist with a braided cord provided the only modesty. Not as tall as the *Indio* men, many of them were taller than the average *Spaniard,* their legs long and lean. The women, like the men, covered themselves with tattoos of all types and designs.

The *Spaniard soldados,* unable to contain themselves, leered at the half-naked women and began commenting among themselves. It was Santo Corral who was most vocal.

"Buenas tetas....mmmm!"

He grabbed his crotch as he eyed a particularly attractive maiden holding a young child close by her side. She saw Corral and stepped further back into the crowd in an attempt to hide herself. To her left, a tall well-built man, probably her husband, eyed Corral with contempt but said nothing.

Castello, seeing the exchange, stepped behind Corral and cuffed him across the back of his head. *"Estupido,* are you crazy? All of you keep your thoughts to yourself. We are surrounded by these *Indios* and we don't need trouble."

Castello was fearful of treachery and warned all of his men to be prepared to fight at a moment's notice.

Many answered, *"Si Capitan"*, but they didn't stop looking.

When Dorantes and the two other horsemen entered the courtyard, there was an audible murmur among the *Indians,* their attention was riveted to these strange animals. Many thought that the horse and man were one creature.

Finally, the two *perros* entered. Even though muzzled, their huge mastiff war dogs snarled and lunged at the line of *Indians*. As a group, the onlookers stepped back, many of the warriors grabbing weapons or fitting their long bows with arrows.

Castello, who was everywhere, saw this and immediately sent the *perros* and their dogs out of the village along with a small contingent of men. With this, the mood seemed to settle, and the attention of the *Indians* was once again directed to the horses and their riders.

In the raised courtyard the *Spaniards* were halted. The *cacique* gave orders for food and water to be brought up for the *soldados*. To Narvaez, he requested that he accompany him to the top of the large mound. Narvaez asked for de Vaca, Xuarez and, of course, Carmona to accompany him. Dorantes and Castello were directed to stay below and remain alert. He also emphasized that they stay apart, as much as possible, from the villagers.

They followed the *cacique* up the well-worn path to the top of the mound. Here a long house of immense proportions had been erected, much bigger than the structure encountered in *Boca Ciega*. Within the structure, several women were busy with cooking fires and a variety of tasks. One older woman seemed to be the matriarch of the *cacique's* family and eyed the *Spaniards* suspiciously. Several young children stood off to the side warily watching these strange men who had entered their world.

From the ridge poles and uprights hung the trappings of village life. Freshly scraped deer skins, baskets, woven ropes, and hideous masks, many with horns, bones, and feathers attached. Some of the bones appeared to be human. Fray Xuarez made the sign of the cross and muttered small prayers as he observed the heathen images.

Entering the long-house, the group sat in a circle, Narvaez and Hirrihigua at opposite ends. The discussion continued into the evening. Carmona, the *Tiano* seaman, struggled to pass the meanings of both parties. Throughout, Hirrihigua, recognizing him as one of his own race, discretely questioned Carmona as to who he was. Carmona didn't pass this information on to Narvaez but talked and signed briefly about his own past and the power of the *Spaniards*. This seemed to gain the *cacique's* trust.

Narvaez asked the *cacique* if they could build a large bonfire by the shore of the bay.

Hirrihigua questioned why.

Narvaez turned to Carmona. "Tell him that we have friends who are lost in the bay and their ship has many gifts that we would like to share with the *Ucitas.*"

The *cacique* thought on this for a moment and then directed his people to construct a bonfire on the shore.

Finally, Narvaez produced a small nugget of gold and asked if the *Ucitas* were in possession of any of this material. Hirrihigua took the nugget and, fingering it thoughtfully, relayed to Carmona that, yes, they had some but that it was obtained in trade with neighbors far to the north, a place called *Apalachen*. He handed the nugget back to Narvaez.

With that, the meeting broke up. The women of the long house passed out food and drink to the visitors. Below in the courtyard, turkey, dried venison, fish, and oysters were offered to the soldiers.

As evening approached the *Spaniards* were led out of the courtyard to a raised field that bordered the bay. Here they would spend the night. Castello, ever cautious, posted double guards and the dogs were brought up to guard the perimeter.

From the shoreline, Alvar de Vaca surveyed the bay. It was a clear evening and the vastness of the scene was overwhelming. Small clouds skudded through the sky, their shadows tracing across the bay. The collection of colors on the water's surface revealed the depth below, the dark blues being deep water, the lighter hues indicating shallows, sand bars, and beds of sea grass. Along the shore, thick collections of mangroves extended in both directions. Further down the beach, the light from the signal fire reflected off the waves and the vegetation on the shore. It was a surreal moment.

Scanning the horizon with the hope of spotting a sail, Alvar found nothing and turned to Narvaez who was close by.

"*Adelantado*, there is no sign of *La Estrella*. From this vantage point, a sail would be easily visible."

"*Si Aguacil*, we can only hope that God will soon deliver *Senor* Miruello to us."

Both turned and walked back to the courtyard where the men, who weren't standing guard or caring for the animals, were relaxing around a fire.

As it grew darker the wilderness around them echoed with the howls, screams, and growls of the many animals that ghosted through the night. Owls, cougars, wolves, coyotes, and the "whoof" of an occasional bear. Some of the noises were unidentifiable and the men imagined the *Indians* calling to each other in the darkness. Few got much sleep.

CHAPTER 14

Miruelo And The Ponce

Miruelo y de Ponce

When you were in his presence...there was a feeling...you knew he was the leader and he wasn't to be trifled with. He had not grown fat like so many others who entered the political world. His face was hard and his blue eyes always seemed to shine with a brilliance, but he was kind and loved by his men. I liked him immediately as did my uncle."

18 April, 1528

Aboard the Brigantine, La Estrella, off the West Coast of Florida

After two days of dead calm, the currents had continually pushed *La Estrella* far to the south. Now, as the sun rose above the water, Angel Jimenez scanned the horizon to the east. There was no sight of land. They had drifted far out to sea and judging from his latest readings, far to the south.

Diego Miruelo moved up next to him. "I would imagine the *Adelantado* has given up on us by now.

"*Buenas dias* friend Miruelo."

"And to you, Senor Jimenez.

Jimenez reacted to the first statement, "As our instructions were given, I would assume he thinks we did not find the Great Bay and have continued on to *Cuba*."

Miruelo answered defensively, "As we have ...only it was not intentional. The weather has made that decision for us.

Jimenez carefully checked his notations. "We are at latitude 25. At first, I didn't believe this reading, but I have taken it several times and found it to be true."

Miruelo laughed, "*La Florida corriente.*"

Seeing the blank look in Jimenez's eyes, Miruelo continued. "There is a river of water that moves about *La Florida. Capitan* de Leon was the first to speak of it."

Miruelo became quiet and stared out to sea.

Jiminez looked at Miruelo with questioning eyes. "You knew *Capitan* De Leon?"

It was a moment before Miruelo answered with a quiet voice. "I only met him once but it was my uncle that will forever be in his debt."

Up until this moment Miruelo had shared little of his life with any-one. But now...he spoke of one of Jimenez's heroes, the great con-quistador, Juan Ponce de Leon. He had to know more.

"Your uncle? Was he a sea *capitan*?"

Miruelo seemed to swell with pride. "My uncle was a great pilot. If not for him I would not have been in this trade...he taught me much."

"What was his name?"

Miruelo laughed. "Friend Jimenez, we shared the same name. My father idealized his brother and named me in his honor...Diego Miruelo."

"If it is not too painful, *Senor* Miruelo, tell me the story."

Diego Miruelo looked long at the young Jimenez and then shrugged his shoulders.

"In the summer of 1513, my uncle was the pilot of the caravel *La Rosa*. At the direction of Viceroy Colon, he had sailed to the Islands of *Bimini* in search of *Indios*."

"A slave ship?"

"*Si*, pilot Jiminez, in those days you took whatever work was offered, but the voyage had another purpose. Viceroy Colon had also sent him to find *El* Ponce and report on his activities."

"He was sent to spy on *Capitan* Leon?"

"Well...yes, that was the directive given. But, remember, no one knew where the Ponce was...it was anyone's guess. So, his primary mission was to gather slaves and, if he found *El* Ponce...so much the better."

Jimenez was eager to hear more. "So, what happened?"

"Around the middle of June, he left *Espanola* and sailed north to *Bimini*." Miruelo stopped, and as an afterthought, he added. "Back then, *Bimini* was the name given to all the land north of *Espanola.*"

He chuckled. *"El* Ponce was given credit for finding the mainland of *La Florida,* but uncle knew it was there long before he ever sailed."

"he did?" Jimenez was captivated.

"Oh *Si*, he had learned of this *Terra Firma* several years before. There were few slaves to be had on the windward islands. We call them the *Lucayos* today. So slavers began searching further west. Reaching the shores of the mainland, they at first thought it to be another island. As weeks passed and they coasted far to the north, it became apparent that this was no island. Even better, the supply of *Indios* was endless."

A short, soft breeze brushed across the deck of La Estrella. Both pilots noted it immediately.

"Friend Jimenez, it looks like this infernal weather is about to change."

"I agree, pilot Miruelo, but please continue your story while we still have time."

"Ah yes, let me see. After leaving *Espanola,* my uncle arrived at the *Lucayos*...I think it was late in July. He had stopped at the largest of these islands, the *Indios* called it *Abaco,* to procure water. As they were loading casks the lookout sighted three sails coming from the southwest. Uncle's sails were furled so I think it was a while before they noticed him. He told me this because it looked as if they would pass by. Not until they made an abrupt course change did they approach and anchor next to *La Rosa.*

"Was it Juan Ponce?"

"*Si,* it was, and what do you think of that? Uncle was looking for him, and Le Ponce found them!"

"What was Juan Ponce like, Senor Miruelo...I mean...how did he look...and...how did he act?"

Another slight breeze wafted across the deck. Overhead, the sails and yardarms reacted ever so slightly.

"I only observed him once and I was then much younger, but from the first time I saw him, I was impressed by his regal bearing. He was about my size...although not as good-looking."

Miruelo laughed and cuffed Jimenez across the shoulder."

"What I mean, friend Jimenez, is that he had a way about him. When you were in his presence...there was a feeling...you knew he was the leader and he wasn't to be trifled with. He had not grown fat like so many others who entered the political world. His face was hard and his blue eyes always seemed to shine with a brilliance, but he was kind and loved by his men. I liked him immediately as did my uncle."

"Did your uncle join his expedition?" Jimenez couldn't get enough.

"No, uncle stayed overnight at this place before embarking the next morning. El Ponce continued on and said he would sail north before returning. He bid uncle 'good hunting' before leaving."

"But why didn't your uncle join the expedition, I thought he was to spy on him?"

"He was, but to join his expedition at this point may have shown his true intentions. Uncle was very impressed by La Ponce and hoped that they would meet again..little did he realize that their paths would cross in a most unusual way."

"What happened?"

Miruello switched positions as he thought about his answer. He swung one leg over the sideboard and steadied himself on a brace rope with one hand. Below him, small waves were beginning to lap the hull.

He called out to the *marineros* who were lounging around the ship. "Prepare to get underway. We will have good winds within the hour. Helmsman, be prepared to steer a course south by southeast." As an afterthought he added, "We are going to *Habana*".

He turned back to Jimenez. "After leaving El Ponce, Uncle arrived at the mainland that evening. It was growing dark so he anchored at the mouth of a river called *Jobe. H*e had been there several times before."

"He had?"

"Si, this *Rio Jobe* was well populated with *Indios* and he had gained the confidence of one of the *caciques*. This *Indio* was very powerful and continually at war with those around him. Uncle would trade worthless beads, worn-out knives, and pieces of glass for the captives he had taken. It was a very good arrangement.

"In the morning he arrived at his village. Seeing them in the bay the previous night, the *cacique* had prepared a feast and insisted that he stay. He had also provided each of them with a woman and I can tell you it was not easy to leave. We were at this place for three weeks."

Jimenez was wide-eyed. "You mean they gave him women?"

Miruelo laughed and winked at Jimenez. "Yes, and uncle said they were some of the fairest creatures on this earth." He held both hands chest high, palms inward, and fingers spread.

Jimenez turned red.

"After securing the slaves Uncle left the village and proceeded northward up the coast. The *cacique* had indicated that there was another large village of his enemies about eight leagues distant. He found the village, but it was mostly deserted. He only captured about 15, and these were mostly women and children."

Jiminez listened intently. Overhead the rigging began to creak and groan as the wind, still non-directional, began to pick up.

Miruelo continued. "At this time he had about 40 *Indios* and the hold had room for a few more so he sailed further up the coast. They traveled for two days. It was then that they saw a village and proceeded to go ashore. The *Indios,* however, had hidden themselves in the mangroves to ambush the landing party. They showered the boats with arrows, killing one man who took an arrow through the throat. After this, they attacked with their war canoes and it was by the grace of God that the boarding party made it back to *La Rosa*."

"Was your uncle injured?"

"Ah! They were all injured. Everyone had suffered an arrow wound of some kind."

"Where was he hit?"

Miruelo gave Jimenez a funny look and then laughed. "It happened as he was bent over to help the *marinero* who had been hit in the throat. There was blood everywhere and the *marinero* was thrashing about...interfering with the other oarsmen. Suddenly an arrow pierced my uncle's leather britches and buried itself in his ass. Right here in the meaty part."

Miruelo turned and pointed to his buttocks.

Jimenez tried hard to suppress a laugh but it escaped through his nose. Miruelo joined him in the laughter.

"When he told me this story we laughed but then Uncle became serious. He told me that getting injured in the ass is very bad. The arrow was in so far he couldn't pull it out and he couldn't sit down. He couldn't stand because he made too good of a target and it hurt like hell."

Jimenez was still laughing, "What did he do?"

"He knelt down on the bottom of the boat and returned fire with a crossbow until they got back to the ship. Two more seamen had been killed by arrows. They left the dead seaman in the boat and hurried up the ladder and across the deck. The *Indios* had surrounded the ship. The *marineros* quickly dropped the sails and lucky for them, the wind was blowing off the shore. Several were injured from arrows shot into the rigging."

"They had taken two boats to shore that day and tied both to the ship when returning from the attack. Uncle's boat had been mistakenly tied to a long rope and it trailed the ship by several lengths. The *Indios* jumped into it and began cutting up the dead seaman."

"They cut him up?"

"They would hack off an arm, a leg, and then his head. They would hold each part for the *Spaniards* to see before throwing it into the water."

"Agh" Jimenez tried to picture the scene in his mind.

"Finally, the *La Rosa* began to outdistance their canoes, and the *Indios* in the boat cut it free. Uncle said he could still see them shaking their fists at them."

Miruelo paused in his storytelling. He sent a seaman high into the *carajo* to keep a watch. "We are far to the south, but how far to the west is only a guess. I don't know, but I suspect we are very close to *Las Tortugas*. Once we can identify something it will allow us to set an exact course, but for now we will continue south by southeast."

The commotion of getting underway settled down, sails were set and lines were drawn up and tied off. The wind was west by northwest and *La Estrella* settled into an easy tack...south by southeast, just as Miruello had ordered.

Jimenez, eager to hear the rest of the story, pressed Miruelo to continue. "Where did he go after escaping the *Indio* attack?"

"Their travels had taken them far north of the *Lucayans*. Those who had been pierced by the arrows were in sorrowful shape. Many required the barbs to be cut out. The screams of pain on that first day after the attack were horrible to hear. When it was over they dressed their wounds with oil and rested. They sailed for four days staying as close to the shore as possible. If they ventured out too far, the Great Current would push them backward. On the fourth day, they sailed seaward and crossed the deep banks hoping to find the *Lucayans*."

At that time a blast of sea spray cascaded down on the two pilots. They laughed and Miruelo noted. "The wind is picking up nicely and the sea is becoming rougher. Let us continue our conversation on the aft deck."

Once on the aft deck Jiminez again pressed Miruelo. "Did they find the *Lucayans*?"

"Not at first, but they found something else, much more terrible!"

"What was it?"

"My uncle related to me that on the morning of the fourth day after the attack, the sky before them was as nothing like they had ever seen."

Miruelo made a broad sweeping gesture with his arms as if he was looking at it."

He continued. "A great towering cloud stood before them. Other clouds were spiraling around it with massive arms that extended to the horizon. Beneath the cloud, the sky was dark as death and split with fearful lightning."

Of this, Jimenez knew exactly what he spoke of. "A *huracan*?"

"*Si*, and a very bad one. They sailed onward hoping to find a port but it was not to be, the storm was upon them just as they sighted an island in the distance. The rains began and the seas were beyond description. They had to reach the island, for a ship in such an ocean is doomed."

Jiminez's eyes were like saucers. "They continued to sail into the *huracan*?"

"It was their only hope. They proceeded on with only the mainsail and lateen. The winds became fierce, but praise to God they remained from the south. They quartered the seas, the bow waves exploding into geysers of spray that fell upon them in great torrents. Over the sound of the wind, Uncle could hear the screams and lamentations of the *Indios* below."

Miruelo had once again become animated with his description of the event, but as he talked of the cargo of slaves below he fell silent and stared out to sea. It was a while before he continued.

"They continued onward as the island drew ever closer. It was large, extending far out in both directions. At its center was a broad open beach. It was about this time that they lost the main mast to the wind. It exploded at its base in a spray of splinters. Uncle joined the *marineros* in the effort to cut it free for it was dragging in the water. Its mass and the wind across the lateen caused the ship to turn abeam to the sea. Waves washed across the deck as they struggled to free the mast. Uncle said they were laid over so far to port that he could have reached out and touched the boiling sea."

Jimenez, who had experienced the force of the *huracan* at *Trinidad*, remained silent.

Miruelo continued, "God was with them, for they finally freed the mast, but not before it had turned *La Rosa* broadside to the wind. It was pushed shoreward and ground heavily into the bottom. Many were thrown clear and landed in the surf."

"Uncle swam as hard as he could at first, but the waves...they were as tall as a horse...kept dragging him under. He could feel the bottom, but then a wave would lift him up and tumbling him forward. His head was bleeding from dragging in the sand and rocks. Uncle said he prayed to God, Saint Peter, the Virgin Mary...all of them. I can't tell you how many times he thought he would die."

Jimenez, his voice lowered, asked, "How many made it off the ship?"

A bright smile flashed across Miruelo's face and he clapped Jimenez on the back. "They all did! Can you believe it? Every *Christian* made it to shore."

"What of the *Indios,* Pilot Miruelo, what of the *Indios*?"

A darkness settled across Diego Miruelo's face and he looked down at the deck. "They were chained below and never made it out. Even as he gained the shore and safety, he could hear their cries over the wind as the ship tore apart like a child's toy."

There was a long silence.

Jimenez finally spoke. "They were heathens, not *Christian*...but no one deserves to die like that."

"Yes, of course, you are right, but there was nothing they could do. It all happened so fast."

"And what of your uncle and the crew?"

"He was eventually thrown onto the shore. The wind was so strong that it was difficult to stand. The incoming waves kept knocking him over. He managed to help other *marineros*. Some were trying to swim, others were holding onto whatever they could find. He dragged them on to the sand. As the waves became higher he thought they would all drown there on the beach. By then the ship was almost gone. They stumbled inland, falling with each gust of wind. Only by joining arms could they make any progress."

"Did they find shelter?"

"They proceeded inland and encountered a small forest that pro-vided some protection. There they huddled under a particularly large tree, wet and miserable until the next morning when the storm subsided."

Miruelo and Jimenez were startled by the call of "T*erra, Terra*" coming from above. Both looked up to see the lookout pointing to larboard. From the deck level, nothing yet was visible.

Miruelo walked toward the ratlines. "I believe this to be the *Tortugas*. A welcome sight if it is true. I will look for myself."

As Miruelo climbed, Jimenez studied his chart. If it was the *Tortugas*, they had drifted almost 65 leagues to the south and west of where they started.

From a position just below the *carajo,* Miruelo called out, "Pilot Jimenez, it is indeed the *Tortugas.* We have but a day's sail to *Habana*. Set the course due south.

19 April, 1528

Aboard the Brigantine, La Estrella, Near Havana, Cuba

Ahead the coastline of *Cuba* stretched across the southern horizon. They were sailing west now, keeping an eye for that familiar indentation in the coast that would signal the harbor at *Habana*. Predictably, the strong Gulf Stream current had swept them toward their destination. Now the winds were on shore and the seas were light. They were making good time.

It had been a long night. Keeping the *Tortugas* well off to port, *La Estrella* had passed into the *Florida* Straits by evening. At Miruello's recommendation, they had sailed all night under reduced sail. At first light, the ship was re-trimmed. Sometime around the hour of Vespers *Cuba* had come into view, and the *marineros* on board raised their voices in celebration. Now the harbor at *Habana* was literally around the next bend.

Almost at their destination, both pilots began to relax. Miruelo balanced himself on the starboard rail and watched the shore slide silently by. Jimenez, just back from a trip forward, sat down heavily on a foot stool.

"Phew! I'm tired. It will be nice to get off this ship and walk normally for awhile."

Miruelo answered, "I look forward to a good meal and a bottle of wine...and maybe the company of a woman." He winked at Jimenez. "We won't have long, the *Adelantado* will expect us to find *Capitan* de la Cerda, resupply, and return as soon as possible with both ships.

Jimenez nodded.

"Pilot Miruelo, What happened after the storm and shipwreck that your uncle experienced?"

"Ha...We were so busy last night, that I didn't get a chance to finish my story."

"You had said that everyone had weathered the storm beneath a tree."

"And they did, a cold and miserable lot they were. All of them clung together in a great mass just to stay warm. They stayed that way all night, shivering and listening to the terrible sounds of the storm. Later the next day the skies finally began to clear and they were able to dry themselves. All they had were the clothes on their backs...some didn't even have that. Many had no shoes. In their swim to the shore, the violence of the water had torn off shirts and even pants"

"And what of your ship," Jimenez asked, "was their anything left to salvage?"

Miruelo shook his head before answering, "They walked to the beach that evening, for hunger was gnawing their stomachs and they looked for anything to help in the quest for food. What greeted them was beyond description."

"The beach was strewn with all matter of planking, barrels, spars, pieces of sail, scraps of this and that, and most horrible of all, the bodies of the captured *Indios*. They were still chained together. Some were buried in the sand...others were partially buried. Uncle said, you had but to follow the lengths of the chain to find the bodies. It was a most ghastly sight."

"Most amazing, however, was the location of the ship...or what remained of the ship."

Jimenez was incredulous, "You mean the ship was still there?"

"Well, not exactly. A single mast had somehow wedged itself into the bottom. It was standing upright with the yardarm still attached...a cross!"

Miruelo pointed seaward as if it was in front of him even now.

"They were hungry and almost naked, and there..in the bay...was the cross of their Savior. It had withstood the fury of the storm and now beckoned for them to repent for the suffering they had caused. Uncle said he fell to the sand and wept."

Jimenez, moved by the story, was silent.

"He vowed at that moment that, if delivered safely from this island, to never participate in the capture and trade of *Indios* again."

For a long while the two pilots were silent as *La Estrella,* sailing easily, continued on a starboard tack along the coast of *Cuba*. Finally, composing himself, Miruelo spoke in a hushed tone.

"They salvaged whatever was useful and then moved away from the awful place. The bodies of the *Indios* were becoming ripe. The crabs and gulls were already hard at work on their corpses. The *Spaniards* moved farther down the beach."

"That night they were able to start a fire. One of the seamen always carried a flint in his pantaloons and it had survived the swim to shore. For this alone, they were blessed. They warmed themselves by burning planking and timbers from the ship."

"By morning our fire had burned down to coals. Their hunger and thirst were severe and they endeavored to move inland in search of water and whatever food was available. It was a particularly clear day and on a high point of land uncle looked back to the bay that was spread out below them. Movement caught his eye, and it was the that his blood ran cold."

"What was it?"

"A line of canoes was moving along the beach. There were twelve of them, each with six men."

"*Caribes*"?

"Of that I am sure. There were only 23 *Spaniards* and not a weapon among them, not even a knife. They crouched there in the grass and watched as the *Indios* drew closer. Uncle knew if they came upon the wreck site they would come ashore to investigate. He resolved then that he would fight until the end rather than end up in their stew pot."

Jimenez made an audible gulp, "What happened?"

"Quite amazingly they turned about and proceeded away."

Jiminez blinked. "They were lucky."

"Our Savior had seen fit to protect them once again, but for the next week they roamed they island in fear and never again ventured a fire at night."

"What about food and drink, how did they survive?"

"There where several springs in the area with good sweet water, but the food was another matter. By the third day, they were growing weak and many returned to the beach to gather small crabs and anthing edible. Quite by accident one of our party found a cache of turtle eggs and then another...and another. They feasted on these as if they were the finest delicacy in all of *Spain*! After that, they became quite good at finding the depressions in the sand where the eggs were located."

"And what of the *Caribes,* Senor Miruelo, did they see them again?"

"It was on the eighth day of their stay on this island. Five of the men were on the beach searching for eggs when a single canoe came upon them. On seeing these savages, our men took flight and returned to camp much out of breath. The *Caribes* had not given chase but had returned from where they had come. Uncle was sure that they would return in force.

"They made a pact that each would fight until the death. They gathered anything that could be used as a weapon...sticks, rocks, even sharpened shells."

"Why didn't they run?"

"Where to, friend Jimenez? This island was narrow and long and they had grown weak eating only turtle eggs. No, they determined to stand and fight."

"Did the *Caribes* return?"

"Oh yes, they returned. Uncle counted eight war canoes. More than 40 of them came ashore and started to advance on their position. Each warrior was splendidly built and covered with hideous tattoos. Their weapons were flint knives and war clubs festooned with rocks and sharpened shells. They set up a fearsome howling as they closed in. At this moment the survivors knew they were dead men.

"Did they attack then?"

"The attack never came! They stopped halfway to the *Spaniard's* position and began to talk amongst themselves and point to the sea. It was at that moment that the three ships of El Ponce appeared, coasting very near the shore. They had been hidden by a bend in the shoreline and a stand of trees. Uncle said the men jumped up and began to wave and shout, hoping that their lookouts would see them."

What did the *Caribes* do?"

"For a moment they stood there and looked confused, not sure whether to attack or not. It wasn't until El Ponce dropped sail and turned towards the island that they retreated back to their canoes. All of the *Spaniards* laughed and jumped about, happy to be alive, for only moments before they knew their lives were lost.

"When the first boats arrived from the ships the survivors gave them great embraces, much to their embarrassment, Ha!"

Miruelo let out a chuckle as if he was reliving the moment his uncle related the story.

"Later Uncle joined El Ponce on his flagship, *Maria de la Consolacion*...He still remembered the ship's name...it was carved in beautiful script just above him as he climbed the ladder."

Miruelo passed his right hand before him as if emphasizing the lettering.

"In the cabin uncle related the story to El Ponce and told him of the cross of our Savior that had survived the storm. El Ponce then related that at this same bay, they had stopped months before to fill their water casks. On this return trip, they had determined to seek out the same bay...a bay that somehow uncle had found in the midst of a great *hurrican.* He was convinced that his rescue was directed by the hand of God."

Jiminez sighed, "Of this, I am certain, friend Miruelo, a truly re-markable story. One of which I will tell often."

Starboard of *La Estrella* the dark silhouette of shore continued to slide by and pass astern. As the light finally faded on this day, an occasional twinkling of lights appeared ahead...the lights of *Havana*.

CHAPTER 15

The Dogs

Los Perros

*T*he handlers released both dogs.

Before the woman had taken three more strides they were on her, tearing at her arms and legs. Dragged to the ground, her screams were cut short as one of the mastiffs tore out her throat.

17 Apr, 1528

Hirrihigua's Village

It was early morning. Standing on the raised mound overlooking the village, Panfilo Narvaez, Alvar Nunez Cabeza De Vaca, and the *Indian cacique,* Hirrihigua, watched with interest a confrontation that was developing below them.

Frays Pietre de Asturiano and Augusto Alaniz could be seen arguing with a group of *Indians.* On the ground around them were scattered what appeared to be wooden boxes. The *Indians,* who had been attempting to restrain the friars, were now being roughly pushed back by newly arrived *soldados.* Voices were being raised.

From the top of the great mound Narvaez in his great booming voice called out, "*Senor* Castello see to the situation over there!" He pointed towards the disturbance.

Below, many eyes turned upward to look at the imposing figure with the great voice who stood above them. Castello, already moving forward, waved to Narvaez.

Hirrihigua, the *cacique* of the village, peering down at the disturbance, did a strange thing. Raising his spear above his head he stood stiff as a statue for several seconds...then...with a sharp scream that startled all the *Spaniards* around him he cast the spear down the hill. All movement in the *Indio* village came to a standstill. Those *Indians* confronting the friars meekly moved back.

By now Castello was in the area and ordered the *soldados* to back off. Next, he confronted the friars who stood their ground. He demanded to know the reason for the disturbance. Not being a particularly religious man, he had no problem castigating the holy friars.

It was Fray Asturiano who addressed Castello. "Follow me *capitan* and you will see the reason for our displeasure." He walked over to one of the wooden boxes and pointed inside.

To Castello, the box looked to be a shipping crate commonly used by *Spanish* ships in the transport of commerce. In fact, many had notations written on them, lists of contents, weights, and quantities. Castello thought it strange that they would be here in this remote *Indio* village. He didn't immediately recognize the contents within until his eyes focused on a human hand partially hidden under an accumulation of painted deer skins, feathers, and linen pieces.

Startled, he stepped back.

Drawing his sword, Castello poked at the skins and tossed them aside. The stench of decay wafted up from the box and he felt the bile rising in his throat. Underneath the skins was the bloated body of a man. The eyes were open...staring, and for a moment Castello felt they were staring at him. What surprised him more was the red beard that covered the man's face.

This was a *Spaniard*!

It was then that Fray Asturiano spoke. "*Capitan*, this is an abomination, all of these contain bodies...*Christian* bodies!"

Turning to look up at the great mound, Castello called out. "*Ade-lantado*, you need to see this."

He then looked to the other men in the courtyard. "Capitan Dorantes, put the men on guard and make weapons ready but do it quietly."

Castello walked to each crate, fourteen in all. His worst fear was that these were the remains of the brigantine crew, but this was quickly rejected as he didn't recognize any of them. There were no wounds on any of the bodies save for some bruising and damage by sea creatures.

One man had both eyeballs missing. "Gulls could have done that," Castello spoke to no one in particular.

Another body was missing half a leg in what appeared to be a shark bite. All had been feasted on by crabs.

"These men drowned, probably from a shipwreck." Again, his comments went unnoticed.

The friars now were systematically going through each crate casting the painted skins, feathers, and other heathen trappings onto the ground.

Fray Suarez now joined the group. He turned and spoke directly to Castello. "These were *Spaniards* and *Christians*, they have been defiled by this work of the devil, this is vile idolatry. All of this..." He spread his arms to encompass the hill top. "All of this has to be burned."

Narvaez joined them, his entourage and Hirrihigua just behind him. By now each of the dead *Spaniards* was clearly visible. Narvaez silently walked among the crates and then addressed the priest.

"Holy Fray, wouldn't it serve a better purpose to just bury these poor souls?"

Suarez shook his head. "No *Adelantado*, for they will dig the remains out of the ground and further defile them. It is best that we burn everything.

Suddenly, Fray Asturiano called out. "Gold, I have found gold." In the corner of one of the crates, he had recovered a small nugget. He held it in the air for all to see.

The word itself was electrifying. All of the *Spaniards* rushed to the crate to inspect the find. They checked the other corners and then overturned the crate to see if anything was under the corpse. Sure enough, another small nugget fell to the ground.

Narvaez called out to the *soldados* standing close by. "Help us empty these crates." Unceremoniously the cadavers were dumped on the ground and each crate was thoroughly inspected for any sign of gold.

More concerned about the *Indians* that surrounded him, Castello and De Vaca backed off and watched the reaction of the *cacique* and the villagers. They didn't like what they were seeing. Many of the men had fetched their weapons and the women and children were falling back to the outer fringes. The *cacique* had a nervous look on his face and he was slowly moving away from the *Spaniards*.

Castello called out to Narvaez. "*Adelantado*, I think we have trouble."

Momentarily forgetting himself during the search for gold, Narvaez quickly took stock of the situation.

"Seize the *cacique*!"

With that, two *soldados* quickly grabbed the chief and bound his hands. They forced him to his knees. One of the men stood guard with a sword poised just above the chief's neck.

The crowd below, now mostly men, began to surge forward.

Again Narvaez took charge. "Capitan Dorantes, have two of the arquebusiers discharge their weapons into the air."

The *Spaniards* below were drawn into a loose circle. Two *arquebusiers* stepped forward. After briefly checking the burning cord or "match," they pointed their barrels only slightly above the heads of the advancing throng and depressed the triggers.

The sound so startled the *Indians* that several fell to their knees. Others dropped their weapons and clasped their ears. The black powder smoke billowed over their heads and its pungent smell filled their noses. All turned and fled.

"Just the effect I was hoping for! *Capitan* Dorantes, have the war dogs brought up and stay alert."

Hirrihigua was still on his knees under the watchful eye of the guard as Narvaez accompanied by the interpreter Marino Carmona walked up to him.

"Help him to his feet," Narvaez ordered the guard. The *cacique* was raised up. A man of about forty, his height matched that of the governor. Lean and graceful like all the men of the village, his black hair was cut off just below the ears and showed early signs of gray. Even bound, he held himself with a good amount of regality. His chin was high as he met Narvaez's gaze.

"Senor Carmona ask our friend the *cacique* about these dead *Spaniards* and from where they came."

Carmona stepped up to the *cacique* and began the hand talk. Immediately Hirrihigua flew into a rage, holding out his bound wrists to Narvaez and stomping the ground with his feet. He then turned on Carmona and began the same routine. Finally, he scooped up fistfulls of earth and flung it into the air. At that he became silent.

Narvaez addressed Carmona. "Well?"

Frustrated, Carmona could only look at Narvaez and shrug. "I think he's unhappy that you have bound him in front of his own people."

"He said that?"

"*Adelantado*, I have no idea what he said, only that I would be upset if the same thing had occurred to me."

Narvaez stared at Carmona a moment and then shifted his attention to De Vaca.

"What do you think?"

Alvar only shrugged.

Frustrated, Narvaez turned to Carmona and the two guards, "Unbind him then and see what you can find out about the dead *Spaniards*. More than that, however, I want to know where the gold came from."

With the bonds removed the *cacique* turned to walk away. He was immediately blocked by the guards. Irritated, he spun around and flew into yet another tirade, only this time he scooped up a handful of dirt and threw it on Narvaez. Very quick for a big man, Narvaez drew his sword and contacted the *cacique's* head with the flat of the blade.

"Thwack"

Hirrihigua dropped to the sand, momentarily stunned.

In the courtyard below, the crowd once more started to surge forward, but this time with a wary eye on the *arquebusiers*. Castello ordered his men to draw their swords and the *arbelestero's* fitted bolts into their crossbows. By now the *perros* had returned. They quickly removed the muzzles from the two mastiffs who, even now, were lunging against their leashes. Dorantes and the five cavalry-men mounted their horses, lances at the ready.

There was silence. Only the growling of the dogs could be heard.

Both camps stared at each other.

Suddenly, from the large mound, a woman began running down the steep hill. Her loud screams were incoherent to the *Spaniards*, but the bow she carried gave cause for concern.

Alvar, standing next to Narvaez exclaimed, "That is the old woman from the long house...I think the *cacique's* mother."

At no more than 100 feet from the column of soldiers she fitted an arrow and, still on the run, let it fly. The arrow arched toward a *soldado* but was easily diverted by his shield.

As soon as the first arrow had been loosed, she fitted another and released it in the same direction. This one impacted the flank of one of the horses causing the cavalryman to temporarily lose control. Horse and rider surged forward, knocking two *arbelesteros* to the side.

"*Mierda*...shit!" Narvaez had had enough. His loud voice carried down and across the courtyard.

"*Perros*!"

The handlers released both dogs.

Before the woman had taken three more strides they were on her, tearing at her arms and legs. Dragged to the ground, her screams were cut short as one of the mastiffs tore out her throat. Stained red from the life blood of the woman, the mastiffs now tore the body apart, pulling against each other. Limbs separated and the entrails spilled across the ground. The crowd of *Indians* watched in stunned silence as the dogs began to consume the woman's corpse.

Hirrihigua, recovering from the blow to the head, wasn't immediately aware of what was happening. Rising from the ground he took in the ghastly scene below he sank back down to his knees and began a mournful wail.

"*Capitan* Castello!"

"*Si Adelantado.*"

"Disarm the *Indios* and search this village."

"*Si Adelantado*, and what should I be looking for?"

"Gold *capitan*, gold...and *capitan...*"

"*Si Adelantado.*"

"Have those dogs leashed!"

Castello barked out several orders. With a military procession, the *Spaniards* rapidly fanned out in two directions, surrounding the crowd of onlookers. Dorantes, leading his cavalrymen, moved rapidly to the right and ran down several men trying to escape. Castello moved to the left with his infantrymen There was little resistance. The *Indians* were herded into the courtyard. Here each was disarmed and searched. The *soldados* took their time searching the women, fondling exposed breasts and the pubic area under the short deerskin loincloths. Any that objected were clubbed to the ground. Having seen the horror that the dogs imparted, many were frozen in fear. A great waling began to emanate from the courtyard.

By the order of Narvaez, the friars began burning the boxes containing the dead *Spaniards*. The smoke from the pyre rose turbulently in the air whipped around by the breezes coming off the bay. The stench of burning flesh filled the village as the Spaniards made preparations to spend the night.

18 Apr, 1528

Hirrihigua's Village

The next morning Santo Corral's squad of six *soldados* moved among the dwellings, again checking for weapons and valuables. Each was entered and thoroughly searched, the contents being thrown out onto the ground. So far, several small pieces of gold and numerous pearls had been recovered. One gold piece was particularly intriguing. It had been hammered flat and shaped into the form of an eagles head. This only whetted the appetite of the men and they eagerly anticipated each new search.

At the next dwelling, Corral was the first to enter. He stopped short at the entrance. There, huddled on the ground, was the woman he had seen earlier in the crowd. She was protecting two young children. Standing beside her, the husband stepped in front of the *Spaniard*.

A lecherous grin forming on his face, Corral called out to the other *soldados* with him, "Take the husband and the children, I will take care of her."

Seeing the soldiers coming for him, the husband charged Corral, catching him with a head butt that split the *Spaniard's* lip and staggered him backward. It was a short-lived attack, however, for one of Corral's compatriots brained the husband with the hilt of his sword. The *Indio* fell to the ground unconscious and bleeding...but not dead. He was dragged outside along with the two children.

Inside, the woman cowered as Corral, wiping the blood from his injured lip, approached her.

"Now we will have some fun *mi chiquita*."

Outside, the five squadmen guarded the entrance. They laughed and made crude comments about the grunts and screams that came from within. Soon, only the soft sobbing of the *Indio* woman could be heard as Corral appeared at the entrance. His sword belt slung over his shoulder, he pulled on his pantaloons.

"Diego, I think she was asking for you next."

And, so it was, each member of the squad took his turn with the young *Indio* woman. When they finally moved on she lay bleeding and bruised on the floor of the dwelling.

19 Apr, 1528

Hirrihigua's Village

Narvaez sat on the ground resting against one of the longhouse support poles. He slowly examined the hammered gold eagle head. Laid out before him were the results of yesterday's village search. The pile of gold was less than impressive...still, there was gold here; that was obvious. Another pile contained pearls, most of which were center drilled and hung on strings made of animal sinew. This was understandable given the huge piles of oyster shells that seemed to line the beach area. There were a few other articles, a copper disk, a small amount of silver, and some turquoise pieces...even a Spanish coin.

Since the death of his mother, Hirrihigua had been unresponsive. He sat on the ground rocking back and forth, babbling incoherently. No amount of physical stimulus could rouse him from this state. They had tried. Slaps kicks...nothing worked.

Frustrated, Narvaez had Hirrihigua's brother, Hiconti, brought in for questioning. Carmona worked hard to make himself understood and to relay the questions of the *Adelantado*. On the question of gold Hiconti would only point to the north and repeat the word "*Apala-cha*". It was a word that the *Spaniards* had not heard before. Anxiously, Narvaez wondered if this "*Apalacha*" was another *Tenoch-titlan* just waiting to be discovered.

Narvaez tossed the gold eagle back into the pile. He was ready to *leave this place*. There had been more than enough time for Miruelo to reach them. He could only assume that the brigantine had returned to *Cuba*. If that was the case, Miruelo should be on his way to *Boca Ciega* with fresh supplies and the other ship.

In the village below, the *Indians* had been disarmed and most had been allowed to go about their business. A few of the men were still being held in the courtyard. Armed squads of *Spaniards* continued to patrol the village, but only to insure that no organized resistance developed. The mood of the *Indians*, however, was sullen.

 Narvaez rose to his feet. "I'm done with this place. Assemble the men and be ready to march within the hour. I want to follow this shoreline further to the north. Possibly Miruelo and *La Estrella* can yet be sighted."

De Vaca nodded his head, "*Si Adelantado*" and headed down the hill to notify captains Castello and Dorantes.

Narvaez instructed the guards to bind Hirrihigua and his brother. Both would accompany the *Spaniards* on their march to the north.

"They can act as guides and will be our insurance against attack."

With that, Narvaez walked out of the long house and peered at the vast bay that spread out before him. He still hoped to see a sail, but none greeted him. With a sigh and a furtive last look he turned and walked down the hill.

19 Apr, 1528

Further Up the West Shore of Old Tampa Bay

As Alvar trudged along the trail, the rain fell in torrents. Like most of the other *soldados,* he had removed his *morion,* tying it to his belt. The helmet was heavy and it trapped the steam and body heat coming off his head. They were moving fast and the exertion was beginning to tell. The rain didn't help. Water ran down his forehead carrying sweat into his eyes. It burned, and no amount of rubbing seemed to help. Underfoot the trail was becoming harder to negotiate. Ahead of him, a *soldado* slipped sideways on the mud, falling to the ground amid a chorus of profanity.

Narvaez was fearful of an attack and did his best to hurry the column along. Three cavalrymen rode at the end of the column making sure that no one fell behind. Behind them, three squads of *soldados* performed a rear guard maneuver that Narvaez had perfected in Jamaica and Cuba. He called it *la rana,* for it resembled the movements of a frog. The squads would conceal themselves at equal intervals along the trail. After a count of 100 the furthest squad would rise and run past the positions of the other two, setting up a new position just behind the horsemen. At the next count another squad would perform the same maneuver, and so on. Using this technique, a surprise attack from the rear of the column was virtually impossible. It was tiring, however, and the squads had to be continually replaced.

At the front of the column, the *perros* led with their huge war dogs. The animals' keen sense of smell and hearing would tip off an ambush long before it had a chance to materialize. It was the flanks that Narvaez was most worried about, however, and he instructed each man to keep a sharp lookout to the right and left.

Alvar looked nervously to his right. The trail led them through a hammock thick with pines and a heavy underbrush of saw palmettos. The rain and mist further inhibited visibility and for a moment Alvar wondered if he should retrieve the *morion* from his waistband. With each step, he braced himself for the shower of arrows that he was sure were coming. There was no attack, and they passed through the hammock, unscathed, to an open grassland. On a sandy rise with a commanding view, Narvaez stopped the column.

Alvar sagged down on the wet sand, glad for the opportunity to catch his breath. The driving rain had not ceased and the strain was showing on the men. To the southwest, the sky was darker still. Lightning traced across the sky like fiery spiderwebs. The continuous roar of the thunder was deafening while overhead the trees swayed in gusts of strong wind. The temperature had dropped.

It was by now the hour of Vespers and Narvaez, backlighted by the flashes of lightning, walked among the men.

"We will make camp here tonight and continue on in the morning."

20 Apr, 1528

The Western Shoreline of Old Tampa Bay

"*Soldados* up, we are moving out!" It was Castello.

Sometime after midnight, the storm had blown itself out and for a few brief hours, the men had managed to huddle together in fitful sleep. Now as morning came upon them the rain started again and the insects were unrelenting. After eating what was left in their haversacks they once again started down the trail. But, now they were moving again and in the open country, and the *la rana* squads were pulled in. Mercifully the rain ended in a magnificent rainbow and a brisk breeze began to blow. The stifling humidity began to dissipate. They marched to the north, at first staying close to the bay but then turning east as they reached its terminus. They continued on for ten or twelve leagues until it was almost dark.

Up ahead at a point of land extending into the shallow bay was another village of about 15 houses. The village was deserted but located somewhat inland was a field of ripe maize ready to be harvested. The men were exhausted and Narvaez made a decision to remain and rest up. From the village there was an unobstructed view of the vast bay and, once again, signal fires were lit in the hopes that the *Spaniards* aboard *La Estrella* would see them.

They stayed two days here, maintaining the signal fires, eating the roasted ears of maize, gathering fodder for the horses, and resting for the return trip.

23 Apr, 1528

Moving South Along the Western Shoreline of Old Tampa Bay

On the morning of the third day, men and horses were gathered up and they began their journey back towards Boca *Ciega*.

Again skirting the bay Narvaez took every opportunity to scan the empty expanse for any sign of *La Estrella*.

There was no sign.

On this day the weather was clear and relatively dry. A brief squall passed over the column but quickly passed on, its remnants dark in the western sky. As they neared the same sandy rise they had camped at only days before a call to make camp was issued. They would rest here tonight and be fresh when they entered Hirrihigus's village tomorrow. This was an ideal defensive position on high ground with sparse vegetation all around. Still, Narvaez set out perimeter guards that were relieved every few hours. The night was uneventful.

Up early, the column moved out, now even more leery of an *Indian* attack. As they neared the village each *Spaniard* was ready for battle. Hirrihigua and Hiconti were placed at the front of the column. Everyone fully expected a major conflict but, strangely, the village was deserted. It was getting late in the day so Narvaez made a decision to spend the night. That evening another violent thunderstorm passed overhead, but this time the *Spaniards* remained dry in the village of the *Ucitas*.

25 Apr, 1528

Sitting Out the Storm in Hirrihigua's Village

At daybreak, the storms continued unabated. No sooner would one squall pass overhead than another would rapidly form and take its place. By afternoon the weather remained unchanged and Narvaez made the decision to stay the day. Finally, just after nightfall the sky cleared and the brilliance of a million stars twinkled in the moonless sky. They would leave in the morning.

26 Apr, 1528

Moving South Along the Western Shoreline of Old Tampa Bay

At first light, the column left the village of Hirrihigua. Everyone was on their guard, for Narvaez was sure that an attack was imminent. Hirrihigua and his brother were again placed at the front of the column under strong guard.

Except for a few isolated hammocks scattered across the grasslands they were in open country. Everyone became more relaxed, even the dogs were quiet.

After traveling two or three leagues the column stopped for a rest in an isolated hammock that offered some shade.

Alvar was tired. He had been sitting in the grass rubbing his feet when an arrow embedded itself into the ground next to him. For a moment he just stared at the shaft, still quivering from its flight. Looking up, the air seemed to be full of missiles. In a single motion, Alvar released the *morion* from his waistband and slammed it onto his head. Drawing his sword, he crouched in the grass hoping to make as small a target as possible.

All around him, men were scurrying to cover themselves with whatever they could find. Curses and commands filled the air. A horse galloped wildly by, two arrows embedded in its rump. Luckily, the arrows had been released in a long arc and their penetrating power was severely limited. Several men had suffered wounds to their shoulders, arms, and backs, but none of the stone points had entered past the barb. Narvaez himself pulled an arrow from his right arm and threw it to the ground in disgust.

Pointing with his sword, Narvaez bellowed, "Capitan Costello, the *Indios* are in the grass to the east. Bring up the *arquebusiers*."

Castello wasted no time. The *arquebusiers* loaded and primed their pieces and waited for the command. Behind them, the *arbalesteros* stood ready with their crossbows. Finally, the *Spanish* sword and pikesmen backed up the formation. It was the typical *Tercio,* or *Spanish* Square, on a much smaller scale.

At about 300 feet from the camp another cloud of arrows launched into the sky. Immediately the *Indians* rose up from their concealment and began running further into the grassland.

Castello commanded, "Fire!"

The concussion of the discharge and a cloud of gray smoke emanated from the line of *arquebusiers*. Lead balls tore through the grass on their way to the *Indians,* buzzing past their ears like angry hornets. One ball was seen to contact a runner and he went down in a tangle of arms and legs. Others stopped to carry him off.

Now it was the *Spaniards'* turn to take flight, for the arrows had begun their downward track.

The *arquebusiers* immediately surged forward, away from the clearing. The *arbalesteros,* behind them, followed closely. Narvaez moved toward the captive Hirrihigua, an area that had purposely not been targeted. All around the *soldados* used their small shields, called *bucklers*, to protect themselves.

Crouching in the grass Alvar winced as an arrow careened off his *morion* and landed harmlessly in the grass. Another embedded itself in the *buckler* that he held shoulder-high.

When the rain of arrows had ceased, *capitan* Andre Dorantes and four of his horsemen quickly mounted but were stopped by Narvaez from pursuing the fleeing *Indians*. Dorantes, his blood still up, reined in but remained in the saddle.

"The horses are too weak and we cannot chance losing any of them," Narvaez called out. With that, the *Adelantado* sheathed his sword.

Narvaez removed his *morion* and turned to watch as several of the men removed an arrow from the horse that had been struck in the rump. It was at this moment that Hirrihigua and his brother made their move. Although chained with their hands in front, the two had been left temporarily unguarded. Hirrihigua jumped to his feet and lunged for the tall grass. His brother followed, but not before hitting Narvaez with a glancing blow with a large rock. Stunned, the *Adelantado* slumped to the ground. The two *Indians* sprinted across the grassland in the direction of their compatriots.

Dorantes, still on his mount, was looking in the other direction when he heard the commotion. He turned and saw Narvaez and then saw the two fleeing figures in the grass. Spurring his horse he lunged across the clearing and into the tall grass after them. Behind him, two cavalrymen remounted and followed their leader.

The brother, trailing Hirrihigua by 50 feet, was quickly overtaken by Dorantes who, with a well-placed kick sent the *Indio* sprawling. Riding on, he passed by Hirrihigua and then, reining his horse, turned to face the *cacique*. Hirrihigua darted to the right and then to the left, but each time Dorantes expertly reined his mount to block the escape. Finally, breathing hard, Hirrihigua stood motionless and waited for his fate.

Dorantes dismounted and looped a rope around the *cacique's* chained hands, remounted, and led him slowly back to the clearing. The other two cavalrymen had already deposited the brother in front of Narvaez who, still holding his *morion*, was sitting on the ground. Slowly he rose to his feet, refusing help from other *soldados* standing by him. The rock wound had opened a gash just behind his right ear and blood matted his hair and beard. His eye came to rest on the brother who had done this to him.

With a contemptible snarl, he threw his *morion*. The helmet careened off the brother's forehead and landed, spinning, in the sand. Next, he walked over to where Hirrihigua was standing and, trembling with rage, grasped him around the neck with both hands.

"*Hijo e' puta*...Son of a bitch, I should kill you right now." Hirrihigua sank to his knees, unable to break the grip of the powerful Narvaez. But...after only a moment...Narvaez let him go. Hirrihigua collapsed in the sand, coughing and gasping for air.

Suddenly calm, Narvaez turned and addressed Castillo. "Capitan Costello, set perimeter guards and have your men build a fire. We will send these two back to their village with a proper message."

The *soldados* began scrounging anything that would burn. A detail proceeded to a small hammock just off the trail to collect bundles of twigs and branches. Soon a brisk fire was burning. The two captives were brought up and ordered to kneel in the sand.

Watching the proceedings, Alvar had no idea what was on the *Adelantado's* mind. He thought it strange that they should be halted here in open country with enemies close at hand. As the fire continued to burn, hot coals were gathered and deposited in the sand next to the *Indians*. It was now that Narvaez approached the captives. He unsheathed his double-edged *montante* and pointed it at the brother.

"Hold him down."

The eyes of Hirrihigua's brother grew wide with fright as two *Spaniards* grasped him from behind.

"Stretch out his arms," Narvaez commanded.

A *soldado* grasped the rope attached to the wrists and pulled.

With a single motion, Narvaez swung his *montante* and severed the *Indian's* hands just above the wrists. The *soldado* pulling on the rope fell backward. The two hands, still attached to the rope, catapulted over his head and landed in the sand. The screams of the victim were like nothing Alvar had ever heard. He stood transfixed.

The two *soldados* holding the brother each grabbed a stump and plunged them into the bed of hot coals, effectively cauterizing the wounds. The *Indio* mercifully passed out.

Narvaez turned to Hirrihigua. "Hold him down."

The *Adelantado* sheathed the *montante* and, instead, pulled a razr-sharp knife from his belt.

"Hold his head tightly." Hirrihigua was a big man and it took two more *soldados* to immobilize him. His screams were continuous, "*Yi, Yi, Aeeeh.*"

Narvaez grabbed the *cacique's* nose between his forefinger and thumb and pulled it as hard as he could. With the knife, he cut through the cartilage septum just forward of the nasal bone and exited just above the upper lip. The tip of Hirrihigua's nose came off with a loud pop. Narvaez threw it in the fire.

The *soldados* released the *cacique* and watched him writhe in pain. Spurting blood from the hideous facial wound stained the sand around him. They finally threw him a rag to staunch the flow of blood.

"Now, release them so they can return to their village. Let this be a warning to anyone who attacks us." Narvaez turned and addressed

Castillo. "*Capitan* Castillo, assemble the men, we need to get moving."

A bucket of water was thrown on the brother to revive him. The severed hands were hung around his neck. Both *Indians* were made to stand and walk down the path. Alvar watched as the two pathetic, shuffling figures disappeared around a bend.

For the next few leagues, the column proceeded cautiously along the trail. Isolated arrow attacks continued but these were from long range and ineffective. Castello had renewed the *la rana* squads and everyone scanned the grasslands intently. Finally, at dusk, they arrived at the original campsite by the bay. Narvaez made a decision to spend the night here rather than continuing on to *Boca Ciega* in the dark.

This time the signal fires were not set for it was feared that they would outline both men and horses. Only small cooking fires were allowed and these were soon covered with green palmetto leaves so that the smoke would help hold off the swarms of mosquitoes.

27 Apr, 1528

Leaving Old Tampa Bay and Traveling East to Boca Ciego

At mid-afternoon, the column passed through the perimeter guards at *Boca Ciega,* much to the delight of the soldiers, sailors, and settlers who watched them stumble in. Entering the village square, all looked to the bay hoping to see *La Estrella* and the supply ship from *Havana*.

They were not there.

Only the three caravels, *Maria de la Meridionales Mares*, *Reina de Napoles,* and *La Doncella de Plata* rode quietly at anchor.

That evening Narvaez called for a meeting.

CHAPTER 16

Black Mouse

Raton Negro

"She babbled of great machines that carried men along the roads....even of flying ships that crossed the skies overhead. Most strange, however, was her continued description of an animal that the inhabitants seemed to worship."

"What animal, s*enora?*"

"...Ah...*Adelantado*...she said, a *gran raton negro*...a large black mouse!"

29 April, 1528

Indian Village at Boca Ciega

Alvar had slept long and hard. The sun was well up in the sky when he stepped out of the hut that he shared with Fray Juan Xuarez and Alonso de Solis. The other two had already arisen and the hut was empty. He leaned on a ridge pole and thought of the last two days.

After arriving back in Boca *Ciega*, Narvaez had called a conference for that evening. The talk of the journey to the *Indio* villages had extended far into the night. Narvaez had even ordered a ration of rum for everyone, and then another, and finally a third. By the time Alvar stumbled to his hut, the sun was coming up and his head was spinning. Yesterday was a disaster. Most of the meeting participants were severely hung over. Alvar himself had not risen until late in the afternoon and then only to piss and drink some water. Even today he felt thick-headed and slow.

From across the court yard Fray Xuarez noticed Alvar had arisen and walked over to join him.

Good morning *Alguacil*, God be with you!"

"And to you padre."

Xuarez stopped and looked into de Vaca's eyes. "Now that you have had a good night's sleep, I'm sure you are feeling better."

Alvar squinted in the sunlight. "A little."

Xuarez laughed, paused, and then became serious. "What are your thoughts on what happened at the *Indio* village?"

"Good friar I have fought men in battle and seen many unpleasant things, but watching this woman torn apart by the dogs was deeply disturbing as was the punishment set on the *casique* and his brother. This is certainly not something that a just and loving God would condone."

Padre Juan, as he was called, was no stranger to brutality. Only four years prior he had been one of the twelve *Franciscan* Friars dispatched to *Mexico*. He had seen, first hand, the destruction of *Tenochtitlan* and the devastation that Cortes' army had caused to the native population. In *Mexico*, Xuarez had been awarded the position of bishop of *Rio de las Palmas and La Florida.* This, of course, was the area granted to Narvaez for colonization, and it was no coincidence that Xuarez accompanied this expedition. Narvaez needed his experience. It also didn't hurt that Xuarez was highly respected by the court of Charles V and the mere mention of his name would curry favor for Narvaez.

The two had first met in *Vera Cruz* when Narvaez was under house arrest by Cortes. Later in *Cuba*, after his release, *Narvaez* and his wife Maria hadentertained the *Franciscan* at their *ranchero* in *Bayamo*. It was there that Narvaez had shared his intentions and asked the priest to join the expedition.

Xuarez had accepted, seeing the expedition as a means…no…a God-given opportunity, to reach the *Indians* under his charge. But his acceptance was conditional. He was well aware of the systematic brutality that Narvaez displayed towards *Indians* in the past. As a result, Xuarez had agreed to accompany the expedition only if Narvaez consulted with him and his coterie of priests on all *Indio* affairs. Narvaez had readily agreed.

The friar responded that he had prayed long and hard about the horrible travesties that had befallen the *casique*, his brother, and his mother. Xuarez was deeply troubled and thinking of leaving the expedition. If he did, he would take the other four *Franciscans* with him.

Now Alvar had learned that he was not the only one concerned about the *Adelantado's* actions.

"*Senor* De Vaca, *Senor* De Vaca!" From across the courtyard Campo was running toward him.

Out of breath, the young page repeated, "*Senor* De Vaca…ah…I have found you."

"So you have, young Campo. What is so urgent?"

"*Senor* De Vaca, the *Adelantado* requests all of his senior leaders for a meeting. Even now they are gathering by the beach. The *Adelantado* himself sent me to find you."

Turning to gather his things, Alvar answered over his shoulder, "Tell the *Adelantado* I am on my way."

Without an answer, Campo took off across the courtyard, his feet raising little puffs of dust as he ran.

Alvar, cinching up his belt, followed close behind, his sword and scabbard temporarily tucked under his arm. As he cleared the courtyard and rounded the last hut, the beach came into view. There on the sand clustered around an overturned boat were all of the officials of the expedition, the ship's pilots, military captains, and the four friars. Also present, Alvar noticed, was the notary, Jeronimo de Alaniz, and a seaman, Bartolome Fernandez. Unlike most of the common seaman, Fernandez was well-educated and was often used as a witness in legal matters.

"Ah, *Senor* De Vaca has decided to grace us with his presence!" It was Narvaez who, at the moment, was sitting atop the boat in loose conversation with comptroller Alonso Enriquez.

"My apologies, *Adelantado*."

Narvaez jumped down. "No matter, let us begin this meeting.

Notary Alaniz sat on a wooden crate and used another crate for his writing table. Behind him, seaman Fernandez politely stood with his hands folded in front. Narvaez looked down at Alaniz. The notary nodded that he was ready.

Narvaez began. "As you know, we sent the brigantine south to find the entrance of the great bay, *Bahia Honda*, which we identified on our first inland journey. After sending out Miruelo we traveled inland again to, hopefully, meet up with the brigantine. This did not happen."

Narvaez paused.

"I can only assume that *La Estrella* did not find the entrance to the bay and continued on to *Habana* as instructed. The other possibility, of course, is that the brigantine was sunk in a storm or ran aground. I do not believe this and I feel sure that Senor Miruello in the brigantine and the relief ship under *Senor* de la Cerda will arrive soon."

Narvaez paused again, checking to see that Alaniz was keeping up.

"At first I was of the opinion that we should begin our settlement here. Friar Xuarez and I even had a name...*La Cruz*!"

Everyone nodded their approval.

"This bay, this *Boca Ciega* as we call it, however, is much to shallow for a permanent settlement and the land around is not suited for crops. The soil is thin and sandy. For these reasons, I propose that we continue northward and split our force. A land force will proceed along the coast while the vessels follow close offshore. Our first objective will be to find the entrance to *Bahia Honda*. It is safe to assume that this entrance is not to the south, as we first thought, for if that was so *Senor* Miruello would have entered it and met with us on the shoreline."

Most nodded their approval but a few, including Alvar, had their reservations about such a decision.

"*Adelantado*!" it was the inspector Alonso de Solis.

"What of continuing on until we reach *Las Palmas* and the *Rio Panuco*?"

There was much nodding and agreement on this statement, for most of those in attendance had not traveled to the *Caribbean* before. Surely they thought, the area of *Los Palmas* was no more than a few days' journey away.

Narvaez listened to the discussion and finally interrupted, "I have made the journey between *New Spain* and *Cuba* twice, once to the area and once returning. Believe me when I say that the distance is considerable."

Looking at Friar Xuarez he continued, "I know the good friar is in agreement for he has made the journey as well. Depending on the wind and weather, it is 10 days or more from *Habana* to *Vera Cruz* by sea. This place were we now reside is directly north of *Habana* and the *Rio Panuco* is nearly north of *Vera Cruz.*"

As he spoke, Narvaez made a rough outline on the sand using his *montonte* as a stylus.

"Going by land, what lies between us and *Panuco* is unknown, but surely the distance is great."

Narvaez stopped and looked around him. Many of the captains and a few officials looked confused. They were military men not well versed in things nautical. They had experience in *Spain* where the distances between areas of importance were relatively short. The magnitude of the New World and the uncharted expanse of *Amichel* eluded them.

Narvaez was perplexed. He looked directly at one of his military captains, Alejandro Tellez, who seemed to be the most confused. "Capitan Tellez, let me ask you. From what direction does the sun rise in the morning?"

Tellez, a bit embarrassed by the question, pointed to the east.

"Correct, *Capitan* Tellez, here the sun rises inland. At the *Rio Panuco,* the sun rises over the ocean. What does that tell you?"

Tellez looked up, unsure of what to say.

Alvar spoke up. "*Adelantado*, the two locations occupy different shorelines. Here the ocean is to the west, at *Panuco* the ocean is to the east. To reach *Panuco* we would have to follow this shoreline around the mass of *Amichel* until it veers to the south. Only then will we observe the sunrise over the water."

"Ah...Senor De Vaca is correct, exactly the point I was trying to make. We are on the wrong side of this continent from *Panuco* and what lies between us is unknown.

Alejandro Tellez stepped back into the crowd, but the confused look did not leave his face.

Narvaez relieved that this part of the discussion was over, now concentrated on his plan to split the force and move northward.

Alvar spoke up, "*Adelantado*, would we not be taking a considerable risk by splitting our force? In our last two forays, we have seen the kind of land through which we must pass. It is thick and overgrown in places. In others, it is trackless marshes and swamps. Deadly vipers are everywhere, *alligartos* abound in the water and poisonous insects hide in our bed rolls. Our horses are weak and following the coast will be difficult. Inlets, tidal marshes, and mangroves extend far inland. Besides all of this, our supplies are low and we may have to deal with hostile *Indios*."

There was some nodding by a few of the group, but it was Xuarez who spoke up next. "I am in agreement with the *Adelantado*. We know that the great bay is close at hand, for we have seen it in our recent adventure. Our journey to its inlet cannot be that far and reloading the horses will only make them weaker still. I for one do not want to return to the ships. Doing so would surely tempt God and subject us to more of the misfortunes we have already experienced. Let us walk upon the land where we have some control, and not at the mercy of the winds and foul weather."

The talk continued, mostly in favor of continuing inland. Besides Alvar only the notary, Alaniz, showed concern at leaving the ships. "I am but a humble clerk but it would seem prudent to use the ships as our base of operation until a suitable site can be found."

There was a strained silence after Alaniz spoke, during which time he sat down, made a few notes, and prepared for the next speaker.

Narvaez had been silent during the discussion, staring at the ground while he doodled in the sand. Now, satisfied that everyone had had their say, he looked at De Vaca.

"I have heard all of your thoughts and it seems that only *Senors* De Vaca and Alaniz have concerns with my plan. I would say, *Senor*

De Vaca, that with your opposition it may be best if you stayed with the ships. I need someone to lead them. Should you arrive at *Bahia Honda* before us, it will be your responsibility to begin preparations for a settlement."

Alvar stepped in front of Narvaez and carefully chose his words. "With respect *Adelantado*, I refuse to lead the ships. I feel your decision to proceed inland is a mistake, but my honor as a soldier demands that I accompany you. I would ask, however, that you bid the notary to note my objections."

Narvaez was clearly perturbed. "*Senor* De Vaca, I will do no such thing. The Commissary and the other officers here are all in agreement with my plan.

What I will do is ask the notary to record my desire to leave this place known as *Boca Ciega.* It is an undesirable location for all of the reasons I have stated earlier. We will proceed with the plan to split the force and locate the mouth of the bay. I would ask again, *Senor* De Vaca, that you take charge of the ships."

Again Alvar looked directly at Narvaez and refused. "I will accompany the land force."

Narvaez was the *Adelantado* but de Vaca had a royal appointment as treasurer and *Aguacil*-mayor. He was the King's designated representative. Narvaez could not force him to comply.

Frustrated, Narvaez turned back to the group of officials. "All able-bodied men will accompany the land force. Only the *marineros* and women will remain on the ships. Let us begin preparations to leave this place. We will leave as soon as that operation is complete."

With that, the meeting was adjourned.

The rest of the day was spent in preparation. Weapons were cleaned and sharpened. The horses were shod. Items on board that could support the land party were off loaded. Anything that could not be taken inland was moved back onto the ships. The bay was a hub of activity. The women on board were allowed to come ashore so that they could assist their men in making ready and be with them before getting underway. Many of the couples slipped away to the *Indio* huts for a few moments of intimacy. There was no feeling of a prolonged separation, however, for every one felt that the entrance to the great bay was close by. In a few days, they could begin building the first settlement. Surely by then the brigantine and the supply ship from *Habana* would arrive as well.

30 April, 1528

Indian Village at Boca Ciega

Although scheduled to leave today, the weather had not cooperated. A violent storm had descended on the expedition bringing with it onshore winds that made it impossible for the caravels to leave the bay. All day long rain squalls had lashed the area with torrents that moved across the bay in inundating deluges. All activities had stopped. Even the ship's boats had difficulty rowing across the once-placid harbor. Finally, at mid-afternoon, the storm dissipated and moved inland. Still, the on shore winds remained strong.

It was only now that the women who had bee allowed ashore could safely return to the ships. Rita La Salvaje hadn't bothered to visit her husband, the ship's carpenter apprentice, Bonito Pina. He had avoided her as well. Being a *marinero*, he was exempt but had volunteered to accompany Narvaez into the interior. It was said that he did this to escape Rita who had taken on one and all aboard ship and accumulated a tidy sum in the process. Pina, unable to control the woman, had decided to take his chances with the land party.

Now it was dusk and time for the women to be loaded onto the ship's boats and rowed out to the waiting caravels. As prearranged, they waited in the courtyard for a *marinero* to accompany them to the boat. As chance would have it, Narvaez, Captain Telles, and Inspector de Solis were crossing the courtyard at the same time.

"*Adelantado*!" It was Rita La Salvaje.

Narvaez and his two companions came to an abrupt stop. "*Senora*, can I be of service?"

"*Adelantado*, your decision to march into the interior will result in the worst of consequences."

Captain Telles and Inspector de Solis immediately began to move away but Narvaez held up his hand. "Wait, I want to hear this."

"But, *Adelantado*, this woman is *loco*. She has been spouting this nonsense for months." It was Inspector Solis.

Narvaez stepped forward, "*Senora*, I have heard stories of your encounter with the *Moorish bruja* and the strange prophecies she related to you...but tell me...why should I believe any of it?"

The other women with Rita stepped back, intimidated by Narvaez's presence.

Not Rita. "*Adelantado*, this old woman who could see into the future...this *bruja*, as you call her, sought me out on the docks of *San Lucar*. I had no knowledge of her before that moment. She was accompanied by a daughter who had brought her from *Hornacho*. The daughter was as unknowing of her purpose as I was." Rita continued.

"The *Moor* woman's name was Talibah and she spoke of a life heavy with loss. Her sons and her husband all died in the *reconquista* and she was forced to a life of poverty."

"She knew my name and where I was from. She spoke of many things that happened in my life...things that only I could know...and yet, she knew of them also."

"*Senora*, of all the people on our expedition..." Narvaez stopped and gestured around him. "All these people...why did this *bruja* pick you?"

"Of that, I do not know, *Adelantado*, but she approached me on two different occasions. The first time on the dock at *San Lucar*, I tried to dismiss her then as a crazy old woman, but as I turned to walk away she talked of my dead son."

"I am sorry to hear of this, *senora*."

"It was in *Seville*. I was young and without a husband working in a filthy *taberna*. I had the child in a back room. He was stillborn."

Rita paused a moment and then continued, "The *bruja* talked of this...she knew everything. She asked...no, pleaded that I listen to her. She looked at me...and yet, she didn't look at me, but rather, through me...like I wasn't there. She talked of our journey as if it had already happened."

Captain Telles and Inspector Solis shifted uncomfortably. Narvaez noticed and bid that they continue on. He would join them later.

Narvaez sat on a log and stretched out his legs. "Proceed, *Senora*. I would like to hear what this *Moor* woman...this Talibah, said of our expedition." The other women moved closer as Rita continued on with her story. From across the courtyard, Alvar noticed the gathering and ambled over to investigate. Narvaez noticed his arrival but did not acknowledge him.

Rita continued. "She spoke of our expedition as if it was cursed, *Adelantado*. She knew of the desertions in *Santo Domingo*. These people, she called them *los afortunados*, the lucky ones." She talked also of a great wind, a *gran tormenta* that would swallow our ships and men."

"She knew of the *huracan*?"

"*Si, Adelantado,* she spoke of it at length, of how only a very few would escape its wrath."

Narvaez looked briefly at Alvar but then turned back to Rita. "Continue, s*enora.*"

"She talked next of our grounding and the endless battles with storms and angry seas, but here I was interrupted and had to leave her, for this was the day before the journey and I had to prepare my berth."

"You spoke of two meetings with the *brujah, senora.*"

"*Si, Adelantado,* it was the next day, the day of our departure. I had stopped at the open market to buy fruit and bread. I felt someone tugging on my garments and when I turned it was the *Moor* woman. I greeted her warmly for she was kindly and very frail."

"And did she speak more of our expedition?" Narvaez was growing impatient.

"*Si, Adelantado,* she implored me, 'I have more to tell you'. She led me to a shady bench and continued her story."

"What did she speak of, *senora?*"

"She somehow knew that we would lose another ship and there would be great confusion before we came ashore. What was most disturbing of all..."

Rita stopped for a moment to gather her thoughts.

"What is it woman, what did she say?" Narvaez stood up.

"The *Moor* woman spoke of a great split in the expedition where some would continue on and others would return to the ships. Those that continued would experience death and deprivation and would vanish from the face of the earth, save for a few who, alone, would tell the horrible story."

There was a collective gasp from the other women. Alvar felt a shiver go up his back but said nothing.

"She spoke all of this to you?"

"Yes, excellency and everything has come to pass. You can imagine my terror when I learned of your decision to separate the forces and march inland."

"Tell me, *senora*, what else did this *Moor* woman have to say?"

"She spoke of many things, *Adelantado*, things of which I have no knowledge of and things I did not understand."

Narvaez's eye squinted as he looked at her. "What...things?"

"This land on which we now stand, this *La Florida* and, indeed, all of *Amichel* will be populated by untold scores, their numbers beyond counting. On the land magnificent stone buildings, bridges and roads will extend in all directions. On the sea, craft of indescribable size will ply the bays and harbors."

Rita stopped a moment, unsure whether to continue, for what she was saying was so unbelievable that it defied comprehension. What she was about to say, however, defied believably.

"Continue, *senora*."

"*Adelantado*, it was at this point that the *Moor* woman's speech became somewhat incoherent. She talked to me as if in a dream. She seemed near collapse and her daughter, who accompanied her, was forced to support her."

"What did she say?"

"She babbled of great machines that carried men along the roads....even of flying ships that crossed the skies overhead. Most strange, however, was her continued description of an animal that the inhabitants seemed to worship."

"What animal, s*enora*?"

"...Ah...*Adelantado*...she said a *gran raton negro*...a large black mouse!"

At this Narvaez exploded in laughter, his cavernous voice carrying across the courtyard and down to the bay. Even Alvar could not hold back his laughter. Rita stepped back, embarrassed by the *Adelantado's* reaction. It was sometime before Narvaez could compose himself. The laughter had been real and he wiped a tear out of his good eye.

"Ah, *senora*, this is proof that this *bruja* is crazy. Ships that fly...and a giant *raton*. Am I to alter my plans on such craziness as this?"

"But *Adelantado*, what of her other prophesies, am I to ignore them?" Rita was becoming indignant.

"*Senora*, this new world we are in is rich beyond belief. Even now I hear of a fabulous civilization to the north with untold riches of gold...a place called *Apalachee*. To realize these riches we must take great risks. There will be losses, and *Spaniards* will die, but those who live and persevere will be the recipients of untold wealth. The great Cortes showed us this when he conquered the *Mexicas*, and with the help of God, we will do it here. Now, *senora*, I must return to my duties, good luck to you and we will undoubtedly meet again in a few days and put all of these stories to rest."

Narvaez turned on his heel and walked toward the beach.

Rita turned to the women clustered around her. "The *Adelantado* is deaf to the warnings that I have relayed to him. The *Moor* woman has been correct in everything she had told me. I truly believe that after tomorrow we will never see these men again."

The women broke into separate discussions, with much shaking of heads and nervous chatter.

Alvar noticed that a *marinero* had approached the group and informed Rita that the boat was ready to return them to the ships. Rita held up her hands and raised her voice. The crowd of females became quiet.

"After tomorrow your men are the same as dead. Do not spend time grieving, for the loss is their choice. Protect yourself and find new *marido's*...husbands, as soon as possible. That is my intention."

With that, the group of women followed the *marinero* to the boats that had been hauled up onto the beach with the crew of rowers standing by. Alvar watched them load and then push out into the bay. He had laughed at the *brujah's* strange predictions, but now he couldn't shake the feeling that this old *Moor* woman in *Spain*, now so very far away, might be right.

30 April, 1528

Indian Village at Boca Ciega

Darkness had fallen. Alvar was preparing his equipment for the march inland and was somewhat startled when Friar Xuarez cleared his throat behind him.

"Fray Xuarez, I didn't hear you approach."

"Sorry, Senor De Vaca, I didn't mean to startle you.

"Probably my fault, good fray. I was thinking of tomorrow's excursion."

"As we all are, may God be with us. Alvar, I am here at the request of the *Adelantado.*"

Alvar paused his activities and studied Fray Xuarez. The fray was uncomfortable. It showed that he didn't like being a messenger.

"What is it that the governor needs?"

"He asks you to reconsider your decision to march into the interior. The governor needs someone he can trust to command the ships."

"My answer to the *Adelantado* is still no, and will always be no. Although I feel that his decision to leave the safety of the ships and move inland is ultimately a bad one, I will serve him in this endeavor no matter what the risks. It has become a matter of honor. My disagreement with his plans was not meant in any way to remove myself from a hazardous assignment."

"I know that, and the *Adelantado* knows that. He apologizes for any misunderstanding and implores you to take command of the ships."

"Again, my friend I must decline this command. I appreciate the *Adelantado's* kind words, but I will take my place tomorrow with the land force. Now, I have a question for you!"

Xuarez seemed to be surprised but smiled pleasantly, "Ask what you want."

"Earlier you expressed many misgivings about the *Adelantado, so* much so that you considered leaving the expedition."

"This is so."

"Why then did you so strongly support the *Adelantado's* decision to split the force and march into this wilderness?"

Xuarez sighed, thought for a moment, and then answered. "After our conversation, I later talked to the *Adelantado* and told him of my displeasure and of my intention to leave the expedition. To this, he begged me not to go and asked for forgiveness. I told him that forgiveness can only come from God and the things that he had done would weigh heavily on his eternal soul."

Alvar sat back. "What did he say then?"

"If I would stay...along with the four other friars in my charge...he would put me in charge of all non-military matters dealing with the *Indios*. Even on military matters, he promised to consult with me before making rash and injurious decisions."

"And you believed him?"

"I had him swear before God that he would honor this promise."

"And he agreed to this?"

"Yes, *Senor* De Vaca, but there is something else that I must relay to you."

Alvar was puzzled. "What is it?"

"The purpose of my presence...and the four other *Franciscans* in my company, is to provide spiritual guidance to the *Christians* on this expedition. More than that I am empowered by his majesty to protect and bring to the cross the *Indios* that we will encounter."

Xuarez stopped for a moment to collect his thoughts. "*Adelantado* Panfilo Narvaez will be taking his army inland whether I am with them or not. Is it not my duty to stay with this expedition and do whatever I can to satisfy the wishes of his majesty and of our Holy Father?"

There was a long silence. Alvar Nunez Cabeza de Vaca stood up and grasped the hand of the friar.

"You are a good man, Padre Juan."

"God be with you, *Senor* De Vaca."

A stiff sea breeze was blowing as embers from the fire swirled about the robed figure of Friar Xuarez walking back across the courtyard. Watching him, it briefly reminded Alvar of stories he had read of Merlin the magician. He laughed to himself. He stayed there until well after midnight just staring into the fire.

To the west, a distant thunderstorm briefly lit up the sky.

CHAPTER 17

CROOKED RIVER

Rio Torcido

The river was very twisted, meandering this way and that as they scouted for a crossing. For this reason, the waterway earned the sobriquet of Rio Torcido...Crooked River...and was duly recorded by the notary Jeronimo de Alaniz.

01 May, 1528

Boca Ciega Bay Aboard the Caravel Maria De La Meridionales Mares

Harmona Caravallo took the stairs two at a time to his position in the aft-castle of the flagship *Maria de la Meridionales Mares*. As he looked across the bay, the last boats were pulling away from the shoreline, the oarsmen making rhythmic strokes in the calm water.

The *Indian* village was now deserted with no sign of life except for a thin ribbon of smoke curling into the air from the embers of last night's bonfire. Further to the north, Narvaez's rear guard was disappearing into a forest of magnificent long-leaf pines. Caravallo could just make out two horsemen and five or six infantry. Soon, all but the horseman had faded into the forest. They seemed to stop, no doubt staring back at the ships. In an instant, the horseman turned and disappeared from view. It was an enduring moment that Harmona Caravallo would remember all his life.

It was only last night that Narvaez had hurriedly approached him and asked if he would take command of the three ships in the bay that were to rendezvous with the land party further up the coast. The offer had surprised Caravallo, for he was only designated a lieutenant in the military hierarchy of the Narvaez expedition, his age and lack of military experience being the primary factors.

Caravallo's father had been a magistrate in the small *Spanish* community of *Cuenca de Huete.* Here Harmona had lived a privileged life and benefited from some of the best educators in the area. He was a bookish young man and it was no surprise that at the age of 17, he was sent to the *University at Salamanca* to study law. A model student, Harmona was retained at the University after graduation to assist the professors and continue his education. Staying until 1515 he resigned his position and began practice as an *abogado*, a lawyer in *Seville,* and eventually served as a minor judge.

In 1520 the political climate of *Spain* was thrown in turmoil when a group of rebels calling themselves *El Comuneros* revolted against the rule of Charles I. Armed conflict began and Caravallo offered his services on behalf of the king.

With virtually no military experience, Caravallo obtained a minor command position but participated in no armed conflict. In the final *Battle of Villalar* in 1521 he fell from a tree while scouting the enemy's position and sprained an ankle. During the battle, his time was spent painfully reclining and unable to walk.

Dissatisfied with his prospects in *Spain*, Caravallo took passage to *Hispaniola* the same year and began practicing law in *Santo Domingo.* In 1523 he was appointed a Licnciado and began to acquire some notoriety. However, with a social status still far removed from the wealthy landowners, Caravallo was easily persuaded to join the expedition when Narvaez arrived at *Santo Domingo.*

Now, staring at the shoreline, Caravallo had mixed feelings. The land expedition would have been an experience and he very much needed to prove himself, but certainly, he would rejoin Narvaez further up the coast and begin preparations for the first settlement. In the meantime, Caravallo couldn't believe his good fortune, because, along with the responsibility of the ships, came a promotion to captain.

The boats had pulled along side their respective ships and the last of the cargo was winched onto the deck. Each boat then took on two or three stout *marineros* and moved toward the anchor locations. Each was marked with a buoy attached by a section of rope that extended down to the anchor. First, they would signal the ship to let out more of the mooring line. This would relieve the tension. Next, the *marineros* would gather in the buoy and begin hoisting the anchor by the buoy rope. This, in effect, would pull the anchor back from whatever it had wedged itself into. Usually, this was enough and today was no exception. The bottom of *Boca Ciega* was sandy and the anchor was quickly drawn in and hoisted onto the boat where it laid across the gunnels. Returning to the ships, the anchor line would then be winched up to the hawse pipe. Finally, the anchor itself was lashed to the gunnel posts and made secure.

Pilot Janero Flores approached Caravallo. "Capitan Caravallo, the wind is favorable. As soon as the bow anchors are raised we are ready to get underway. The other ships will follow our lead."

"Then let us leave this place, Pilot Flores, and set a course to the north. Keep us as close to the coast as you feel practicable."

When the bow anchor cleared the water line, the foresail dropped into place and *Maria de la Meridionales Mares* slowly advanced towards the narrow inlet from which they had entered this *Boca Ciega Bay* two weeks before. Behind *Maria,* the other ships of the expedition followed in line.

Clearing the inlet, Flores gave the order for all sails. Today the wind was southwest and they would be running with it. Standing on the aft deck, Caravallo turned and watched the last ship, *La Docella*, as it passed though the channel. Even from this distance, he could make out the *marineros* clambering through the rigging, balancing on foot ropes. In the blink of an eye the sails dropped into place, their whiteness sharp in contrast against the azure sky, turquoise sea, and green shoreline.

They were underway.

02 May, 1528

The West Coast of Florida

Alvar led his horse along the trail. Actually, it wasn't even a trail but a barely visible footpath, seldom used. He thought of yesterday when he had paused with Friar Xuarez to watch the ships as they sailed out of *Boca Ciega*. The last of the soldiers had moved past them, the noise of march and the boisterous camaraderie all around. With a furtive look at the ships Alvar and Xuarez turned their mounts and followed the soldiers into a heavily wooded pine forest.

Where before, Narvaez had explored to the east of *Boca Ciega,* this time he had taken his small army northward along the coast. He hoped to find a northern entry to the bay and then meet up with Caravallo and the three support ships. The idea was to parallel the shoreline and maintain access to the ships and their supplies. After emerging from the pine forest, however, the bay turned northeastward and bifurcated into two estuaries. They could see the separating peninsula just across the water. They continued along, calling this arm of the bay, *Cruz de la bahia*...cross of the bay. Heavy marsh and mangrove inhibited their movement and their path turned increasingly to the northeast.

To the north, sawgrass and mud confronted the expedition, and they were forced further inland. At one point the line of march turned back to the southeast, the huge wetland in front of them simply too large to cross.

Continuing in this direction, Narvaez became increasingly agitated, but there was nothing he could do. Finally, the marsh began to narrow. Across the expanse, pines and hardwoods began to appear. At a promising site, Narvaez sent three men to test a crossing. The mud was thick and, at times, the water was to their thighs, plume grass all but obscured their progress, but the three managed to slog across to the higher ground on the other side. In their wake, a muddy, beaten-down path showed the way for the others.

Anxious to reacquire the coast, Narvaez ordered the men and horses across. It was a mistake. The horses became mired in the soft mud and teams of men had to wade into the ooze to free them. Shoes were sucked off the soldiers' feet as they labored to cross the expanse. It wasn't until the afternoon that the crossing was completed. Horses and men were utterly exhausted and it was with some effort that the expedition again got underway.

Well inland, their route to the ocean was now blocked by the wetlands to the west, the same ones they had skirted before the crossing. They were, however, able to turn further north and progress continued on relatively dry ground. After a league of travel in this direction the marsh began to thin until, finally, a faint trail guided them across the remainder of the wetlands. The line of march was now to the northwest and as the day's light began to fade, the camp was established in a pleasant hammock of hardwoods.

The night was one of the darkest Alvar could remember. Thick clouds had obscured any trace of star light and even the light from the camp fires seemed to be absorbed by the inky blackness. From somewhere out in the wetlands the piercing cry of a cougar sounded. Even in the company of hundreds of well-armed men he had felt isolated and exposed. So had ended on the first day. They had only managed to travel a little over 2 leagues.

Now, on the second day, they trudged along, the good-natured banter of yesterday had subsided considerably. Before leaving *Boca Ciega*, each man had been issued only two pounds of biscuit and a half pound of bacon. At most, this salted ration would only last fifteen days, but more than enough time if they would be resupplied along the coast. The few pigs that remained were kept on the ships. Narvaez felt that for such a short journey herding them would be more trouble than they were worth. At dinner last night, and breakfast again this morning, each man unconsciously curtailed his intake.

Moving north and following the faint path, they stayed on the high ground, thickly populated with tall pines and a saw palmetto understory. The pines, many reaching three feet in diameter and towering to a hundred feet or more, had trunks that were blackened with soot. It was obvious to Alvar that this area had experienced a fire, but the trees seemed unaffected. Somehow a fire in all this lush vegetation surrounded by water seemed out of place. Still, one only had to brush up against the tree's bark to see the evidence on their hands and clothes.

The land expedition totaled 300 men and 40 horses. Of the 300, there were 283 armed *Spaniards*. Most of the men traveled alone, but a few of higher social standing brought their slaves or personal servants. These were an assortment of black Africans, *Indians,* young boys, and "white slaves," Muslims captured in the *reconquista* or other skirmishes on the coast of *North Africa.*

There was Garcia de Parades, a rich land owner in *Extremadura* who had jumped at the opportunity to make a personal investment in the *Indies*. His four blacks accompanied him everywhere. Most notable was a huge *Abidji* that everyone called *Toro*. In the Parades family since birth, *Toro* had grown up with Garcia and was extremely protective. Without question, the strongest man on the expedition, his feats of strength were legendary. In his own way, Parades was fond of *Toro*, the relationship more like two siblings rather than master and slave.

Accompanied by four Muslim slaves, Diego de Solis was a cousin of the expedition's royal inspector Alonso de Solis and a minor official of the court in *Andalusia*. He had made his fortune in the spice trade, and like Parades wanted to expand his holdings into the New

World. A cruel and demanding man, Diego de Solis was unforgiving of the four young boys who catered to his every need. They, in turn, were terrified of him...that is...all but one, who suppressed a burning hatred for his *Spanish* master. Called Aldo by de Solis, the boy had not forgotten his *Muslin* name of Mudar Salameh and vowed to himself, that one day, he would kill the *Spaniard*.

Pedro Lunel had left *San Lucar* with four Africans but had sold two in *Santo Domingo* where premiums for blacks were particularly high. With some of the money, he had purchased a fine three year-old gelding. Astride the horse, Lunel was apprehensive of attack and had the remaining two slaves, Caesar and Rizado, walk on either side of him while on the trail.

Doroteo Teodoro was a Greek boat builder who had made his home in *Cadiz*. Doroteo's family had been taken by the plague in 1524 and his business had fallen on hard times. Quite by accident he had encountered Narvaez in a tavern and learned of the expedition. Having nothing to hold him in *Cadiz,* he had sold what remained of the business and taken his one remaining slave apprentice, a mixed-race *Moor* boy he named Loannes, to accompany him.

Fernan Estrada, a young cavalry lieutenant, was from a well-to-do noble family in *Extremadura.* His father had served Ferdinand II and Isabella during the *reconquista* of 1492. Awarded land and slaves for his services, the father had given Fernan one of his most trusted servants to look after him during the expedition. Older than Fernan, the black *African* had had his tongue cut out by a previous owner and only evaded death by the intervention of Fernan's father who bought and nursed him back to health. A *Kikuyu* warrior from *East Africa*, he held the Estrada family in the highest regard. His loyalty was beyond doubt. Unable to speak, he had changed his name to Kamau which translated to "quiet warrior" in his native *Bantu* language.

Guillermo Avellaneda had served side by side with Capt Alonso Castillo throughout *Spain's Comuneros Revolt*. At *Tordesillas,* he had decapitated an attacker who was about to skewer Castillo with a lance. Busily engaged with another combatant, Castillo had not seen the threat. The engagement at *Tordesillas* had been short, but without Avellaneda's intervention, it could have been Castillo's last. Satisfied to serve under Castillo, Avellaneda had taken the title of *Sargento mayor* and had the respect not only of his commander but of the troops that served with him. Each with a bondsman accompanying them, both men had joined the Narvaez expedition to make their fortune in the New World. Castilo's Pietro was young and gregarious while Avellaneda's Yago was quiet and reflective. Both served their masters well and were well treated in return.

The three cousins, Pedro de Valdiviseso, Diego, and Andres Dorantes de Carranza were all on the expedition. At 34, Pedro was the oldest of the cousins and the most experienced, having served with Cortes from the beginning of the *Mexica* campaign. In the final battle for *Tenochtitlan*, cousin Diego had joined him only to be severely wounded. Returning to *Spain*, Diego recovered sufficiently to join the youngest cousin, Andre, battling the *communeros*. At *Villilar* Diego was again wounded, but only slightly. After the revolt, both had returned to *Salamanca* where they heard of the Narvaez expedition and immediately joined.

After *Tenochtitlan*, Pedro accompanied Cortes to *Honduras* and then, returning to *Hispaniola* in 1526, was convinced by a rich landowner, Lucas Ayllon, to accompany him for the purpose of establishing a colony along the east coast of *Amichel*. The expedition was a disaster and Pedro, along with the few survivors, returned to *Hispaniola*. Besieged by creditors, he had sold most of his possessions and was on the verge of bankruptcy.

Upon the arrival of the Narvaez expedition, the three were joined in an emotional reunion. Over tankards of rum, Andre and Diego agreed to cover his debts and convinced Pedro to join them. Accompanied by two personal servants, Andre's Estevan and Diego's Manalito the three cousins began their journey together.

Including Narvaez's page Campo, these seventeen, mostly non-*Spaniards*, represented only a small part of the land force but performed the greater part of the menial labor. Tending horses, maintaining equipment, clearing obstacles, and preparing meals were activities looked down upon by the *Spaniards*. The challenges of this strange land and the threats of a common enemy, however, would all but eliminate this social order.

The expedition badly needed to regain the ocean, but whenever the course was adjusted westward another line of marshes and meandering waterways greeted them. Continually forced back to the faint footpath, they trudged ever northward.

Like all of the horsemen, Alvar would stay mounted for only short periods of time. The animals were still noticeably underweight and nowhere near being in a condition to stand the weight of a rider for a full day. During rest stops the horses would be set out to graze, the slaves holding the reins while they ate. Guards were always posted around the horses, but, so far, not a single *Indio* had been seen. Still, Alvar couldn't shake the feeling that they were being watched.

For Alvar, the days seemed to run together with nothing to differentiate one from the other. Moving amongst grassland and marshes the expedition would encounter vast tracts of pine and palmetto woodlands. On the higher ground, deciduous oaks, magnolias, ash, hickory, and trees unfamiliar to Alvar, would abound. In the wetter areas and along waterways towering Cyprus, festooned with moss, blocked the light and imparted an eerie twilight on everything below. Here, only ferns grew in lush clumps of greenery. Ever present throughout the landscape were the stately cabbage palms, always recognizable from afar and invariably populated by birds of all types.

After a week the expedition was still well inland and most of the biscuit and salt pork had been consumed. Occasionally a deer would be taken but the *Spaniards* were uncomfortable leaving the safety of the group to hunt. Narvaez did assign several crossbowmen to walk in the lead of the column to get a shot at the occasional animal that was surprised along the trail. Even when hit, however, the deer were amazingly impervious to the shaft that usually passed all the way through them. Unless it was a killing shot through the heart, the wounded animals would bound away and elude the *Spaniards*.

Coveys of quail would explode out of the brush startling the men and spooking the horses. One soldier, charging his arquebus with bits of nail and iron filings, had managed a shot at these birds as they took to the air. Two were hit and quickly consumed but Narvaez severely rebuked the man for wasting powder. More than that the loud report of the firearm had echoed across through the woodland and undoubtedly advertised their presence to a, as yet, unseen enemy. Strangely, not since leaving *Boca Ciega* had they encountered any *Indio* or even signs of habitation. Only the faint trail that they followed north gave the slightest indication that they were not alone.

To help curb their appetite, many had begun eating the base of the saw palmetto stalk. Grabbing the stalk just below the frond it could easily be pulled from the core. The small amount of core material removed was tasty and nutritious. In time the men learned to dig up the entire core and slice it into edible sections.

On the ninth day of their journey, a black bear was encountered foraging for food along a small stream. Four cavalrymen surrounded the animal and attacked it with their lances. All were amazed at its ferocity. Skewered by two lances the wounded beast lunged at one of the attackers and unseated him from his mount. Falling to the ground, the man was momentarily winded and in great danger of being mauled when another lancer rapidly dispatched the bear with a killing thrust to the heart. Cut into strips and roasted, each of the 300 men was given a small portion that was rapidly consumed.

The land had opened up somewhat and the expedition again left the trail and set a westerly course for the ocean. On the tenth day, however, they were besieged by thunderstorms so severe that all forward progress was halted. In a grove of trees, they huddled in a circle under whatever shelter was available. The horses, corralled in the center, became restless when hail as big as marbles began to fall. Milling around, their agitation increased and several, encumbered by hobbles, fell to the ground. Men rushed forward to calm their mounts. Holding bucklers over their heads as protection from the stinging ice balls, they became part of a widening melee. The ground underneath became a quagmire of mud, grass, and ice. More than one man was knocked to the ground by flailing hoofs and the press of bodies.

Alvar, peering out from under a thick palmetto, thought of assisting but changed his mind when an ice ball contacted his forearm, leaving a stinging welt.

"Hijo de puta!"

Friar Xuarez joined him under the palmetto.

Branches and leaves fell to the ground, severed from the limbs above. All around a landscape of white covered the ground, severely cooling the air. Quite suddenly the hail and rain stopped altogether. A strange calm seemed to hang in the sky. Soaked and miserable, the two *Spaniards* huddled under Alvar's leather *cuerra, but* the jacket provided little protection from the elements.

Darkness descended rapidly on the campsite.

Alvar and Xuarez shivered as the rain once again began to fall, softly at first and then in torrents. The intensity of the lightning increased. With each flash, the forest seemed to dance in eerie hues of green. The effect was terrifying. Alvar thought he saw movement in the trees, at one time conjuring up a face peering at them. By the next flash, it was gone and he wondered if he had seen it at all. He grasped his sword tighter.

Well into midnight the storm, now spent, receded to the east, cleaving the sky with trailers of electricity that extended across the horizon. Soon only a distant rumble testified to its passage. The sound of frogs and other night creatures filled the air with a deafening crescendo. Insects buzzed about their ears and things, unseen, crawled on their skin. Wet, cold, and exhausted, Alvar finally managed to fall asleep.

In the early morning, the sun rose in a cloudless sky. As the air warmed, however, a steamy vapor rose from the ground and obscured everything further than a few feet distant. Soon, the sun became only a faint ember glowing through the mist. The air seemed to drip with moisture. Their departure on this day was delayed until just before noon, many of the men exhausted from the onslaught of the storm. Once underway their westward movement was again blocked by a line of impassable marshes and thick forests. The mood of the men was becoming surly. They were tired and hungry. All had lost weight marching in the unrelenting heat and humidity. Worse still were the scores of insect bites that covered their exposed arms, neck, and legs. Even some of the captains began to question the decision to abandon the ships.

Only a few miles out Narvaez called a conference. It was decided to return to the northward leading trail and follow it to its terminus. They reasoned that it must lead somewhere and further attempts to regain the coast would only delay their progress.

It was at this meeting that Alejandro Tellez began to think that their original destination to *Panuco* couldn't be that far off. After all, they had been marching for almost two weeks and covered a considerable distance. Many in the meeting nodded their heads in agreement. Alvar looked at Tellez in disbelief. They had already discussed this while still in *Boca Ciega*. *Panuco's* location was on the other side of the great Gulf and many miles distant. Ready to protest such thinking, Alvar looked at Narvaez who made eye contact and, ever so slightly, shook his head no.

"He knows," Alvar thought, and then he understood. The men needed hope and if it was their belief that *Panuco* was close, well...so much the better! With that, the expedition altered course and on the 13th day regained the faint foot path.

Later walking beside Xuarez and discussing *Panuco*, the Friar clapped Alvar on the back and said, "I think you are beginning to understand what it takes to be a leader."

Continuing northward, their travel was continually impeded by fearsome storms that seemed to come upon them in the late afternoon and through the night. Fires were impossible and sleeping was difficult. The fatigue and lack of food were beginning to tell on the men, but they trudged on.

16 May, 1528

Crooked River

After fifteen days the bedraggled expedition came upon a great river, its current running strong from the rains. Narvaez immediately ordered horsemen to scout the river in both directions for a more suitable location.

The river was very twisted, meandering this way and that as they scouted for a crossing. For this reason, the waterway earned the sobriquet of *Rio Torcido*...Crooked River and was duly recorded by the notary Jeronimo de Alaniz. After a considerable amount of searching, a site was located about half a league up river. Here the river looped back on itself, the channel widened and the current was not nearly as swift. One of the horsemen, an intrepid young man named Juan Velazquez, plunged his horse into the water, and although drifting downstream for a considerable distance, made it across. Climbing the steep bank with some difficulty he waved to his comrades and then rested for a short time. Moving up river, he again entered the water and emerged directly in front of the column. The horse was blowing hard and exhausted by the ordeal but Velazquez reported that the depth had been no more than five feet until he reached the middle of the river. There the bottom dropped abruptly and remained deep until only a few feet from the far side. Further up, where he had made his second entry, the bottom was much shallower but still dropped off at midstream. The expedition would make their crossing here, adjusting their entry upstream so as to exit at the shallowest point.

Velazquez's steed was a strong stallion and in the best shape of any in the expedition. Many of the other mounts, however, were in a much more weakened state and would not be able to negotiate the crossing on their own. Indeed, many of the men could not swim and there were weapons and supplies that needed to be moved across. Tools, crossbows, swords, lances, arquebusiers, armor, and most importantly, gunpowder. The carpenter of the expedition, Alvaro Fernandez, and apprentice Bonito Pina began constructing small rafts and directed the others in felling trees and gathering lashing material. Narvaez made it clear that all were expected to help. Although no *Indians* had as yet been encountered, he did not want his forces divided for long on both sides of the river.

Juan Velazquez, the horseman who had made the initial crossing, objected, "I will not do the work of common laborers, *peons,* and slaves." With this, he turned on his heel and began to walk away. Narvaez, his face flushed with rage, stepped up behind the young *hildago* and with a well-placed kick sent him sprawling. The camp erupted in laughter until Velazquez jumped up with his sword in hand.

Slowly, Narvaez drew his *montante* from its scabbard. It was a fearsome weapon, too large and unwieldy for most men, but in Narvaez's powerful grip, it was lethal.

"I suggest that you sheath your sword and assist in crossing the river, my young Cabellero, or you will die here today."

Captains Castillo and Tellez, with swords also drawn, moved up in support of Narvaez.

For a lingering moment nothing happened, but then, slowly, Velazquez lowered his sword.

Narvaez quickly turned and hailed carpenter Teodoro, "Give this man a task to assist you, I want to be across this river before nightfall."

By late afternoon the construction of the crude rafts was complete. The first to cross was a five-man contingent of skilled swordsmen led by Captain Castillo. They would provide the initial security while the others crossed. Hopefully, it wouldn't be necessary to beat a hasty retreat. In their support, Narvaez lined up the crossbowmen and arquebusiers to provide covering fire should they be attacked.

Their crossing was without incident and the raft was hauled back with a ship's line that had been brought along for just such a purpose. Several of the stronger horses were ridden across, including Juan Velazquez who was still quiet and sullen from his earlier confrontation with Narvaez. The weaker horses were lashed to rafts on either side and led across. Two or three swimmers accompanied them.

As evening approached only the rear guard of four swordsmen, Fray Xuarez and Alvar were left to cross. With a last look behind them, the six waded into the water and stacked their accouterments onto the remaining raft. The water was cool and Alvar thought of his times as a child wading in the streams around his native *Andulacia*. Xuarez removed his robe and heaped it onto the raft. It struck Alvar as amusing seeing the holy man standing there with his skinny white legs, attired only in his undergarments. Alvar unbuckled his sword and dropped it onto one of the wooden rafts. Attached to the sword belt was his headgear. The *morion* was heavy and hot and he avoided wearing it unless absolutely necessary. As an afterthought, he removed the *cuerra* that protected his chest and back. The three of these items combined would have sunk him to the bottom of the river like a stone.

The water remained knee-deep for the first few yards and then began to drop rapidly. The muddied water blocked any view of the bottom and each step was a sensory experience. Both men had removed their sandals and hung them from a cord around their necks. A mixture of mud and vegetation greeted every step. Small fish pecked at their legs and although not painful were a distraction. Alvar wondered what else was sizing them up under these dark waters. At waist deep it became hard to fight the current. Pushing the log rafts in front of them, they began kicking for the other shore. At mid-stream, the current carried them rapidly along. Two of the swordsmen, both non-swimmers, clung to the rafts in abject terror while the others in the party kicked their legs and moved the rafts across the deep channel. Nearing shore, thick grasses carpeted the bottom and it was a while before they could regain their footing in the shallow water. Fighting the current, half walking, half swimming, they pulled the rafts toward shore. Several of the men on the other side waded into the water to help.

Still knee-deep in the river and pulling his raft, Alvar stepped into a deep hole. Unprepared, he fell forward and momentarily disappeared underwater. Regaining his feet he rose up coughing and sputtering.

"Ah, mierda!"

He had ingested a lot of water and for a moment a coughing spasm racked him as he willed his legs to continue moving forward. Still coughing, he tripped again and fell forward in the now ankle-deep water. For a moment he remained there on hands and knees trying to clear his lungs. His eyes were still watering from the coughing exertion when Fray Xuarez reached down to help him up.

It was strangely quiet. Xuarez hadn't relinquished his grip and Alvar felt it tighten around his arm. He looked up at the priest. Xuarez was looking into the heavily wooded area just beyond the river's edge. At first, all Alvar could see was the tangle of tree limbs and thick shrubs. Scanning to his right and left, the others of the expedition were also staring into the forest. Many had their swords drawn and seemed to be moving into the line of battle.

He saw them then.

Materializing through the trees were the faces of men. Actually, it was the whites of their eyes that Alvar first detected, for their faces and bodies blended so well that they seemed to be part of the environment. They were everywhere. Alvar tried to count the *Indians*, but with their constant movement behind the cover, he gave up.

To no one in particular he mumbled, "I think maybe there are two hundred of them."

Slowly a group of about twenty *Indians* moved into the open area, but the rest remained concealed in the thick vegetation.

Cautiously, Alvar recovered his sword from the raft and moved forward. They were in a bad position. With their backs to the water, the *Spaniards* had no chance of retreating. If the *Indians* attacked they would have to fight to the death.

The *Indians* moved further into the clearing. They were unusually tall men, perfectly proportioned, their faces hideously painted in a variety of designs. Most were completely naked with only amulets around their arms and ankles. Tattoos seemed to cover every appendage. The designs varied; lines, swirls, circles, and caricatures of animals. They were the fiercest-looking warriors Alvar had ever seen. Some carried long-handled clubs while others brandished powerful-looking bows with quivers of arrows held in animal skin pouches.

He wished he hadn't removed his *cuirass.*

At first, the two sides merely sized each other up. To Alvar's right, the *arbelesteros* had formed a line and each man had his crossbow trained on the group of *Indians*. The *arquebusiers* were hurriedly working at loading their weapons and setting a flame to their primer cords. Some were still damp from the crossing. It looked as if the battle would break out at any moment.

It was then that Narvaez mounted his horse and spurred it forward. Riding behind the line of *Spaniards* he turned abruptly towards the *Indians*. Reacting to Narvaez's spurring and hard reigning, the horse was agitated, its nostrils flared and its eyes were wide. From the saddle hung numerous little bells that kept up a constant din as the animal surged forward. Narvaez had not drawn his sword but the sight of this huge redheaded man on an animal they had never seen was too much. The *Indians* pulled back into the forest.

Narvaez reigned in his mount and called for Marino Carmona to come up. The *Tiano* seaman had been pulled from his duties aboard the *Maria de la Meridionales Mares* and brought along to assist in translation. Narvaez stayed on his mount as Carmona arrived.

"Seaman Carmona, I need to talk with these *Indios*."

"I will try, *Adelantado*."

Carmona moved forward. Ahead of him and partially hidden by the thick cover, the *Indians* watched intently as he stopped and out-stretched his arm, palm up. Nothing happened.

Narvaez turned and ordered the men to lower their weapons. The *Indians* seemed to be arguing amongst themselves as to what to do.

Carmona thumped his chest and called out in his native language, "*E-oh tay Teeana!*" His arm remained raised in the sign of peace. To the *Indians,* Carmona was different than the *Spaniards*. The dark copper skin, straight black hair, and slashing tattoo across his right cheek made it evident, he was one of them.

Six men emerged from the line of trees and walked towards Carmona. The tallest of the three starred directly ahead at the *Tiano*, the others looked right and left, keeping a wary eye on the line of *Spaniards* and particularly on the mounted Narvaez.

The leader was a fearsome individual. Multiple scars covered his upper chest, their pale whiteness in contrast to the weathered skin. Braided into his hair were eagle feathers and the fibulae of small animals. He was armed with only a war club, a smooth stone lashed to a wooden handle. The others carried a bow and one arrow in their left hand. Hanging loosely at their sides were quivers made of deerskin, each containing several more arrows.

Stopping in front of Carmona, the leader studied him for a moment and then with an audible huff looked up at Narvaez.

"*Je tah le le atta wanne.*"

Narvaez looked to Carmona who shrugged his shoulders. "It is a language I do not understand, *Adelantado*. I will try the hand talk." With this, Carmona lightly touched the *Indio* on the shoulder to get his attention.

It was a mistake.

The leader reacted immediately, grabbing *Carmona* by the throat and raising his war club. The five companions rapidly fitted arrows to their bows. Narvaez, however, spurred his horse forward and with a kick sent the *Indio* leader sprawling before he could strike a blow.

Several *Spaniards* rushed up.

"Seize them!" Narvaez bellowed. Drawing his *montante*, Narvaez used the flat of his weapon to swat at the nearest *Indian* companion. The *Indian's* bow clattered to the ground. The other companions hesitated and were quickly subdued by the advancing *Spaniards*.

The *Indio* leader jumped to his feet but was immediately surrounded by three men, swords drawn. He crouched low, war club in hand, slowly turning to face each in turn. For a moment it was a standoff until *Capitan* Castello came up and entered the circle. He and the *Indio* leader warily circled each other with weapons poised. His attention diverted by Castillo, the *Indio* did not see one of his other assailants come up behind him. The *Spaniard* swung his shield and caught the leader full on the back of his head. The leader fell to the ground unconscious.

The six were rapidly unarmed and tied with their hands behind their back. The other *Indians,* still partially hidden in the thick trees, were visibly agitated, many hollering curses at the *Spaniards*. A few rushed forward into the clearing to shake their weapons but quickly returned when the *Spanish* horseman came to the front and formed a line.

The six sullen captives sat cross-legged in the sand surrounded by a group of four swordsmen. Narvaez dismounted and walked up to the leader, now conscious but obviously still feeling the effects of the blow to the head.

"Stand him up and release his bonds. He is their leader, and we must treat him with some respect."

One of the swordsmen moved forward and turned the *Indio* around. He stiffened and thrust his chin out, surely expecting to die. But, as the ropes restraining the *Indian* fell to the ground the whole area became eerily quiet. Only the sounds of the horses and equipment noises hung in the air.

A basket of trinkets was brought up and sat next to Narvaez. He reached down and pulled out several small copper bells and handed them to the leader. Both men were of equal height but Narvaez, being of much heavier build, seemed larger. The *Indian* studied the bells closely for a moment and then, grasping one between thumb and forefinger, began ringing it. He turned towards his compatriots and said something. He turned back toward Narvaez and bit on the bell, feeling the soft metal give way under his bite.

Narvaez ordered the other *Indians* released and offered them bells and brightly colored beads as well. Reaching into the basket once more, Narvaez pulled out a rusted knife. The conversation between the *Indians* came to an abrupt halt as each eyed the weapon suspiciously. Narvaez turned the knife, hilt forward, and handed it to the *Indian*. Gingerly, the knife was accepted. He had never seen iron and the strange metal seemed to fascinate him. Biting down on the blade he discovered the hardness of the iron blade and grimaced. He hefted it from hand to hand and then passed it to the other *Indians* who inspected it one by one.

Carmona was brought forward once again. The *Indio* leader, standing aloof, let the others struggle with communication. They, however, frequently gestured to him and seemed to ask for advise. At one point he seemed frustrated and stepped forward. Loudly thumping his chest he repeated over and over what sounded to the Spaniards as *Teo-toh-tah.*

Another member of the expedition joined the conversation. His *Christian* name was Don Pedro and although serving as one of the *capitans,* his position was strictly honorary. Don Pedro was an *Aztec* prince whom Narvaez had befriended while a captive in *Vera Cruz.* A nephew of the great Montezuma, he had been captured early by the forces of Cortes and converted to *Christianity* by the man who now accompanied him, Friar Juan Velazquesz de Salazar. They had become good friends. Both had accompanied Narvaez back to *Cuba* and then on to *Spain*. He had become Narvaez's protectorate, following him everywhere. His dress was a mixture of *Spanish* armor and *Aztec* weaponry. From his belt hung an obsidian-tipped war club, a *macana*. Early on both Don Pedro and Friar de Salazar had made the decision to accompany Narvaez on his expedition to *Amichel*.

"Senor Carmona, perhaps I can help, I seem to recognize some of their gestures."

Together the two came to understand the captives.

The leader, the one the *Spaniards* now called Teo, was indeed the head man, a *casique*, of a village not too far distant. Narvaez communicated his desire for peace and only asked for food to feed his men. Teototah tried to explain that they had only planted enough maize to feed his own people but Narvaez was insistent and the *Indian cacique*, perhaps realizing this was the only way to appease these powerful invaders, agreed to lead them to his village.

And so the column of *Spaniards* and *Indians* moved off to the east. The six captives, surrounded by an accompaniment of *Spaniards*, led the procession. Partially concealed behind trees, grasses, and palmettos, the other warriors of the tribe followed on the flanks. Periodically, small groups would break from the cover and approach the *Spaniards*, studying with wonder, the strange clothing and armament. They were particularly curious about the horses and would nervously retreat each time one of the animals made a sudden move. The *Spanish* cavalrymen, sensing this, would abruptly spur their steeds and rein them around to face the intruders. It was comical to watch the terrified *Indians* fall over themselves in terror trying to get away.

After a march of less than half a league the *Indio* village appeared next to the trail, a cluster of crude huts surrounded by a single long house constructed in the middle of a large open area. The inhabitants had chosen well, for the ground here was raised and not subject to flooding in the wet season. To Alvar, it looked very much like the village they had encountered to the west of *Boca Ciega Bay*. The inhabitants, wary of the newcomers, stood and silently watched as the *Spanish* columns moved into the open area and proceeded to set up a loose perimeter.

Further east and on the other side of the trail was a field of maize. Amongst the maize, a variety of pumpkins and squashes grew on vines that partially encircled the stalks. The field was well-tended and the ears were full and ready to be harvested.

For a moment Narvaez lost control. The hungry *Spaniards* fell upon the maize field, stripping the stalks. Consuming ears as fast as they could be husked, the empty cobs were tossed to the side. The mood of the *Indians* became sullen. As a group, the warriors began to close on the *Spaniards,* weapons at the ready. The inhabitants of the village, mostly women and children moved back. Narvaez, sensing that hostilities were imminent, called for his captains to regain control and ordered up a line of *Arquebusiers* to fire over the heads of the *Indians*.

The loud reports and the smoke terrified the *Indians*. This was something they had never experienced and they fell back in confusion. The inhabitants of the village rushed to the surrounding trees for cover. Many covered their ears, the women screamed and the babies cried.

Narvaez turned to Carmona and Don Pedro who had accompanied the captives on the march to the village.

"Senor Carmona, have the *cacique* tell his people that we only want food to feed our hungry soldiers. Tell them that no harm will be done to them and we will reward them with gifts."

It took some time for Carmona and Don Pedro to communicate these thoughts but finally, Teototah seemed to understand and was led to the center of the open area. In a loud lilting voice, the *cacique* addressed his people. He turned while talking so that everyone might hear. What he said, of course, was not understood by the *Spaniards* but it seemed to calm the warriors and village inhabitants. Weapons were lowered and slowly the people filtered back into the village.

Narvaez had the basket of trinkets brought into the open area and assigned the friars Alaniz and Asturiano to distribute the gifts. Additionally, the friars were to keep a sharp eye for gold that may be in the possession of the villagers. To his captains, he directed the control of maize collection with only enough taken for what they actually needed. He further ordered that there would be no fraternization with the natives. They were in a precarious situation here and did not need to initiate a running battle in this trackless wilderness.

From his position at the rear of the column, Alvar noticed that not all of the *Indio* warriors had re-entered the camp. A group of about fifty moved back just out of sight. Alvar brought this fact to Narvaez who answered in kind.

"This *cacique*, Teototah, is wise. We must remain vigilant."

In fact, what Teototah had told his people was.

"These bearded ones have great power in the beasts they ride and the weapons that they carry. To attack them would be foolish and cost us many lives. We will swallow our pride and while they are here our best warriors will watch them from afar. For now, treat them as our guests, feed them until they leave our land."

CHAPTER 18

Damn Little Vampires

Pequenos Vampiros Malditos

Now with the lengthening shadows, the ever-present swarms of mosquitoes began their rise from the vegetation.

"Pequenos vampiros malditos!" The damn little vampires were unrelenting. The only thing that really seemed to help was a very smokey fire.

16 May, 1528

Teototah's Village Near the Withlacoochee River

Like the rest, Santo Corral was tired, hot, and hungry, but most of all, he was miserable. The promise of making his fortune on this expedition was not coming to pass. He had endured months at sea on the stinking ships, overcoming seasickness, disease, and boredom. Sailing along the coast of *Cuba,* he and his compatriots had endured those terrible storms, crammed below decks without fresh air and only a greasy lamp for light. In *La Florida,* there was no evidence of a great *Indio* civilization like that which Cortes discovered in *New Spain.* He had spent days traipsing through this infernal wilderness beset by hunger and attacked by insects of every imaginable size. His sandals were worn and rotting from the ever-present humidity that sucked the energy out of you before the day was half over. Now, beside a fire, he sat with a company of men parching maize from the *Indian's* field, the only thing he could see of value since they arrived. There were only five cooking pots on the whole expedition and these had to service 300 men Whatever else was available was thrown into the pot as well. Part of a force assigned by Narvaez to collect anything edible in the camp, Corral and his companions had commandeered four deer, five rabbits, two turkeys, and a quantity of fish from the surly natives.

Corral had been impressed by the size of these people. All of the men were well over six feet and finely proportioned but their arms, legs, torsos, and faces were covered with hideous tattoos. Into their pierced ears many had inserted pieces of bone, or wood, or lengths of animal sinew tied to a feather, a clam shell, or whatever caught their fancy. Upon their heads was a cap made from animal skins that fit tightly to the head and terminated at a point, not unlike the stocking caps worn by *Spanish* sailors. To these caps, the men attached a variety of feathers, plumes, and other animal parts. These *Indio* warriors brandished a bow that was almost as tall as them. Their arrows were tipped with sharpened stones or sea shells lashed to the shaft with sinew. Others carried a spear and, like the arrows, it was tipped with stone of shell points. Finally, their genitals were concealed with only the briefest of a covering bound at the waist and running up the crack of their buttocks. All were barefoot.

Although somewhat intimidated by their fierce countenance, Corral knew that the *Indians* were no match against the *Spaniards'* training, horses, and weaponry. What most interested him, however, was the women. Like the men, they were tall and well-proportioned and wore only the briefest of clothing. Although he didn't care for the multitude of tattoos on their bodies, he was enthralled with their bare breasts, long legs, and buttocks. He was not alone. Most of the *soldados* felt the same way. During one food-gathering sortie they had entered one of the dwellings that contained three comely females, one in particular had caught everyone's eye. That evening they talked far into the night about what they would do to this little *chiquita* if given the chance.

17 May, 1528

Teototah's Village

It was a restless night. Narvaez had kept Teototah as a hostage to insure they wouldn't be attacked in the darkness. A large body of *Indio* warriors still patrolled in the woodland surrounding the village. Narvaez ordered large bonfires maintained during the darkness hours. In a protected area, a squad of *arbalesteros* kept their crossbows at the ready, and in another, the *arquebusiers* had loaded their weapons with horseshoe nails and rocks for maximum effect. The horses were saddled and the men laid down with their swords by their sides. The captains slept in two-hour shifts, getting up to check their men and oversee the bonfires. They talked in whispers to each other, and to the men on watch. The night was unusually still and quiet with only the crackling of the fires and the forest noises breaking the silence. Occasionally a horse would blow and stomp its feet.

Earlier in the evening, Alvar had cleared an area next to a large pine tree and along with Friar Xuarez had laid down. He had fallen into a fitful sleep only to wake up sometime after midnight. Next to him, Xuarez was softly snoring. Unable to fall back asleep he propped himself against the tree and watched the flicker of the bonfires. The fire's light danced on the tops of the trees making the forest appear to be moving. Overhead the moonless sky was wonderfully clear, the stars seemed to shine with an unusual brilliance. Alvar scanned the constellations, trying to remember their names. A faint flash of light caught his eye. It was almost imperceptible. At first, he thought it was a reflection from the fire but then his peripheral vision detected another. Sitting up, he stared at the sky intently. Nothing happened. He settled back against the tree.

Another one.

Once again he sat up. There was another, but this time his eye picked up the low line of clouds far to the west that were momentarily illuminated. It was lightning, and it was very far off. Now fully awake, Alvar stood up and stretched. Here and there lone figures could be seen moving about...some checking the fires others getting up briefly to urinate behind a tree. He noticed Captain Castello moving across the open area.

Castello nodded, "*Alguacil* De Vaca."

Like Castello, Alvar answered in a whisper, "Captain Castello, do you mind if I walk with you, I seem to have trouble sleeping?"

"Not at all *Alguacil*, I would welcome the company."

With a tilt of his head toward the west Alvar noted, "I think it will be a wet morning."

Castello shook his head, "Let us hope it holds off until first light."

It didn't.

An hour before dawn the storm was upon them, preceded by gusting winds that released swirls of bonfire sparks that drifted high into the air. Lightning flashed continuously and the temperature fell. Men rushed to calm the horses and secure equipment. Just as quickly as it had started, the wind dropped and a strange calm settled in, even the lightning abated. Like everyone else, Alvar stopped what he was doing and looked to the sky.

"Was it over?"

It was then that the distant rumble of rain could be heard moving across the trees, louder and louder as it rolled ever closer. To Alvar, it sounded like an approaching waterfall. It started with a few enormous drops that splatted hard on the ground. Then, as though someone opened a floodgate, the rain was upon them, falling in torrents.

Alvar thought he had never been so uncomfortable. The rain was cold. He began to shiver. The bonfires dwindled to a flicker and then snuffed out. It was unbelievably dark...only the occasional lightning flashes gave a hint of their surroundings. Sharing the space below the tree, both he and Friar Xuarez squatted in the mud, absorbed in their own thoughts, dealing with the situation as best they could.

17 May, 1528

Teototah's Village

At dawn's first light, the camp began to come alive. The storm had passed and now a steamy humidity hung in the air. The captains checked on their men and the horses were tended to. Alvar removed his garments, rung them out, and placed them on a tree limb to dry. Others were doing the same. The sky cleared and the storm moved off to the east. The remnants of one drowned bonfire emitted a tiny column of white smoke. The arquebusiers had stacked their weapons, the powder and priming cords soaked beyond use. The *arbalesteros* still kept guard but it was obvious that the *Indians'* intentions were not warlike. Cooking fires began to spring up all over the camp. To Alvar, it was amazing there was anythng burnable after the storm. A crowd of children gathered at a safe distance and intensely watched the horses only to be shooed away by their mothers.

Narvaez was already in conference with Teototah. While Carmona and Don Pedro struggled to interpret, Narvaez reached into a small leather bag and held up a piece of gold.

"Senor Carmona, see if they have any gold and from where they get it."

Teototah reached for the nugget but Narvaez quickly withdrew his hand and placed the piece back in the leather bag. Frustrated, Teototah turned to his companion and motioned for him to come forward. Reaching out, Teototah grasped the man's arm and held it up. Around the *Indio's* bicep was a thin gold armlet. This immediately got everyone's attention.

Narvaez had the bag of trade goods brought up and directed Carmona to deal with Teototah so that they may obtain the armlet. "Senor Carmona, make it understood to the *cacique* that we will trade for this armlet and any other such gold that might be in the village. More than that, we need to know from where they obtained it."

The communication with Teototah had been frustrating and difficult, but slowly, ever so slowly, Carmona began to pick up a little of their meaning. The hand talk helped, but even it was difficult. The *Tiano* sign for water, for example, was the right hand brought across the face in a wavy motion. For Teototah's people, who called themselves *Et tah Potano*, the sign for water was both hands raised together and then brought slowly apart. For the *Aztecs*, and Don Pedro's people, the sign for water was a swimming motion, like a breaststroke. There were similarities, however, and as the two interpreters worked through them, their understanding of "*Potano*" improved.

Carmona had successfully bartered for the armlet. It had cost four copper bells and a rusted ax head. He handed it to Narvaez. The talking continued. Suddenly Teototah uttered a word that the *Spaniards* had heard before, "*Apalache*" and pointed to the north. Narvaez, who had been talking with captain Tellez turned and prompted Carmona.

"Find out all you can about this...*Apalache*. We have heard this name before."

19 May, 1528

Teototah's Village

It was the third day at Teototah's village. Narvaez had given orders not to antagonize the natives in any way. He directed all of his captains to come down hard on any *Spaniard* who disobeyed. On the second day, Jose Pedero was caught stealing a turkey and was administered 5 lashes in full view of the village. Narvaez however, had ordered that the lash, the *gato de nueve colas*, be reduced to three strands rather than the usual nine. Since that time the mood of the *Indians* had changed dramatically.

The expedition had used the time to rest, repair equipment, and purchase food. The *Indian* hunters were awarded silver bells, beads, and small pieces of metal for anything that they brought in. The *Spaniards* had eaten well during their stay. Wild Turkey, deer, and the rabbit had been among the main stays on their menu, with an occasional squirrel, alligator tail, and oysters.

Seeing the oysters and other seafood, Alvar began to question the hunters as to the proximity of the ocean. To this, they all pointed to the west and indicated less than a day's journey. He had discussed this with the expedition comptroller, Alonso Enriquez, Alonso Solis, the royal inspector, and Friar Juan Xuarez the commissary. Together they approached Narvaez. It was Alvar who spoke first.

"*Adelantado*, we know from the hunting parties that the sea is not far off. We think it would be in our best interest to send out a scouting party in search of a harbor from which to contact our vessels."

To this, Enriquez, Solis, and Xuarez nodded their heads in agreement. Narvaez, however, was slow to answer, even somewhat agitated. He had been busy planning the next leg of their journey. A quest to find this *Apalache*, the so-called source of the gold that the *Indians* had all talked of...it pervaded his every thought. This city of gold would save his expedition. An expedition that was already wrought with bad luck and over expenses. Narvaez himself had gone heavily into debt mortgaging much of his property in *Baymo* to cover the cost of ships and equipment. To fail at this endeavor would be a disaster. More than that, however, he had to prove that he was the equal of Cortes, that he, Panfillo de Narvaez, could find a source of riches equal to the great *Aztec* city of *Tenochtitlan*. Yes, and with it he would curry much favor from the king.

Although he wanted to continue as fast as possible in search of *Apalache* he had to consider the wishes of these four royal appointees now before him, and what they said did have merit. Linking up with the ships would provide much need supplies and additional man power.

"Senor de Vaca, I feel that the sea is probably very remote from the place where we now are, but it would be wise to investigate it. Take forty foot soldiers and go with these *Indios* to see if what they speak of is the truth. If, however, you do not find the sea we must not speak any more about it until we have marched upon *Apalache*."

With that, Alvar began to make preparations. As the noon hour was approaching, he didn't think it prudent to leave immediately. It would take the men time to prepare and he would have to take at least one interpreter. Since Don Pedro was a soldier and seemed to be well along in understanding these *Potanos*, it would be him. Alvar approached captain Castello and asked him to pick the forty foot-soldiers that would accompany them. They would leave in the morning at first daylight.

20 May, 1528

Scouting Party on the Trail to the Sea

All had awoken well before sunrise. Captain Castello had chosen 40 good men and the party was well under way as the sun rose into a clear morning sky. The dogs, cavalrymen, and arqubusiers had stayed with Narvaez. With only fourteen *arbalesteros* and 23 foot soldiers, Castello wanted to move as fast as possible. Alvar,

Don Pedro, and two *Indio* guides accompanied them.

The trail was well-worn and easy to traverse. It was obvious that this was a commonly used thoroughfare. By mid-morning, they had traveled what Alvar estimated at four leagues. They had moved fast in a southwesterly direction. Here, the woodlands began to give way to sandy scrub. The further they traveled, the more open the land became. Large sandy patches void of any vegetation were scattered all about. Small *serpientes de cascabel* – rattlesnakes – were a problem here. No more than two feet in length their coiled bodies dotted the ground as far as the eye could see. Now, instead of keeping watch for possible attack, each man intently studied the ground where he was walking. Only the barefoot *Indo* guides seemed to have a sixth sense for avoiding the reptiles and walked along quite unperturbed. To their south, a line of shrubs and small trees marked the river location. It was the same river they had crossed to get to Teototah's village.

Sometime after noon, the environment began to change. It was not an immediate transition. At first, the sandy substrate became soft and spongy. Patches of shallow water appeared, each with its own population of insects, frogs, and small mammals that scurried away as they approached. It was the multitude of birds, however, that most impressed Alvar. Vast flocks filled the sky around them, gulls, pelicans, cormorants, and ducks of all types. In the trees, great plumed egrets seemed to rest on every branch. High overhead vultures and other raptors glided on thermals rising from the grasslands below.

Soon, they were splashing through ankle-deep water and aquatic plants began to appear. Shellfish became abundant and the sharp shells of oysters began to cut their feet. Alvar bent down and scooped a palm full of water into his mouth. He spit it out...it was brackish and not drinkable. After only another half league did the party stop. The water was now to their knees and in front of them was the strong current flow of the main channel of the river. Beyond it, the river's mouth and the broad expanse of a bay.

Castello joined Alvar at the front of the column.

"*Algucil*, it seems to be a large bay but to reach it we would have to cross this torrent, which, of course, is impossible since we are so poorly prepared for such an endeavor."

Together they scanned the horizon. There was no sail to be seen.

Alvar spoke next, "I agree Capitan. We will return to the village and report our findings to the *Adelantado*."

20 May, 1528

Teototah's Village

They sat cross-legged around the fire pit. Green palmetto fronds, leaves, and grass piled on top of the hot coals produced a thick white smoke that provided some protection from the hordes of mosquitoes. Only occasionally would the flicker of a flame show itself. These smoky fires, *fuegos humeantes*, where scattered throughout the camp, each surrounded by a group of *Spaniards*. In the still evening air, a hazy pall hung in the air below the trees. Eyes watered and breathing was difficult.

Narvaez listened intently as Alvar and Castello described the bay.

"Senor De Vaca, in your opinion was the bay adequate to receive our ships?"

"*Adelantado*, we only observed the bay from the far side of the river. At our location, we could make no determination of its depth, obstructions, or accessibility. It did, however, appear to be a large body of water well set in from the coast."

"And you, capitan Castello, what of the *Indio* presence in the area?"

"*Adelantado*, we saw no one. No villages, no people, no canoes in the bay. We did, however, see many paths leading to the coast with evidence that all had been well traveled. "

Narvaez stood and stretched. He walked over to the pit and nudged a few unburnt sticks into the fire. The smoke shifted and he hurriedly moved to the other side of the pit. He rubbed at his eye and blinked several times.

Narvaez spoke to no one in particular. "I think we will send out another party in the morning. If our comrades are searching the coast for us, as I suspect they are, this may be our chance..." He abruptly turned to one of the young captains sitting by the fire.

"*Capitan* Valenzuela!"

Somewhat surprised, the young captain stood up. "*Si Adelantado.*"

"I want you to get together another company of men and be ready to march in the morning to the coast."

"*Si Adelantado.*"

Narvaez turned and formally addressed Alvar.

"*Agacil* De Vaca, please pass your thoughts to *Capitan* Valenzuela on approaching the bay from the other side of this river.

"*Si Adelantado.*"

Narvaez, head down, paused and began pacing before the fire. He rubbed his red beard as if in deep thought. The camp was quiet, for all could clearly hear the governor when he spoke. Somewhere deep in the woods, a cougar screamed. The horses became visibly nervous and several men jumped up to quiet them. Narvaez watched for a moment and then turned again to Captain Valenzuela.

"Capitan, I want you to take a squad of cavalry on the chance that you make contact with the ships. If you find a suitable site I want a signal fire set on two successive nights. At all times, day and night, keep a sharp watch for our ships. If this happens, have the cavalry squad return immediately and notify us."

"Si Adelantado."

"Get busy *capitan*, for there is much to do and I want you leaving at first light."

"Si Adelantado." Valenzuela, turned to leave.

"Oh, *Capitan* Valenzuela."

"Si."

"Have Senor Carmona accompany you on this trip, we will need Don Pedro here."

"Si Adelantado."

Sitting back down on his bedroll Narvaez spoke to Alvar.

"De Vaca, you and Capitan Castello will remain here. You and your men have marched enough. Have them rest."

"Si Adelantado." Alvar, very fatigued from the day's ordeal, had no problem with this order.

With that, Narvaez laid down and was quickly asleep.

21 May, 1528

At the Mouth of the Withlacoochee River

*C*apitan Diego Valenzuella sat easily upon his mount and scanned the expanse of water. Before him was the bay that *Agucil* De Vaca and *capitan* Castello had seen from the other side of the river.

To the north, he could see the broad delta area where the river's fresh water surged across the numerous mud flats and sand bars. He tried to judge where his companions were when they surveyed the river from the other side. It was indeed a sizable bay, but what he saw before him was disappointing. It was shallow, very shallow.

Earlier that day they had left Teototah's village and marched only a short distance before reaching the river. Luckily, the rafts used the week before were still at the water's edge. The river had dropped and the horsemen crossed without incident. With the horses across, ropes were attached to the rafts and they were rapidly pulled to the opposite shore. The process was repeated until all had crossed. Only one foot soldier had fallen from his raft, but he was quickly pulled back by his comrades. By the time the party had wrung out their clothes and regrouped on the other side of the river, the sun was well up.

The route to the sea had roughly followed the river, only moving inland when the river widened into impassable sloughs and swamps. The *Indio* guides kept to the high-ground and a well-worn path. When only half a league from the coast the river bifurcated into several tributaries. One in particular stood in their way. To avoid another crossing, they were forced further to the north. At last, there it was in front of them, the unmistakable horizon of the sea and a broad bay. Valenzuella had smelled the salt air wafting in on the breeze. It had been late afternoon when they arrived and the next few hours were spent investigating the area and finding a suitable location for a signal fire.

Valenzuella shielded his eyes from the setting sun, now a large fiery ball just dropping into the horizon directly in front of him. There was not a cloud in the sky and the day had been hot...very hot. Now with the lengthening shadows, the ever-present swarms of mosquitoes began their rise from the vegetation. He waved his hand in front of his face and slapped at a particularly annoying sting on the back of his neck. Even the foul-smelling mixture of animal fat burrowed from the *Indians* didn't seem to help.

"*Pequenos vampiros malditos!*" The damn little vampires were un-relenting. The only thing that really seemed to help was a very smokey fire.

Valenzuella sighed, spending the whole evening breathing smoke was only marginally better than being preyed upon by these insects. Even now, his men were gathering sticks and dried grass for the signal fires directed by Narvaez.

He squinted and scanned the horizon from north to south. Not a sail in sight.

Above, across the land, on the water, in the water, life abounded all around him. In the distance, he watched two deer effortlessly bounding through the shallow water and over clumps of saw grass. Overhead a cacophony of sound pierced the air from the wheeling waterfowl preparing for the evening roost. Some of the birds he recognized, but it was the variety of ducks and smaller birds that amazed him. Growing up in his native *Castellon,* he thought of the pleasurable times duck hunting with his father, uncles, and brothers.

To his right, in a quiet estuary, what appeared to be a half-submerged log suddenly exploded in a deluge of spray and movement. When it was over *El Caiman* lifted its head above the surface, a flopping fish tail dangling from its fearsome jaws. With two gulps the tail disappeared down its throat.

Valenzuella shivered. He thought to himself, "Father will not believe me when I tell him of these things."

The sun edged below the horizon. In the west, the afterglow cast a red hue on the water and across the land. The sky was clear and already a few of the brighter stars began to show in the darker eastern sky behind him.

Horseman coming up from the beach towed huge bundles of drift-wood behind them.

The first licks of flame jumped up from the signal fire.

Out on the water, Valenzuella saw several canoes, their occupants adorned with elaborate feather headdresses. Although they slowed their traverse across the bay to stare, the canoes stayed at a safe distance. They glided into the growing darkness of the bay and out of sight.

"These will be a concern," Valenzuella thought and made a mental note to increase the perimeter guards.

Finally, the darkness closed in around them and only the crackling of the fire and camp noises defined their small group. Valenzuella dismounted and led his horse to the makeshift corral hastily constructed by the men. He removed the saddle and hobbled the front legs, then removing the bit from the horse's mouth he let the bridle hang at its neck. The horse, relieved of the burden, worked its tongue and mouth as if trying to regain feeling. Slobber dripped from its mouth.

Valenzuella grabbed his bed role and tried to gauge where the smoke from the fire would be accumulating. Tonight the light breeze was shoreward. He dropped his blanket downwind and as close to the fire as possible. Here he would be very visible and at risk should they be attacked, but he didn't care, he would do anything to rid himself of the *vampiros malditos.*

23 May, 1528

Teototah's Village

Alvar submerged the wooden canteen into a clear flowing eddy of the little stream and carefully shielded its mouth to keep the many water bugs from being sucked inside. Next to him the *Moor* slave, Estevan, had just finished filling the last of several that now hung around his neck. Sitting on a log to their right Andres Dorantes lazily drew circles in the sand with the tip of his sword.

Alvar was still chuckling from a story Estevan had been telling them of his exploits on the island of *Menorca*.

Still a young man, and before he had been pressed into slavery, Estevan had worked the fishing boats that plied the waters of the eastern *Mediterranean. Menorca* was a little island just off the coast of Spain and the fishing had always been productive in its rich waters. On one particular evening, the weather had been unusually rough and the owner of the boat had elected to enter a protected harbor on the island's north shore. He and the first mate had then proceeded to row ashore, leaving Estevan to secure and clean the boat. Sometime after dark they had returned, both roaring drunk, and accompanied by three prostitutes. They had continued their party on board until both the owner and the first mate passed out.

Up until now the protected harbor had been like a mill pond, but as the storm increased in intensity even the harbor became unusually rough. All of the women became seasick and begged Estevan to row them back to town. He had agreed, but only on the condition that he could have his way with them first. What had particularly amused Alvar was Estevan's description of mounting one of the prostitutes as she retched over the side.

Dorantes just shook his head, "*Alguacil*, I have heard these stories of Estevan many times before, and every time they get a little better."

There was a commotion on the trail and Dorantes quickly stood, his sword ready.

Campo appeared, "Senor De Vaca and *Capitan* Dorantes, the *Adelantado* requests your presence, Valenzuella's party has returned."

As they made their way into the *Indio* village some of Valenzuella's foot soldiers were still straggling in. At the center of the village, a knot of *Spaniards* and a few *Indians* were clustered together in a rough semi-circle. Valenzuella's horse, with the reins on the ground, stood motionless except for an occasional swat at flies with its long tail. At the center of the circle, Valenzuella knelt on one knee to draw a rough diagram in the sand. Narvaez stood just to his right.

"The harbor is shaped thus, *Adelantado*. It is wide and, unfortunately, very shallow. From where I stood reeds and mangroves could be seen growing far out from shore. The surface of the water is a mixture of colors, indicating reefs and sand bars not far from the surface. At times we would see many plumed *Indios* spearing fish far out from shore."

"And did you see any sign of our sails upon the horizon?" Narvaez asked the question like he already knew the answer.

"No, *Adelantado*, I kept several lookouts posted throughout the days and maintained a strong signal fire for two nights. At the end of our time there I had the men construct a large cross at what I thought to be the most visible point on the bay. To the cross, I attached a note giving the date and a description of our location."

"And what of the men, Valenzuella? Where there any injuries?"

"No *Adelantado*, save a few blisters and one bite from an *escorpion*."

Narvaez paused and stared blankly at the lines in the sand, then, seemingly coming to a decision, looked up to his officials and captains who were now clustered around him.

"It is unfortunate that we could not make contact with the support ships but tomorrow morning we will leave this village and continue our journey to the north. We will seek this place they call *Apalache*. With that Narvaez reached into his shirt and pulled out a nugget of gold about the size of a large grape. He held it up for all to see.

"This, according to our *Indio* guests, comes from *Apalachee*, where they say it is plentiful."

There was a murmur among those gathered around the *Adelantado*, for this was the reason they had joined the expedition...to become rich, to find another *Tenochtitlan* as Cortes had only ten years previous. Surely in the endless land, this *Amichel*, there were many more *Tenochtitlans'*.

CHAPTER 19

River Of Death

Rio de la Muerte

Alvar, standing a short distance away, felt the sadness and struggled with the thought of Velazquez dying so far from home. He would remember this day and this river of death that brought "grief to us all."

24 May, 1528

Teototah's Village Near the Withlacoochee River

Santo Corral's feet slipped in the loose mud and he slid on his backside down the steep incline to the creek.

"Hijo de perra," son of a bitch!

There he sat, feet in the water and a muddy ass. Grabbing a small sapling, he hoisted himself and stood for a moment wiping off the dirt and loose vegetation. With a sigh, he tugged at the six straps around his neck. The expedition was leaving within the hour and Corral had pulled the short straw for replenishing the canteens. Yanking the first cork out with his teeth, he lowered the canteen into the water and held it under with his foot, all the while holding on to the sapling and trying to maintain balance. When the bubbles stopped he hoisted it up and, still holding the cork in his teeth, re-inserted it...all with one hand. The first two were easy, but now the added weight around his neck made for difficult balance. On the fifth canteen, the strap snagged on a root. As he bent to retrieve it, the four full canteens swung out. Reacting to this he jerked upright, but in so doing his right foot again slipped on the muddy bank. Still holding onto the sapling, Corral fell hard to the ground. Now in water to his waist, he watched helplessly as the fifth canteen floated out of reach. Frustrated and angry he spit the cork, still in his mouth, in the direction of the wayward canteen. Sitting in the water he removed the cork from the final canteen and shoved it under water. When full he pushed in the cork and rolled over onto his hands and knees. Santo crawled back up the muddy bank.

On flat ground, he rolled over to a sitting position and caught his breath. He scanned the stream below looking for the missing canteen, but it was nowhere to be found. Now he would have to give up his to replace the missing one. He contemplated walking downstream to look but decided against it.

He felt someone watching him.

Moving cautiously, he located the hilt of his dagger that was jammed into his belt. He had left his sword back at the camp. Slowly, ever so slowly, he rose and turned to look up the trail by which he had come.

At first, he saw nothing, but then a slight movement to the right brought his attention to the presence of an *Indio* girl. Almost perfectly camouflaged with her back to the trees, it was the whites of her eyes that had betrayed her presence. Around her waist was a short deerskin wrap, a *falda*, and nothing else. She was barefooted and bare-breasted with tattoos on her arms and thighs. Dark black hair fell just below her shoulders, she was maybe 14 or 15. In each hand was an empty water bladder. Like Santo, she was also at the stream to collect water.

A leer spread across the *Spaniard's* face as he stared at her breasts. This was the same girl that he and his companions had seen when they first entered the village. Now they were alone and desire overwhelmed him.

Sensing her danger and blocked by the stream and heavy underbrush, the girl bolted for the trail. Even with the weight of the canteens Santo was quick. Diving forward he caught her by the ankle. Both fell to the ground in a clatter. The girl kicked at Santo with her free leg. Her heel caught Santo full in the face and bloodied his nose. He loosened his grip and she almost tore free but Santo managed to grab the ankle with both hands and drug her toward him.

Kicking wildly, she began to scream. Santo straddled her and clamped his hand over her mouth. She bit down hard on the soft muscle tissue just below the thumb.

"Mierda puta!" Santo withdrew his hand. Blood spurted from the deep bite wound. Beneath him, the girl's face, neck, and chin were awash with blood. She bucked hard and Santo, distracted by his gushing thumb, fell to the side. Quick as a cat, the girl turned and was on all fours. Clawing at the ground she struggled to get to her feet but Santo once again caught an ankle and pulled her prostrate. Straddling her, he pushed her face into the dirt while tearing at the deerskin around her waist.

Surprisingly strong, the young woman managed to turn on her side and raked Santo's neck with her fingernails. She began to scream again, her teeth still stained with blood. It was then that Santo balled up his fist and hit her hard, the blow landing slightly below the right eye socket.

The girl's body went limp. All resistance ceased. For a moment Santo, breathing hard, stared down at the girl. Her eyes, wide open, were rolled back in her head. Her breathing was shallow and an occasional moan gurgled out of her blood-stained lips. He sat up and looked around. Only the sounds of the stream, gurgling behind him, permeated the stillness. Santo dropped his pantaloons.

He rolled the *Indio* girl over and tore off the remainder of her deer-skin *falda*. Santo straightened her legs and, lifting them up, held one on each of his shoulders. He entered her then, stroking violently. With the adrenaline up, the passion was short in coming and he exploded inside her. The relief was immense. Santo slumped forward, momentarily overwhelmed with fatigue. He released the hold on her legs. They thumped to the ground. His eyes were closed and with his forehead resting on the girl's shoulder, he waited for the throbbing to stop. Suddenly, the girl's lungs seemed to fill with a monumental effort, and just as suddenly the air was released with a gush. Her throat emitted a strange rattle that rapidly faded away. Santo jumped backward in surprise. Her breathing had stopped.

Standing, he stared down at the lifeless form. Her eyes were open but unfocused; they seemed to stare through him. He prodded the body with his toe. Nothing. He prodded again. Now, standing there in his nakedness, he began to realize the enormity of his actions. Should the *Indians* discover this they would surely want retribution.

What would Narvaez do to him for jeopardizing the expedition?

Santo, now panicky, wondered if anyone had heard the girl's screams and, even now, was coming to investigate. He stuffed himself into his pantaloons, mindful of the sticky body fluids that ran down his thighs. Grabbing the girl's ankles, he pulled her off the trail and into the underbrush. He noted her skin was still warm.

He blundered about looking for anything that would cover her. Sticks, grass, leaves. Then, glancing over at the trail he noticed the canteens and the young woman's water bladders still laying on the ground. He rushed to them and tossed the bladders into the stream. The canteens he hung around his neck. Turning back to the river he watched the bladders as they quickly floated downstream. An idea came to him. He rushed back to the body and began dragging it to the stream. He continued out into the water. At about midstream, the water was to his waist and the corpse was floating on its own. He released her and then watched as the current carried the remains of the young woman along.

Santo looked about until he was satisfied that no one had seen him. He quickly hurried back up the trail, stopping briefly to throw dirt over the dried blood on the ground. Nearing the village he moved into the surrounding cover. Hurrying along, his legs were cut on the sharp palmetto stems and he had to reverse direction frequently to get through the dense underbrush.

Sensing he was close enough to the *Spanish* campsite he moved cautiously forward. He could hear men cursing, the farrier's hammer, and horses moving about. Santo cautiously moved out into the clearing. He was in luck, two horses were tethered close by and masked his emergence from the thicket. The thumb was throbbing and he tore off a strip of his tunic to wrap it.

No one saw him.

Moving as nonchalantly as possible he strode toward his companions. If asked about the injuries, he would say that he had fallen at the river bank.

Across the clearing, Narvaez mounted his horse and held his *montante* high in the air,

"*Caballeros*, follow me, we march to *Apalachen*".

Santo handed out the canteens, gathered his things, and quickly got in line for the march. In the confusion, no one even noticed his injuries. With a quick look over his shoulder, he moved out with only one thought. He regretted losing the canteen.

24 May, 1528

On the Trail North From Teototah's Village

The stop at Teototah's village had reinvigorated the expedition somewhat. The supply of maize had been plentiful, even enough to feed some to the horses. They had responded well, and even though most were still severely underweight, the animals seemed to move with new vigor. The men also moved along easily, joking and talking of the riches that would greet them at *Apalachen*. The six *Indio* guides that Narvaez had "borrowed" from Teototah led them north. The columns of men and horses moved slowly at first. The heavily forested trail obscured men marching only a few feet from each other. The threat of ambush was great, and Narvaez had once again initiated the *la rana* maneuver to protect the rear of the column.

Finally, the forested area ended abruptly in a broad river flood plain that seemed to extend far to the west. Here they turned northeast and skirted the area until firmer ground let them proceed north once again. Even so, sloughs and small streams abounded everywhere. Movement was slow. Most amazing were the many forested hammocks that covered the wetlands. Alvar could identify great stands of oak, maple, cedar, and elm. Many of these trees towered a hundred feet or more into the air and their trunks were as thick as a man standing.

The expedition camped in one of these hardwood hammocks for the evening.

The next day it was late afternoon when they came to a small river that flowed into the wetlands. The expedition stopped here and made camp. They would cross in the morning and continue north.

26 May, 1528

Crossing the Wekiva River and Approaching the Wacasassa River

It was one of the most miserable nights Alvar had ever experienced. All around them were swamps, rivers, streams, and lakes. The mosquitoes were so thick that they completely covered any exposed skin. They were not slapped, but instead scrapped off. The men covered themselves with cooking fat, mud, and grass. They dug holes in the sandy soil and covered their legs...anything to fend off the insects.

In the morning the river was crossed without incident. At its deepest, the water only came to the horses' bellies. Men and supplies made it across with relative ease. Still, it wasn't until the noon hour that the expedition again got underway.

After this crossing, the trail led to higher ground and somewhat easier travel. The guides, however, related to Carmona that they would soon come to another river, this one larger and deeper. After half a league they stood, again, at the water's edge. The *Indians* called this river *Waccassasa,* the word meaning *"river of rain."* In the dry season, it was a meandering lazy stream. During the summer deluges the "River of Rain" would swell outside its banks flooding the entire area. Today it was running high in its banks and Narvaez sent a scouting party upstream in search of a favorable crossing.

The scouting party struggled through the deep undergrowth and thick vegetation, many times having to make wide detours just to get back to the stream bed. Finally, at a league from where they started, there was a broad delta where a smaller stream entered the main river. Here a sandbar cut across most of the river with only a narrow area of deep water between them and the other bank. The search had taken longer than expected and by the time the search party returned the shadows were growing longer and the hour of Vespers was close at hand.

Narvaez heard the report and immediately instructed the scouting party to lead the expedition to the crossing point. As it was growing late they would camp there and cross in the morning.

After the sun had set a clear, star-filled sky twinkled above them. Before he retired Narvaez looked to the heavens and commented to Campo.

"The sky is clear, God willing, we will have a good day for crossing tomorrow."

What Narvaez could not have known on this evening was that a tropical depression had formed over the *Gulf of Mexico* and was moving rapidly to the east. As he was observing the clear evening sky that night, an intense storm was just coming ashore seven leagues west of their campsite. As the camp slept, conditions rapidly worsened. By midnight the low rumble of distant thunder reverberated in the air. The stars disappeared behind a blanket of low scudding clouds. At about two o'clock the first strong winds began to blow, and by daylight, the deluge had started. The rain fell in sheets that pounded the forest floor below. Within minutes the *Waccassasa* spilled over its banks and threatened flooding the campsite. Slipping and sliding in the mud the men struggled to gather supplies and horses and move them to higher ground. Lightning crackled across the sky and the crescendo of thunder was deafening. In the woodland trees crashed down and huge branches, sheared by the wind flew through the air. The tropical depression, now at full force, had stalled directly over them.

The rain continued for three days. Even after that, intermittent squalls blew across the landscape for two more days. During this time everyone in the Narvaez expedition suffered immeasurably. Fires were not possible, horses could not forage and the remaining hardtack that each man carried was rapidly consumed.

Finally, when the storm had passed the days became unbearably hot. The sun heated the ground and sent billowing clouds of water vapor that hung heavy in the air, stifling everything below. The roar of the bloated *Waccassasa* was unending. Huge trees, uprooted in the flood, rolled in the swift- water, their branches clawing at the sky above. For two more days, the expedition sat idle while the river continued its purge.

03 June, 1528

Crossing the River of Rain

Today Narvaez walked to the edge of the river and determined that to try a crossing here would be suicide. He gave the order to move further upstream hoping that the volume of water would lessen. Progress was slow. Another day passed. The expedition had to make frequent detours around vast flooded areas. Finally, the scouting party that had been sent on ahead rode into camp with good news. A short distance ahead the river widened in a vast alluvial plain. There was only one deep channel and it was only 25 feet wide. The horseman had easily ridden their horses across the expanse.

The expedition arrived at the crossing site in the late afternoon and Narvaez, fearful of another setback, insisted they begin crossing at once. A small group of *Spaniards* went first. All of these men could swim and they made it across the deep area without problem. Others swam their horses across. Once on the other side, they set up a defensive perimeter to protect against attack.

Now the remainder of the expedition started across. Two crude rafts were rapidly constructed to transport the supplies, gunpowder, and non-swimmers. Even for such a small crossing the whole process took time. Finally, as darkness fell, the last of the expedition had made it across "the river of rain." They camped for the night.

05 June, 1528

The Trail to Apalachen

Starting out the next morning the trail split. One path led northwest, the other north. Narvaez called up the guides and questioned them as to which direction they should go. They explained that the north trail led far inland while the trail to the northwest stayed closer to the coast.

After hearing both descriptions Narvaez addressed his interpreter.

"*Senor* Carmona, ask them which is the best trail to *Apalachen*."

After hearing the word "*Apalachen*" and not waiting for Carmona's translation all the *Indian* guides pointed to the northwestern trail.

"We have our answer!" That was all that Narvaez said and directed the expedition towards the trail that led to *Apalachen*.

That evening the guides informed Narvaez that at the next river encountered they could go no further. They called it *Seno sah Aucilla* and explained that it marked the boundary between the *Timucuan* and their fierce enemies, the *Apalachee*. They further explained that the *Seno sah Aucilla* was a sacred river that flowed through a strange heavily forested land besieged with caves and dark swamps that could swallow a man as if he never existed.

As the evening fires were lit the men gathered around the pits and discussed the day's events. Alvar sat with Marino Carmona and listened intently as the *Indio* guides talked of the country through which they would be passing. Communication was slow, a mixture of sounds and hand talk that Carmona would have to translate into *Spanish*. As the last visages of light faded from the sky, Captain Andres Dorantes and his slave Estevan joined the throng.

All through the translations Estevan listened intently, leaning forward to catch all the nuances of the *Indio's* speech and mannerisms. The conversation ebbed and flowed, sometimes laboriously, with Carmona struggling to understand.

Then, something strange happened.

During a particularly difficult translation, both sides were becoming frustrated. The five *Indio* guides talked in unison, all waving their arms. Carmona couldn't grasp their meaning. He dropped his head in exasperation.

"Senor Carmona, the *Indios* are trying to tell you that at this river they call *Seno sah Aucilla,* their enemies, the *Apalachee,* will meet you in force. They are very protective of their border. These guides are much afraid."

With that, Estevan looked at the *Tumucuan* guides and tested a few words on them. *"loa dechi mi twana."*

They understood him, and for a moment the *Indians* and the black *African* seemed to connect.

Everyone around the fire became silent. They stared. Estevan finally stepped back into the shadows.

It was Captain Dorantes who finally spoke. "I knew of Estevan having a gift for many languages but I had no idea that this would include this strange tongue of the *Indios*."

He turned. "Estevan, come forward into the light and help Senor Carmona so that we may know everything of which these *Indios* speak."

It was a good alliance, for although Estevan was a talented polyglot, he had no knowledge of the hand talk for which Carmona excelled.

Narvaez, who was watching the proceedings raised his hand for silence.

Capitan Dorantes, I think it is time we allow Estevan to wear a sword and armor. He will, from this day forward, be an emissary for our expedition. I want his presence to be of some note as we bargain and make valued decisions with these people.

From that moment on, Estevan the Moor, or Estevan de Dorantes as he was more commonly called, became a valued member of the expedition.

13 June, 1528

The Trail to Apalachen

It had been a week since they had moved westward from the bend of the *River of Rain*. The heavily forested and narrow trails severely delayed their progress. On the occasions when the lead horsemen and soldiers came upon a clearing or grassy opening, they would pause and let the horses graze while the trailing columns caught up. The delays could last for hours. The men were tired and food was very scarce. All had lost weight and many suffered from chronic diarrhea. Narvaez was frustrated, it was taking too long. He also felt that the guides were unnecessarily stalling. He called the interpreters to bring the guides before him. As they approached, Narvaez directed that one of the *Indians* be tied securely to a tree. The man, actually a boy of about 16, became very agitated, his eyes wide with fear. He commenced with a strange screeching that unnerved the *Spaniards*. Narvaez ordered him gagged.

The remaining guides commenced a wailing of their own. One of them stepped forward. He looked at Narvaez while addressing the interpreters in his strange tongue. The *Adelantado* listened, but, of course, understood nothing of what the *Indio* guide was saying. When the man became silent, Narvaez expectantly turned to Carmona and Estevan.

It was Estevan who answered. "*Adelantado*, the *Indio* is much afraid. He asks why you are doing this while he and his *companeros*...his companions...are aiding you."

Narvaez looked directly at the *Indio* spokesman as he answered. "Tell him that he should delay us no longer. I grow tired of their treachery."

Estevan repeated the words of the *Adelantado* to which the *Indians* began making very loud vocal denials. Narvaez was having none of it. He turned and ordered his blacksmith, Jorge Nazario, forward.

As Nazario approached the *Indians* fell silent. A large man like Narvaez, Jorge was known for his skill with a knife. He carried two with him at all times. His face and arms showed the scars of many a fight. With horses, he was gentle and compassionate, with men he was quite the opposite. He enjoyed inflicting pain and he would do anything that Narvaez requested of him.

"*Si Adelantado*." Nazario looked over at the bound *Indio* and a smile curled his lips.

"Ah, friend Jorge, I have a little job I need you to perform...are your knives sharp?"

"My knives are always sharp, *Adelantado*, how can I be of service?"

With this, the blacksmith pulled one from his waistband and lightly ran his thumb along the glistening blade. For all to see he held the thumb up and showed the slit that was now flowing with fresh blood. He turned toward the *Indio* boy and licked the blood away.

"Jorge, our friends here have decided to delay our journey to *Apalachen* and take us in unnecessary directions."

Narvaez motioned for Estevan to interpret as he spoke.

"Jorge, I want you to cut a small piece of this *Indio's* nose off so that his...ah...*companeros* will know that we are unhappy with their delays."

Narvaez waited while Estevan completed the translation.

Nazario moved toward the captive. "Only a small piece *Adelantado*?"

"*Si*, only a small piece my friend, but for each day after this that we do not reach *Apalachen,* one of the other five will also have their noses cut."

"And what if we don't reach *Apalachen* after all their noses are cut, *Adelantado?*"

Narvaez thought only a moment. "Then Senor Nazario you will cut off their balls!"

The five guides began to wail and had to be subdued by their guards. The young captive struggled against his bindings. His screams of protest could be heard even through the wad of cloth that had been shoved in his mouth. Two *soldados* moved up and held his head tightly against the tree. Nazario grabbed his nose between thumb and forefinger and pulled. At the same time, he sliced upward through the skin and cartilage with a single movement. The severed piece came off with a small pop.

Turning to Narvaez, Jorge held up the small section of skin and gristle. "Is this small enough *Adelantado?*"

Narvaez laughed and answered, "Yes, Jorge, it is just the right size."

Nazario threw the severed piece at the five guides and returned to his duties with the horses.

Narvaez, satisfied that he had made an impression with the *Indians,* walked away from the proceedings calling out over his shoulder, "Release the captive and guard all six well. We will camp here tonight."

16 June, 1528

The Trail to Apalachen

Alvar looked down at the dead mastiffs laying alongside the trail. Each had several arrows in it. Somehow the dogs didn't look quite so fearsome laying there on the ground. This loss was significant, for their keen smell provided an early warning of ambushes. In battle, they were absolutely fearless and the *Indians* greatly feared them. These were the first deaths suffered by the expedition at the hands of the people inhabiting this land. Somehow Alvar sensed there would be more. Those responsible for the deed had scampered off through the trees. Several riders had charged after them, but Narvaez called them back; the risk of ambush being too great.

The attacks had started three days ago and, up until now, had been ineffectual. Over the days several arrows had been shot at the *Spaniards*, but all had been from long range. One such arrow had glanced off Alvar's *morion*. The force had momentarily stunned him and left his ears ringing, but the arrow had fallen harmlessly to the ground. When he inspected the headgear, there was a large impact dent. He could only imagine what it could have done to his head.

As the column passed by the dead canines Alvar took notice of the men. Many were thin and haggard-looking. The equipment was rusty and deteriorating. Clothing was frayed. The leather shoes and boots were rotting away. Some suffered from a bowel ailment and had to stop frequently along the trail to relieve themselves. This, of course, caused delays. A detail of men would have to stop with the afflicted to provide security. As the line became increasingly extended Narvaez would be forced to call a halt. Once regrouped, the stragglers had barely any time to rest before the head of the column was up and marching again.

Alvar shook his head. They badly needed to be resupplied, and yet Narvaez continued inland looking for this city of gold...this *Apalachen*. They should be moving toward the coast. Surely, the vessels they had left behind were looking for them. He thought of Janero Florez aboard the *Maria*. And, what of his friend Angel Jiminez and the little brigantine *La Estrella?* What were they doing at this very moment?

Looking out into the forest he answered his own question. "Probably plying the coast in search of us."

The country had become heavily forested. The wetlands and grassy expanses, experienced early in the march, were replaced now by thick forests. The ground was drier but frequently interspersed with lakes of all sizes. The expedition glided along these forest paths screened by a canopy that imparted a twilight existence even at mid-afternoon. Occasionally, they would emerge into a clearing, and here the *Spaniards* would pause, either to rest or to camp for the evening. They would set up perimeters and gather wood for the fires. The horses would be sheltered at the center of the camp. Slaves would be sent out to gather fodder while Narvaez and his captains conferred as to the next day's order of march.

Concerning the guides, Narvaez had kept his promise and three more of the *Indians* had felt the sting of the farrier's knife. He had relented, however, on the final guide, the oldest of the group. As an incentive, he gave him three additional days.

This evening seemed no different than any of the others. As Alvar rejoined the column he could see ahead a lightening in the forest canopy...another clearing, and probably the end of today's march.

17 June, 1528

The Trail to Apalachen

The morning dawned gloriously bright and clear. They would be getting an early start. As the columns were lining up and preparing to move, there came a disturbance from the far side of the clearing on which they had camped. Immediately the captains formed the men into lines of battle. Swords were drawn, bolts were fitted into the crossbows and the arquebus priming cords lit.

There came from the treeline a line of magnificent warriors, all armed and painted in the most hideous of colors. The *Spaniards* fell silent as they watched the *Indians* advance. They took notice of their long bows, each with an arrow fitted into the string. Others brandished primitive clubs and spears. The numbers of the two armies looked to be about the same but it was anyone's guess how many were hidden in the trees. The *Spaniards* nervously looked behind them, expecting more to materialize out of the forest at any moment.

But, the *Indio* advance stopped. The center of their line parted and pulled back, creating a sort of pathway. For a time both armies stared at each other, neither moving. The *Indians* were silent, and from the *Spaniard's* side, only the sound of the horses permeated the clearing.

Fully expecting a desperate battle, the *Spaniards* were surprised when the sound of flutes drifted out of the forest behind the *Indio* horde. It grew louder and seemed to be coming toward them. From the path that the *Indians* had formed, a strange procession came into view. Six very large men were carrying a litter supported by two limber poles. Atop this litter sat a splendidly attired man reclining on a cushion of rich furs, his shoulders wrapped in a painted deer skin. On his head rested a lavishly plumed bonnet highlighted with eagle feathers. In his right hand, a beautifully carved shaft with a massive obsidian point lashed to one end. On either side of the litter, a line of flute players continued to emit the strange resonance that was at once eerie and annoying.

The procession continued forward, passing the line of warriors.

Narvaez, astride his horse, sheathed his *montante* and turned towards the men. "This is the *Indios cacique* who comes toward us. They wish only to talk, lower your weapons."

There was a collective sigh.

Narvaez addressed the captains that had assembled around him. "*Capitan* Castillo, I want you and *Aguacil* De Vaca to accompany me, but on foot. Also, have *Senor* Carmona and Estevan come up."

Looking down, he spied Captain Alejandro Tellez standing with his men. "*Capitan* Tellez, if these *Indios* betray us do not hesitate to attack, but use your best judgment."

"*Si Adelantado.*"

Narvaez spurred his horse through the front ranks and then halted as he waited for his retinue.

The *Indio* procession came to a halt about 200 feet from the *Spaniard's* front line. The flute playing stopped as well, and the six porters carefully sat the litter onto the ground and stepped to the side. The *cacique* remained seated.

Narvaez moved forward. To either side walked Alvar and Captain Castello; behind them, Carmona and Estevan. Trailing four or five paces from this front contingent were two armed flag bearers followed by two additional soldiers. Narvaez had picked all of these men for their height and bearing. The flags, flapping nosily in the morning breeze, were somewhat soiled and faded. The largest was the *Spanish* standard for *Castille* and *Leon*, the castle, and the lion. The other was a bright red heraldic conquistador banner. Most called it *"la Bandera Narvaez."*

As they closed, Alvar studied the *cacique* closely.

Like all of the *Indio* men, he was tall, but his body showed the results of luxury, the fat accumulating around his neck and midsection. His fingernails had grown to an unbelievable length, the ends of which had been filed to a point. His arms, legs, and face were heavily tattooed with zigzag patterns and circles. Still, he was impressive by the shear magnitude of his trappings. The litter on which he sat was constructed with an overhead framework thatched with palmetto fronds. Around his shoulders was draped a brilliantly painted deer skin. From the limber poles hung an assortment of dressed otter and fox pelts.

When only a few feet apart, Narvaez ordered a halt and rode slightly forward toward the *cacique*. He stopped and gestured for Carmona and Estevan to join him. The *cacique*, in turn, remained seated, apparently unmoved by the approach of the *Spaniards*. The other *Indians* in the party, however, watched the approaching horse with some apprehension. This was an animal they had never seen before. They could only compare it to a deer, but it was so much bigger. Narvaez took advantage of the native's ignorance. Holding the reins tight, he lightly spurred the animal. Agitated, the big stallion pranced and blew. Slobber and foam dripped from its mouth, some of it was flung onto the bodies of the litter bearers who winced and moved back. It was exactly the effect that Narvaez wanted.

Finally, controlling his horse, Narvaez instructed Carmona and Estevan to start a dialogue, to welcome the *cacique* and tell him that they came with no malice to do harm. The two interpreters approached the litter and a murmur passed through the *Indio* ranks. Even the *cacique* leaned down to confer with one of his advisers. All eyes were on Estevan.

Carmona and Estevan stopped.

The *cacique* rose from the litter and walked toward Estevan, stopping directly in front of him. He cocked his head and examined the young *Moor*, lifting his hand to look at the whiter palm and rubbing his arm, hard, as if trying to remove something. He touched Estevan's nose and turned to make a comment to those behind him. There was some laughter. Quite unexpectedly, the *cacique* grabbed the hem of Estevan's pantaloons to have a look at his privates.

Estevan balked and moved back.

From the saddle, Narvaez chuckled. "*Senor* Estevan, they have never seen a black man before."

Estevan stepped forward again and tried a few words that he had learned at Teototah's village. "*Te-ah so, yanta*". Welcome friend.

To his surprise, the *cacique* seemed to understand but then commenced into a lengthy diatribe of which Estevan could only pick out a few words. He turned to Carmona for help, but Carmona just shrugged his shoulders.

"I will try the hand talk, Estevan." Carmona stepped forward.

Together, the two interpreters worked with the *cacique* to establish some communication, while Narvaez and the rest of the party stood idly by. A bag of trinkets was brought forward by one of Tellez's men. Alvar and Captain Castello presented it to the *cacique*. He studied the glass beads, tools, and small copper bells with interest, but a small mirror seemed to intrigue him most of all. He turned and showed it to several of his people who grimaced and made faces into it, to the amusement of the others. Abruptly, he gathered the gifts and had them taken away - all but the mirror.

Stepping forward the *cacique* thumped his chest and repeated the word Dulchanchellin over and over again.

" Dulchanchellin, Dulchanchellin"

Carmona turned to Narvaez to interpret, but the *Adelantado* held up his hand. He understood the *cacique* was identifying himself. Standing tall in his stirrups, Narvaez also began to pound on his chest. With his great booming voice, he mimicked the *cacique* and repeated, "Narvaez, Narvaez." Then, pointing at the *cacique* he repeated Dulchanchellin several times.

With that, the big *Spaniard* dismounted and walked to the *cacique*. Narvaez was slightly the taller of the two and heavier built. He grasped the hand of the *cacique* and shook it. Narvaez noted that his hands seemed soft and his grip weak. The *cacique's* life of luxury had taken its toll.

Turning to his people Dulchanchellin removed the painted deerskin that he wore and held it up for all to see. Then he turned and draped it over Narvaez's shoulders.

It was a good start. For the next hour, the two leaders talked through the interpreters as best they could. With each passing minute, Estevan's grasp of this strange language seemed to improve until he alone was talking with the *cacique* and conveying his messages. Narvaez pressed him to ask about *Apalachen*.

Dulchanchellin was well acquainted with *Apalachen* but relayed that it was more than a town, it was the name of his enemies. Gesturing to the northwest he described how his people had been at war with the *Apalachee* for as long as he could remember.

As the meeting was breaking up, Narvaez held out a piece of gold between his thumb and forefinger, a gesture that would indicate it was not meant to be a gift.

"*Senor* Estevan, tell the *cacique* that this is something that we value more than anything. Ask him if it is true that the *Apalachee* have great quantities of it."

Dulchanchellin leaned forward and studied the small nugget. He began to nod and then turned to Estevan. "This is true."

For Narvaez, his hopes once again soared.

17 June, 1528

Journey to the Suwanee River

The meeting between Narvaez and the *cacique* had ended on good terms. Dulchanchellin would lead the *Spaniards* to his village and feed them. The *cacique* had remounted his litter and the procession proceeded back up the path from which they had come. The warriors followed next, walking loosely in ranks of four abreast. Finally, the Spaniards followed with a strong contingent of infantry forward, and the cavalry following close behind. At the end of the column was a strong rear guard. Narvaez had learned long ago to always be prepared for treachery.

The day had passed uneventfully until they came upon a great river. A wide, deep river whose current ran strong. Most strange was the color of the water...it was a dark amber, the color of tea. The *Spaniards* would call this "The River of Tea." The *Indians* called it *Su-han-ee*.

The men congregated on the bank and looked to the other side. It would be a formidable crossing. A canoe was waiting to carry Dulchanchellin across the expanse while the rest of his procession simply dove into the water. These people were strong swimmers and soon a mass of bobbing heads, flailing arms, and legs attended the *cacique* as he was paddled across.

For the *Spaniards,* it was a different matter. Most could not swim, and even if they could there was the matter of heavy armor, saddles, supplies, and weapons. They would have to construct rafts. The process began immediately. The woods rang with the sound of axes. The downed trees were quickly de-limbed and cut to length. These sections were then slid into place to be lashed together. The slaves did much of the heavy work but Narvaez was able to cajole most of the lower class *Spaniards* to help. Dulchanchellin even sent about twenty men back across the river to help. The higher class of *Spaniards,* the *hidalgo's,* however, were content to sit under shade trees and watch the others work.

Sitting with a group of friends, Juan Velazquez was becoming bored. He had been the first to cross the *Rio Torcido*, jumping his stallion into the water. It had been a show of bravado, and surely he could do it here. He tried to convince his friends to join him but all had demurred saying they couldn't swim and they would take their chances with the rafts.

"*Mis Amigos*, the horse will do the swimming, all you have to do is hold to the saddle."

The others, however, would not budge and even ridiculed him for being ostentatious.

Irritated, Velazquez rose to his feet. "I will show you." He quickly mounted his horse and spurred it forward.

Supervising one of the raft constructions, Alvar was startled to hear a horse approaching at full gallop. Everyone turned to look. It was Velazquez. Riding hard, he rode toward several of Dulchanchellin's men who were standing in a group. The terrified *Indians* scattered in all directions. A much amused Velazquez laughed out loud as his horse approached the raised river bank and leaped high into the air.

The horse and rider landed in the water with a huge splash. The force of the landing threw Velazquez out of the saddle, over the horse's head, and onto his back. Still wearing armor, he thrashed wildly as the weight pulled him under. Still grasping tightly to the reins he managed to pull himself to the surface. The current began to move man and animal downstream. On shore, *Spaniards* and *Indians* raced along, trying to keep Velazquez in sight.

Hand over hand, the terrified Velazquez pulled himself back to the horse but not before being dragged under several more times. Coughing water and gasping loudly, panic quickly overtook him. Holding tightly to the horse's neck he actually tried to remount, but the added weight forced the horse's head under water. This happened several times, both man and animal disappearing only to emerge seconds later in flailing, desperate anguish. Finally, both slipped from view around a corner of the river. Those on shore were hampered by roots and vegetation and could follow no further.

Alvar was stunned. Everyone had come to the river's edge to watch, and now, a desperate silence hung over the expedition. It was Narvaez who finally broke the mood.

"Capt Tellez, organize a search party and travel down river. Senor Velazquez was very much alive when he passed out of sight, we can only hope that he made it back to shore."

Tellez was quick to respond, "*Si Adelantado*." Within ten minutes three horsemen and six soldiers passed out of sight along a thin trail that paralleled the river.

The work on the rafts continued.

By early evening the horses, men, and equipment were being taken to the far shore. The passage, as in previous crossings, was crude but effective. Two horses accompanied a raft, one swimming on either side, their heads supported by a halter rope and their bodies by a girth belt. On board the raft two men held the horse ropes, two men pulled on a line that was attached to the far shore and one man played out the rope that would pull the empty raft back. It was time-consuming.

As the shadows grew long, Tellez and his search party returned empty-handed. they traveled far downstream and had seen no sign of Velazquez or his horse. Disheartened, they unsaddled their mounts and prepared to make the crossing. Theirs was the last raft to cross the river.

17 June, 1528

After Crossing the Suwanee River

The hour of Vespers had arrived. By the river, Fray Xuarez was just finishing a short mass for the safe return of Juan Velazquez. Other soldiers were preparing the evening fires. Further out, Narvaez and his captains were discussing their defensive strategies in the event of an attack although Dulchanchellin and his people did not appear to be aggressive. They had set up their own camp several hundred yards from the *Spaniards* and things seemed quite peaceful.

There was a commotion off to the right and all rushed over to see what was the matter. From the treeline, a very large *Indio* stepped into the clearing. On his shoulders, he carried the lifeless body of Juan Velazquez. He walked to where Narvaez was standing and laid the dead *Spaniard* on the ground.

Estevan was close by and hurried over to translate for the *Adelantado*. The *Indio* explained as best he could that a search party, sent out by Dulchanchellin, had found the body and the dead horse several hundred yards down river, hidden from view by a large tree that had collapsed into the water.

Narvaez thanked the *Indio* and then asked if he would lead his men to where the body of the horse was lying. Lest it not go to waste, they would drag the horse back to camp and butcher it for the evening meal. The *Indio* complied and a small body of men and two horses headed back down the trail accompanied by Estevan.

With Narvaez looking on, Fray Xuarez came up and knelt by the lifeless body. He reached down and closed the blank staring eyes, crossed himself, and then taking the silver cross from around his neck, pressed it to the forehead of Juan Velazquez. After a short prayer he rose, replaced the cross, and directed two slaves owned by Garcia de Paredes to bury the body. Paredes, standing nearby, stepped forward to protest, but thinking better of it, remained quiet. The two slaves followed Xuarez as he looked for a suitable grave site.

Juan Velazquez had been the nephew of Diego Velazquez de Cuellar, the former governor of *Cuba* and the very man who had sent Narvaez to arrest Cortes in *Mexico* many years before. As a favor to his former leader and old friend, Narvaez had agreed to take the young man, but had found him impetuous and difficult to handle. Still, the two had remained friendly even after several minor confrontations. The young man had a quick temper but was even quicker to make amends. He had been well-liked by all, and everyone felt a sense of loss. A line of his compatriots slowly walked by the body, each stopping in turn as they gave the sign of the cross before moving on.

Alvar, standing a short distance away, felt the sadness and struggled with the thought of Velazquez dying so far from home. He would remember this day and this river of death that brought "grief to us all."

18 June, 1528

Dulchanchellin's Village

They had been walking all day, closely following the *Indian* procession ahead. Dulchanchellin had indicated that his village was a day's march from the river and as the sun arced lower in the sky, Alvar felt that they must be getting close. He marveled at the *Indians'* resilience. Even with the burden of Dulchanchellin's litter, the column moved along briskly without stopping for rest and seldom for water. The *Spaniards* strained to keep up, and now as evening neared it was obvious they were spent.

Many had removed the hot armor and carried it slung over their back. All of the canteens were empty. Footwear had deteriorated badly and now many had elected to march barefoot. Even the horses walked with their heads down, only occasionally grabbing a shrub or a fleeting mouthful of grass as it passed by. The path at times became quite narrow, passing through dense woodlands and criss-crossed by numerous streams and rivulets. Here progress slowed. Men crowded single file onto the trail. The high woodland canopies filtered out the sun, but in this cool forest twilight, the lack of wind and high humidity was most unbearable. The previous evening's meal of roasted horse had been welcomed by all, but now the benefits of this meal had long since passed. During the march, there was the usual number of stragglers and Narvaez was compelled to send a strong force of ten cavalrymen to ensure no one was left behind.

As they swung further east, the thick forest gave way to stretches of grassland. The sun beat down, but at least here a breeze would occasionally cool them. Reaching back, Alvar rubbed his shoulder. Like the others he had gathered the burden of armor and thrown it over his back, but it was now chaffing the skin and he couldn't find a comfortable position.

Quite suddenly, the sound of flutes once again filled the air. Alvar looked up and scanned the horizon. Far ahead the grassland seemed to come to an end. There, in what looked to be a shallow wooded valley, he could just see the top of several structures. The *Indians* ahead had picked up the pace and many were waving their hands in anticipation of returning home.

Captain Castello came riding back through the column, urging the men forward.

"The village is just ahead, *mis amigos.* Try to look sharp. We don't want *los indios* to think we are tired...this will only show weakness."

There were groans and curses within the column but the men unshouldered their armor and slipped back into it. They straightened their backs, held their heads high, and quickened the pace.

CHAPTER 20

Apalachen

Apalachen

Across a cleared expanse of ground, fields of maize could be seen growing on either side of the trail. At a distance of 500 yards, the thatched roofs of forty or more huts rose above the stalks.

Narvaez turned to La Mancha. "This is Apalachen?"

La Mancha only spoke two words. "Si, Apalachen."

18 June, 1528

Camp Near Dulchanchellin's Village

At Dulchanchellin's direction, the expedition camped on high ground somewhat distant and east of the village. The area was shaded by tall trees and cooled by a constant breeze. Not far away a clear spring pushed up through the ground, the water meandering along a rocky bed before it eventually widened into a low wetland populated by saw grass. From their vantage point, the village appeared much bigger than anything encountered before. Fields of maize were spotted in the immediate area around the central area where a long house dominated all of the other structures.

Dulchanchellin was no fool. He would keep the newcomers at arm's length. As his procession filed into the village, warriors spread out and took up permanent positions between the village and the *Spaniard's* campsite. In time, a delegation appeared with food, and baskets of maize, which were quickly distributed among the men of the expedition. Fires sprang up and the parching process began. Kernels were stripped from the ear and heated in a pan. When sufficiently brown the cooked kernels were ground into a coarse meal which was consumed while drinking water. This mixture would then swell in the stomach giving even the hungriest *Spaniard* the feeling of fullness. The mixture was nutritious and light. Any left over meal was gathered for future consumption, each soldier storing it in whatever contrivance was at hand, leather bags, pieces of gathered linen, dry canteens, and even helmets.

As darkness drew near Narvaez and his captains were not entirely comfortable with their situation. The contingent of heavily armed warriors remained just outside the village and Dulchanchellin had not returned to parley with Narvaez. Extra guards were set out and the arquebusiers were told to keep their match cords lit throughout the night.

In the half-light just before darkness, Silvio Gutierrez again reached for his canteen. The heat of the day had severely dehydrated him and he had been drinking constantly. His canteen was empty. Leaning against a tree he turned to his companion Diego de Huelva.

"Diego, do you have water to spare?"

Diego de Huelva was a hawksish-looking man, with deep-set eyes and a nose that seemed much too large for his face. He had always been thin - some would say emaciated - but strangely, his countenance hadn't changed that much, even after these exhausting days on the march. That is, except for his head. Like everyone else his beard and hair had grown long, but on him the added mass exaggerated the size of his head in comparison to the thin body. His companions had taken to calling him *cabeza arbusto*...bush head, or *arbusto* for short.

"Silvio, my friend, I have been drinking almost as much as you. My canteen is empty as well. Let us go together to the spring and fill them up."

The two men began their trek toward the spring. It was only a short distance away, but somewhat secluded and downhill from the campsite. It was a quiet evening. Only the sounds of the camp a short distance away and a pair of barred owls calling to each other in the treeline could be heard. It was almost dark as they carefully moved down to the water source. All around fireflies, *la luciernaga*, signaled their presence with pale bursts of eerie green light. These were not the only insects about. Nearer to the water swarms of mosquitoes attacked the men. They would have to hurry so they could get back to the campfires and the mosquito-repelling smoke. At the edge of the spring, Gutierrez knelt down to fill his canteen. Next to him de Huevla idly looked about. Back toward camp the glow of the campfires could plainly be seen above the hill. Further west only the outline of a few trees were profiled against the faint afterglow of sunset. Overhead, the stars were beginning to shine in all their brilliance.

His canteen full, Gutierrez brought it to his lips and drank deeply.

"*Madre mia*, Silvio! Hurry or there won't be any blood left in me." De Huevla swatted at a particularly painful bite.

Gutierrez finished drinking with a loud sigh and then refilled the canteen. Rising up he made way for de Huevla who remained standing as he removed the plug from his canteen. He knelt down to fill the canteen.

"THWACK"

De Huelva jumped up, "What was that?"

It was now almost completely dark but Gutierrez thought he had seen something fly across his field of vision. He had his sword out. De Huelva had forgotten his.

Gutierrez had dropped down to his knees, head turning in all directions, "I think it was an arrow, check that tree behind you."

De Huelva, also staying low, moved to the base of the tree and slowly slid his hands up the trunk. With just the stars for light, the tree was barely visible but as he felt higher his hands came in contact with a shaft. Not sure whether it was an arrow or a branch he followed the shaft outward until he felt the feathers.

De Huelva dropped to his knees again, "*Santo Cristo*, it was an arrow, and right at the level of my head. If I hadn't bent down..."

"Sssssshhhh!" Gutierrrez was listening. Something had caught his attention out in the darkness.

Both men listened intently. It was quiet...too quiet.

Somewhere out there a twig broke and then the sound of a body moving through the grass. With that, both men panicked and bolted back up the trail. Running blindly, De Huelva tripped on a tree root and stumbled to his knees, but just as quickly was up and running again. Gutierrez, now far ahead and running hard, was the first to enter the clearing.

"To arms, to arms, we are under attack!"

The men, some already asleep, quickly mobilized. Weapons were grabbed and armor hastily donned. The captains lined them up into several hastily formed *tercios* or *Spanish* squares. The horses were moved to the interior of the defensive formations, for cavalry was virtually useless in the dark.

The noise and clatter of the mobilization gradually subsided. Everyone was peering out into the dark just beyond the fire light. Now, the only noise was the sound of the captains giving an occasional command. They waited.

Nothing.

Narvaez stepped into the fire light. "Who gave the warning that we were under attack?"

Sheepishly, Huelva and Gutierrez stepped forward. "We did, *Ade-lantado*."

After hearing their story, Narvaez and a squad of men proceeded down the trail to the spring to investigate. Four *ballestero* led the procession, their crossbows ready. Behind them, two torch men and finally Narvaez and four swordsmen.

It wasn't long before the procession returned. Narvaez walked up to de Huelva and presented him with the arrow. It had embedded itself a hand's length into the tree. Narvaez had used his *montonte* to hack at the tree and remove the shaft. With the men assembled around him, Narvaez addressed the group, his voice booming across the clearing.

"We must be prepared for treachery. Tonight was a warning. From now on, all men leaving the safety of the camp must be accompanied by two companions and you will carry your weapons with you always."

Narvaez then instructed the captains to stand down, but not before doubling the guard. It would be a long night.

18 June, 1528

Dulchanchellin's Village

From his vantage point, Dulchanchellin had watched the *Spaniards* as they reacted to the arrow attack. He was impressed and not a little concerned. They had rapidly formed a formidable military formation and their weapons were different from any others he had ever seen. Although the bearded ones looked bedraggled and starving, there was no doubt in his mind they could cause terrible damage.

Dulchanchellin had not ordered the arrow attack. In fact, he knew nothing about it until later when two young boys had bragged about it. He had them brought before him.

"Why," he asked, "have you done this thing?"

The boys, not yet warriors, shifted nervously in front of him. They looked to the right and to the left. If it hadn't been for the guards restraining them, Dulchanchellin had the feeling they would have run off.

"Answer me!" He banged the shaft of his spear into the ground.

Cowering, the taller of the two boys answered, "Great Chief, no one has ever killed one of these white men. We wanted to prove that we are ready to become warriors."

With a sigh, Dulchanchellin sat down. "You are both foolish boys. What you have done has put us all in grave danger. You have broken the trust between us and the bearded ones with your actions."

Dulchanchellin paused. He considered what to do next. Surely the bearded ones would want revenge and with first light, they would use their weapons and riding deer to attack the village. He couldn't take a chance.

"Let the boys go, I will deal with them later. Now, as quickly as possible we must leave this village tonight. We will quietly take the north trail and go to the land of our brothers the *Utina*. The women, children, and elders will leave immediately. The warriors will follow close behind and protect us from attack."

19 June, 1528

Camp Near Dulchanchellin's Village

It was the longest night that Alvar could remember. He slept with his armor on and sword close at hand...that is when he slept at all. Everyone expected screaming hordes of warriors to come crashing through the camp at any time. Every night noise was suspect. Dawn finally broke calm and clear. From their vantage point, the village looked tranquil, nothing was moving; even the line of sentries, so prominent the day before, were gone.

Narvaez quickly gathered a group to parley with Dulchanchellin. Captain Tellez, Marino Carmona, Estevan, and three soldiers. Narvaez and Tellez would be mounted, and the others would follow on foot. Alvar was left in charge of the remainder of the forces with orders to charge the village if things went badly.

With everything in place, Narvaez led the group a few hundred paces from the camp and stopped. He wanted to insure that his actions were interpreted as peaceful. From their vantage point, both Narvaez and Tellez surveyed the village.

"*Adelantado*, I see no sign of the *Indios*."

Not seeing movement of any kind Narvaez was troubled. "Be on guard *Capitan* Tellez, this could be a trap."

Slowly they made their way into the village.

Still nothing.

They entered the large court yard. It was eerily quiet. At that moment a small dog scampered across the the open area, upsetting a stack of kindling wood that clattered to the ground. Startled, all of the men reached for their weapons and instinctively formed a protective circle.

Back at the camp Alvar saw the defensive movement and prepared the men for a charge.

Narvaez, *montante* in hand, could see no other movement. He motioned to the three soldiers. "Search the village!"

The three rapidly went from structure to structure while Narvaez and Tellez investigated the long house.

The village was empty.

"Captain Tellez, ride back and have Senor De Vaca bring the men forward. We will gather what we can and then continue on for *Apalachen*."

"*Si Adelantado*."

Narvaez dismounted and walked over to a fire pit, the coals still hot. Skewered on a spit, an overcooked rabbit had been left by the *Indians* in their haste to leave. The expedition leader helped himself and sat down on a log.

19 June, 1528

At Dulchanchellin's Village

The *Indians* had fled, and the men of the expedition took the opportunity to gather as much of the ripe maize as possible; in fact, anything in the village that was useful was quickly collected. Narvaez had sent a party of horsemen to investigate the trail. In two hours they had returned, reporting that Dulchanchellin and his people were a league to the north. The horsemen had encountered a strong rear guard and backed off when several arrows were launched in their direction. One horseman displayed an arrow that had deeply embedded itself in his *doubler*. Luckily, he had seen the missile in time to raise the shield.

Narvaez, anxious to get moving, had the expedition form up and by noon they were marching north on the same trail that was heavily imprinted by the mass of *Indians* moving just ahead of them. By mid-afternoon, the village was far behind and they again encountered remnants of Dulchanchellin's rear guard. The warriors would launch arrows and then quickly disappear into the countryside. It was frustrating to the *Spaniards* who knew the dangers of ambush if they pursued the attackers.

The assaults continued. A mount ridden by Lieutenant Pepillo Sotomayor took an arrow to the flank. Sotomayor had fallen heavily to the ground when the animal, reacting to the pain, stumbled and fell. Gaining his feet, Sotomayor complained of pain in his side. A rib had been broken. A non-lethal injury, but one that was painful and would take time to heal. The horse was tended by Jorge Nazario who dug out the point with his knife and dressed the wound as best he could.

The *Indians* had begun to move around the expedition, attacking the flanks in small groups. They moved quickly, blending into the foliage so well that the *Spaniards* had little time to react. One *ballistero* had been able to lose a bolt at one of the fleeing figures, hitting him in the shoulder. The warrior had spun around and fell to the ground but, amazingly, he jumped to his feet and disappeared from view.

A group of four black slaves had lagged a few paces behind the column. This was understandable because each carried heavy loads for their owner Garcia de Paredes. Bundles were strapped to their back on a wooden framework...a *mochila*...with crude rope shoulder straps that dug deeply into their skin. These loads contained the trifles of Paredes such that he could travel with as much comfort as befitting a member of the gentry class.

Concealed from view as the column passed by, a group of five warriors sprang up and rushed the group of blacks. Terrified, three abandoned their loads and ran. Only one remained to face them. He was Toro the massive *Abidji* who feared nothing. The *Indians,* distracted somewhat by the discarded packs, slowly began to circle the lone black man. Each was armed with a long-handled mace with a heavy stone lashed to the end. The *Spaniard's* called these weapons *quauhololli's*.

Toro, unarmed, released his pack and turned slowly with his attackers. Behind him one of the warriors lunged forward, his *quauhololli* descending in an arc towards the *African's* head. For a big man, Toro was exceptionally quick, his huge hand catching the weapon in mid-swing. The other hand wrapped around the warrior's neck and snapped it like a twig. With one motion he lifted the body and threw it at the other four. It landed in a clump by the side of the trail, the head twisted grotesquely. Now, armed with the dead man's *quauhololli*, Toro turned to meet the other four attackers.

They hesitated. This huge black man had just killed their comrade in the blink of an eye and now, with a weapon, he would be even more dangerous. Their hesitation was quickly interrupted by the clatter of hoofs. Warned of the attack by the escaping slaves, four horsemen from the column were approaching rapidly.

The *Indians* bolted from the path and disappeared from sight.

Noisily, the riders clattered to a stop beside Toro, billowing dust up around him. Two forced their mounts a short distance into the brush, poking here and there with their lances. Several soldiers, breathing hard, arrived after a long run. Ahead, the column had stopped and taken up defensive positions, but it was to no avail, for the *Indians* had made good their escape and there would be no further action.

Now, Narvaez and Garcia de Parades rode up and surveyed the scene. Narvaez dismounted and kicked at the *mochilas* that had been carried by the slaves; then he walked to where the dead warrior lay. He poked at the body with his *montante* and then approached Toro. He examined the *quauhololli* and then threw it into the brush.

Turning to one of the cavalrymen he commanded, "Get this man a sword, he has proven his right to carry it today."

Walking up to de Parades, Narvaez was less complimentary. "Senor Parades, no longer will my column be held up by these men carrying your slippers and silk underwear."

Gesturing at the packs he continued, "You will only carry the necessities to fight and stay alive. The rest you will leave on the trail where it lays."

Narvaez remounted his horse and rode back to the head of the column.

The other horsemen formed a protective barrier while an angry de Parades supervised the recovery of his "necessities".

Ambling over to the side of the path with his heavy *mochila*, Toro slung it into the brush, and then, bending down, retrieved the *quanuhololli* that Narvaez had tossed away. He shoved it into the belt that now held his new sword as well.

19 June, 1528

On the Road to Apalachen

At the head of the column, Narvaez stopped to confer with his captains. These attacks were becoming a bother and something needed to be done. It was Andres Dorantes who stepped forward.

"*Adelantado*, I will take six of my horseman...*mi caballistas*...and conceal them in the cover such that after the column passes and anyone should be following, we will fall upon them."

Narvaez thought this a good idea and Dorantes proceeded to pick his best men.

At a favorable location, a diversion was created at the back of the column. Two riders were told to engage in mock battle while a group of soldiers gathered noisily around them. There was to be loud yelling, banging of shields, and even the discharge of two firearms. During this time Dorantes and his *caballistas* would slide unnoticed into the cover and wait for the column to pass by.

Everything went as planned. Once Dorantes and his men were in position, Narvaez stopped the mock battle and instructed the procession to continue on.

Concealed in a grove of trees Dorantes and his men stood by their mounts. They had chosen the downwind side of the trail. The smell of horses was new to the *Indians* and would immediately alert them to the *Spaniard's* presence. Amongst them was an *arquebusier* with his weapon ready to fire. This sound would alert the rear of the main column where another group of armed *caballistas* waited.

It was only a few minutes after the column passed that movement was noted on the trail. A band of twenty warriors seemed to glide along the fringes, moving stealthily from one tree to the next. Every now and then one would break away to the center of the trail for a better view and then, quickly, rejoin his companions. They were well-armed. All had a *quanuhololli* in hand or tucked into their breech cloths. Others had long powerful-looking bows and still others carried a short spear for thrusting. Their passing was almost noiseless.

The *caballistas* quickly mounted and broke out of the clearing. As planned, the *arquebusier* fired his warning shot. The six mounted *Spaniards* thundered toward the *Indians* with their swords drawn. All of the warriors were experienced fighters, but none had ever experienced a threat like this. Some jumped back into the trees, but others broke and ran up the trail. Only two warriors stood their ground to meet the charge. Dorantes, riding in the lead, swung his sword in a short arc, decapitating the first, the other disappeared under the hoofs of the riders, his body lay in a mangled, bloody heap.

The *Indians*, running hard, came to an abrupt halt when the other contingent of horsemen from the main column appeared in front of them. Frozen in fear, they threw down their weapons. Strangely, the warriors dropped to their hands and knees as if waiting for execution. Dorantes and his men warily circled the group until it was obvious that there would be no further resistance.

"Bind them. We will take them back to the *Adelantado*."

The weapons were taken and each warrior had his hands tied behind him. They were set in a rope line, each with a noose around his neck, and led back to the main column in a single file.

Briefly, Dorantes and another rider returned to the crumpled forms in the trail. Dismounting, he walked to the trampled corpse and drew his sword. With one swing he removed the head. Using a short piece of rope he died both of the decapitated heads together and handed the gruesome trophy to the rider who remained mounted.

Narvaez had halted the march. Soldiers had been placed in defensive positions. As Dorantes' *caballistas* rounded the trial, with their prisoners in tow, the defensive lines parted and let them through. There were cheers and several taunted the prisoners.

"Bravo! Capitan Dorantes and his *cabillistas* have captured the *Indios."*

"Hang the *bastardos*!"

Beside Narvaez, Alvar de Vaca and Alonso Enriquez watched the *caballistas* approach. The prisoners were brought in front of Narvaez and told to kneel. Dorantes rode up and threw the two heads onto the ground. To Alvar, they made the sound of a gourd when dropped onto a rock. For a moment he starred at the surprised dead eyes that seemed to be starring back at him.

"Adelantado, we killed two and captured these five. Several escaped us, but I doubt they will be back." Dorantes looked back at his men who laughed loudly and brandished their swords.

"What would you have us do to them?"

"Capitan Dorante, you and your men have performed well." Narvaez walked down the line of prisoners looking carefully at each one.

"We will keep these four as guides." Narvaez then stepped over to the remaining *Indio*. He appeared much younger than the others.

"This one we will send back to Dulchanchellin with a message and a gift. The message is that we only want peace, but if they fight us we will kill them all...and as for the gift!" Narvaez picked up the rope with the two decapitated heads and hung it around the young warrior's neck.

More cheers from the men.

23 June, 1528

Approaching the Aucilla River

Grateful to be alive, the four *Indians* captured in the ambush seemed to work well with their *Spanish* captors. They were even given *Christian* names. The oldest and most knowledgeable was the warrior Latakneona, a cousin of Dulchanchellin. The *Spaniards* called him *La Mancha*...the spot...for a large birthmark that covered the right side of his face. Estevan, especially, seemed to form a friendship of sorts with him. They would talk late into the night, each describing his own life and culture. Estevan talked of the wonders of the modern world in *Spain* and the *Mediterranean* while La Mancha related stories of his people, their beginnings, and the great battles he had been in. At first, the conversations proceeded slowly, with much hand talk and repeating of words and gestures. As time passed, however, Estevan, seemed to master the language and talked easily. Alvar, ever curious, at times would sit in on these conversations, frequently interrupting so that Estevan could interpret for him. La Mancha, in turn, learned many *Spanish* words and soon could make himself more or less understood. His greatest desire, he related, was to ride one of the *Spaniard's* large deer. When this was relayed to Narvaez, he agreed, providing that La Mancha led them as quickly as possible to *Apalachen*.

The country through which the expedition now passed had changed dramatically. Forests with extraordinarily tall trees towered high into the air, dwarfing the expedition as they moved along. A man with his arms outstretched could not reach half way around them. Looking in any direction, this sea of behemoth trunks seemed endless. Far out into the forest darkness, one could only imagine what was looking back. The vegetation on the forest floor was sparse, each species seeming to fight for the small amount of light that filtered through the leaves and branches above. Smaller trees were thin and spindly as they strained to find an opening in the canopy.

They came to a river that was most strange. The guides turned and followed the river bank to the south and then, suddenly, the river disappeared into the ground. Here they crossed over. When questioned, the guides related that further south still the river reappeared out of the ground and continued to the sea.

Thunderstorms frequented this area and passed rapidly from west to east, the violence of these *tormentas* such that the expedition was forced to stop and cower in fright. Even the *Indio* guides were wary of the storms, describing them as angry spirits looking for victims to appease their wrath. Lightning would split the skies. Many of the trees were rent from top to bottom with ugly black scars that showed the effects of these *rayos*...thunderbolts.

Not having a clear view of the sky, the storms would come upon the expedition almost without warning. Perhaps only a single clap of thunder would announce the tempest's arrival before clouds covered the sun and titanic winds lashed the upper branches. On the ground the air was still, but high above a battle of natural forces waged. Limbs, leaves and deluges of hail and water would cascade down upon the *Spaniards*. Often the expedition would encounter blow-downs, clear evidence that the wind had won many of these battles. The trail would be blocked in tangles of limbs and fractured megaliths that, in their collapse, took others with them. Here, the trail would have to be rerouted, many times for as much as a league or more in a circuitous route around the affected area.

The expedition had stopped at midday to rest after a hard morning of bypassing one of these blow-downs. It was the sixth hour after dawn and Fray Juan Xuarez had assembled the other holy men to give thanks and pray for their safe deliverance. They had cleared and rounded the blow-down, but La Mancha and the other guides had struggled to reestablish the trail. The going had been unusually rough and required a line of men leading the march with swords and axes to clear the way. Finally, the thin path had reappeared.

Guards were posted. At the center of the clearing, the *Spaniards* circled Xuarez and his group of friars. Xuarez raised his hand for quiet. After a moment of contemplation, he began the short prayer, but the first words were hardly out of his mouth when a low, almost inaudible rumble sounded to the west. Had they not been silent for prayer it may have even gone unnoticed. All looked to the sky, but what could be seen through the heavy canopy was clear and the sun seemed to shine brightly. Still, they knew what was coming and the men rose to their feet albeit with their hands still folded and their heads bowed. Interrupted in his entreaty, Xuarez began again but to all that attended it was the shortest and fastest prayer that the good friar had ever given. After the "Amens" men rushed in all directions to prepare themselves for the onslaught they knew was coming.

It wasn't long.

Another clap of thunder resounded through the woodland, this one much closer. Alvar hunched himself underneath a large tree with heavy overhanging limbs. It would provide some protection from the heavy rain he knew was coming. Being under a tree during a thunderstorm was not a good idea, but here he was in an endless forest of trees; what were the chances of his tree, amongst all the others, being singled out?

"Senor De Vaca, may I join you?" It was Friar Xuarez.

"Good friar, I will never turn down a man of God at a time like this."

Xuarez laughed, "Let us hope it passes us by."

Just then the forest grew perceptibly darker and far overhead the winds descended on the tops of the trees. Limbs and leaves began to fall to the ground.

"Is there room under there for another?" It was Friar Augusto Alaniz.

"Two men of God, I am surely safe now," was Alvar's reply.

Looking out across the forest floor Alvar could see all manner of *Spaniards* crouched under trees or bushes, many with their coats over their heads. Even the *Adelantado* had found a choice seat amongst some downed trees that would afford protection.

The horses were hobbled and set in one large group at the center of the gathering; around them, slaves and some of the cavalrymen kept watch.

The rain came upon them in a rush, falling straight down in torrents, for here underneath the canopy, there was no wind. Above, lightning seemed to split the sky with almost continuous discharges. Over the din of the thunder and rain, an occasional sharp crack could be heard somewhere out in the forest. A large limb or tree had succumbed to the power of the wind.

Staring out into the clearing, Alvar was momentarily blinded by a searing flash.

Crack-Boom!

Something stung his jaw. The flash and the noise were instantaneous. His ears rang.

Beside him, Friar Alaniz called out, "*Madre de Dios*!"

Alvar blinked and rubbed his eyes. Light spots danced about and he couldn't seem to focus. His ears were ringing.

Again, "*Madre de Dios*, the tree is burning." Alaniz again.

His vision returned, and a blurry point of light danced in front of Alvar's watering eyes. He blinked the water out again and again, each time the vision clearing a little more. Finally, it returned well enough to see a fire burning in one of the towering pine trees just across the clearing. It was about half way up. The rest of the tree was gone.

Scattered about on the ground were the remnants of the tall trunk, some still smoking. Many of the horses had been hit by the flying debris, some with deep cuts in their flanks and shoulders. Terrified by the noise and fire, many had fallen to the ground, tripped up by their shackles. The scene was utter confusion.

Fray Xuarez jumped up, "There is a man down over there."

The rain was still falling heavily.

Crawling out from under his concealment Alvar was surprised to see blood in the puddle that had formed just under him. He stared at it a moment. A drop of red fell as he watched; the blood was coming from him!

"Senor De Vaca, you are bleeding." Alaniz gently turned his head for a better look.

"There is a piece of wood embedded in your jaw about the size of a small nail. I will have to pull it out."

With the rain coming down even harder, Alvar sat down in the mud and as gently as possible Velasquesz grasped the piece between forefinger and thumb.

"Are you ready Senor De Vaca?"

"*Si Padre*, do what you have to do."

Almost before the words were out of his mouth, Alaniz jerked backward with all his strength. So much so, that he lost his balance and fell backward into the mud. The splinter had exited the wound with a loud sucking pop as Alvar screamed in pain.

"Ahhhhhhhhhhhh!"

The blood now flowed even more freely from the wound. Alaniz stood up and tore a piece of cloth from his vestment.

"Keep pressing on this *Senor* De Vaca until the bleeding stops."

The rain was abating and the sounds of the storm were moving to the east.

After a moment both men walked over to the still burning tree to survey the damage. Alvar was holding his throbbing jaw with one hand. Friar Xuarez was administering to a man laying on the ground, a large section of the tree lay by his side. The man was barely conscious, his chest rose and fell rapidly as if struggling to get enough air. Blood trickled from the corners of his mouth.

Xuarez looked up at his two companions, "This is Juan Avero, a soldier with *Capitan* Pantoja's company. I found him with that log on his chest." Xuarez nodded towards the large section of trunk that lay beside him. "It was with difficulty that I was able to lift it off."

"Will he live?" Alvar's jaw hurt when he talked.

"*Alguacil*, the piece of tree crushed his chest and I fear the wound is mortal." Tears formed in the friar's eyes and he turned away.

Alaniz touched the shoulder of Friar Xuarez. "I will remain here with you my friend so that *Senor* Avero will not die alone."

Suppressing his own emotion, Alvar made the sign of the cross and turned away from the sad scene.

The rain had stopped.

25 June, 1528

Approaching Apalachen

Traveling through this megalithic woodland had been difficult. Food was scarce. Occasionally, in clearings close to lakes or streams, small villages would be encountered. The terrified inhabitants seeing these strange men and animals, would flee into the woods. Meager fields of maize would be decimated. Many of the men were sick and the horses had deteriorated badly. Swords, armor...anything containing iron, was rusting. Leather rotted and fell apart. The occasional deer killed was immediately skinned and the hide cut into strips to repair saddles, shoes, and armor fastenings. Buckskin, however, was not as strong as cowhide, and without proper curing, these repairs quickly rotted as well.

All had felt the debilitating effects of diarrhea. At times the entire column was forced to stop as men fled to the bushes to relieve themselves. Some were beginning to feel the effects of another malady. It was a general feeling of fatigue, aching of the joints, and rashes. The worst cases complained of soreness in the mouth and even bleeding gums. Those among the expedition with sea experience recognized it as the dreaded *escorbuto*...scurvy, so common on long voyages.

Narvaez was ever present, pushing the expedition on. Most days the column traveled five or six leagues. On other days, when conditions were better, they would complete seven or even eight leagues. The best day had been ten leagues, but that had been early on. Conversely, the worst day had only been two leagues...the day they had buried Juan Avero.

The column had stopped. Alvar was thankful. Shedding his armor and sword, he rushed to a low overhanging tree that would, more or less, give him some privacy. The gurgling in his stomach was growing worse and he squeezed his rectal muscles as tightly as possible. Moving branches aside he stepped to a clear spot and fumbled to untie his pantaloons. His skin was hot and he felt a little unsteady. He dropped the pantaloons to his ankles and then kicked them aside. Grabbing a branch he squatted and balanced himself as best he could. The release of pressure was instantaneous. He could feel the gas and foulness release the bloat in his stomach. The relief was immediate but the dizziness grew worse. Still squatting, he dared not move. Previous experience had shown that the spasms would return until he was completely empty.

There was noise coming from the column. Something was happening.

Alvar grabbed fist fulls of grass and tried to clean himself. Rocking forward he dropped to his hands and knees and crawled over to the pantaloons. Rising to a crouch he slipped them back on and leaned against the tree for balance. Finally, stepping into the open, a breeze cooled his forehead. Feeling somewhat better he moved to retrieve his armor and sword. He was desperately thirsty.

"*Senor* De Vacca!" It was Campo and he was breathing hard. Alvar turned toward the young page.

"*Senor* De Vaca...ah...his excellency requests...ah...your presence."

"*Senor* Campo, if that canteen of yours holds any water I would be in your debt if you would share it with me."

Campo freed himself of the canteen and handed it to Alvar. "*Si*, I just filled it no more than a few minutes ago, but we must move forward."

"We will young Campo, but while I am drinking tell me what is happening." Alvar raised the vessel to his lips and drank deeply.

"The *Adelantado* has requested you to come forward because we have arrived at *Apalachen*!"

Alvar drained the canteen and then, with his eyes closed, stood there a moment.

"*Alguacil*, are you all right?"

"I am now, young Campo. Go and tell the *Adelantado* that I am on my way."

Alvar strapped on his sword, slipped into his *cuirasse,* set the *morion* on his head and slung his *rodela* over his shoulder, and hurried toward the front of the column.

25 June, 1528

Arriving at the Indian Town of Apalachen

The column stretched for a considerable distance and Alvar had been close to the end when Campo had found him. Hurrying forward he stepped around the men, horses, and equipment who were lounging on the trail.

"*Alguacil*, what is the news, why have we stopped?" The men asked.

Alvar nodded at the men, shrugging his shoulders, and continued on.

Ahead, there was a break in the trees. A line of cavalry was facing forward in battle formation. He pushed between two of the horses.

Narvaez was standing with his captains. Also present were Inspector Solis, the *Indio* guide La Mancha, Estevan, and the comptroller Alonso Enriquez. All were looking to the west. Across a cleared expanse of ground, fields of maize could be seen growing on either side of the trail. At a distance of 500 yards, the thatched roofs of forty or more huts rose above the stalks.

Narvaez turned to La Mancha. "This is *Apalachen*?"

La Mancha only spoke two words. "*Si, Apalachen.*"

The huts themselves abutted another treeline that began anew and appeared very dense. Scattered about were many small lakes, their perimeters obstructed by large trees that had fallen into them.

Like the others, Alvar stood and stared. His first thoughts were not positive, but he was also relieved, for now they were at the place they wished to be.

"This is not the great city that we have been led to believe."

Just outside the village, some of the inhabitants could be seen rushing out to look at the strange gathering of animals and bearded men. Just as quickly they would disappear into the surrounding woodlands.

"Ah, *Senor* De Vaca, join us!" it was Narvaez.

"*Adelantado*, I came as quickly as I could. Is this the place called *Apalachen* to which we have been marching?"

Narvaez seemed embarrassed. "It is not what I expected." Just then several arrows could be seen arching towards them.

"On Guard! On Guard...*en Guardia*!"

The men squatted down to make as little targets of themselves as possible. Those with shields held them over their heads. The four or five arrows having been shot from so far away clattered among them without doing damage.

Narvaez stood. "On your feet men, those arrows were spent, they had not the power to kill a beetle!"

There was laughter as everyone again stood upright.

"De Vaca, you and *Senor* de Solis accompany *Capitan* Dorantes into the village to see what threat we are facing."

Turning, Narvaez addressed his captains. "*Capitan* Castillo, you and *Capitan* Valenzuela proceed back down the trail. Ensure our men are prepared for an attack and place a strong rear guard at the rear of the column. *Capitans* Tellez, Penalosa, and Pantoja will remain here should an attack come from the front or we need to go to the aid of *Senor* De Vaca."

Everyone fell to their assigned tasks. Horses were brought up for Alvar and Alonso de Solis. With a total of nine mounted men, ten crossbowmen, and forty-foot soldiers...*rodeleros,* the advance party moved toward the village.

The horsemen...*caballistas,* advanced in line, De Vaca, Dorantes, and De Solis at the center. The path to the village was wide here and able to accommodate nine horsemen abreast. Directly behind the horsemen marched the ten crossbowmen, their bows drawn and the bolts in place. Behind were the forty-foot soldiers holding their shields and weapons at the ready.

There was a single hut, at the outskirts of the village. Alvar concentrated on it as they approached. He was sweating underneath the armor and his senses were on edge trying to pick up any unusual movement or noise. Holding the reins and the shield with his left hand he squeezed tightly onto the sword with his right.

If they were going to attack it would be now. They had reached the first hut.

Nothing. They stopped. Dorantes ordered men to search the hut.

A woman and two young children were brought out. They uttered not a sound.

The horsemen started forward again.

The next hut yielded two women and an older male of some status. He was extensively tattooed and wore a headdress of multicolored feathers. A quick interrogation by Estevan and Carmona determined his position as shaman of the village. Hand talk was the only communication, for these people spoke a much different language.

Another hut yielded a group of young boys, none over fourteen years of age. In their possession were small bows and a supply of arrows, most probably the source of the earlier attack.

At each successive hut, a detail of foot soldiers would bring out women and children, but no warriors. There were forty huts in all. The inhabitants were herded to the center of the village and held on guard. The shaman was held separately.

To Captain Dorantes, Alvar shared a thought. "*Capitan*, it appears these people had no knowledge of our coming."

"I agree *Alguacil,* and we should remain alert, for their men may not be far off and undoubtedly someone was sent to fetch them."

Alvar, Dorantes, and De Solis dismounted and walked to a hut that had been cleared. Just to the outside, a cooking fire was burning. Alvar and Dorantes poked their heads through the opening. Inside was only the most meager of possessions - hides, cooking implements, baskets, blankets of poor quality, and vessels for grinding maize.

"These people have no riches *Alguacil*. I see nothing here that should interest us."

Quite unexpectedly De Solis' horse reared and fell to its haunches. Still holding the reins, there was a look of surprise on the Inspector's face. Dorantes saw it first, an arrow was deeply embedded in the animal's side. Blood was oozing out onto the sand.

"To arms, to arms, we are under attack!"

Thirty or forty warriors brandishing bows and clubs were approaching from the deep line of trees. Dorantes leaped to his horse, followed by De Vaca.

The crossbowmen were the first to react and return fire, their bolts finding at least two targets. One *Indian* dropped to the ground, dead before he hit, and the other limped back to the forest cover. A charge by Dorantes and four other horsemen routed the warriors and they quickly disappeared into the thick undergrowth. The fight was over.

Alvar approached Dorantes, his blood still up from the charge. "I guess we know where the men of this village are now."

Dorantes looked at Alvar and laughed. He turned to one of his horsemen. "Ride back and tell the *Adelantado* that this village of forty huts is secure."

CHAPTER 21

Ghosts In The Trees

Fantasmas en los arboles

Shortly after the party of Spaniards had returned to their ranks, the line of warriors, just outside the treeline, seemed to evaporate.

Alonso Enriquez spoke for all the Spaniards, "They disappear like ghosts in the trees!"

27 June, 1528

The Indian Village at Apalachen

The army had moved rapidly into the village. For the next two days, the soldiers populated the dwellings and ate the food that was on hand. There were great quantities of maize in the field ready to be harvested. Each hut was searched, the contents rudely thrown into the open courtyard at the center of the village. To the delight of the discoverers, there was some gold and even a few pieces of silver found, but the quantity was not great.

On arrival, Narvaez had directed Captain Castillo to set up a defensive perimeter and then, strangely, retired to one of the huts.

On this day, Alvar, spied Campo scurrying across the courtyard and called out to him.

"Campo, a moment!"

"*Si Alguacil*"

"Young Campo, the *Adelantado* hasn't been seen for two days, is he ill?"

Campo looked about him, not sure how to answer the question.

"What is it, boy?"

"*Senor* De Vaca, the *Adelantado* asked that I not tell anyone but he has been feverish and seems to be losing strength. Last night he sweat so profusely that I had to help him change his tunic three times. I am very worried."

"Young Campo, we have all been sick. I myself have had spells. We can only hope and pray to our savior that he soon recovers. Take care of him, I will do whatever I can to help with the tasks at hand."

"*Si Alguacil.*" Campo hurried away.

There was a commotion at the center of the village.

At the prisoner compound, twelve soldiers had forced themselves into the area holding the *Indio* women and children. Other soldiers were cheering them on. The women were being accosted, but not without opposition, they were fighting back. One *Spaniard* was doubled over, the victim of a well-placed kick to the groin. Another had a hand full of hair and was dragging an *Indio* woman to a nearby hut.

Alvar recognized the soldier. "*Senor* Corral...enough!"

Santo Corral stopped but maintained his hold on the writhing woman.

"Ah, our *Alguacil*. Surely *Senor* De Vaca will not prevent me from claiming a spoil of war."

"*Senor* Corral, you will release this woman at my command"

"Look about you *Alguacil*, there are many of us and only one of you.

There was movement to Alvar's right. "You are mistaken *Senor* Corral. There are two of us!" It was Captain Alonso Del Castillo.

Corral had not seen Castillo's approach but was still belligerent. "We have marched until our feet have bled, we are tired and many of us are sick. We only want what we deserve!"

He looked back to his compatriots for support, but they began to drift away. Castillo was respected by all on the expedition and his prowess with the sword was indisputable.

"You will release that woman, *pendeja,* or I will carve you into little pieces. Castillo began to move toward Corral.

It was at that moment that Narvaez exploded out of his hut, *montante* in hand.

"Enough of this!" He was dressed only in a soiled tunic, he was bathed in sweat and his eye patch was not in place, but he was big, and he was mad, and he was coming at Corral in full stride.

Santo Corral released the woman.

Narvaez grabbed Corral by the neck and it looked for a moment that he would kill him outright, but he relented. Turning to Castillo he said, "Put this *hijo de puta* under arrest, we will deal with him later."

With that, Narvaez stalked off and re-entered the hut. Campo was there to help him through the door, for it was clear that he had exhausted himself. It was soon after this incident that the men of the village appeared again at the treeline.

"To arms, to arms!"

The *Spaniards* rushed to form up in their ranks. First, the *rodeleros* with their swords and shields. Behind them were the *ballesteros,* their crossbows fitted with lethal bolts. On the flanks, the *arque-busiers* struggled to prime their weapons while the *caballistas*, the horsemen, formed in the rear.

For a moment it seemed utter confusion, but the lines assembled quickly. *Alguacil*

De Vaca, *Contralor* Alonso Enriquez, and the captains moved to the front. With everyone in place, a quietness fell over the village. Both sides eyed each other with anticipation.

Three unarmed *Indio* warriors stepped forward, their arms raised in supplication.

Alvar turned. "Estevan! We need Estevan and La Mancha forward at once!"

Estevan and the captive La Mancha quickly passed through the line of *rodeleros*.

Alvar addressed Estevan. "You will accompany me forward to talk with the three *Indios.*" Addressing the captains, he continued, "Should we be betrayed and attacked, *Contralor* Enriquez will take command."

Alvar turned to the captains. "*Capitan* Pantoja I would be honored if you would accompany us as a witness."

The five stepped forward and walked toward the warriors that were now halfway between the lines. The three warriors were all a head taller than any of the *Spaniards* or Estevan. Only La Mancha was their equal in height. All were adorned with massive headdresses of brightly colored feathers which seemed to make them even taller. Their faces, torsos, and upper thighs were replete with hideous tat-toos of all designs. Wearing only the briefest of covering over their genitals, all three were barefoot.

Estevan and La Mancha stepped forward to begin the discussion. Alvar, Enriquez, and Pantoja stayed in the background, alternately looking to the right and left for signs of an attack.

After a short discourse, Estevan turned and addressed Alvar. "*Alguacil*, they have come to ask for their people."

Alvar answered, "Tell them that I will consider this only if they agree to leave us in peace."

Estevan and La Mancha entered into further dialogue with the *Indians*. There seemed to be some argument. Finally, Estevan related what was discussed.

"Alguacil they would like their shaman, women, and children returned and are unhappy that we have occupied their village. They ask us to leave."

"Tell them that we will consider their request, but first we must be assured that there will be no more attacks." Alvar looked directly at the warriors as he spoke to Estevan.

Again they conversed, at which the *Indians* abruptly returned to their lines.

"What did they say?" It was Enriquez.

"*Senors*, the *Indios* are clearly upset that we have invaded their village, but they will take our requests back to their *cacique* for consideration."

"As we must also to the *Adelantado*." Alvar spun on his heel. He hurried back to the lines and walked to the hut where Narvaez was resting.

From outside he made his presence known. "*Adelantado*, my apologies for disturbing you, but I must ask your advice on the *Indio* prisoners."

"Come in De Vaca, I am not dead yet."

Inside the hut, Narvaez lay upon a crumpled blanket. He had raised himself on one arm. Campo was mopping the sweat from his forehead.

"*Adelantado*, the *Indios* request that we release their shaman, women, and children. This request, I told them, we would consider if they would insure us of their peaceful intentions."

Narvaez thought a moment. "We must release the women and children, this will demonstrate our good intentions, but we should retain the shaman. Do they have any other concerns?"

"Yes, they are most opposed to our occupying their village."

Narvaez sighed and lay back down. "Wouldn't you feel the same way if it was your village?"

"Most assuredly *Adelantado*."

"Give them back their families and tell them we will camp outside their village if they will provide us with food and ensure that there will be no more attacks. We will show the shaman the proper respect that his position requires, but he will remain with us until we are satisfied that they will not betray us."

Alvar got up to take his leave.

"*Senor* De Vaca, there is one more thing."

"Pray-tell me *Adelantado*."

"This issue of the soldier...this *puta* Corral...in the old days I would have killed him and thought nothing of it."

Alvar nodded but remained quiet.

"We can not tolerate insubordination and insurrection such as he displayed. When this incident with the *Indios* is over, he will receive 100 lashes at my command. You will ensure that this is done."

"*Si Adelantado.*"

With this Alvar rushed back to his captains, briefing them, and the interpreters, of the *Adelantado's* wishes.

After a time, the three warriors again emerged from the trees and walked to the meeting place. Alvar, the *contralor* Enriquez, *Captain* Pantoja, and the two interpreters soon joined them.

Alvar spoke first. "Estevan, see what they have to say of our proposal."

After a few exchanges, the talk between Estevan, La Mancha, and the warriors seemed to become heated.

Alvar held up his hand and Estevan stepped back. "*Alguacil*, they claim they will not negotiate until their families are released."

"I see."

Alvar stepped back and signaled back to the line of *Spaniards*. The ranks opened up and the women and children filed forward. The negotiators stood silent and watched as they streamed past and disappeared into the trees.

Turning to Estevan, Alvar directed him to continue. "Tell them we have demonstrated our good faith by releasing their families. We will leave their village if they agree not to attack and assist us in the procurement of food so that we may renew our journey.

On hearing this, the *Indians* indicated that they were pleased that their women and children had been returned but still demanded the release of their shaman who was much venerated by the village.

Framing his response carefully, Estevan ensured the warriors that their shaman would be treated with respect but that he would be held until peaceful relations were established.

To this, the *Indians* requested a *Spaniard* of high rank to be held by them under the same conditions.

Alvar on hearing this demand, flatly refused, saying that this was unnecessary.

The *Indians* were clearly agitated. They countered that they would rejoin their lines and present these proposals to their *cacique* for consideration after which they would return with an answer.

They did not.

Shortly after the party of *Spaniards* had returned to their ranks, the line of warriors, just outside the treeline, seemed to evaporate.

Alonso Enriquez spoke for all the *Spaniards*, "They disappear like ghosts in the trees!"

27 June, 1528

The Indian Village at Apalachen

After the *Indio* warriors had left, the expedition settled into the village for a very uneasy night. Alvar had the soldier, Santo Corral, brought to him. He also summoned the notary Jeronimo de Aliniz and Diego Valenzuela, Corral's captain. Corral, with his hands tied behind his back, stood there visibly shaking.

Alvar began. "*Soldado* Santo Corral, because of your insubordination and treasonous actions the *Adelantado* has directed me to administer 100 lashes to you. Let it also be known that, if your vile actions had occurred anywhere else but here, where we need every man, you would have been executed."

Corral sunk to his knees. "No *Agucail*, I beg of you."

Alvar looked at the pathetic creature in front of him with disgust. "The punishment is 100 lashes which I would normally have carried out freely. Because of our situation, however, I am reducing the punishment to 25 lashes. In the coming days, we will need every able man to defend this camp."

Alvar turned to Jorge Nazario who was standing close by. The farrier had a maniacal leer on his face as he stroked the multi-stranded whip...*azote*...in his hands.

"*Senor* Nazario, you will carry out the sentence."

Placed against a large tree, Corral's arms were wrapped around it and securely tied. Stepping forward Nazario lightly ran the rawhide over Corral's arms, across his shoulders, and over his neck.

"I want to acquaint you with my little kitten...*pequeno gatito...Senor* Corral."

Corral was now sobbing, much to Nazario's delight.

The first blow came as a surprise to everyone, it was so sudden that even De Vaca jumped.

He continued, counting after each blow had fallen, "*uno, dos, tres...*"

At the count of five Nazario paused a moment as though he was confused.

"I have already lost count...let me see, was that number five or number four."

Contorted in pain, Corral began screaming when he heard Nazario's quandary, "Five you dirty pig...*cinco cerdo sucio.*"

Nazario guffawed and the soldiers around laughed openly.

Alvar spoke up, "*Senor* Nazario, continue with the punishment."

After Corral was dragged away, guards were posted around the camp with the heaviest presence at the west end of the village. Here the tangle of downed timber, marsh, and small lakes was the ideal staging point for an attack.

This moonless night was extremely dark. Heavy clouds covered the sky like an enveloping blanket. The *Spaniards* sensed the presence of the *Indians*. Beyond the light of the fires, strange calls emanated from the darkness. To the unaccustomed ear, it was difficult to separate which were animal and which were human.

In the early hours just before dawn, the attack came.

At first, the darkness of the treeline just beyond the village was illuminated by numerous small fires that twinkled like fireflies. This puzzled the *Spaniards* for they could not determine for what purpose they were there. Suddenly, a wall of flaming shafts launched into the sky, and the reason for the fires became apparent. The fire arrows arched high and then fell onto the thatched huts, tinderboxes of dry palm leaves, and cedar bark.

"To arms, to arms...*a las armas*!"

The camp was thrown into confusion. The huts erupted into towers of flame as the *Spaniards* hurried to defend themselves. Now, silent and invisible arrows began to impact the men that were silhouetted against the flames. The terrified horses, hobbled for the night, lost their balance, and fell to the ground. Many were also impacted by arrows. The handlers struggled to control them.

Narvaez, struggling to walk, pulled on his armor and gave commands.

"*Musketeers*, fire into that treeline."

But, there was no treeline...only darkness, the sun had not yet risen and the cloud cover masked the morning glow. The *Spaniards* could only guess where to aim. Tongues of fire erupted from the ends of the muskets and the smell of black powder mixed with the acrid smell of burning vegetation. Shot and ball could be heard impacting trees and branches. Only once did they hear a scream of pain in the darkness.

Firing at will, the *musketeers* kept up a steady, although uneven barrage. By now the *soldados* had formed up. Crossbowmen and *Rodeleros* waited in their ranks for the attack they were sure was coming. Horseman, the *caballistas*, remained unmounted, preferring to not make an even larger target of themselves against the flaming huts.

The arrow attack stopped.

Narvaez, kneeling on one knee and supporting himself with his *montante* called out, "Enough! We must save what powder we have."

All was quiet except for the crackling of the fires. These had even begun to die out, their source of fuel now burnt to the ground. The village of forty huts was now reduced to smoking ash. Many of the Spaniards who had beaded down in the huts had only seconds to escape the raging inferno. They lost clothes, shoes, blankets, and weapons.

As the sun rose the dark line of the woods materialized out of the darkness. Only an occasional *Indio* could be seen moving amongst the trees and swamps but it was enough for Narvaez. He ordered the *Spaniards* forward, but it was a futile advance. The *Indians* had pulled back and disappeared.

"*Adelantado*, over here!" It was Captain Pantoja. His company of *roleleros* had come across a body partially hidden in the grass. It was an *Indio* warrior shot through the lungs, the exit wound exposed the backbone and torn tissue. He was long dead.

"Probably the scream we heard as our *musketeers* were firing into the darkness."

Walking over to view the body, Narvaez sagged against a tree and had to be helped onto a horse for the return to the village, or, what was left of it. He was burning with fever.

There were no *Spanish* deaths, but many had not fared well in the night attack. Fourteen *soldados* had been injured by the rain of arrows. These had to be cut out of arms, legs, shoulders, and thighs. The most serious was an arrow taken by Rolando Prieto, a crossbowman in the company of Captain Enrique Penolosa. As he had looked up to watch the fiery trail in the sky, an arrow entered his mouth, partially exiting the neck on the right side and narrowly missing the carotid artery. The amount of blood flowing down his throat had almost drowned him. Others had suffered burns while escaping the huts, including Narvaez whose red beard and eyebrows had been singed.

Seven horses had also been hit, but none seriously, for they had been corralled some distance from where the majority of arrows had impacted.

A meeting of the expedition officials and captains was called. Narvaez did not attend, he lay under a makeshift cover burning with fever. Campo was watching him closely.

Captain Pantoja was the first to speak.

"Compatriots, we must delay our journey and rest ourselves. Our men are greatly fatigued and many are sick, most importantly the governor, even now, rages with tertian ague. Our horses grow continually weaker and our weapons and equipment are in need of attention."

Most were in agreement, but Alonso Enriquez, the comptroller, raised an objection.

"*Senors,* here we are under attack and the *Indios* are most aggressive. I fear that by remaining here we put ourselves in jeopardy."

Alonso de Solis, the quartermaster and inspector, was quick to answer. "I share the concerns of the comptroller, but where should we go, and in which direction? Here we are surrounded by fields of maize to feed our men and horses."

Captain Castillo stepped forward. "Although this village presents us with a defensive challenge we have the advantage of ample food and water. By remaining vigilant and sallying forth to attack the *Indios* before they attack us we can gain the advantage."

There were nods all around.

As they were talking Alvar studied each of the men. They were all thin, some more so than others. The looks on their faces betrayed fatigue and frustration. They were filthy, their shoes were worn...some were barefoot, and a few were injured. It was obvious what must be done.

The meeting had deteriorated into several individual conversations. Alvar raised his hand for recognition. As *Alguacil* and second in command, his words would carry some authority.

"*Caballeros*, I think that most are in agreement to remain here. We will remain at this location and rest ourselves while maintaining a strong military vigilance. While here, we will attempt to learn as much as possible about these..." Alvar made a gesture towards the thick forest, "...these *Apalachee*!"

Alvar paused. "Unless there are any objections." He looked about him; there were none.

He continued. "I will leave it to the *capitans* to formulate our defensive strategy. Now, I will take this decision to the *Adelantado* for his approval."

29 June, 1528

Indian Village at Apalachen

It had been another tense night. Few of the *Spaniards* had got much sleep, the *Apalachee* had made sure of that. Periodically, arrows would fall into the camp, shot from somewhere just outside the village. The men tried to sleep under their armor or pulled up next to a log or rock, anything that would cover them. Once a nervous musketeer had fired his arquebus at a sound just in front of his guard position. It had alerted the whole camp. The *Spaniards* hurriedly assembled into their assigned positions expecting an attack, but none came.

Sometime in the early morning, the arrows stopped and for a few hours, some were able to relax. This calm continued into the first light of dawn. The air was thick with fog and a heavy wet dew covered everything. Even as the sun rose in the sky the visibility was limited to just a few feet.

Captain Alonso del Castillo was up early. Leaving the main campsite he moved out in the direction of the sentry stations closest to the tangle of woods and swamps. He knew the men would be edgy and was careful to make his approach known.

"Hello, the guard!"

There was no answer.

He repeated himself. *"¡hola! el guardia."*

In a hushed tone, the reply came. "We are here."

There, directly in front of him, four figures materialized out of the gloom. They were hunkered down behind some small saplings and a clump of palmettos. One of the soldiers, Alonso recognized him as Juan Soldado, and raised his finger to his lips.

Quietly he whispered, "*Capitan* Castillo, we were just about to send a runner, there is considerable movement to our front. I fear the *Indios* are massing for attack."

Listening intently, Castillo also heard the noises; snapping of twigs, rustling bushes, an occasional grunt...things that shouldn't be heard unless a large body of men were assembling. He didn't hesitate.

"*Senor* Soldado, how close are the other guards?"

"At fifty-foot intervals, they are both to the left and right of us."

"As quickly as possible have them move back. I will alert the camp."

Castillo hurried back. He moved among the men shaking them awake and directing others to quietly alert the camp. From prior experience, he knew the attack would be preceded by an arrow barrage. He directed the men to don their armor and stay hidden behind obstacles and keep their *bucklers* at the ready. The horses were saddled and moved to the far end of the camp with a heavy guard. Realizing he had ventured out bareheaded, Castillo located his *morion* and placed it securely on his head.

Quickly the lines formed up. Castillo moved among the anxious crossbowmen and musketeers directing them to hold their fire until sure of a target. The nervous guards quietly called out *"Santiago"* in an attempt to identify themselves before crossing the lines.

Then, all was quiet. Not a breath of air moved.

At his station, Alvar De Vaca, sword in hand, crouched down behind his buckler wishing he could make himself even smaller. He and twenty other *rodeleros* formed a protective shield around the *Adelantado* and the other sick men of the expedition. Narvaez, still burning with fever, could barely lift his head. Campo, by his side, grasped a dagger and stood ready to defend his protector and friend.

On the right flank, Captain Dorantes and his dismounted cavalrymen joined the other rodeleros standing with Captain Pantoja.

Captains Tellez and Penalosa secured the left flank. Captain Diego Valenzuela remained behind the line to protect the rear and provide a reserve force should the line be breached.

A veil of white permeated the air around the *Spaniards*; fog so thick that moisture condensed on their swords and helmets and dripped to the ground.

Somewhere out there a sound...almost inaudible...fell upon the ears of those with the best hearing. It was the hiss of arrows launched into high trajectories.

"Arrows!"

The call rang out up and down the lines.

"Flechas, flechas!"

Falling like hail, their arrival was announced by a loud clattering as shafts bounced off helmets and armor. Most were embedded into the ground, trees, shields, and anything the *Spaniards* could crawl beneath. Some struck flesh. Luckily, only five received wounds of any consequence, the most serious striking a soldier high on the right side of his back. It was a painful wound and the man's cries of anguish were unnerving. Fray Xuarez ran to his assistance and with the help of two others pushed the shaft through until the point exited just above the clavicle. Breaking off the point, he pulled the shaft back through the wound until it was clear.

"Let it bleed for a while, so that it may cleanse itself and then push this hard up against it!" Xuarez handed the wounded man a wad of moss and then scampered back to cover.

"Flechas, flechas!"

Again the arrows came and this time only one man was slightly injured, the arrow slicing off the tip of an exposed finger.

"Enough of this!" De Vaca stood up and instructed the musketeers to discharge their weapons in the direction of the trees. In the half-light of the fog, the blaze of black powder leaped out like serpent tongues. Although out of sight, the double loads of shot rattled against trees and brush. Several screams emanated out of the murk.

"Now forward!" The front line surged.

"Quickly men!"

Keeping their shields high they advance rapidly expecting an enemy to appear at their front at any moment. But, other than a few stray arrows, the *Spaniards* reached the tree line with no opposition. They could clearly hear the *Indians* retreating through the dense woodland, swamp, and brush. On the flanks, the attackers used the big fields of maize to mask their withdrawal. Volleys were fired into the field. The balls noisily crashed through the stalks, tearing paths until their inertia was spent.

By now a slight breeze had begun to blow and the dense fog began to dissipate. It was eerie. The huge old trees that bordered the swamp began to appear, their tops still obscured by the thick mist. More and more the arboreal environment materialized until the depth and density of the wilderness was all around them. Further out, steam rose from the small lakes and swamp areas that punctuated the woodland.

"*Alguacil*, we have a dead one!"

As in the last attack, a single dead *Indio* was found. This one had a clean hole through his forehead. On exiting, however, the ball had removed most of the back part of the skull. Brain matter and blood coated the surrounding vegetation. Other blood trails were found as well, but these only led into the swamp and the *Spaniards* did not follow.

Moving back to the camp the sky above began to open, the bright orb of the sun alternately appearing as clouds skudded across the sky. Wisps of blue appeared. The heat on their shoulders felt good. The moisture that clung to everything began to burn off and soon the coolness of the morning was replaced by the hot oppressive heat and humidity of mid-morning.

30 June, 1528

The Indian Village at Apalachen

The leaders of the expedition determined to conduct forays into the enemy's territory. These reconnaissances were made in strength...*en la fuerza*, a force strong enough to thwart even the most determined *Indio* attack...the purpose was twofold. They would scout the country to see if there were other villages worth exploiting and, to find and kill the attackers who were constantly besieging them. Narvaez had partially recovered from his illness, and was, once again, totally in charge of the expedition. The *Adelantado*, however, was not the same man as before the sickness. Arms and legs once described as "tree trunks...*troncos de arboles*" were half their size. His face was gaunt and the endless energy that characterized him in the past had dissipated.

The first reconnaissance to the east was led by Captain Alonso Pantoja. Twenty horsemen...*cabeleros*, thirty swords...*rodeleros,* and five crossbowmen...*ballesteros* ventured out. For three days they passed through a sparsely inhabited land. The trails were poor and their way was frequently blocked by lakes, large and small, swamps and blow-downs...enormous trees bowled over by the wind. The lakes were deep and difficult to cross; all manner of poisonous snakes and insects frequented the grasslands, swamps, and lakes.

On the fourth day, the first reconnaissance party returned and reported to Narvaez. No great cities had been found, in fact, all that was encountered was an occasional cluster of three or four huts containing family groups attending their maize fields.

That night another attack had occurred and dissipated just as fast, leaving several *Spaniards* injured, but none seriously. Narvaez called for another reconnaissance to the west. This group, led by Captain Penalosa moved out as soon as it was light, but unlike the first party encountered a series of small villages on the second day. These were different people from the *Apalachee* who, although similar in appearance, wore their hair long and braided. Intertwined in the braids were all manner of bones, shells, and strips of fur.

They were the *Thimogona* sworn enemies of the *Apalachee*. After some discussion with Marino Carmona, who accompanied the scouting party, they asked to send twenty men back with Captain Penalosa to fight their enemies.

Of course, Penalosa readily agreed.

On the return to *Apalachen,* it was a strange procession that entered the barricaded village. Twelve *cabelleros* led the procession followed by the weary *rodeleros*. Just behind them ambled the group of wide-eyed *Thimogona's* with their long-bows. Behind this procession, eight additional *cabelleros* followed at some distance to guard against attack from the rear.

At the village, the *Spaniards* had rebuilt some of the huts for protection from the frequent storms and cool temperatures. The nights were especially uncomfortable with the temperatures, at times, dropping rapidly. Winds blowing across the flat, featureless land added to the discomfort. This puzzled Alvar, for the longitude of this place was far south of *Spain* from whence they had begun their journey over a year ago. On clear days, however, the temperature would rapidly rise and become uncomfortably hot. It was these drastic changes that caused the *Spaniards* to suffer greatly, for their clothing had become worn and threadbare. On the two excursions the *Spaniards* had collected animal skins from the villages, but it was not enough.

The abundance of maize at *Apalachen* allowed the men and horses to regain some of their fitness, but the almost daily attacks were exhausting the *Spaniards*. Double guards had to be posted each night and the threat of arrow barrages was always present. The guerrilla tactics used by the *Indians* had changed somewhat. Under cover of darkness, a lone warrior would make his way as close to the camp as possible and wait, unnoticed, until someone passed in range of a bow shot. Two *Spaniards* had taken wounds to the upper torso; neither lethal, but only because the body armor provided by their *cuirasse* had impeded the penetration of the projectile. Still, at this close range, the arrowhead had penetrated and the resulting wounds were painful and debilitating.

Daily, a force of four horsemen, sixteen-foot soldiers, and the *Thimogona* warriors would venture out to scout the area. The number of *Thimogona* varied with each day. Some would disappear for days and then suddenly reappear. When questioned about this, their *cacique*, a magnificent warrior named Guanicota, explained that his men returned to their village to care for their families.

Within the camp, men began to complain of missing possessions and on July 10th a *Thimogona* was discovered leaving camp with a stolen *Spanish* sword. Narvaez had the *Indio* brought before him and called for Guanicota. who appeared before the *Adelantado* with twenty of his warriors. Quickly, these were surrounded by *Spaniards* and an uncomfortable stand-off ensued. Narvaez called up Marino Carmona to interpret.

"*Senor* Carmona, tell the *cacique* that this man was caught stealing from us."

While Carmona was attempting to convey the *Adelantado's* message, the accused, with hands tied, began to jabber at Guanicota in their native tongue. Lieutenant Fernan Estrada, who was standing over the prisoner, stepped up and cuffed him smartly on the head. The conversation abruptly stopped. The line of warriors, clearly agitated, moved forward. The surrounding *Spaniards* closed ranks around them.

It was Guanicota who diffused the situation. Knowing that his warriors would be quickly annihilated in such a confrontation, he spread his arms and commanded his men to back away. To this, they reluctantly complied. Narvaez waved for his men to back off as well. Turning back to Narvaez, Guanicota relayed through Carmona that he had no knowledge of his men stealing from the *Spaniards*.

Narvaez looked directly into Guanicota's eyes as he addressed Carmona. "Tell the *cacique* that I think his men have been stealing from us ever since they arrived."

To this, Guanicota stiffened, for essentially Narvaez was calling him a liar. Returning the *Adelantado's* stare he asked, "What would you have me do?"

Narvaez sat back as if contemplating his next answer. "Tell the *cacique* that our punishment for stealing is to cut off a hand."

Guanicota was shocked at such harsh retribution. When Narvaez's words were communicated to the warriors they began to surge forward. The prisoner began to wail.

Narvaez, seeing this, stood up and pointed at the line of warriors. "One more step and there will be more than a hand cut off this day."

Below him, Carmona was busily translating.

On hearing the translation, Guanicota immediately instructed his warriors to back off.

Carmona spoke, "*Adelantado*, the *cacique* asks that you will consider a lesser punishment."

At this point, Fray Xuarez pulled Narvaez aside to have a word. "*Adelantado*, wouldn't it be better to not anger the *Thimogonas* and keep them as our allies?

"Padre, I know these *Indios*, they will steal us blind if given a chance. They only respect power. I must set an example."

"Perhaps less of an example is warranted."

Seeing an opportunity, Narvaez thought a moment before answering. He turned to Carmona.

"Tell the *cacique* that if they remain our allies against the *Apalachee* I will spare this man's hand, but...he still must pay for his crimes. We will remove only a finger."

Narvaez held up his hand and pointed to the right ring finger.

Reluctantly Guanicota agreed.

Narvaez addressed Campo who was standing next to him. "Set an iron in the fire to cauterize the wound and summon *Senor* Nazario."

"*Si Adelantado!*"

"And have him bring his hammer and chisel."

The soldiers holding the *Thimogona* captive drug him closer to the fire and set his right hand on a wooden block. It took three of them to hold him steady.

Jorge Nazario stepped forward and placed the cutting edge of the chisel on the man's ring finger just below the knuckle. Slowly he raised the hammer high above his head, hesitated, and then brought it down with a resounding "Whack!"

Everyone jumped and the *Thimogona* captive screamed....but...Nazario had intentionally not contacted the chisel and, instead, hit the wooden block. The man's finger was still intact.

Everyone was still wide-eyed and Nazario let out a huge belly laugh. The soldiers were the next to laugh and even Narvaez had to stifle a grin.

"Blacksmith, carry out your duty!" It was Fray Xuarez and he was not amused.

Quick as a cat Nazario swung the hammer again. The *Thimogona's* finger flew off the block and landed in the sand. Campo stepped up with the heated iron and pressed it to the spurting wound.

Narvaez stood and addressed the gathering. "Now, let us join together in fighting the *Apalachee*."

It was on the 13th of July that the expedition suffered another death. In the early morning hours a slave of Pedro Lunel, known only as Bonero, had been tending the fires. Piles of firewood, gathered the previous day, had been amassed near the center of the village. During the evening hours, all of the camp-fires were supplied from this one pile. Unbeknownst to anyone, a lone warrior had penetrated the defensive perimeter and hid in this pile of sticks and logs. During the evening Bonero had made several trips to the pile without consequence. On his last, he had bent over to lay out the straps on which to bundle the load. On raising up, Bonero had looked into the eyes of death; an *Apalachee* warrior with his bow at full draw. Before he could blink, the arrow had passed through his body and embedded in a tree. His aorta had been severed. The *African* was dead before he hit the ground. Unnoticed by anyone, the *Apalachee* warrior had bounded across the open area and disappeared into the darkness. Only then did he emit a loud series of yelps that alerted the whole camp.

At daybreak of the next day, Narvaez called a meeting of his captains and officials. The fever had left him, but the man before them now was gaunt and sallow-skinned. The fever had taken its toll. The voice of Narvaez, however, had not been affected and it boomed across the village clearing. The captains and officials were invited to present their ideas. Many talked long and hard about the deprivations forced upon them and the constant attacks by the *Apalachee*. The general consensus was to return to the coast and wait for the relief ships who, everyone agreed, must be frantically searching for them. Alvar did not speak as the discussion circled around him. He could not help but think that he and only a few others had warned Narvaez about setting into the wilderness without support from the sea. He so badly wanted to remind the *Adelantado* of this fact, but remained silent.

Narvaez listened patiently while everyone spoke, only intervening when the discussion became heated. Finally, he stood up and requested silence. "We have made two reconnaissances. One to the east and one to the west." Narvaez pointed for effect sweeping his hand over the broad expanse of countryside that surrounded them. "I agree that our presence in this village is not one we wish to continue. We suffer daily from attacks that we cannot use our power to thwart. These...*Apalachee*...flee into the swamp before we can give fight...and we have suffered losses." At this, Friar Xuarez got up to offer a prayer. The circle of *Spaniards* fell silent. Fray Xuarez clasped his hands and looked to the sky. "May Christ who called you, take you to himself."

Making the sign of the cross, Narvaez lamented. "Ours is a most unfortunate and humiliating situation."

Then he turned and pointed north. "We have no knowledge of what lies to the north of this place. I think before we leave, one more reconnoiter should be made in this direction. With this, we will assure ourselves that a great prize has not slipped through our grasp."

There was general agreement and nodding of heads.

"I assign *Aguacil* De Vaca to lead this mission with *Capitan* Dorantes to accompany him with twenty *caballeros* so as they may travel as quickly as possible."

Turning to Alvar, he made his final instructions. "Senor De Vaca, proceed north and question everyone as to what lies further ahead. Proceed in this direction until you are assured that there is nothing to be gained by further travel. If, however, something of interest is found, repair back to this location as quickly as possible."

"*Si Adelantado*, we will be leaving within the hour." Alvar motioned to Andres Dorantes and together they hurried off to make preparations.

16 July, 1528

Third Expedition North of Apalachen

It had been two days. They had traveled fast along paths that were well-worn, hunting trails used by the inhabitants of this land for millenniums. Large forests predominated the landscape, some with trees so large and so tall that the *Spaniards* would gaze up at their immensity in amazement. Always present in this arboreal environment were areas of blowdown, huge trees toppled like matchsticks in a tangled maze. These blowdowns...*derribar por el viento*...seemed to frequent the margins of forest and grassland where the force of great winds would be at their strongest.

As they rode, wild animals of all manner would be encountered. Startled deer would spring from the side of the trail and dart into heavy cover, white tails flashing a warning as they bounded high into the air. Occasionally a bear or even a cougar would be encountered, their presence causing the horses to snort and sidestep. In the grasslands wolves would be seen from afar moving away from the column of men and horses, frequently looking over their shoulders to ensure that these newcomers weren't in pursuit.

On this day threatening darkness had risen in the southern sky, sub-tle at first, the gray haze transforming into a black presence that slowly crept northward. At noon the first distant rumbles of thunder drifted over the grassland, but overhead the sun continued to beat down with unrelenting heat. The air became still and oppressive. Even astride their horses, the *Spaniards* were sweating profusely. Mosquitoes and insects of all manner swarmed around their heads and bodies while the horses were particularly tormented by legions of deer flies...*moscas del venado*...who, besides leaving bleeding wounds on the horse's ears, attacked the riders as well.

They rode on, seeing not so much as a single *Indio*. At mid-after-noon, the stillness of the air was interrupted by the first light breezes bringing the smell of rain. The darkness had moved higher into the sky. Wispy tentacles of dark clouds drifted across the sun. The tem-perature began to drop. Overhead, flocks of birds took to the air to escape the approaching storm. They were now on a vast grassy plain that extended to the horizon. Inter-spaced here and there were lonely islands of trees and shrubs, usually on a raised hillock or ridge. The gentle breeze that had brought the first smells of rain now combined with periodic gusts that flowed across the top of the grasses like ocean waves.

Close to one of these wooded hillocks, Alvar stopped the column and turned his horse to look at the advancing storm. Captain Dorantes joined him.

"*Alguacil*, the storm is close upon us."

"I see that *Capitan*. It would be best if we moved into these trees and set up camp for the evening."

Dorantes nodded and then dismounted. He turned to the column of men. "*Cabelleros* we will camp here for the night. Move quickly, for the tempest is almost upon us,"

With swords out the men hacked at the palmettos and other undergrowth to clear a space. Others wandered through the grove looking for downed limbs or dead trees, anything that might be used for a fire.

Cavalryman Diego Torres yanked at a large limb that had fallen into the undergrowth. It wouldn't budge. Drawing his sword, he stepped further into the brush and chopped away at the vines and other vegetation. He tried pulling on the limb with his free hand. Sheathing his sword, Torres reached down close to the ground to get a better grip. Closing his hands around the limb he felt a sharp pain just above the right wrist. Yanking his hand out from under the limb he jumped back. Looking in horror at the arm, a small snake was hanging from his wrist, its fangs still embedded in the skin. Desperately Torres shook it free. The snake fell to the ground and coiled for another strike, the rattles on its tail held high as they vibrated their high-pitched warning.

Pulling his sword, Torres severed the snake in two, but the damage had already been done. Blood flowed down his hand onto the hilt of the sword, but in his veins, the blood carried the viper's venom throughout his body.

Alvar had remained on his horse to observe the oncoming storm. It had dogged them all day long, advancing slowly northward. Now, it approached with demonic furor. He watched as shafts of rain moved diagonally across the front and lightning split the sky. The thunder was almost continuous now.

There was commotion behind him.

Turning, Alvar saw one of the *cabelleros* being carried into the clearing. He dismounted and walked toward the disturbance.

To no one in particular he asked, "What has happened?"

Dorantes came up to him. "It is Torres, one of my best riders; he was bitten by a serpent through the large vein in the wrist. He walked over to tell his compatriots and then fell down at their feet. He is in great pain and unable to move his arm."

The darkness of the storm was upon them. The bright afternoon was now a somber twilight. Crescendos of thunder exploded all around while forked tentacles of supercharged lightning arched through the sky. A few hail stones impacted the ground and bounced along like white marbles. Then, a blistering deluge of the ice balls came in a torrent. Horses reared and men dove for cover, holding their bucklers over their heads for protection. Those nearest Torres tried to cover him with whatever was close at hand, but they too felt the sting and strove to cover themselves. In his pain, Torres rolled under a bush and tried to shield his head with the uninjured arm.

Severed by the hail, limbs, and leaves fell from above. The hailstones hitting Alvar's helmet were deafening. Large welts formed on his shoulders and arms from the impacting spheres. Around him, the ground turned white. The temperature now dropped again.

Just as quickly as it had begun the ice storm passed over them, its progress visible on the grassland like a giant sickle laying everything before it. There were moans and curses all around. Men rubbed their bruised bodies and slipped about on the layer of ice beneath their feet.

Now it began to rain.

The deluge continued through the night and the temperature continued to plummet. When they had left *Apalachen* and throughout their journey, the heat had been oppressive, now in the early hours of the morning the men shivered uncontrollably. Just after midnight, Torres became delusional, his cries adding to the crescendo of rain falling around them. The night was so dark that no one could even evaluate the state of his injury. Just before dawn, the moans ceased and there was great concern for the state of his health.

The first blush of light revealed the terrible ordeal of Diego Torres. He was dead. The arm was swollen three times its size and colored a dark black that extended into his chest and neck. Near the bicep, the skin had split and secreted a mixture of blood and body fluids. The fact that he had suffered was obvious. Dark scratches from his fingernails creased his face, abdomen, and legs. Alvar would never forget the look of anguish that still looked up at him from the man's dead, open eyes.

They buried Torres in that clearing as best they could for the ground was a quagmire of mud. Mostly they covered him with the sicks and firewood they had collected before the storm. After a brief memorial, Alvar conferred with Captain Dorantes.

"There is no sign of any great culture in this land. Indeed, we have not seen a single inhabitant in the last two days. Inform the men that we will be returning to *Apalachen*."

16 July, 1528

The Indian Village at Apalachen

Don Pedro rose early. The sun wasn't up yet, but the sky was clear and the morning glow gave the promise of a clear day. It was warm and he hadn't slept well. The mosquitoes had pestered him all evening. His arms and legs showed the results of the insect's blood feast. The last straw had been a large flying roach that had landed on his mouth just as he was inhaling. He had almost swallowed the thing. Quickly rising he sputtered and spat to remove the foul taste from his mouth. He reached for his canteen but it was empty. Only a few drops fell on his tongue as he raised it into the air. Disgusted, he threw the strap over his shoulder and started toward the spring just a short distance away.

As he strolled through the camp most of the men were still asleep, their snores, farts, and heavy breathing punctuating the cool morning air. Close to the spring he could see four of the perimeter guards; two were playing some kind of game in the sand, lobbing pebbles at a nearby stump. Another watched the game with disinterested eyes while the fourth stared into the distance, fighting sleep, his head falling forward and then jerking upright in a start. Don Pedro stopped and turned in a circle, surveying the camp around him.

It had been twenty-three days since their arrival at *Apalachen*. The decision was made to stay at this location and recuperate before continuing their journey. The fields of maize had been ready for harvest and the famished expedition fed themselves and their horses. Half of the fields on either side of the village had already been harvested and flattened, improving the defensibility of the camp. Now, the only real threat came from the forested swampy area to their west. Here the *Indians* tormented the camp every night, moving just close enough to launch their arrows and then withdrawing into the wilderness behind them.

"Don Pedro, it would be best if you would shield yourself behind something. This is the time of morning when these *Apalachee* become most active."

It was Miguel Casares, a *rodelero* with Captain Tellez's company, one of the two playing the pebble game.

"Senor Casares, I am in need of a drink of water. Would you have a canteen available?"

"Sorry...*lo siento*...Don Pedro, we are dry as well, but soon it will be light and safe to go to the spring.

The spring bubbled from the ground just to the west of the village, the water exceedingly clear and pure. The runoff flowed toward the swamps in a meandering rivulet that was bordered on both sides by laurel, water oak, and low palmettos. For protection, the *Spaniards* had flattened the area immediately around the spring and for some distance out. Still, it was uncomfortably close to the heavily for-ested labyrinth of swamps and small lakes that provided cover for the marauding *Apalachee*.

The spring was just visible from where Don Pedro stood, the area beyond dark and foreboding in the morning half-light. His thirst was great. He moved warily toward the spring clutching a sword in one hand and canteen over his shoulder.

Behind his makeshift bastion of sticks and branches, Casares watched as Don Pedro moved slowly toward the spring. He slid his finger close to the crossbow release. From what he could see, there was no movement in the trees and the area around the spring was clear except for a couple of small bushes. It looked safe.

He scanned far to the left and then to the right. Streaks of dawn colored the sky. He could see the treetops now.

Something wasn't right. Something had moved.

Peripherally he sensed a change in something to the left of his field of vision...but what?

As if in a trance Casares watched with unbelieving fascination as one of the shrubs rose up. He blinked and looked again and then, in a moment, he understood. He swung his crossbow to take aim, but even before pulling the lever, he realized he was too late.

Don Pedro had reached the spring and was just loosening the strap around his shoulder to free up the canteen. As he was beginning to bend forward, a searing pain shot through his body. An involuntary shriek pushed upwards from his esophagus and exited his mouth with frothy bubbles of blood.

He dropped his sword.

He was confused, the pain was overwhelming. He turned to see what had happened and caught a brief vision of a man running into the bush. There was a noise behind him...*Spaniards* were calling to him...but he had trouble understanding what they said. Don Pedro tore at his tunic to see what was the source of this terrible pain. Sinking to his knees he saw the hole in his chest just below the right nipple. It was oozing blood and pink matter.

Suddenly the pain was gone, replaced by a quiet dullness. His thinking remained clear.

"It must have been an arrow...but where was the shaft?"

Slowly he looked around him on the ground. Nothing, only his life-blood puddling on the sand.

His eyesight began to fade. The darkness closed upon him and his last conscious sight was the spring gurgling just in front of him. He knelt there, now blind and his consciousness ebbing. From far down in his soul his *Aztec* heritage called out to him. He was no longer Don Pedro but again Prince Azitonichatez son of Cietaquota, favored concubine of the great Montezuma. He tried to chant the death song, but the muscles in his throat would not respond. Oh, he was cold....so cold....and then...nothing.

In that millisecond of realization, Miguel Casares had loosed his bolt at the camouflaged attacker, but it had missed, passing only inches from its mark. He immediately sounded the alarm and then, sword in hand, jumped over the parapet to attack the intruder. His confused compatriots watched for a moment and then joined him in the attack.

Holding their bucklers in front at arm's length they sprinted toward the spring.

From the swamp, a mass of arrows arched toward them. Casares felt an arrow slice into his right shoulder, but it only left a deep gash before passing on. One of his compatriots fell heavily to the ground, a shaft passing through the soft calf muscle.

Reaching the spring Casares slid to a stop beside the still kneeling Don Pedro. He held out the buckler as best he could to protect them both, but, strangely, the arrow barrage had stopped. Behind him, there was movement in the *Spanish* camp. A musket discharged. Out in the bush, Casares could hear the balls striking the vegetation. Another musket discharged, its loud report echoing through the swamp.

The attackers had disappeared.

It was then that Casares shifted his attention to Don Pedro. He was kneeling, both hands at his side and head down. There was much blood.

"*Senor* Don, can you hear me?" Casares touched his shoulder.

Don Pedro's body fell forward, his face impacting only inches from the spring.

Casares quickly rolled him over, but the *Aztec* prince turned *Christian* was dead, shot through by that *Indio* lying in ambush only a few feet away.

"*Ah, Madre de Dios*!" Casares made the sign of the cross. He sat there for a long time thinking of how he should have stopped Don Pedro, of how he should have seen his attacker just a little sooner. Miguel Casares was consumed with guilt.

He cried.

Around him, other *Spaniards* closed in and shook their heads when they saw the body of Don Pedro.

It was Frey Xuarez who finally knelt beside Casares and talked him into returning to the camp. Others were gathering up the body.

They would bury Don Pedro in the village.

19 July, 1528

The Last Day at the Indian Settlement of Apalachen

The camp had marching orders. No sooner had the reconnaissance mission returned than Narvaez made a decision to move to the south. In the four days that Alvar and Captain Dorantes had been gone the camp at *Apalachen* had suffered no large-scale attack but men and horses had been continually preyed upon whenever they went for water.

Watering the horses was the most hazardous. Even under heavy guard, the procession of men and horses would initiate an attack. The spring that bubbled up just outside of the village flowed down to a small lake that was thick with reeds. The perimeter of the lake and indeed much of the surrounding area was populated by large trees whose branches and trunks littered the surface. Further out the lake degenerated into a broad marshy swamp that expanded into a dark morass of blow-downs and impenetrable forest.

The *Spaniards* had cleared a large area at the lake's edge to bring the horses. *Musketeers* and crossbowmen would set up on the higher ground while the handlers in full armor would lead the animals in groups of four to the water's edge. The horses would be saddled and covered with whatever protection was available. Rising from the water or concealed behind a floating log the *Apalachee* would unleash a barrage of arrows and then disappear into the morass almost before the *Spaniards* could react. Still, a few of the attackers had suffered injuries. One fleeing *Indio* had taken a musket ball to the shoulder, the force of which bowled him over. As he arose the crossbowmen had riddled him with the short steel bolts loosed from their powerful weapons. The bloated body, now half submerged, still floated in the deeper water. Although no *Spaniards* or horses had been killed in these attacks, many had been injured. Farrier Jorge Nazario spent a good part of every day cutting out arrows and bandaging both men and beasts.

It was apparent that they must leave this place.

Narvaez, Marino Carmona, and Estevan had spent much time questioning the captives and allies while De Vaca and Captain Dorantes had been away. All had said that the land surrounding *Apalachen* was poor and with few inhabitants. When questioned about what lay to the south, however, they talked of a village named *Aute*...somewhat larger than *Apalachen* and rich in maize, squash, and beans. More importantly, it was close to the ocean and a possible site for reuniting with the caravels. La Mancha talked of it with some knowledge for as a young boy he had journeyed there with his father to trade for shells. These talks had convinced Narvaez to move south as quickly as possible. A peace delegation was sent to the *Apalachee* asking for a cessation of hostilities if the shaman was returned and the village abandoned.

The *Apalachee* had agreed.

That night the *Spaniards* had spent their first quiet night in weeks. In the morning they assembled and moved out. Just outside of the village, a contingent of *Apalachee* met them and the shaman was released. The *Indians* walked off without a word.